BEING BONARELLI

BEING BONARELLI

Alan C. Iannacito

ISBN: 1511433175
ISBN 13: 9781511433174
Library of Congress Control Number: 2015904829
CreateSpace Independent Publishing Platform
North Charleston, South Carolina

Cover Art: By the author's eighteen-year old alter ego.

To: Sherril, Lisa, Paul, Sophie, Cynthia and the Iannacito/Cito extended families.
To: frustrated crafters of words and to stories that want airing.

Acknowledgements

Winston Churchill said, "Writing: it begins as an amusement, becomes a mistress, then a master and finally a tyrant."

Over the last thirty years, I have written stories, poetry and non-fiction for several different publications. This is my breakout novel started twelve years ago with as many rewrites and serious edits. Finally it gets down to just getting it done. It is never done, and when you think you have done the weeding you find that the weeds are intricate to the entire garden and are never completely eradicated. Writers call this cutting out your babies. Sometimes this process removes other important parts, too.

Good books, good instructors and inspiration help. Inspiration is where you find it be it a piece of string or an entire yard full of ideas. My characters have always written themselves, I only type the words.

Inspiration started with my mother Ellen's voracious appetite for books that rubbed off on me. I spent days with Laura Lee Hope and The Bobbsey Twins books, Mark Twain, The Hardy Boys mysteries, Nancy Drew mysteries and comic books. So I think and write in the visual images of my characters.

Guidance, as I recall, came from Miss Margaret Oyler, my North High School English teacher. It is not only English and writing but the liberal arts like band with Mr. Richard Culver and art with Mrs. Jeannette Lacey, and Boys Advisor Mr. Eugene Garner who kept my head on straight and worked together to influence my senses. This was over fifty-years ago and I still carry their good council and teaching.

Later I tuned into all of the usual classics, college literature teachers, wonderful writers, great musicians and unfathomably brilliant visual artists. I was able to study at MSU, CU and DU with the likes of Colorado's *Poet Laureate* Joseph Hutchison; professors and mentors including Robert Pugel, Bruce Ducker, Rex Burns, Sally Stich and a myriad of 19th and 20th Century writers. Influence also by old Colorado authors with international credentials, Gene Fowler and John Fante.

Later in my quest for the writing craft I studied stories, attended conferences and seminars about writing and communication. It's all about the writing and butt to chair. I have the Jackalope Writers at Denver's Buckhorn as sounding boards: Irv Sternberg, Jerry Drake, Bruce Most, Michael Allegretto, and Doug Hawk

I would like to thank my many friends and associates from Rocky Mountain Fiction Writers Southwest critique group. Leader of the pack Mary Ann Kersten kept us in order; Kathy House, Ed Hickock, Kathy Reynolds, Jerry Drake, Liesa Malik, Andrea Catalano, Kevin Wolf, Z.J. Zupor and a host of other critique partners.

Editors Monica Baruth and Anita Mumm helped me over the rough parts. And, the very accommodating publisher, CreateSpace, made it smooth and professional onto the Yellow Brick Road.

Thank you all.

Before Carlo, "Charlie," Bonarelli evolved from an undisciplined teenager to an iron-hard-warrior, he was like most boys of the post WWII era and like the "Cold War," cynical, irreverent, and uncertain. This is his story.

Denver, Colorado: Fall, 1958

1

Charlie picked up the morning paper and read, *Girl Murdered in Park*. It was real then. He wasn't dreaming. He read the newspaper story as fast as he could. There was no mention of Carlo, "Charlie," Bonarelli, by name, but a line read: *The body was discovered by a North High School boy on his way through the park*. Charlie thought the cops didn't tell the press his name or age. He knew it was a matter of time before reporters learned he was the boy, eighteen-years-old, old enough to be treated as an adult. "Did they have to name North High School?" He didn't understand any of it yet, but it was serious enough to bring him out here on the cold sidewalk this morning, to read the paper where he imagined himself impaled on the end of an enemy's spear.

He re-read the story as he treaded back into the house, hoping that it was all a farce. Disgusted, he tossed the paper on the kitchen table and stared at it, wishing the content to go away. A clock alarm sounded from his parent's bedroom.

He heard his dad, Vince, "Damn clock."

His Mother, Bea, didn't need the clock. Charlie heard the toilet flush and the water run from the front bathroom between his parent's room, his brother Sam's and sister Jody's rooms.

Bea came out of the bathroom wrapped in a thick terrycloth robe. "Good morning, Charlie." She tried to smile. "Are you okay? I mean, after last night? How's your hand and shoulder?"

He answered a groggy "Hi, Mom, I'm fine. My hand and shoulder will be okay, not much pain this morning." But, Charlie recognized physical pain in his mother's eyes. "And how are you this morning?"

Bea answered, "I'm okay. How about I make French toast for breakfast?"

Inwardly Charlie knew the, "I'm okay," answer from his mother who suffered from a reoccurring illness was a gloss-over.

"French toast," Charlie blanched, "Yeah great, Mom."

Bea ran a hand through her son's hair. "God Bless you, Charlie, and that beautiful wavy black hair, my handsome lad." She hugged him.

Charlie thought that he detected a sob from his mother. She nodded at the paper on the table. "There's a story about last night? Was she . . . ?"

Charlie still found his mother's quaint British accent amusing. He refused to comprehend that Bea fought a disease that could take her wonderful voice forever.

"Murdered, yeah," he answered, "The story is on the front page." *The way I found her as if it could have been anything else.*

Bea clutched the robe around her neck, "Charlie, that poor girl. At first, I couldn't understand what your father was telling me last night, when he called from the police station. Thank God, you have Matt."

"Yeah," Charlie pointed at the paper. "I think he's the only cop that believes I had nothing to do with it."

Bea leaned over to read the headline.

"How awful," tears welled in her eyes. Bea was sensitive to the press. She never liked the tabloid style of reporting even though she grew up with it in her native London.

Charlie saw her put her hand to her mouth and continue to stare at the paper, afraid to touch it. Her constant physical pain and mental anguish forced her to look for diversions. She looked back at her son.

2

"You're ready for school? What's that you're wearing?"

Charlie shrugged. "The usual, you know."

Bea looked him over and wrinkled her nose. If you didn't have your dad's olive complexion you'd look like a breadstick. Are you eating? You can't weigh more than 135 pounds."

Charlie stood tall and straight, all five-foot-nine-inches. "You would say, 'growing like a reed'."

"Those clothes, they're unkempt."

"Well, you know, Mom, my favorite shirt and jeans."

"That's what I mean Charlie. You're wearing that shirt, fresh out of the laundry, and I haven't ironed it yet. And those dungarees are ready to fall off your butt. Let me have that shirt. I'll heat up the iron. My son isn't going out of this house looking like a laundry bag." Bea pulled at his shirt as he finished unbuttoning. "I'll be back in a jiffy." She took the shirt downstairs.

Charlie felt a chill through his T-shirt as he reached to the small shelf near the kitchen sink and turned on the radio. The overcast sky outside the kitchen window mirrored his feelings. He wondered how many people see a dead body while doing a good deed. He waited for the newscast.

"Now the news and weather," the radio announcer said, "Last night, a murdered girl was found in North Denver's Highland Park, behind Woodbury Library. Police have no suspects. The girl, as yet unidentified, may have been raped according to the Denver Police Department."

"Raped?" Charlie tried to remain calm as he went to the table and looked for the story again. "Did you hear that? She may have been raped, but the cops didn't say for sure." He often thought out loud leaving himself vulnerable to those within earshot. "How can the news make the assumption without verifying the story? She may have been isn't the same as she was -- bastards. And how come it just had to happen when I was in that park last night? What happened to the guy with the flat tire? Who were those two other guys?" He thought about last night.

2

Boy Meets Girl -- Dead

Carlo, "Charlie," Bonarelli heard a voice, barely audible, from someone in the moonlit park punctuated by scudding clouds and old growth trees.

Seconds earlier he had seen someone, illuminated by a light from the adjacent library's rear window. The person was limping. Then a voice, and he saw the corner of a jacket just visible from behind a momentarily backlit tree, another person.

As the clouds parted for a few seconds the tree threw a shadow over a picnic table. Charlie, in a hurry to get into the library to use a phone, didn't see what lay crumpled to one side of the table. He rushed into the building and found a librarian sorting over a cart of books. She looked up as he approached her.

"There's a man, injured out on the back street. We need some help."

"I'll call the police." The librarian went behind the main desk and picked up the phone, found what she was looking for on her desk and dialed a number. While she waited for someone on the other end she asked, "What happened?"

"I was driving up the street when I see this guy. It looks like he's trying to change a tire near the curb. It's thick ice where he's working. The tire looks a little flat on the front right side. His car jack must have slipped out from under the car because it was lying in front of the car. I run up to the guy and he looks hurt.

"Then he's hollering at me to move the car away from his leg. One of his legs looks like it's trapped between the car and the curb. I tried to push the car away from his legs."

The librarian saw Charlie's right hand. "You're injured."

He felt a sensation in his hand and examined a bloody cut across his right palm.

The librarian grabbed a box of tissue from behind the counter, and pulled out a handful.

Charlie took the tissues and clenched them tight into his hand. He grimaced, feeling pulling heat in his right shoulder.

The librarian looked at the phone as if it should come alive, "This is taking a long time."

"Anyway, I couldn't move the car. The guy hollers for me to get some . . . ."

The librarian held up her hand to indicate that someone was talking to her. She watched Charlie clench the tissues then spoke into the phone and reported what Charlie had told her, "In back of the library . . . Highland Park Place, right?" She looked at Charlie.

"Yeah, almost at the corner," he squeezed the wad of tissue tightly.

The librarian held up her hand again. "Okay, I'll tell him." She cradled the phone. "The police are sending a car to meet you at the corner. What about that hand?"

"I must have cut it on the guy's fender when I was trying to move the car. Maybe you could give me a few more tissues. He took the offered tissues jamming them into his hand with the already bloody wad.

Charlie ran out of the library's back entrance and cut across the park. He had to pass the picnic table again. The clouds had opened more illuminating the area better lighted with the bright moonlight. He saw something on the ground near the picnic table. He ran to the table but stopped like a quick-braking truck and almost slipped. He reached for the table to steady himself.

"Jesus." He saw someone on the ground. He smelled a flowery perfume. There was no movement. He leaned down hoping that the person would say something.

"Hey, you okay? Hey." He reached to touch the person with his right hand and the blood soaked tissue dropped onto the ground by the body. The person didn't move. Charlie didn't know what to do, but tried shaking the inert form. It was a female. He thought he recognized her. She wasn't breathing.

Charlie jumped up and thought about going back to the library again, but he saw a car approaching near the corner. He ran towards the Denver Police patrol car as it rolled to a stop.

He looked up and down the street as he ran to the curb where the squad car pulled up. He didn't see the car or the man whom he tried to help earlier. "What the hell?"

"Hey, kid." A policeman spoke from the passenger side of the car, "You the one that the library called about?"

"Yeah, that's me. But, the car and the guy are gone. Hey, and there's somebody down in the park, by the picnic table." Charlie pointed towards the trees and the table.

The policeman got out of the car. He clicked on a flashlight and pointed it at Charlie, blinding him. The cop quickly swept the beam across the area then put the light on Charlie again. "The guy and his car are gone?" What do you mean, there's somebody by the picnic table?"

"Over there," Charlie pointed toward the picnic area, "About midway between here and the library. I just saw a girl, a woman, I'm not sure."

"What're you talking about, kid?"

Charlie felt his hand bleeding again. The tissue was gone. He pulled out his handkerchief and wrapped it around the cut. "When I was coming back from the library to meet you . . . ."

"Riley, what's up?" The driver of the police car spoke through the window.

"The kid says there's someone in the park, on the ground. Let's go take a look."

The cop's partner got out of the car and followed Charlie and Riley towards the center of the park. Both policemen swept the area with their flashlights.

"Over here." Charlie walked to the side of the picnic table where he had found the body.

Riley shined his light around the table, and resting the beam on the motionless person lying on the ground he reached down and touched her neck. "No pulse -- deader than yesterday's news."

The two officers shined their lights over the body making an iridescent-like image of death. The odor of flowered perfume again wafted around the site.

Riley said to his partner, "Joe, a girl, woman, maybe raped? Look at her clothes. "Call it in. I'll stay here with this boy, maybe get some answers."

Joe ran towards the police car. Riley looked at Charlie with more interest than Charlie felt comfortable with. "Kid, you're staying here for now. We need to talk a little."

"Huh?" Charlie felt like he had just stepped in some dog's droppings. He instinctively looked at his shoes.

Riley played the light around the body again. He shined the light on her face. "You know this girl, kid?"

Charlie recognized the face. He had seen the girl or woman; it was hard to tell if she was a student or what? "I've seen here around the library, but I don't know who she is. I don't think she goes to the high school. Maybe she lives around here?"

He thought back on the few times that he had seen the girl. He didn't think that she was quite right, like she was brain damaged or afflicted. Remorse, the reality of this poor girl's death, enveloped him. The thought of her violated ending made him queasy.

Charlie had seen dead people before, at family funerals, but he had never seen a person violated as this poor girl on the ground had been. Her dress was ripped and pulled up around her neck. She was wearing a bra, but her underwear was gone. Her right shoe was off and lying on the ground at one end of the picnic table.

A piece of clothing was on the table. He got sick to his stomach. He thought, Jesus, what happened here? Who were those two guys that I saw earlier? One of them limped like Ralph Jay.

Despite a sick stomach, Charlie took quick looks at the body. His mind dwelled on the voice he had heard. The limping person, was it Ralph Jay who some kids at school called "The Animal?"

"Hey, kid," Riley grabbed Charlie's right shoulder. He shined his light over him again.

Cops and flashlights. Charlie reached up to rub his sore shoulder.

Riley put the light on Charlie's right hand. "You're bleeding through the hanky around your hand. Let me see that."

Oh shit. I touched the girl with my bloody hand, the tissue?

Charlie reluctantly showed his hand.

Sensing something, Riley asked, "What's wrong? What's your name, kid?

Charlie tried to hide his hand. He thought of the man in the street, where did he go? "I cut my hand when I was trying to push the car away from the guy's leg."

Riley looked puzzled. "Oh yeah, the guy with the car huh? You better keep the hanky on the hand then. So what's your name?"

"I'm Charlie, uh, Carlo Bonarelli. I'm called 'Charlie.'"

"Okay, Charlie." Riley shined his flashlight in Charlie's face again. "You got anything to do with this?"

"I don't know what you mean."

"You got some identification kid?"

Charlie couldn't see Riley's face for the light in his eyes, but he didn't like the inflection in the cop's voice.

He reached in his back pocket with his left hand. "I have a driver's license." He flipped open the wallet to show the license. A silver foil packet fell out.

"What's this?" Riley bent down and picked up the foil covered rubber. "A little young to be worrying about this sort of thing ain't you? Here." He dropped the little package into Charlie's wrapped right hand. "The license?" He paused as he looked at Charlie's license and then at him. "So you got a vehicle, 'veee-hickle,' around here?" Not waiting for an answer Riley read the name on the license. "Carlo Bonarelli, that a Mexican name?"

"No, Italian."

"Eye-talyin? So that's a wop name, huh."

Before he could answer, Riley pushed on the middle of Charlie's back and guided him toward the library. "Let's go over here where the light is better."

Charlie heard sirens increasing in volume. Clouds covered the moon again.

"This park is darker 'n hell. Hold up a minute, Bonarelli.

Riley waved his flashlight at two police cars, arriving at the corner where the other police car had found Charlie.

He waited with Riley. He heard the cop breathing, and smelled sulfur as Riley, who had pulled a cigarette out of his front pocket, struck a match. The flash caught someone's attention.

"What's up?"

Riley turned towards the voice. An official looking man, carrying a medical bag approached. Two men in plain clothes exited the library's back entrance.

More police cars arrived in front of the library. More flashlights appeared and a Denver Fire Department truck, siren howling, drove on the street nearest the picnic area. A powerful spotlight played into the trees and the picnic table.

"Christ, could you get that spotlight a little brighter, goddamn-it, that'll put my eyes out." The man with the medical bag complained. "Where's the body?" He walked off without an answer towards the now brightly lit picnic area.

"Sorry, Examiner." Two men in suits, who Charlie guessed, were detectives came up to Riley. "Officer, ask the fire department to tone that light down for the Coroner please."

"Okay Detective." Riley turned to Charlie. "This eye-talyin kid found the body." Riley left Charlie with the detective.

"I'm Detective Lieutenant Matthias Grueber, this is Detective Jimmy Burns. Tell us what you've seen. First, who are you?"

"Matthias, you mean Matt?" Charlie asked. It's me, Charlie Bonarelli."

Grueber hesitated a moment then took the wallet still dangling in Charlie's left hand. He examined the license and handed the wallet back to Charlie. "What're you doing here, Charlie? Sorry, I didn't recognize you at first in this darkness."

Charlie felt the tightening vise of the law. He was skeptical of any authority, especially the police, but he knew and trusted his father's friend, Matt Grueber.

Trust or not, Charlie had never forgotten the photo from years before in *The Rocky Mountain News* of a police detective with a rubber hose and a man bent over a rail. The image remained fresh in his mind even after several years. He could barely read then, but never forgot his mother's reaction to the story. There was that stain of black and white brutality, the ugly scar across the front page of the paper.

"I . . . ."

Someone interrupted.

"Hey Detectives, what gives?"

A man appeared into the light, wearing a suit and hat. A "PRESS" card stuck in the hat band. A second man, baggy suit, and carrying a huge press camera trundled behind the reporter.

Charlie recognized newspaper photographer, Harry Rhoades.

Detective Grueber stared at the reporter and the photographer. "Stobber, Rhoades? Hope we didn't take you guys away from anything important."

"Nah," Stobber spoke, "We were watching a pretty good Golden Gloves though -- preliminary bout. You know, kids beating the shit out of each other. But, don't let that concern you. So where's the victim?"

Grueber answered, "Not yet you two. I haven't seen the victim yet. The Coroner is looking the area over now." Grueber looked at Charlie. "I want to talk to you, but later. Don't go away."

"But, I've got my boss's truck. I was making a delivery. I'm working. He's expecting me and I'm already late."

"Sorry, Ch . . . ." Grueber stopped. "You two, out of here." He pointed at the reporter and the photographer who had already flashed a photo.

Charlie's eyes reacted violently. "Damn-it, enough lights already."

"You see something kid?" The reporter asked. "What's your name, kid?"

Harry Rhoades brought the kitchen cabinet sized camera up again and a flashbulb popped.

"Hey, f . . . ." Charlie caught himself.

Detective Grueber grabbed Charlie's right shoulder.

"Shit, that hurts. Lay off of that. I have to use the toilet, okay?"

"You need to come with me." Grueber hustled Charlie away from the newspaper men. He saw two more people, one with a camera exit the library, flash bulbs popping.

The detective led Charlie towards the picnic table but away from the body.

"Stay here." Grueber took a small pad and pen from an inside coat pocket.

Charlie saw the dull metal from the man's holstered revolver.

Grueber stopped writing. "I need to take you down to the station, Charlie."

"The station -- what for? I really need to pee."

"We want to know what you saw. I'll call your father to meet us. Stay here."

"Can I call my boss, I've got his truck?"

Detective Grueber talked to a uniformed policeman.

The policeman went to Charlie. "I'll take you over to the library to use the toilet, and the phone. Let's go. Oh, and I'll take the keys to your truck."

Charlie looked back at Detective Grueber. "Matt, am I in the deep stuff?"

3

Grilled and Served

Vince Bonarelli stood at the reception desk of the police station when his son Charlie was escorted in by two Denver police officers.

One of the cops pointed Charlie to a bench. "Wait there."

Charlie sat on the hard wooden bench lost in thought. He hadn't noticed his father who came over and stood silent at the other end of the bench. He looked up to see Vince steaming.

Vince put out his hands, palms up, with a look to match his question. "Charlie, what the hell happened?"

Charlie looked around before he answered. At this time of night, a week night, the precinct house was a hollow shell of peeling paint and green tile floors. His stomach grumbled and odors of puke, old shit, stale food and body odor threatened to make him retch. The Desk-Sergeant ignored a muffled noise from a back office. Poor lighting pulsed like a heart and then stopped, and then started again. Charlie imagined the cops had electrocuted someone. This was a nightmare and he was part of it.

"Geez, Dad, I stopped to help someone and I found this girl, dead, in the park behind Woodbury Library." Charlie felt an unexplainable guilt as if he was the cause of the girl's death. He felt like a criminal earlier as he rode to the station in the sour smelling police car.

Vince repeated himself, "So what the hell is going on, Charlie? I got very little information from Matt when he called me."

Charlie winced when Vince put his hand on his sore right shoulder. He felt the pain now from the earlier damage.

In a daze, Charlie repeated himself. "I stopped to help somebody in Highland Park, and I found a body." Charlie worked to rub the sting out of his shoulder as they waited.

Detective Lieutenant Matthias Grueber came into the police station with his partner.

Matt Grueber, Vince's old wartime pal. Charlie knew that the man with the German name was a war hero from what he had heard about him from his father. But, forgetting who he was, and what he represented, he wasn't looking at Grueber like a hero. He thought of the tall, rugged-looking blonde cop with the craggy smile as *Tedesco*, a "Kraut." All the cop needed to complete the picture was the *sfregio*, the saber scar, the true mark of a German villain. But Grueber was an American. The image went away as Grueber spoke perfect English. He looked at Charlie and then addressed Vince.

"So Charlie, all grown up?" He shook hands with Vince. "It's been a couple of years since I've seen Charlie. I almost didn't recognize him in the poor light at the library."

Charlie watched Vince. He knew his "Dad" could control his temper when it was absolutely necessary. He understood Vince was trying to remain cool, but he heard his increasing irritation when Vince asked, "Matt, what's going on with Charlie? He's supposed to be working. His boss called me looking for him and is mad as hell the truck is being held, and searched, for what?"

Grueber answered, "It's a formality, Vince. Your boy found the body of a girl in Highland Park, behind Woodbury Library." He held out a small notebook. He had to squint in the blinking lights. "Shitty light, you'd think they could at least fix the lights.

"Charlie says he was trying to help a motorist. The patrol car got there, the motorist was gone and there's a body. He says he thinks that he saw two men, or boys, in the park earlier, where the body was found. There are too many loose ends. Oh, and here's a problem, there was a bloody tissue dropped near the body. The lab will be checking the blood type, probably right now."

"Hey, I probably dropped that when I was checking the girl." Charlie held out his hand. "I mean, look at this. The librarian gave me some Kleenex to stop the bleeding."

A phone rang at the front desk. The Desk Sergeant listened to someone on the other end of the phone. He motioned to Grueber to come over and spoke quietly to the detective.

Charlie watched Grueber scratching his cheek. *Shit, I dropped the Kleenex right there where the girl was.*

Grueber returned to Charlie and Vince. "The truck's clean, nothing to implicate either the truck or Charlie with the girl's body in the park, right now. The tissue will be a problem though. Oh, and I asked a patrol team to take the vehicle back to the market where Charlie works."

Vince bristled like a porcupine. His neck turned red. His cool was off. "Hell no there'd be nothing to connect Charlie with the body. He explained about the Kleenex."

Charlie looked at Grueber. "I recognized the girl."

Grueber stared at Charlie then at Vince, "Okay then, let's go to my office." He pointed the way. "I need to know what happened, and why you were in the park, Charlie. Take your time before you answer, think about it."

Charlie knew this was more than a friendly chat between old buds. He tried to remain calm and specific. He held his breath for a moment. How could he be rational and calm about the dead girl? He had recognized her.

"About 7:15 P.M., my boss, Max Irving, asked me to deliver ten pounds of hamburger to the Barrel Drive Inn. 'Use the panel truck,' he said, 'Take it easy, the streets are pretty damn slick out there.'"

"He was right. I almost slipped and fell with the package of meat when I walked out the back door of the market. It was dark. A cold, Halloween-like darkness when you'd of thought that bats should be flying and bones rattling.

"Lou, the butcher, was out near the alley. He says to me, 'Slicker 'n snot, huh?' I saw the red glow of his cigarette against the darkness and I wondered why he would stand out in the cold freezing his butt for a smoke? I told him that I was taking an order to the Barrel.

"Lou flipped the cigarette, and I watched its glowing arch before it hit a clump of snow. He says to me, 'Make it quick kid, I need you to stuff the sausage.'"

"Sausage," Matt smiled at Charlie. "You make sausage?"

"Yeah, I have to grind up the meat, mix in the boss's secret spice recipe, and stuff the casing. I had to get back pretty soon." Charlie thought about the sausage and how he hated slipping animal gut on the end of the grinder, watching the machine extrude the big meaty turds.

"Anyway, I managed to get the load into the truck without falling. I eased the truck out of the alley, and followed the ruts in the icy street. I remembered to be careful on the drive down Speer Boulevard. Despite the slow driving, the truck did the slip-and-slide."

"Okay, so you drove to restaurant, right?" Grueber wrote in his notebook. "What did you do on the way?"

"I switched on the radio. Max's favorite talk station came up with someone talking about 'danger . . . Cold War,' you know, more B.S, so I found this jazz program that I like, *Cool Bill Davis*."

Grueber's eyebrows arched. "I thought that all of you young guys like Rock-N-Roll?"

"Yeah, well, I like a little bit of everything, and I remember Cool Bill announcing, "It's 7:30 P.M., and you're listing to the *Cool Bill Davis Show*. Here's a ballad by Chet Baker.'

"The DJ was spinning, *My Funny Valentine*, a little too dreamy for the icy drive." Charlie didn't mention that had Karin Delaney on his mind and difficulty concentrating on the road. He didn't think Vince and the detective needed to hear about his hard-on when the music made him dream nasty thoughts about his neighbor, Karin.

"Okay, Charlie," Vince interrupted his son's thoughts about Karin. "So you're driving to the restaurant, and then what? Get to the point."

"Easy, Vince," Grueber held up a hand. "I want to hear the whole story why Charlie was at the park."

Charlie remembered that at an intersection, a jolt of adrenalin woke him from his thoughts about Karin when the truck slid on the pavement. Cool Bill Davis finished a sponsor's announcement and came back on the air with an upbeat Duke Ellington tune. He tapped the rhythm on the steering wheel and managed not to crash before he pulled into the big, barrel-domed roof drive-in known for their root beer and cheeseburgers. He wanted to hang around awhile, but remembered the sausage.

"I delivered the meat. I had to get back to the market. I took a different route back and drove behind North High School. I thought the streets wouldn't be so slick there. I cut across Federal Boulevard to pass next to the library and Highland Park."

"Northwest of the library, I made a left turn from Highland Park Place when I saw a car near the corner with its lights on. A person was hunched between the car and the curb.

"I thought something was wrong. I pulled over and parked the truck, got out, and went towards the car that had slid against the curb. I heard some noise and a shout.

"The person was curled over. I could see by the suit, no overcoat though, and a big hat, that it was a man. He looked up briefly. I saw the man's eyes but I couldn't distinguish the man's features under the hat. It was that strange darkness, like a cloak. The moon was in and out of the clouds. The man looked down again as he spoke to me.

"He said, 'My foot is stuck here.' There was a car jack lying in front of the car. Then the guy says, 'The jack slipped when I was changing a flat.' The voice sounded familiar, but I couldn't place it. I forgot about it as I bent over and grabbed onto the fender of the car, a late model Oldsmobile, it wouldn't budge. I pushed and pulled like crazy and my feet slipped from under me. I lurched into the car's fender, smacked the hell out of my right shoulder when I fell into the car. I pulled myself up from between the car and the curb. I wasn't getting anywhere.

"I told the guy I'd get some help. I'd run over to the library and use the phone. I ran towards the library, but got stopped short."

"'Who are you going to call?' The guy sounded concerned. You'd think he'd have wanted me to go as fast as I could, but I stopped. 'The police I guess. I'll be right back.' I turned to run across the park towards the library. A breeze caused the tree tops to move against an on-again-off-again cloudy sky. I felt a pain in my right shoulder, but I didn't see the cut in my hand." Charlie looked down to see that the handkerchief he had wrapped around his right hand had stuck to the cut.

Grueber asked, "What about the two guys you told me about earlier? You said that you saw two guys when you ran to the library to call the police. Can you identify anything at all about them?" He leaned across his desk towards Charlie. "You mentioned that one of them limped. Do you have any details like, height, weight, complexion, hair color? Were they white, Hispanic?"

"I don't know." Charlie leaned back and tried to collect his thoughts. "Maybe white. The moon threw a little light, not much though. The guy I actually saw looked about six-feet tall. It must have clouded over again. There wasn't much light through the trees."

Charlie thought about the limping person. He thought of Ralph Jay from school, and the creepy little bastard, Joe Birch, who ran with Jay. He hesitated, "I can't be sure who it was."

"You can't be sure -- any ideas? Maybe it was somebody from the market, from school, the restaurant, what?" Grueber sensed something, but he wasn't sure what it was. "Okay, you think of anything, anything at all, Charlie, you'll let me know, right?"

Charlie thought if it was Ralph Jay, the other guy would definitely be Birch. But what would Ralph be doing in the park at night? He sure as hell wasn't at the library. Charlie knew that Ralph Jay read nothing but Becky Morris's ass.

Jay had a thing for Becky. He knew that Jay salivated over Becky who never returned his ardor. Complicating the standoff was one of Becky's friends who wanted to put the moves on Ralph.

Becky had invited Charlie to the Jr. Prom the year before this. That was a surprise. He didn't think he would be going to the prom much less have a girl invite him to the dance. And, Becky always seemed to be around to walk with him between classes. She did her family's shopping at the meat market when he was working after school.

Maybe Becky's the reason Ralph Jay is always dogging me. He wants Becky. That's it, Ralph Jay is jealous of Becky's attention to me.

"Charlie, Matt is talking to you." Vince shook Charlie's shoulder, causing searing pain up to his neck.

"Ouch, Dad, that hurts."

"What about the girl, Charlie. You said you recognized her? Who is she?"

"I don't know her name. She hangs around North and the library. There is something wrong with her, like an injury or maybe a mental problem. She doesn't attend the high school. I think maybe she lives by the library. That's all that I know."

Grueber wrote in his pad, "Okay, we'll check it out. We need to have that shoulder and your hand looked at."

Charlie recognized that this was an order, not a request, nor a particular concern.

"Nah, it's just a pulled muscle."

The detective rolled his eyes. "Maybe, but the hand doesn't look too good from here. I want you to go over to Denver General

Hospital." He looked at Vince. "You want to take him? We need to have that hand and shoulder examined."

"Matt, you sure that's all, the shoulder and the hand?" Vince's tone had changed. It was clear Grueber had more in mind than the shoulder and the hand.

"He looked at Vince again. We have to do this Vince. If you weren't a trusted friend, I'd have a police car take him to the hospital for a thorough examination. You know it's part of the routine."

Charlie's attention was on his father and Grueber.

"On second thought, just to avoid complications, I'll have an officer take Charlie down to Denver General. You can meet him there and take him home after. Sorry for the inconvenience."

* * *

As he was escorted into the hospital, Charlie, sensed the weight of the situation. He was a suspect sure as hell.

The eerily lighted emergency entrance framed a cop standing inside who opened the door as they went in. Vince followed a minute later. They waited for people ahead of them. The emergency room stunk of alcohol and vomit. A woman came in screaming about her split ear and a damaged eye. Two drunks stumbled in escorted by another cop. One of the drunks lost it on the floor.

"Shit, Leonard, you did it again." The cop at the door pushed the sick man into a restroom. "Clean up for Christ's sake."

Vince looked at his watch and complained about how long it was taking. The cop who had brought Charlie in moldered on the waiting room bench. He yawned as he watched an orderly clean up the drunk's puke.

The cop looked relieved as a nurse led Charlie into a space with a curtain around it.

An emergency room doctor examined Charlie's shoulder and ordered a film of the shoulder and hand. He asked an orderly to take an external photograph the hand too. After the photo, a nurse cleaned and bandaged his hand. It didn't need stitches. She took blood samples and gave him a Tetanus shot.

"Let's get that x-ray," the doctor motioned to the nurse.

* * *

It was like Charlie thought. The shoulder injury turned out to be a pulled muscle. The doctor didn't stop with the shoulder examination. The nurse handed Charlie a hospital gown. "Strip, put this on."

Charlie balked. "What's all this about? I've got a cut hand and a sore shoulder, that's all?"

The doctor ignored the question. "Take off your clothes and put on the gown please."

"Shouldn't you have done this for the x-ray? Now what?" Charlie realized the futility and started to remove his clothes. The nurse left.

"Okay, young man, let's see the hands again." He checked the fingernails, looking for other abrasions or scrapes. "Okay drop the gown."

"What the hell?" Charlie's face reddened.

"The genitals, I need to take a look. Orderly, bring the camera again."

"Bullshit, Doctor. What's going on? I pushed the car with my hands, not my dick."

After the doctor's examination the orderly came in and took two scrotum shots.

Bastards. Charlie quickly retrieved his gown and wrapped it around his waist. *And, fuck you both.*

"No bruises, no body trauma." The doctor wrote something on a form attached to a clipboard. "Stay here." He left the area.

Charlie grabbed his clothes and quickly put them on.

A few moments later the doctor and the cop entered.

23

"Oh, see you've got your clothes on already. Okay, you can go home now." The cop motioned Charlie out of the room with a nod of his head.

In the emergency room corridor, Vince scrunched up his eyebrows. He wanted answers. "Well?"

"Everything's cool, Dad. We can go now – fuckers."

A surprised Vince asked, "What happens now, Charlie?"

"I don't know, but I guess we're going to know soon enough. They took pictures of my dick."

4

Hey Jay

Charlie sat at the table and reread the article about the girl. *This is going to go badly once the kids at school* . . . . The phone rang. He heard his mother's voice.

"Oh hello Bobo . . . yes, he's right here. Charlie, it's your cousin."

Charlie went to the phone, his shirt still warm from Bea's iron. "Hey, Bobo, yeah, that'll be great. I'll be ready. See you in fifteen." He hung up the phone and went back into the kitchen.

"Bobo's picking me up this morning."

Bea held out a plate of French toast. "You've got time to eat. Sit down, and let's not *mangiare fare colazione* like *il lupo.*"

Charlie always got a kick out of her Italian. "How do you do that, Mom? I mean, manage those Italian words with the British accent?"

She laughed. "I'm a continental Brit, baby. Now eat."

Vince walked into the kitchen. He made a wry face. "French toast, again?"

"You love it, Vincenzo. Sit and eat before you're late for the office. And don't drip syrup on that clean white shirt."

Vince wrapped Bea in his arms. "Why don't you sit down and I'll give you your breakfast instead?"

"Thanks, Sweetie." She playfully pushed him away. "You better get going. I'll endure." She put a dramatic hand to her forehead.

Vince sat at the table and picked up the morning news. He studied the headline and read the first paragraph of the story. "These reporters write a lot into an event, don't they?"

An anguished Bea replied, "I haven't read the story yet. What does it say? No, never mind, I'll read it later. Right now I need to get Sam and Jody up."

She left the kitchen as Vince read the paper. "This story doesn't sound good for, 'A North High School boy who found the body of a girl . . . .'"

Charlie picked at his breakfast.

"Better eat, Son. I have a feeling that you're going to have a long day." Vince held up the paper and tapped the story with a finger. "It's probably a good idea to keep this to yourself."

A horn honked. Charlie ran downstairs to his room to get his books.

Bea's voice came from another room. "Brush your teeth, and don't forget your lunch and jacket, Charlie."

"Yeah, don't forget your lunch, Charlie." Jody hollered from another room.

Charlie's cousin, Roberto, "Bobo," Marcantonio hit the car horn again as Charlie bolted out of the front door teetering a stack of books and a sack lunch. Bobo's car radio blared Elvis Presley's latest hit, *I'm All Shook Up*. Charlie got in the car as Bobo sang with the music.

"Oh-yah, oh-yah. How's it going, Charlie?"

"Bobo, can you turn the radio up just a little louder, I've still got eardrums in my head."

Bobo grinned and turned the radio volume down.

"Thank you. You're upbeat this morning, cuz. How come you've got the car today?"

Bobo scrunched his 165-pound boxer's body over the steering wheel with a sly sideways glance. "I'm taking my Nonna to the doctor after school. You wanna ride along, or you gotta work? You know she always treats us to a malted after we take her somewhere. Hey, what's with the bandaged hand?"

"Later, man. Anyway, I like your grandmother, but I think I got something to do after school – I'm sure of it." Charlie zipped up his jacket. "Man, it's cold in here. You got a heater or what?"

"Heater's on the fritz. So what did you do last night after work? You get that bad hand feeling-up Karin in her parents game room? There's nothing like warm tits on a cold night."

"Hey, Bobo you think too much about Karin. She's a good girl. Anyway, I was detained. I didn't get home until ten last night."

"What's that mean, detained? You mean you were getting laid, right?" Bobo bulged his eyes and licked his lips like a hungry child.

"Christ, that's ugly when you do that, Bobo. I was detained by the Denver Police. Geez, man, open the fucking windows. It's warmer outside than it is in this meat locker. Your Nonna's going to freeze to death in this car before you even get her to the doctor. You can take her to the mortuary instead."

"What the hell do you mean? What about the police? You do something, and I wasn't involved?"

"Bobo, watch where you're driving. You're going to hit the curb. Anyway, you know that retarded girl who was always hanging around school?"

Bobo bobbed his head back and forth as they had seen the girl do when she walked. He extended his tongue. "Ah-ah-ah."

"Shut up, Bobo. I found her last night in the park -- dead."

Bobo swerved to miss a parked car. "Dead? No shit? You found her dead? Where'd you find her dead? No shit?"

Despite Vince's warning, Charlie told Bobo what happened, and about Detective Matt Grueber, and his suspicions of seeing Ralph Jay and his pal in the park where he found the body.

"Ralph Jay, The Animal, no shit? So the police took you in. So how's your hand this morning? No shit? You found the girl, dead? No shit?"

"Bobo, you'd better wipe yourself when you're done shitting. Hey, think about driving us to school without killing us, okay?"

"Wow, Charlie. I can't believe that somebody killed that poor girl. She was harmless; screwed up, but harmless. So you didn't tell the police, Detective Grueber, Uncle Vince's friend, that you suspect Jay and his monkey-butt friend, Birch?"

"No. I don't know for sure if it was those two."

"Well, what if it was Jay, and what if he recognized you in the park? What's the possibility that he tries to beat you to death like he almost did that kid at school?"

Bobo found a place to park. They quick-stepped to meet up with their friend Zellie Goldfarb.

"Zel, wait till you hear the latest." Bobo blurted, "Charlie found a dead girl in Highland Park last night, and he thinks that he saw The Animal there too."

Ralph Jay, "The Animal," regularly bullied, beat on, and intimidated kids at school. He once menaced a teacher until the baseball coach cornered him. Nobody knows what the coach said to Jay, but he backed off like a puppy with his tail between his legs. The threat quickly wore off though and Jay continued to terrorize the school.

How Jay managed to avoid juvenile hall was a question pondered by anyone who knew of him and his friend Joe Birch. An early childhood affliction left Jay with a limp and a chip on his shoulder.

Jay was tall, handsome, and menacing. School hall traffic parted like the Red Sea when Jay and Birch flowed through.

Jay and Charlie usually went out of their way to avoid each other. Unlike most of his classmates, Charlie didn't feel so threatened by Jay as he was more concerned that his own temper might get the better of him. He realized early that he was unable to think straight if he got mad. He didn't just "go mad," he went haywire. Charlie worked hard to contain his ill feelings and use the energy to his advantage.

Bobo jumped up and down. "Jay may have a limp, but he's got arms like a windmill fucking gorilla." Bobo scratched under his arms for effect. He visualized himself as an up-and-coming Golden Gloves boxer. He couldn't tolerate bullies. He shadow-boxed an imaginary opponent, "I'd like to get the son-of-a-bitch in the ring."

Charlie reminded Bobo and Zel about Jay. "He's stronger than a bull. He's worked out since he was a little kid to fight whatever bugs him, and now he's mad at the whole world."

"Right," Zel agreed.

Zel Goldfarb, was from the "West Side," across Sloan's Lake which he constantly reminded anyone who would listen. At six-foot, two-inches high, he should have towered over Jay. But, Zel slouched; his kinky red hair looked like rusty steel wool. Freckles and wire-rimmed glasses inspired him to self-depreciate.

"I look like a Jewish Howdy Doody now, but when I'm old and gray haired, wearing a black suit and have *tachlis*. When I've done it all, made my mark, then it'll mean something when I tell you to stay the fuck away from Ralph Jay. He's nuts-o, out of control, *meshuge*, and he wants to crack your heads."

Bobo looked cockeyed at Zel. "Whadya mean? You think The Animal don't like me and Charlie?"

They walked into the school to their lockers.

"Speaking of Beelzebub," Zel nodded down the hall.

Jay and Birch walked toward the three boys.

Zel mumbled about a movie he had just seen, *Gunfight at The O.K. Corral.*

Jay and Birch glared at Charlie and Bobo.

"Hey, assholes, how's it going?" Birch gave the finger.

"Fuck you twice, monkey-butt." Bobo gave the finger back.

Jay said nothing, but grabbed Birch by the collar. He whispered loudly into Birch's ear. Charlie thought he heard Jay say, "Stupid shit, shut up."

"What does that tell you guys?" Zel asked.

Birch shoved his hands in his pockets, lowered his head and huffed down the hall with Ralph Jay pushing him along.

"Hey, Jay, how's it hanging?" Bobo called after.

5

Gimpy and Limpy

Charlie thought all morning about the incident with Ralph Jay in the hall. He unconsciously squeezed his sack lunch into a ball as he walked to the cafeteria. Something was up, and it had to do with the girl in the park. Was it a coincidence that the voice Charlie heard last night in the park and Jay chewing on his pal this morning sounded familiar? If it was Jay and Birch in the park last night, why were they there?

Charlie felt a slight pain when someone gently touched his right arm.

"Hi Charlie, you going my way?"

Becky Morris smiled. She was almost his height, slender, blonde hair, long and neat. No poodle skirts for Becky. She designed and made her own clothes, and was dressed in a matching, tight-fitting, top and skirt.

Despite his preoccupation with what happened the night before, Charlie's libido kicked in. He didn't quite understand, yet, the complete mental and physical affect that high school girls and young women had on him except they caused his erections.

"Hi, Becky. You're looking delicious. So are you on your way to lunch?" Charlie thought about licking her neck.

"Yeah, c'mon, you can walk me to the lunch room."

They saw Ralph Jay walking fast without Birch in tow. Jay, who stalked Becky relentlessly, scowled when she took Charlie's arm and they walked away.

Becky asked, "Did you hear what happened in Highland Park last night? That retarded girl who always hung around the library. She was murdered in the park behind the library.

"I was supposed to study there with Ruthie last night, but I had to take care of my little sister. It's creepy to think what may have happened if I had been walking back there on my way to meet her."

"Ruthie? You were going to meet Ruthie at the library?" Charlie knew that Becky's best friend, Ruthie Grey, had a crush on Jay, of all people. She probably told Jay that she was meeting Becky at the library. That might explain what Jay and Birch were doing there if it was them.

"Anyway," Becky continued," our teacher read an article from today's *Rocky Mountain News* in Civics class. Some guy from our school found the body. The article didn't give a name. I wonder who he is. Would you think that he might have something to do with the girl's murder?

"Charlie, you're staring a hole through my head." She looked at him with a sudden comprehension. "Charlie, what's the matter? You're turning red. Hey, what happened to your hand? Oh no, was it you? Did you find her?"

Charlie realized that the name of the person who found the girl's body would soon be all over the school. "Look, Becky, I was making a delivery to the Barrel last night." He told her the story but left out the two people he saw. "It was gruesome."

Becky blurted, "God, Charlie, how awful. God, I'm sorry what I said about the guy . . . you know, that maybe he had something to do with it."

"That's okay, the cops thought the same thing. They questioned me and took me to the hospital to check me out, thoroughly. I'm not sure yet that I'm not a suspect. My dad asked me to keep this quiet, but it'll be all over school by last bell."

As they walked the noisy halls towards the cafeteria, the assistant principal, Mr. Greyer, came toward them. He waved to get Charlie's attention. A limp slowed him as he tried to stay ahead of two people following him.

"Bonarelli, these people insist on talking with you. Let's go to my office and sort this out."

Becky let go of Charlie's arm, "I'll meet up with you later, Charlie."

"Are you Carlo Bonarelli?" A woman interjected herself between Charlie and Mr. Greyer.

Mr. Greyer put up a hand to stop her. "I wanted to find you, Charlie, before others like these two get to you, they're reporters. I read the *Rocky Mountain News* article about what happened last night. These people are from *The Denver Post*. They told me you found the girl. Somebody from the police gave them your name."

Mr. Greyer turned on the reporter. "This is highly irregular. You can't interview students without parental permission. This is harassment."

The woman objected, "Mr. Greyer, I believe the boy is eighteen, and the public has a right to know."

"To know what?"

The reporter glared at Mr. Greyer. "We want to talk to the boy alone if you don't mind."

"Absolutely not. You can't come into a public school and harass the students, or the staff. We'll go to my office. Nothing's going to happen here."

"Come, Charlie." Mr. Greyer limped as he took Charlie in tow. The two newspaper people followed them to the school office.

Mr. Greyer lead the way into the school's main office and into his private office behind the counter.

Charlie's internal alarm cautioned him about talking to reporters. "Wait a minute, I'm calling my dad."

"Good idea," Mr. Greyer pointed to his phone.

"Bobby," the reporter told her partner, "Get a shot of, uh . . . ." The reporter took a pad and a pencil from her purse and looked at something written. "You're called 'Charlie' not Carlo. Is that right?"

She didn't wait for an answer. "Charlie, what were you doing in Highland Park last night?"

The news photographer focused on Charlie.

"Stop," Mr. Greyer cautioned. "Charlie's going to call his father. You two can wait. Either have a seat or get out."

Charlie dialed a number and waited. "Dad, please." He waited another ten seconds then spoke. "There are two people here from *The Denver Post*." Charlie held the phone close to him and turned away from the reporters, "Yeah, a reporter and a photographer." A camera flashed. "Okay, yeah, I'll be okay. See you later, bye."

Charlie hung up the phone. "My dad says that I don't have to talk to you. So, excuse me please."

Mr. Greyer nodded his head in agreement. "You two can leave the school now. And, if you ever barge in here again, I'll call the police."

The photographer made ready to take another photo. The reporter grabbed his sleeve. "Let's go, we'll see Mr. Bonarelli later." She turned and winked at Charlie.

Mr. Greyer stood by his desk, "Smart lady crime-reporter. That's a new one. Oh, Charlie, I want to talk with you a moment. Please sit down. I need to know what's going on. It may affect the school and the student body."

Charlie told the assistant principal the details. He mentioned the two people by the picnic table, but he didn't speculate to Mr. Greyer who they might be.

Mr. Greyer's face was stone-like before he spoke. "Watch yourself, Charlie. It's possible the person who killed the girl might think you can identify them. Be careful of people whom you don't know, and maybe even those you do."

This last statement struck Charlie as strange from the assistant principal. He hesitated a moment and replied, "Okay, Mr. Greyer, I'll be all right. Thanks."

"Better get to lunch while you still have a few minutes, Charlie."

As Charlie walked out of Mr. Greyer's office he recognized Mr. Truwet, a substitute psychology teacher. He was on crutches. He stared at Charlie and nodded.

"Hello, Mr. Truwet." Mr. Greyer limped over to the man. "How's the leg?"

*   *   *

Becky waited for Charlie outside the school office. "Charlie, those two from *The Denver Post* are hanging around outside the front door of the school. I don't know what you told them, but I heard the woman tell the guy with the camera that they would find you later. I think they're going to ambush you. It looks like they're asking questions of any kid who passes by."

"Questions? Who knows about it except us and Mr. Greyer? He'll chase them off. How did you know that they're from the *Post*?"

"Uh, Ruthie, you know she works in the office part time. She was there when you went in. I guess she must have heard you talking or she figured it out. Hey, do you have a way to work tonight after school? I can drive you."

"I'm not working tonight. My boss isn't sure that he wants me there right now. I'll take the bus home."

"You better not take the bus. Those newspaper people will find you. I'm driving Ruthie home, you should ride with us. I'll drive you home, too."

"Thanks Becky. Where will I meet you?"

"Meet us at the side door, near the teacher's parking lot. I'm parked close to school. Anyway, I doubt the newspaper people will expect you to exit by the teacher's door. Hey, if we hurry we can still get lunch."

"Damn, my lunch. I left my sack lunch in the office. You go ahead, Becky. I'll grab my lunch. See you later. Thanks."

Charlie ran back to the school office and saw Mr. Greyer still talking to Mr. Truwet.

"That was some fall. You know, I've heard that our highest domestic fatality rate is from home accidents. You've got to watch those ladders, Mr. Truwet.

"Maybe you should have the school nurse take a look at those face scratches too. How long do you have to keep the cast on your right leg?"

The two men turned and looked as Charlie walked near them.

"I forgot my lunch in your office, Mr. Greyer. Okay if I go get it?"

"Sure, Charlie."

As Charlie went to retrieve his lunch, he thought about Mr. Truwet's condition. What about the cast and the crutches?

On his way out of the office, Charlie followed Mr. Greyer and Mr. Truwet. The substitute teacher gave a backward glance, causing him to almost trip over his crutches.

* * *

The two girls approached Charlie. "Hi, Becky. Hey, Ruthie, how's it going?" He leaned against a wall nearest the door to the teacher's parking lot. School was out for the day, but the teachers usually stayed an hour after the students left.

Becky waved, "Hey, Charlie."

Ruthie grinned and stole a sideways glance at her friend. Becky colored, but didn't say anything as they walked through the teacher's parking lot toward the street behind the school.

Charlie saw a familiar car, an Oldsmobile, the same model he thought he saw in the park the night before. He stopped. The girls waited while giving him a questioning frown as Charlie examined the right fender-well of the big car. He put a hand on the right hubcap, checking for, what? He wasn't sure himself. The car only looked familiar. He couldn't tell if this was the same vehicle that he had cut his hand on.

Sloppy streets had caused grime to stick around the fenders and the wheels. Charlie walked around the car looking and thinking about the fresh scratches on the chrome front bumper visible through the road dirt.

He took out his pencil and wrote down the car's license number on the back of a book cover.

"What's going on? What are you doing at my car?"

The two girls and Charlie looked around to see Mr. Truwet. The girls gave a questioning shrug.

"Nice car, Mr. Truwet." Charlie put his pencil behind his ear. I was just writing down the model, 1958 88-Coupe, nice."

"Get along now. I need to get into my car please." The teacher avoided eye-contact as he searched his pocket for the keys. He slipped but recovered as he tried to maneuver the crutches.

"How'd your hurt your leg, Sir?" Becky asked.

"Never mind. You kids get along now."

"Come on ladies." Charlie feigned a grimace at the two girls.

Ruthie chuckled as they walked. "Did you notice that both Mr. Greyer and Mr. Truwet have damaged right legs? Gimpy and Limpy. What do you think crawled up his nose?"

6

Temporary Insanity

The three friends walked to a 1949 Cadillac sedan with a car dealer's temporary license plate. Becky's father was a used car dealer on West Colfax Avenue, and he let her drive the inventory.

Charlie gave the big car his critical assessment. "Wow, is this your boat?" He rubbed the bandaged hand along the car's body and snagged on one of the tail fins. "Very cool. It's nice to have a steady supply of wheels. What mob did your Dad get this one from?"

Ruthie hooted. "Charlie, you're terrible."

"I've got to keep up my image."

Becky retorted, "Charlie, my boy, Daddy is convinced that this car once belonged to the Baldino Brothers. I'm pretty sure that he had the blood stains cleaned out of the trunk, though." She raised her eyebrows. "Care to ride back there and find out?"

"Cool Becky. Maybe you and me . . . ." They saw Mr. Truwet drive by in the big 88.

"What do you think of Mr. Truwet?" Becky asked.

"Mr. Twerp, that's what the boys in psychology call him." Ruthie interjected. "He's just subbing, doesn't know neurotic anxiety from his navel."

"Wow, you're one deep chick, Ruthie -- scary." Charlie laughed.

Becky grimaced. "Ruthie wants to major in psychology when she goes to college."

"Yeah, that's me. But then you know about psychologists, huh, Charlie? Oops."

Becky glared. "Ruthie, c'mon let's go before those reporters find us."

While Becky searched in her purse for her car keys, Ruthie looked at Charlie and mouthed, "I'm sorry."

He was sure he turned purple. *Damn your big mouth, Ruthie.*

Ruthie, an office assistant between her classes, was often sent with messages for the students. Every Thursday for the last few weeks she had carried a message for Charlie, usually during the history class he hated to miss. Charlie knew Ruthie read the notes excusing him from class. He was asked by the school nurse to see the school system's visiting psychologist. He knew by Becky's reaction that Ruthie had told her about the notes. Ruthie probably told Ralph Jay too, that Charlie saw "the shrink."

"Charlie, you want the back seat?" Becky stood by the door of her car looking at Charlie who stood like he was on the moon. "We better get going. Those reporters will find you."

"Huh, yeah." Charlie got into the back of the Cadillac and slouched down in a corner. He seethed internally about how he was railroaded into seeing a school psychologist. *How the hell did I get into that crap?*

He was lost in thought about what happened after he made the mistake of saying too much to, Miss Sutton, the school nurse. It was a routine visit. She asked him questions. "So, Charlie how's your appetite?"

"Pretty good."

"Pretty good, you eat a balanced meal or pretty good, you don't eat so well?" She wrote on a form.

"My mother's been ill. Sometimes we eat on the run or snack, you know."

"Oh, your mother, she serious?"

"Ummm, I'm not sure."

"Well does your mother's illness bother you?"

"Sure. It bothers all of us."

"How's your father taking it?"

"I don't know. He doesn't say much. But, I'd bet he's concerned. He seems sad at times."

The nurse wrote something on the form.

"You sleep well, Charlie? You look a little worn out."

"When I sleep, I do okay, three, four hours a night."

"That's all? Four hours a night? No wonder you look haggard."

The series of Thursday sessions started with Charlie's visit to Miss Sutton, the school nurse. She looked wonderful. They sat in chairs facing each other. The stiffness in his pants as he sat in front of her caused him to cross his legs. She spoke, "Charlie, your homeroom teacher thought you might be having a little melancholy and asked me to talk to you. So, Charlie, do you have any problems studying, you know, concentration, you must be tired staring at the books all night."

"I don't stare at the books all night. I work some nights at the market. I also work some band jobs, maybe two, three times a month. I study in between."

"You're wearing yourself out, Charlie. I think maybe there's a little depression there, too." Miss Sutton stared at Charlie like she could see inside of his skull.

He squirmed in the chair trying to cover his erection. "We about done here, Miss Sutton?"

"Charlie, I'm going to have you see our visiting school psychologist. I'd like to follow up with this."

"Psychologist -- that's a shrink, right?"

"Oh no, Charlie, she'll just listen to you. Maybe she can help you with sleep habits, appetite. Maybe something about your parents is upsetting you. Maybe you are suffering depression? We're studying that now."

"I don't think so, Miss Sutton. Thanks, but I'll take some aspirin for a couple of days."

"Miss Sutton smiled and patted Charlie's knee. Now, just a couple of sessions with the Doctor, okay, please? She's made some progress with melancholy."

Charlie left Miss Sutton's office thinking this was the end of the conversation. *What was she talking about, melancholy, nah, not me?* He left humming *Melancholy Baby.*

* * *

Two days after Charlie's visit with Miss Sutton, Ruthie appeared in his history class with a note to the teacher. The teacher looked at it, raised his head and motioned to Charlie. "Something for you, Charlie," he handed the note over.

Charlie read the note asking him to report to a room and meet with Dr. Schwingle.

"What's this about?" He handed the note back to the teacher.

The History teacher shrugged, "I don't know. Guess you better check it out."

Charlie sat in the back of the car staring at Ruthie's neck. He held Ruthie almost responsible for Dr. Schwingle.

The psychologist was a short, stocky woman, with long black hair. She wore nylons over what Charlie imagined was an equal length of black hair on her legs. It was tough concentrating.

"Tell me about your family, Charlie. I'd like to know all about your mother, your father; do you have siblings?"

Charlie answered that he had a younger brother and sister.

"Do you get along with your younger brother and sister? You told Miss Sutton that your mother has not been feeling well lately. Does that bother you? What about your father? Do you have a good relationship with him?"

Dr. Schwingle's crossed, black-wormy-haired-looking legs intrigued him. He spoke to her shoes for thirty minutes each Thursday.

He wondered if Dr. Schwingle had a boyfriend. Did he get turned on by those underarm-like legs?

"Do you like girls, Charlie?"

"What? Oh, yeah, sure. I mean, why wouldn't I like girls?"

"What do you like about girls, Charlie?"

Charlie thought about Sigmund Freud who had titillated half of his graduating class. He thought he should shock Dr. Schwingle, give her a Freudian thrill. He was convinced he could end these sessions.

"They give me a hard on." He looked at her face – like a stone.

The sessions went on for two more weeks and then he never heard from Dr. Schwingle again.

*   *   *

Charlie continued to stare at the back of Ruthie's head in the front seat of the sedan. She turned on the radio as Becky drove.

"Oh Elvis, don't you just love him?" Ruthie looked like she would melt. "You guy's wanna go get a Coke? My treat."

Charlie sat up. "I need to get home, things to do."

Becky turned to the back seat. "Ah come on, Charlie. Ruthie's treating; she's got a whole dollar."

"Yeah, come on, Charlie. We'll go to the Barrel for a soda. It won't take long."

Becky didn't wait for an answer. She pointed the car towards the drive-in a few blocks away.

Becky studied her rear-view mirror for a few seconds. "Somebody is following us, probably reporters."

She drove into the Barrel's lot. Patrons kept their car engines running on this cold, gray afternoon. The car Becky had seen drove past and disappeared. Loud radio music sounded through open windows into the already noisy parking lot.

Becky and Ruthie waved to every other car as kids from school passed through the restaurant's lot. Ralph Jay's 1950 yellow Chevy sat across the concrete island that jutted from the restaurant's new glassed-in front.

Jay spotted Becky. He almost spilled his tray getting out of his car. A soda toppled over. Jay swore as he righted the drink and closed his car door with the tray on it.

He came over to Becky's car. He didn't notice Charlie sitting in the back seat. Becky didn't put the window down for him, but Ruthie opened her window. "Ralph, come on over here."

Jay walked around to the passenger side and stuck his head in. He ignored Charlie or didn't see him. He didn't acknowledge Ruthie either. "Hey, Becky, nice car."

Becky gave a wry smile. "It's one of my Dad's."

"Hey, Ralph." Becky asserted herself, "Watcha doing?"

"Just hanging out." Jay looked past Ruthie again. "Becky, you want to go a movie with me on Saturday night?"

"Thanks, Ralph, but Ruthie and I have something to do."

Ruthie turned her face towards the back seat. Charlie saw her teary-eyed.

Jay looked into the back seat. "Shi . . . . Hey, Bonarelli. Looks like you got the night off, huh? I heard that you found that girl in Highland Park last night. Did you whack her?"

Charlie looked at Jay, "Maybe, I saw you and the other jerk there, too. What do you think, Jay? Maybe you had something to do with that?"

Jay's face hardened. He turned and went back to his car.

"Asshole," Ruthie colored and gave Jay the finger.

Charlie tried to lighten up the offended Ruthie. "Geez, Ruthie, you've got a surly attitude."

She hung her head like an admonished puppy and cried.

Becky put a hand on her friend's shoulder. "Ruthie, it's okay. Ralph Jay is a creep. I don't know what you see in him anyway."

A carhop started for the Cadillac when Becky announced, "Let's get out of here."

Charlie moved to get out of the car. "Wait, I need to make a phone call."

"I think we'd better leave here, Charlie." Becky started the car and pulled out. I'll stop at the drugstore up the street. They have a pay phone."

Ruthie wiped her eyes. "C'mon, let's go please."

Becky checked her mirror as she pulled out of the parking lot, "Same car."

Charlie looked back, but didn't recognize the car, "Probably reporters waiting to get me alone."

Becky found a parking place on the street near the drugstore. Charlie got out and walked into the small corner store. The car they thought was following them turned down another street. He saw some students he knew sitting at the soda fountain. They waved as he found the wooden phone booth. A girl hung up the phone and exited the booth. Charlie entered, closed the bi-fold door, and dialed his father's office.

"Dad . . . yeah. Funny thing happened at school today. We've got this substitute teacher, Mr. Truwet. Uh no, he's not my teacher. Anyway, this Mr. Truwet drives a big Olds 88, like the one that I saw last night. I don't know if it is the same guy, but his car is scratched just about where it should be if it is the same car. Another thing, the guy's on crutches and has a cast on his right foot. Oh, Dad, those two guys that I saw in the park, I think it might have been . . . ."

The phone booth door pushed in and hit Charlie just between his knees. Jay and Birch stood outside the booth.

"Hey, Bonarelli, funny running into you again so soon."

"Damn it, Jay, break my knees why don't you?"

"Yeah, why don't I do that?"

"I'm on the phone jerk-off."

Jay stuck his head into the booth. "Talk'n to Karin, I'll bet. You're the one jerking off."

Charlie pushed Jay's face out of the booth and put the phone back to his ear. "Dad, I'll have to talk to you later. Yeah everything is okay. Bye." He hung up the phone.

Charlie wondered how could Jay know anything about his relationship with Karin. He knew that if Jay really knew anything he would put the information in front of Becky if it would sour her on Charlie.

"Bonarelli, what I want to know is what or who you think you saw in the park last night?"

"Yeah," Birch blurted. You didn't see us – did'ja?"

Jay smacked Birch on the back of his head. "Shut the fuck up will you."

Jay reached a hand into the phone booth and tried to grab Charlie. Charlie was quick enough to shut the folding door catching Jay's forearm just before his hand grasped Charlie's neck.

"I won't break your arm if you agree to back off, Jay." Charlie pushed harder on the door.

"Excuse me boys. I'd like to use the phone please."

"Mr. Greyer." Birch pulled on Jay's free arm and tugged. "It's Mr. Greyer."

Charlie pushed harder on the booth door until Jay gave a cry of alarm.

"Christ, let go, Bonarelli." Jay yelped.

"That you in there, Charlie?"

Charlie recognized Mr. Greyer's voice and released the door. Birch pulled Ralph Jay out with enough force to cause the pair to fall.

"Anything wrong here, boys?" Mr. Greyer pushed up his glasses and stared at the two on the floor.

Charlie exited the booth. "Not a thing, Mr. Greyer."

Jay and Birch picked themselves up and backed away.

"Then I guess you boys better get along. I'd like to use the phone please."

Charlie watched Jay and Birch leave the store. "Don't let the door hit you in the ass on the way out, girls."

Mr. Greyer sat in the phone booth. "Sure everything is okay, Charlie?"

"Yeah, it's cool, Mr. Greyer."

"Okay, then, I'll use the phone."

Charlie left the drugstore for Becky's car and got in. Jay and Birch were gone.

Becky called through an open window. "Charlie, what's going on?"

"Nothing, Becky."

"You sure? We saw Ralph Jay and that Birch character go into the drugstore after you, and nothing's wrong?"

"Nothing's wrong, Becky. I need to get home, okay?"

Charlie looked back at the drugstore. He saw Mr. Greyer looking out at them from behind the drugstore window as they pulled away.

"Why do you suppose he showed up just when he did?" Charlie asked no one in particular.

7

Lust or Love?

Charlie was deep in thought again when Becky drove him home after dropping Ruthie off at her house.

"Charlie, we're here." Becky pulled to the front of his house stopping abruptly.

He sensed that something was wrong. She wanted to talk. He didn't.

"What're you thinking about? Who're thinking about, Charlie?"

"Uh, nothing. Thanks for the ride. See you tomorrow." He got out and closed the door.

"Charlie?" Becky's anger went straight to the gas-peddle. The car's back tires sprayed debris from the street as she drove away.

He didn't say goodbye but hollered, "Thanks, Becky" as she peeled down the street. Charlie's mind was on Karin Delaney, and what did Ralph Jay know?

Inside the house he dumped his books and said, "Hi Mom," gave her a kiss and went to the back door.

"Where are you going, Charlie?" She knew the answer and gave a worried look. "Charlie, I know where you're off to. Darn kid, you don't know what you're getting into. If I thought it would do any good, I would stop you."

"See you in an hour, Mom."

"What about your homework?"

"It's cool, Mom. I did most of it during study hall at school. I'll finish up after dinner." He started out of the back door.

Bea raised her voice. "*Testa dura*, just like someone else I live with."

"Hard head, me — nah." Charlie went out the back door, bolted down the alley, cut through a new house construction site and crossed the street to the Delaney's.

Karin Delaney's parents worked while she stayed home with her fourteen-month-old boy, Joey. She answered Charlie's knock while holding her son in her left arm.

"Hey, Charlie, c'mon in. I'm just feeding Joey. He gets hungry a little early. Here," she handed him to Charlie who took the child without thinking much about it except that the kid smelled like food.

Joey's face was smeared with sauce and strained peas. Charlie shucked his jacket while trying to avoid rubbing the boy's dirty face.

"I'm making him some chocolate milk. C'mon back to the kitchen."

"Geez, Karin, the kid looks like a finger painting."

She turned and gave Charlie a killer smile. He could never get enough of looking at the copper-haired beauty. Worldly at barely twenty-years old, the unwed mother raised a child and went to night school.

Charlie followed her into the kitchen with the boy over his un-damaged left shoulder. Karin's books were spread out on the kitchen table. A bowl was turned over on Joey's highchair tray, and an open can of Chef Boyardee near the stove cautioned Charlie about getting too close to Joey again.

Too late, Joey rubbed spaghetti sauce and peas on Charlie's cheek.

"There's a wet rag there." Karin pointed at a stained cloth near the highchair. "Wipe his face, will you please?"

The cloth felt clammy in Charlie's hand. He cleaned Joey's face.

Charlie watched Karin as she stirred chocolate syrup into a cup of milk. She was barefooted, had on tight dungarees and a sweatshirt.

Unlike all of the other girls Charlie knew, Karin didn't bother with a girdle, and seldom wore a bra at home. He marveled at her body under the loose shirt and tight pants.

He smoldered as she turned around to take Joey and put him in his highchair. She gave the boy his milk and he slurped at it like a piglet in a trough.

"Chocolate, Joey, you love chocolate milk," she gleamed at her son. "Charlie, you've got spaghetti sauce on your cheek."

Charlie put his left hand to his face.

Karin grabbed his hand, leaned over and licked the food from his face. She placed Charlie's left hand under her sweatshirt.

A sucking noise emitted from Joey as he slurped his milk. Karin kissed Charlie hard on his mouth.

Blood pumped through Charlie like a hydro-plant. He would split his jeans if this continued.

Karin pulled away and took Charlie's hand from underneath her sweatshirt.

"Karin, honey," Charlie grabbed her arm and quickly went into the tunnel of lust.

"I have to put Joey down for a nap before my folks come home."

She picked up her son. "You've finished your milk. Good boy. Here let mamma wipe your face." She picked up the empty cup with one hand and the wet rag with the other hand almost losing Joey, "Oops, pumpkin, almost dropped you."

Karin trundled Joey, the rag and the cup to the sink. Still clasping her son, she rinsed the rag and wiped his face. He gave her a raspberry for her trouble.

Laughing, she came back to the highchair with the cloth and wiped it clean. She turned and threw the rag into the kitchen sink. Joey giggled.

"Charlie, your face is red. What's up?"

He didn't answer.

"Let's go into the living room. I'll put Joey in his playpen."

Charlie followed like an obedient puppy. He thought that he was panting. He felt spittle at the corners of his mouth.

Karin bent over to put her son into the playpen. She laid him down and covered him with a small blanket. "Nappy-Nap, Joey. You'll be all fresh when Grandma and Grandpa come home."

Joey lay down and stuck part of the blanket into his mouth.

"So, your parents expected soon?" Charlie went to pull the front curtain back and look into the street.

"They'll be here later. Want to watch TV? There's a great new program on -- a bunch of kids dancing to all the new music. It's a kick, it's called *American Bandstand*.

"What about Joey?" Charlie nodded towards the playpen.

"We'll keep the volume down. Besides, he's good for a little nap after he eats, a real little man. C'mon, let's do it."

"Yeah, okay." Charlie's ears felt hot under his long hair. Karin's smell, her looks, her terrific boobs primed Charlie for an immediate sex fix. He was hooked, addicted, inflicted and wet clay in Karin's hands.

She turned the TV on and adjusted the volume. "Joey's going to sleep." She cooed softly to her son who was already snoring in his playpen.

"C'mon, Charlie, let's try this new dance."

The MC, Dick Clark's voice announced, "Here's the latest Elvis Presley hit, *All Shook Up*."

"Jesus, Elvis again, does anybody else sing or play anymore?"

"C'mon." Karin grabbed Charlie's hands and pulled him from the sofa. He felt the pull in his right shoulder. He wasn't quite sure of himself yet but followed Karin as she danced. She made a quick look at his bandaged right hand, but said nothing.

She moved around him, rubbed him; played him. Charlie wiped the back of his hand over his mouth. "God, Karin, this dance makes me slather like a quarter-horse."

"What do you know about quarter-horses, mister? C'mon let's do it."

"You mean dance, right?"

"Yeah, dance." She grinned. She enjoyed teasing Charlie, but she also liked rewarding him. She was earthy, candid, but often remorseful.

"Shit, Charlie, I'm depressed as hell, but horny too. What's that mean?"

"I don't know, fast?"

"You bastard," she laughed and continued to dance.

She could laugh and cry and the same time while trying to make light of her situation, "caught with my pants down."

Charlie knew it was all show, a good face for him and his friends. He knew better by the tear stains in her books from when she studied late at night, her son in a crib near her desk.

He knew she hurt, but he couldn't resist the sensuality of this girl-woman. She'd get him boiling with her sex then turn down the heat with her guilt. She stopped dancing and wanted to talk. She slumped on the couch.

They sat on the couch. She habitually started a conversation in the middle of another thought. Charlie could follow her conversation without a prelude.

"At first I had the feeling that I might never hold my head up again, but then I figured that the bastard left me pregnant, on my own, he could go to hell. I'll show him and his snotty family."

She mimicked, "'Jimmy can't be married now, Karin. He's got a full football scholarship to the university.' Like they could even give a damn about their grandchild. So now they want to see him. I told them to screw off. No support, no affection, they just want to see if he has all of his parts."

Karin watched her sleeping son. "I love Joey beyond anything or anyone, but what could my life have been?"

53

Charlie saw that he needed to change the subject. He couldn't understand maudlin women.

"Oh, heck, Karin, let's have a laugh. Let's dance, shake it up a little. Get off of it sweetie, you just get weepy."

Karin wiped her eyes. "It was a fling. Jimmy's parents said, 'fling.' Can you believe it? Right in this very room, they told my parents, 'it was just a fling, Jimmy has to go on to school.'"

"What about me? I had to leave school that year. Finished my studies at home and took the GED. I work part-time, go to school, and my parents help." She cried. "I'll be damned if Jimmy and his family will ever get to see my Joey now. He's my son. Jimmy never even called about him."

Charlie grabbed Karin up from the couch. "Okay, kiddo, let's lose the long face. The music, the new show, okay?"

"Anyway, Charlie, you know the rest, I can't have any more children." She twisted her sweatshirt.

"It's okay, sweetheart, now quit thinking and let's dance." Charlie pulled her up and twirled her to a new song coming out of the TV. Charlie knew the whole story, Karin's difficulty with Joey's birth, the hysterectomy, the long recuperation.

"Okay, don't get sad, Karin. See this, he held up his bandaged right hand. I've got some trouble of my own, but I'm not going to burden you with that. Let's dance."

Charlie thought he might be in love with Karin. He was confused between her and Becky. Becky was nice too, but they never seemed to get together long enough before she got her feelings hurt.

He knew that soon enough, they'd be parting. Becky to college and himself, "who knows?" was his standard answer to anyone that asked.

"Hey, Charlie let's do this one." Karin pulled on his arms and him out of his own funk.

Karin put her arms around his neck and gave him a long kiss. She let go and danced away. He followed and caught her from behind.

He pulled her loose sweatshirt from around her neck and hair-line. He kissed her where the thick copper colored hair made a "V" at the back of her neck.

His hands went up her sweatshirt and clasped her breasts.

She reached back and put her hands into his long hair.

"Charlie, what's in your hair?"

"What?"

"Your hair, Brylcream or something?"

She pulled away from Charlie. She reached into his back pocket and pulled out a clean handkerchief. She wiped her fingers and hands, then dropped the handkerchief on the couch.

Karin's hands went to Charlie's belt. She unclasped the belt and unzipped his pants. The pants dropped and his boyhood shot out of his shorts.

She giggled. "Oops, it's the purple-throbber."

Charlie pulled Karin's top off over her head to expose her breasts and he gently squeezed her full hard nipples.

"Better than *National Geographic* huh, baby?" She dropped her dungarees and pulled down her panties.

Charlie kicked his loafers off, and dropped his shorts. He was naked except for his socks.

"Charlie." Karin put a hand around his erection. "Take it slow, baby."

"Sure," Charlie choked. The top of his head was about to erupt.

"I wonder how long I'll be good for." She said off-handed.

"What?"

"I just don't know, Charlie."

"What?" He was ready to explode.

There was a noise in the back of the house.

"Oh—God—oh—God, my parent's, it's early."

"What?"

"I think that my parents are home." She had already found her dungarees and pulled them on."

"Charlie, get your clothes on."

He tripped over his jeans, but managed to pull them on. He grabbed his shirt, shoes and jacket. "Christ," he quickly scooped up his underwear.

Karen already had her sweat shirt on. She jammed her panties into a pocket. She pushed on Charlie's back while guiding him towards the door.

They heard the back door open.

"Hello, we're home."

Karin had run to the back door. "Hey you're early. Be quiet now, Joey's still taking his nap."

Charlie was out the front door and able to duck behind a large bush and jammed on his jacket. He had never removed his socks. He tried to walk and put on his shoes at the same time. He got on the jacket and carried his shirt and underwear.

"What the hell am I doing?" He wadded up the shirt and shorts and jammed them inside of his jacket.

At that moment, Charlie felt as if he had lost more than his underwear. His lust and sexual release came with a cost – guilt. He was a Catholic. He had committed mortal sin, again. He wondered if sex was sinful why did it have to feel so good? Catholic, damn it, he thought. He would have to go to confession while he still lived with his parents. They expected him to take communion with them every Sunday.

He was going to have to tell a priest again that he, an unmarried boy, was banging somebody's mother. The last time had cost him five rosaries for penance and a knowing look from his dad.

He hitched up his pants, zipped up his jacket and combed his duck-ass hair. A clouded sky and darkness added to the gloom of the late afternoon.

"Crap." His eyes reacted from a flash of light. "What the . . . ?"

"Mr. Bonarelli." It was the female reporter and the photographer who he had seen earlier at school.

Caught like a cat in a mad dog's jaws. He ran across the street with the two newspaper people racing after him. Neighbors, returning from work drove by, gawking at the scene.

Charlie cut through the construction site and across the alley past the garage. The back door was unlocked. He bolted through. Before he could close the door and lock it, he heard a horn honking and his father shouting, "Get the hell out of here before I call the cops."

Vince came into the kitchen as Bea prepared supper. "We better circle the wagons. There's a woman reporter and guy with a camera out there. I think that maybe I chased them off though."

The front doorbell rang.

"Damn it. I told those two to get the hell out of here." Vince went to the front door and opened it.

"Oh, Matt, it's you, c'mon in."

Vince opened the screen. Detective Matthias Grueber and another detective walked into the front room.

"Hello, Vince. This is detective Bill Shay. We need to talk to Charlie."

"Oh yeah, what for?"

8

Like Rats

Bea, holding Jody, welcomed the detectives, "Hello, Matt." Matthias Grueber had served with Vince and Bea's brother Bernie in London. The families were old friends, but with last evening's events they all knew that tonight wasn't a social visit.

Bea put Jody down. Grueber and his partner entered the room and removed their hats.

Grueber spoke for the pair. "Hi, Bea, we need to talk to Charlie."

Vince asked them to sit in the front room. Bea had the kitchen table set for the evening meal.

Charlie was hungry. He managed to get his clothing back in order, but he needed to use the bathroom to clean up before dinner.

"It'll just take a few minutes." Grueber looked at Charlie. "Hey, Charlie, you doing okay? I don't know how the reporters found you today. Somebody in the department gave your name out. You're eighteen so we can't really stop the reporters once they smell blood. Sorry, bad choice of words. If they keep dogging you, don't tell them anything other than what you told us, what you saw. We're here to ask you a couple more questions."

Vince asked, "Bea, will you take Jody and Sam into the kitchen, please? I think we'll just be a few minutes, Hon."

Charlie remained standing, leaning against the doorway between the kitchen and the front room.

Vince motioned, "Charlie, have a seat."

Grueber opened the conversation. "Charlie. An officer found a car jack this morning, in the street, just about where you said that you tried to help the motorist. Do you have a better recollection now of what that motorist looked like?"

"I really couldn't see him that well, with the shadows and all. But, funny thing, this morning the assistant principal, Mr. Greyer, called me into his office. He wanted to know what was going on. He tried to fend off two newspaper people. It was the same two that just followed me up to our back door."

Grueber's partner looked up. "Yeah, we saw them too; told them to get the hell out."

"Anyway, when I was in the office, this substitute teacher, Mr. Truwet, comes hobbling in on crutches. He had a cast on his right foot. I heard Mr. Greyer, the assistant principal, ask about the leg. Mr. Truwet told Mr. Greyer that he took a fall from a ladder.

"Later, when I was leaving school, I walked through the teacher's parking lot and I see this hot Olds 88; brand-new. Turns out it's Mr. Truwet's car, and he's not too happy that I'm looking at the car. He comes up and shoos me away. But not before I see this scratch on the bumper where maybe a jack slipped."

Matt took out a notebook. "Truwet. That's T-R-U-W-E-T?"

"Yeah, I think so. The kids call him twerp."

Matt's partner chuckled.

Matt Grueber wasn't amused. "Why's that Charlie, what about Mr. Truwet?"

Charlie explained, "I don't have him for a class, but he's subbing for the psychology teacher while she's in the hospital. Anyway, the kid's call him twerp because he's small and mousy. I heard he had some kind of tantrum in class. A couple of football players teased him, like baited him, man. He flipped. He told the class that 'rats pee on the floor, but you don't have to act like rats.' He can't control the class; it makes him mad I guess."

"Okay, so what about the car, Charlie?" Grueber wrote something in his notebook. "You said a new Oldsmobile 88. What about the color?"

"Well, yeah, the color is greenish, maybe pea green."

Grueber's partner belched. "Sorry," he grinned.

"Hey, that reminds me." Charlie brightened up. "The guy in the park, the one who was caught between the curb and his car wheel, belched; it sounded more like a squeak. Funny thing again, Mr. Truwet, in the parking lot, he belched; sounded like the same squeaky noise that I heard from the guy who was stuck."

Matt asked again, "So you didn't get a good look at the guy or the color of his car? Maybe like Truwet's car?"

Charlie thought. "It was night. The park was dark except for the street lights. Those lights make car paint almost yellow. Yeah, the car could have been that green color, but I'm not sure."

"Okay." Matt closed his notebook. "We'll talk to this Mr. Truwet."

"Thanks, Vince, Charlie -- Bea," Matt Grueber called into the kitchen. "See you sometime."

Bea came from the kitchen. "Want some dinner you two?"

"Thanks, but we ate before we came."

Vince showed Matt Grueber and his partner out.

Charlie ran down the back stairs to his room. He hollered up the stairwell. "I'll be right back."

"Charlie, dinner's on the table. Get back here."

He called back. "It's cool, Mom. I'll be right back. I need to wash my hands."

Vince called down the stairs. "Hustle your butt, Charlie, we're hungry."

"Yeah, hustle your butt, Charlie." Jody yelled.

Charlie appeared. "Hey, Sis, watch your mouth."

Vince admonished Jody.

Bea gave Vince a wry look. "Look who's talking now." She went to the stove and turned off a pot. She suddenly grabbed at her left breast.

Vince got up from the table and went to his wife. "What's wrong, Honey?"

"Whew! I don't know. All of a sudden I have this pain in my left side, and I feel faint."

"Here, come and sit down. I'll take care of dinner."

"No, it's okay. I'll just get some aspirin. It's okay. Come now, everyone." Bea looked at her family, "*mangiare*."

"*Mangiare*," Charlie, we're hungry." The two children said in unison. They made sounds like hungry birds. "Cheep, cheep."

Bea left and returned with the aspirin bottle. Her skin flushed, her forehead wet, she wiped her napkin over her face and took her place at the table.

Charlie stared at his mother, then a questioning look to Vince.

"Let's say Grace." Vince made the sign of the cross.

Charlie watched his mother struggle with pain through Grace. He helped dish food for Jody.

Sam reached both hands for the bread.

"Sam, mind your manners." Bea gave a pained look at her younger son. "You know how to ask for things."

Everyone started talking at once.

"Yeah, Sam, you're a piggy."

Sam stuck his tongue at Jody.

Vince talked to Charlie across the table. Bea listened, taking only small portions of the meal for herself.

"Charlie, did you ever tell Matt Grueber about your suspicions? You know, who this kid is that you saw in the park? Ralph something?"

"Well I may have mentioned it, but I don't really know if the guys in the park were Ralph and his asshole buddy. Matt never really pressed me for details."

"Not supposed to say asshole, Charlie." Jody shook a fork full of food at him.

"Jody, put your fork down." Bea pointed a finger at her, and directed the pointing finger to Charlie. "Charlie, you're getting to be a potty-mouth and a cheeky shit."

"Oh, oh," Sam pointed at Charlie. "Mom's got the finger out."

"Hush, and eat." Bea almost laughed, but her pain came back in small stabs; perspiration beaded on her head.

Charlie saw his father's concern.

"Charlie, let's talk about the guys in the park after dinner."

They finished dinner in silence until Sam got out of his chair to rummage in the refrigerator. "Got something for desert?"

"There are cookies in the jar." Bea answered. "I didn't feel like making desert today."

Charlie saw his mother's painful expression. He picked up the plates.

Vince put his arms around Bea. Tears came to her eyes.

"I'll do the dishes tonight." Charlie put the dishes on the counter. "Sam and Jody can help."

Vince gave Charlie an appreciative look as he helped Bea stand up. "Let's get you into the bedroom. It looks like you could use some rest."

Bea leaned on Vince as he helped her out of the kitchen into their bedroom.

"What's wrong with Mom, Charlie?" Sam had a handful of cookies.

"She's sick silly." Jody was in no mood to help with the dishes.

"C'mon, Charlie, let's go, Jody." I'm going to miss *The Rifleman*." Sam crunched a cookie.

"Let's move it then." Charlie took the pots off of the stove. He looked at the contents, "Now what?"

"Don't look so dumb, Charlie." Jody pointed towards a cabinet. "Tupperware, don't ya know nothing?"

"Okay, Miss Nasty-Wasty." Charlie dished warm leftover food into the plastic containers.

"Let me whoosh the Tupperware, Charlie." Jody reached onto the counter for the plastic containers.

"Okay, I'll get the dishes going. Here," he handed a dishtowel to Sam. "I need to call Zellie about some homework."

The phone rang.

"I'll get it." Jody rushed over to the phone in the hallway near the kitchen.

"Hello." Jody waited a moment. "Oh." She handed the phone towards Charlie. "It's that lady."

Charlie knew she meant Karin. Anybody over eighteen-years of age was an older person to Jody. He took the phone.

"Hi." He listened. "Okay." The phone went dead. "Karin?" He listened for a few moments then cradled the phone. "Shit."

Sam and Jody watched Charlie but said nothing.

Charlie went to the sink and started the dishwater. "What do you suppose that was all about?"

9

What Is Love?

Enveloped in a mental fog, Charlie finished cleaning up the kitchen. He asked Sam and Jody to start their homework. "Sit at the kitchen table. I'll help you if you need me to, but right now I'm calling Zel." He picked up the kitchen hall phone and dialed the number. His brother and sister fidgeted at the table.

Charlie pointed a finger at them. "Okay you two, you've got to get that schoolwork done." He waited for Zel's phone to pick up. Jody and Sam went to their rooms to get their books. He heard Sam tell Jody that "Charlie points his finger just like Mom". They still lingered when Zel's phone picked up.

"Yeah, Zellie please," Charlie put his hand over the receiver, "you two get at it now. Mom's . . . yeah, Zel, you won't believe what just happened. I just got a call from . . . ," He watched Jody and Sam as they sat at the table, no books open, no paper out, staring at him on the phone.

"Hang on Zel." Charlie pointed the handset at the two. "Do it! Open the books and get to it."

He put the phone back to his ear, taking the phone further down the hall stretching the cord to the breaking point.

Jody whined, "I don't want to do my homework."

Sam hollered, "Mom lets me watch TV for a half-hour. I'm going to miss *The Rifleman.* C'mon, Charlie, I'm gonna watch TV."

Alan C. Iannacito

Charlie ignored his brother's and sister's whimpers. In a low voice, "Zel, Karin called me. We've been busted. Her parents came home early; one of them saw me walking from the house when I was trying to avoid a couple of newspaper people. Yeah, those newspaper jerks are dogging, nosy bastards, won't leave me alone. The problem now is Karin's parents. Nobody's supposed to be there when they're at work. They found my handkerchief on their couch.

"They raised all kinds of hell with Karin, threatened to kick her out; called her a slut, really read her off. They told her they knew that I had been there, you know -- really chewed her. She was crying, and I could hear her Dad yelling at her Mom."

Charlie listened to Zellie who told him he should stay away from Karin for now.

"Yeah, I guess you're right. Man, I don't know what to do. I'm thinking that maybe I love her, but I don't get out of school for another few months. I don't have a real job." He whispered under his breath so only Zellie could hear. "I get horny just saying her name. Is that love?"

Vince hollered from the bedroom. "Charlie, come on in here."

"Dad, I'm on the phone."

"Get the hell off of the phone and get in here — now."

"Gotta go, Zel, see you tomorrow." Charlie went to hang up the phone and saw Jody and Sam fake their efforts.

"Daddy wants you, Charlie." Jody pointed to the bedrooms.

"Charlie, get in here. I need you to call the doctor for Bea."

At this, the three of them quick-stepped into their parents' bedroom.

"What's wrong, Mommy sick?" Big tears welled in Jody's eyes.

"Yeah, what's wrong with Mom?" Charlie went over to the bed near where Vince sat comforting Bea.

Sam stood still in the doorway.

"Charlie," Vince gave his oldest son a concerned look, "Call Dr. Morrow. The number's in the book, in the kitchen drawer nearest the phone."

"Sure, I know where it is."

"Let me know when you've reached him."

Charlie rushed to the kitchen and fumbled for his mother's phone directory. He found Dr. Morrow's phone number written on the front of the worn book and took the book to the phone where he dialed the number. There was an answer. He listened.

"Dad, he hollered towards the bedroom, "it's the answering service. What'll I do?"

"Tell them who you are, and that your mother is Dr. Morrow's patient. I think we need to get her to the hospital. Wait, I'll come in there and take the phone. You come in here with Bea."

Vince rushed to the phone grabbing the phone from Charlie. "This is Vincent Bonarelli, Bea is very ill. I want to talk to the doctor."

Vince could be heard in the bedroom. "Okay, I'm staying by the phone. Please make it quick." He hung up and stood by the phone in anticipation.

Charlie sat by his mother's side. Jody brought a damp cold rag from the bathroom and wiped Bea's face.

Sam asked, "Charlie, Mom's going to be all right isn't she?"

They all saw the great pain in their mother's ashen expression. The aspirin hadn't relieved the pain greater than the little pills could handle.

The phone rang. Vince picked up before the second ring. "Dr. Morrow? It's Vincent Bonarelli. Bea's really ill. She has bad chest pain and she can't even function now. She took aspirin about thirty minutes ago. She's pale and . . . okay, I'll wait, oh, okay, temperature."

Vince called to the bedroom. "The doctor is calling for an ambulance. He wants us to take Bea's temperature, too. Charlie, get the thermometer and take your mother's temperature."

"Where's the thermometer?"

Bea's pain brought tears to her eyes, but she was able to point to the bathroom.

Jody jumped up from her mother's side. "I know where it is." She ran into the bathroom and returned with the thermometer. Just like her mother, Jody had brought a bottle of alcohol and a wad of cotton.

Charlie reached for the thermometer.

Jody retorted. "I'll do it." She took the thermometer from its case, opened the bottle of alcohol, dabbed the cotton with the liquid, wiped and shook the thermometer, and inserted the glass tube under her mother's tongue.

The two brothers watched their little sister with new respect.

"Yah have to let it stay for two or three minutes."

Vince called from the phone. "What's going on?"

"We're getting Mom's temperature." Sam called back.

"Hurry up."

Sam looked back to his sister. "Hurry up, Jody."

"It takes two or three minutes. You're impatient just like Daddy."

Charlie fidgeted for another minute then grabbed the thermometer out of Bea's mouth and read the temperature, "Dad, 102 degrees."

They heard Vince on the phone for another minute. "Okay, we'll be ready when it arrives."

Vince came into the bedroom and took his wife's right hand. "Dr. Morrow wants you to be taken over to Saint Anthony's, he's called an ambulance."

She gave him a questioning look. Charlie, Sam and Jody stood dumbstruck.

"Mommy has to go to the hospital?" Jody cried. "Can we go, too?"

Vince sat silently, rubbing his wife's brow.

Sam asked. "Dad, can we go to the hospital with you?"

"No. You three better stay here. I doubt the emergency room wants kids around. Charlie, you'll need to take care of Jody and Sam. I'll call you from the hospital when I know something."

The ambulance company was two blocks away from the house. They listened to the approaching siren.

"I'll ride in the ambulance with your mother. Charlie, you may have to pick me up later. You kids get your homework done. Everything will be okay."

"Vince?" Bea asked in a weak voice. "Can we afford an ambulance? Can't you just drive me over to the hospital?"

There was a knock on the door.

"Charlie, open the door for the ambulance people."

As Charlie walked around the bed to the door, Vince got up to gather Bea's purse from the top of the highboy. He had a second thought and put the purse back. He bent down and picked up her slippers from near the bed.

Charlie opened the front door for two ambulance attendants who wheeled in a gurney. One of the attendants followed him into the crowded bedroom.

"Hi there, we're here to take you to the hospital. Let's get you comfy."

The attendant spoke to his partner who was now at the bedroom door. "Bob, I think that we can get the gurney in here. Family, can you give us some room, please?" The man in charge looked at Bea. "What's your name dear?"

"Bea." They all answered in unison.

"Okay, Bea, we want to lift you onto the cart here. Just rest easy. That's the girl."

The two attendants carefully placed her on the padded cart, put two blankets over her, strapped her down and wheeled her out.

"Saint Anthony's, right?" Bob asked the family.

Vince walked behind carrying Bea's slippers. "Yes, Saint Anthony's. I'm riding along. You kids get your homework done. Charlie, make sure Jody and Sam are in bed by 8:30, okay."

"Right, Dad, I'll take care of everything. You'll call us as soon as you can? You want me to call the family yet?"

"No, I'll call everyone." Vince went out of the door after the ambulance crew. "On second thought, Charlie, you'd better call Mama and Papa. Ask them to call the rest of the family."

Charlie, Jody, and Sam watched from the front door to see their mother loaded into the big white ambulance with flashing lights. Vince got in while the one of the attendants closed the door behind him. Despite a cold night neighbors congregated outside their homes. The flashing red lights reflected off of home exteriors as the cold white vehicle headed down the street.

Charlie went to the front porch and watched the ambulance as it turned the corner towards the hospital. "Okay, you two into the house and work on your books. I did my work at school but I'll bring my book up and do a review."

A neighbor walked up with several people trailing behind. "Is that Bea, Charlie, did she have a heart-attack or something?"

"We don't know what it is yet, Mr. Fellows. Dad will call us from the hospital, we just don't know. We'll let you know sometime tomorrow. Goodnight."

* * *

Charlie called Nonna and Papa Bonarelli, and then sat at the kitchen table with Sam and Jody. Lost in thought, he couldn't concentrate on his book. Jody and Sam watched him fidget with his pencil and turn the pages in his book without looking at them.

"You're not studying, Charlie." Jody pouted.

The phone rang. Charlie jumped up expecting to hear his father on the other end.

"Dad, is that you, Dad?" The line was open but there was no answer on the other end. "That you, Dad, is Mom okay?" The line went dead.

"What the hell?" Charlie looked at the phone as if it should answer him. He put the hand-piece back on the cradle. The phone rang again.

Charlie heard Vince's voice. "Charlie, who you been talking to?"

Puzzled, Charlie asked, "That wasn't you who just called? I thought you were calling, but there was no answer when I picked up."

"No, that wasn't me. Your mother was admitted to the hospital. The emergency room doctor mentioned pain killers, but they can't give her anything until a diagnosis. Dr. Morrow will be here shortly."

"The hospital has started some tests. She's getting an electrocardiogram and some other things. I'll know later."

"What about you?" Charlie asked. "Can I come and get you?"

"No, I'm staying with your mother. I'll call again later. Are Sam and Jody getting their homework done okay?"

Jody and Sam's questioning looks told Charlie that they were struggling to concentrate.

"I'll make sure that they get their homework done, Dad. You sure you don't want me to come over to the hospital. Sam and Jody are old enough to stay by themselves for a while. I can ask one of the neighbors to keep an eye on the house."

Charlie listened to Vince, "No, I'll be okay. Gotta go now. Did you call Momma and Papa?"

"Yes, and Dad, tell Mom that we love her, okay."

Charlie hung up the phone and went back to the table. His brother and sister asked at the same time, "How's Mom?"

He told them what their father had said then grabbed his book. "Okay, let's finish this."

Jody and Sam pestered Charlie as he helped them finish their homework. He was looking over an algebra solution when the phone rang. He jumped up expecting to hear from a family member checking up on them.

"Hello."

No answer.

Charlie lost patience. "Son-of-a-bitch." He slammed the phone back into its cradle and went back to the table.

"You two, get ready for bed." They got up from the table.

Sam whined that he missed *The Rifleman.* Jody cried that, "Mommy's not going to be here tonight to read me my story."

Charlie closed his book thinking he would check the problem later. "Get ready for bed. I'll read you your story, Jody. Sam, maybe you can catch the tail-end of another program while I get Jody ready for bed, but then you gotta go to bed. *Capisce?*"

Sam grumbled that he understood and left the table.

The phone rang again. Charlie let it ring four times. "Better not be another phantom." He picked up but remained silent.

"Charlie?"

10

You Killed That Girl

"Charlie? It's me, Bobo."

"Hey, Bobo, did try to call earlier?"

"No, man, my mom just heard from Nonna Bonarelli that Aunt Bea's in the hospital?"

"Yeah, Dad's with her. I'm just waiting to hear back from him. They're doing some tests."

"Man, I hope everything is all right."

Charlie felt uneasy talking about his mother, even to his cousin and trusted friend. "Geez, Bobo, I knew that Mom had been ill, but I didn't understand the full meaning of it until now. Man, she's really hurting."

"Remember, she was in the hospital two years ago? I was just sixteen. You know, it was to remove a lump from one of her breasts. What does that mean? Now I'm asking myself about that operation; no one ever talked about it. I remember I sat for a long time in the hospital waiting room while Dad talked with Mom's surgeon.

"You know, Bobo, I've never told anybody this, when Dad returned to the waiting room, he was crying. He says to me, 'Your mother's biopsy came back, it was malignant.'

"'Malignant?' I'm thinking. What is that? I didn't know what to say, except, 'Oh.' I didn't want to appear dumb, but I knew the sound of the word, 'malignant,' meant something bad was wrong with Mom. Later, I looked the word up in the dictionary. It took me awhile to figure out that the definition meant something about evil. Something, 'very harmful,' and then I saw the word, 'cancer.'"

"Jesus, Charlie. That's serious shit isn't it? I mean don't people die from that? Oh, I'm sorry, man."

Charlie didn't understand cancer except like Bobo, it was associated with death. Shocked, the realization that his mother might die, "God-damn-it, Bobo, Mom's not going to die." Charlie couldn't believe that his vibrant mother was stricken with an evil disease that could kill her.

He remembered when his mother returned home after the surgery two years prior, it took her weeks to recuperate. He heard her tell his Dad that she had to be fitted for a special bra. He thought about when she went to the hospital, periodically, for treatments that left her sick for a couple of days after each treatment.

"Christ, Bobo the last time she was sick as hell. Her hair fell out, remember?"

Bobo answered, "Yeah, I remember that. It took awhile, but she got all of her hair back, right?"

"Yeah, then after several weeks things seemed okay."

Charlie remembered how his mother regained her strength and became the funny and witty Bea again. But lately he had noticed she was withdrawn, and a few days ago she had taken ill. One day he saw her curled up in a chair in her bedroom; she was crying. He startled her when he asked if she was alright. She got up and put her arms around Charlie.

"I'll be fine, Charlie. I am just a little tired right now."

He hadn't seen his mother cry often. It made him worry for her. What if the cancer was still there in his mother's body? He didn't want to ask his Dad about it. He wasn't sure how to express himself.

"Charlie -- you still with me?"

"Uh, sure, Bobo," he listened to his cousin.

"So what's going on now?"

"Uh, we don't know until the tests come back."

"You going to school tomorrow?"

"I'm not sure what's going on with that yet either. I'll call you in the morning before you leave, you taking the bus or your Mom's clunker?"

Charlie listened again to his cousin. "Hey, that's one of the reasons I'm calling, too. My Mom's getting a new car -- well it's a used car. Dad picked it up from one of his buddies. Anyway I get her old car. Pretty cool huh? I can get down to the GG, no problem now."

The GG, Golden Gloves, was Bobo's passion. He was a fair boxer, but Charlie thought that his cousin wasn't going to gain national status anytime soon. Bobo was an uncontrollable hothead.

"Bobo, take the bus to the GG. You can't think straight anyway after those other boxers knock your head off. You'll drive into a tree."

"Oh, yeah, thanks a bunch pal. Hey, smart-ass, I'm on the card for the bout next month. You think you can come? I could use you in my corner."

"Bobo, I'm not sure. I think I might have a gig with the band. I'm not even sure what I'm doing tomorrow. I'll probably have to pick Dad up at the hospital."

"Yeah, things are a little crazy right now. We'll check with each other in the morning."

"Right. Hey, you sure you didn't try to call me earlier?"

"No -- how come?"

"We had a couple of calls but no one answered on the other end."

"Maybe just a wrong number, see you tomorrow maybe."

Charlie hung up the phone. He went to make sure that Jody and Sam were ready for bed. Jody wanted a story and Sam whined again about not getting to see his TV program.

"Tomorrow, Sam. You'll see the rest of it tomorrow. Those shows drag on anyway. You probably didn't miss much."

Sam threw a stuffed toy horse at Charlie who picked it up and stuck it under Sam's pillow. "Get to sleep, Sam.

"I'm going to read a story to Jody, *Raggedy Ann & Andy*, you want to listen in?"

Sam stuck his tongue at his brother as Charlie switched off the light. He went to Jody's room. She had her book out in anticipation. He sat on her bed.

"Okay, sis, were did Mom leave of last night?"

*   *   *

When he was sure that his brother and sister were asleep, Charlie turned on the kitchen radio. He tuned it to his favorite station. The *Cool Bill Davis* show was still on. He heard the sax of Coleman Hawkins, and took a seat at the table.

He wanted to finish his homework before his eyelids drooped, but things about this day nagged at him.

Charlie leaned back, *Lousy day, Mom's sick, Karin's upset, those reporters, the thing at the drugstore, and I haven't practiced at all today.*

He put his mind back on the last algebra problem and finished his review. He leaned back to stretch when the phone rang. It was Vince.

"Hi, Dad. How's it going with Mom?" He listened to his father.

"She's still undergoing tests. It's late. The hospital has a room for her. I'll stay with her tonight, but I'll call you early before you go to school. Your Aunt Theresa is coming over to the house in the morning to help get Jody and Sam going. You can pick me up later. I'll let you know.

"Anyway, Charlie, try to get some sleep. I've got a feeling that tomorrow is going to be a long day. I'm worried about, Bea. They've given her something, but she's still having some pain."

"Dad, are you sure that you don't want me there with you and Mom?"

"Yeah, it's okay, Charlie. I'll give your mother your love. Are Jody and Sam okay?"

"Everything is fine, Dad. I'll take care of them. Want me to bring you anything – no? See you tomorrow then."

Charlie hung up, switched off the radio and the upstairs lights. He went to his bedroom in the basement where he undressed for bed. He padded barefoot past his bathroom and onto the cold cement floor of the laundry room to put his shirt into the hamper. He groped for the overhead light cord and pulled.

At that moment he felt a strange connection to the yellow light. Shadows from a detergent box and the bleach bottle increased the feeling. He recognized each family member's freshly laundered clothes stacked neatly on a table. He thought that he would put them away in the morning.

A sudden depression enveloped him. What about his mother, who would take care of her? What if she didn't feel better? How would the family cope without Mom? Who would take care of Jody and Sam? What about his Dad?

Charlie put his shirt in the hamper and pulled the light cord. He lingered in the dark, feeling the cold air against his skin. The slightly opened window blinds faced the back towards the garage and drive from the alley.

For a few seconds Charlie saw car lights through the blinds and then they were gone. It was probably a neighbor coming home late. He thought it was strange though that a passing car's lights would shine directly into the window unless they pulled into the driveway. He took the shirt from the laundry hamper, put it back on and went back to his bedroom for his jeans.

Hurrying up the stairs, Charlie fumbled with the pants buttons. He switched on the back light and opened the back door. The car was gone. He stepped out and almost tripped on a large piece of cardboard that had been leaning on the door. He picked up the cardboard. Something was written on one side. He tried to read it under the light but had to take it inside to see it.

Bonarelli you killed that girl!!

Dumbstruck, Charlie pondered over the message. "Who wrote this crap? What the hell is somebody thinking?"

Charlie thought whoever left this message was long gone by now. He closed the door, shut the light, and took the cardboard to the laundry room where he put it on top of the dryer. He removed his clothes and went to his bathroom to shower.

He soaked in the shower thinking about the girl in the park and the message at the back door. Once he got out and dried, he walked back to the laundry room to read the cardboard again. "I'll bet Ralph Jay did this, the prick."

In bed, Charlie couldn't sleep. His mind festered with incrimination against Ralph Jay. He was sure that Jay was dogging him for no other reason than to get under his skin. He thought that the message on the cardboard sneaky, "like Jay and his pal, Birch," he voiced.

*   *   *

Charlie slept fitfully only to be wakened by his internal clock. He felt drugged, but he had to get up to get Jody and Sam ready for school.

Drowsily, he tried to shave. "Damn, cut my ear. Damn, damn." He grabbed for a piece of toilet paper to staunch the blood. The ear kept bleeding. He tore off more toilet paper, applied it to the cut and squeezed until the pressure finally worked. He left the toilet paper stuck to his ear knowing that the bleeding would start when he removed the white pennant.

The doorbell rang. Charlie wrapped a towel around him and ran up the stairs. He opened the front door to feel a cold rush of air hit his bare chest and arms.

"Charlie, put some clothes on."

"Hi, Theresa, Dad said you'd be over to get the kids moving. Thanks for coming."

Aunt Theresa came in with the morning paper, a fresh loaf of Italian bread and a sack of food. "I picked this up at Carbone's on the way over here. Joe let me in the back door. God, that bakery smells heavenly. I didn't want to leave."

Theresa nodded at her nephew's ear. "Charlie, did you stick your head into the disposer?" She headed for the kitchen to put the groceries on the counter. "Kids up yet?"

"Hi, Auntie," Jody walked sleepily into the kitchen. Charlie watched as Theresa gathered Jody up in her arms and almost paralyzed her with hugs and kisses.

"*Madonna,* but you are getting big. I can barely pick you up now. What have you been eating, stones?"

"Auntie, you're squeezing me to death."

Theresa's laughter carried through the house. She put Jody down and went to the cabinets looking for utensils.

Sam came into the kitchen. "What's so funny -- Hi, Auntie."

"Sammy, come on over here and give your Aunt a big hug." Theresa held out her arms.

"Watch out, Sammy she'll crush your bones," Jody giggled.

Sam got a hug from Theresa and scurried out of the room.

"Okay, you guys, I brought some sausage and peppers cooked up last night?"

"Yeah, and French toast with lots of syrup," Jody beamed.

Theresa turned to the sink to wash her hands.

Charlie blanched at the thought of sausage and peppers for breakfast. He was already feeling queasy.

The phone rang. Charlie picked it up. "It's, Dad."

Everyone quieted while Charlie spoke. "Yeah, Theresa is here. Okay, I'll come over in about an hour."

"He wants to talk with you." Charlie handed the phone to Theresa and walked downstairs to dress.

After breakfast Charlie found the keys to the family car. Theresa had a worried look on her face.

"Charlie, call us as soon as you can."

11

Fried Peppers

Charlie drove into the hospital parking lot. He felt a rumble in his stomach. "Oh-oh, Aunt Theresa's jumbled breakfast concoction of sausages, eggs, tomato sauce and fried peppers."

As he parked and got out of the car, another car pulled up behind him. A man got out of the passenger side. Charlie voiced, "Cops?" Even on this cold day the guy had no jacket, and he wore a short sleeved-shirt with what looked like a clip-on tie. A shoulder-holstered, short-barrel revolver hung under his left arm. Cigarette smoke emitted from the driver's half-open window of the unmarked car.

A voice inside the car hollered, "Bonarelli?"

Charlie stopped and looked at the smoking window then at the detective walking towards him, "Yeah."

The approaching detective asked, "Charlie Bonarelli, right? I'm Detective Brawley. We want to ask you a few questions, down at the station."

"Why – about what?"

Brawley answered "About the park a couple nights ago."

Charlie asked, "Where's Matt Grueber?"

"Grueber's off the case, you're with us now. Get in the car."

"I just got here. I came to see my mother. My Dad's expecting me to pick him up."

The smoking window belched more smoke. "He came to see his mommy, that's nice. Hey looks like you cut your ear, kid."

Charlie reached up to pull the paper of off the cut ear. Brawley grabbed his sore shoulder. "That'll wait. Get in."

"What about my Dad? I've got his car?"

The driver got out of the car. The cigarette in the corner of his mouth did little to distract from his pocked and smashed nose. "You want to get in maybe? Or maybe you want a set of cuffs to make the point, kid."

"Easy, Mickey, we're just taking him in for questioning."

"Okay, kid." Detective Mickey opened a back door of the car. "Get in."

Brawley pushed Charlie in. Both men got back into the car.

"What about my Dad? He's expecting me and he needs his car?"

Mickey belched. "Screw the car kid, we're rolling."

Brawley intervened. "We need the kid to let his old man know about the car, Mickey. Pull in front of the hospital entrance, I'll find his father."

Brawley leaned back over the front seat. "What's the room number, kid? What's your Dad's name?"

"The room is four-something. I'll have to ask the front desk. My Dad is Vincent Bonarelli."

They pulled up in front of the hospital, and Charlie opened his door.

"You stay. I'll get your Dad." Brawley opened his door and looked in at Charlie. "What's your mother's name?"

"Beatrice, 'Bea,' Bonarelli."

Brawley got out of the car. "Right, Bea Bonarelli."

Charlie looked at the rear-view mirror to see Mickey's heavy eyebrows and gray eyes staring back at him.

"Bea Bonarelli. Haw." Mickey lit another cigarette. "You kill the little chickadee, Bonarelli?"

"Get bent."

Mickey got out of the car and opened the back door. He reached in and grabbed Charlie's coat collar. He pulled him out of the car. "How about I just slap the shit out of you right here, punk?"

"Go ahead – go ape, Daddy-O."

Mickey raised a hand to smack Charlie who instinctively lifted a hand to block the slap and hit his cut ear. The bleeding started again.

"What the hell are you doing?" Vince Bonarelli grabbed the detective's up-raised hand.

"Wha . . . ?" Detective Mickey didn't like the interference. He turned on Vince when Brawley stopped him.

Vince saw the blood on Charlie's ear. "What are you doing to my son?"

Brawley pulled Mickey away. He spoke from the side of his mouth into Mickey's ear. "What are you thinking? We got witnesses, watch it." He nodded at two nurses exiting the hospital.

Mickey protested, "This is a mouthy kid."

Brawley held onto Mickey. "You got a handkerchief, kid? Use it on the ear."

Vince examined his son's bleeding ear. "What's going on here? Why do you need Charlie? I'm calling Matt Grueber. God-damn-it I want some answers, and right now."

Brawley stepped between Vince and Mickey. "Mr. Bonarelli, we're just taking your son down to the station for some more questions about the girl in the park. You know, it's just routine stuff."

"This is bullshit." I'll drive him to the station when it's convenient. Right now is not convenient."

"We'd like to talk to him now, sir, while it's fresh in the kid's memory." Brawley let go of Mickey and guided Charlie back to the police vehicle.

"It's okay, Dad. I'll be alright." Charlie felt the grumbling again in his stomach.

"Charlie, where did you park the car? I'm following you down to the station. We'll see about this crap."

"What about Mom?"

"She's sleeping now after a dose of painkillers."

* * *

The detectives drove in silence to the central police station. Charlie watched out of the back window, reassured that Vince was in sight.

Charlie's stomach continued to rumble. Aunt Theresa's breakfast caused erupting sounds like Vesuvius. He felt a sickness that signaled a trip to the toilet. "I've got to get to a bathroom, quick."

"What's the trouble kid?" Mickey looked into the rearview mirror just as he drove into the station parking lot. "You shit your pants? You'll be shitting them soon enough I'm betting. Haw."

In the station, Charlie held his stomach with one hand and a handkerchief with his other hand over the cut ear. He looked for the men's room, "I gotta go."

Vince came into the station. "What's the matter, Charlie?"

"Something I ate. I've got to go – now."

Brawley pointed down the lobby towards the men's room. "Don't be long, Bonarelli."

"I'm calling Grueber." Vince went to a pay phone in the front lobby.

Detective Brawley called after him. "You're wasting your nickel, Mr. Bonarelli." He's off the case. The entire investigation is in Central District now."

"How come you're treating Charlie like a suspect?"

Charlie heard his father, and he saw Mickey as he entered the men's room. The detective reminded him of Quasimodo but less intelligent.

He made the toilet in time. When he returned, Vince was talking at the two detectives. "You guys are investigating what?"

Mickey piped, "The murder of the little chick in the park, whadya think?"

Vince's stare met Mickey's emotionless eyes. "Charlie found the girl in the park after he reported the automobile and the incident with the motorist. The librarian called the cops before he found the body. That's it, end of story."

"We'll see if that's the end of the story." Mickey started to say more when Brawley looked at him and shook his head.

"Uh, Mr. Bonarelli, we just want to clarify some details. You know, the other night was kind of fouled up."

"Who fouled it up?" Vince was tired from the night before at the hospital with his wife. He was ready to explode when the cops noticed Charlie.

"Better, I think." Charlie belched.

Brawley pointed the way. "We'll go down into that room on the right."

"I'm going with you." Vince followed.

"How old are you, Charlie?" Detective Brawley knew the answer, but was making a point.

"Eighteen."

Mickey smirked. "He's eighteen, Mr. Bonarelli. He's legal and he's all ours. You can wait in the hall."

The detectives directed him to a wood and opaque glassed door. Brawley led the way, with Charlie then Mickey following him into the room.

The sparse room was a picture of an empty soul. Charlie felt a resurgence of the stomach grumbles as his mind made a slide show of images from the last two days.

Mickey motioned to a table with two chairs on either side. "Have a seat, young man." The slug-nose detective grinned like a wolf contemplating a morsel.

Brawley pulled a tablet from the table drawer. He placed his short-sleeved arms across from Charlie, preparing to write while Mickey leaned against a wall behind Charlie.

Mickey's image stared across from where Charlie sat facing a mirrored window. He felt the detective's eyes on the back of his head. Charlie's mind went from fast-forward to slow-motion as he tried to compose himself. He felt the fog of depression invade his skull.

"Bonarelli, Bonarelli, you with us?" Mickey's voice blurted from behind. "Detective Brawley just asked you a question."

Brawley started again. "Okay, Charlie, let's do this again. What were you doing in the vicinity of the park behind Woodbury Library two nights ago?"

"Uh, well it's like I said, I was driving around the park back to the market where I work."

"Where were you driving from?"

Charlie scooted in his chair. "From the drive-in on Speer Boulevard, you know like I said before."

"Like he said before," Mickey chimed from the back wall. "Haw."

"So, Charlie, why did-yah come back that way and not directly up Speer Boulevard to the market? See, we figure that the quickest way between two points is a straight line, like that, see?" Brawley drew an imaginary line in the air.

"Yeah, like the crow flies, Bonarelli. Haw."

"Just taking a different way, you know. I like to alternate the route just to break up the night. I thought it was less slippery maybe."

"See," Mickey raised his voice, "We figure you broke up the little girl, huh? You know, kid, the little retarded girl."

Mickey came around to the side of the table, leaned on the end and breathed into Charlie's face. "We figure you saw the chickadee in the park and maybe thought you could have a little fun, a little action maybe -- right?"

Charlie almost threw up from the strong tobacco smell and breakfast emitting from Mickey.

Brawley intervened. "Back off Mickey, let the kid talk. Now, Charlie, why did you stop at the corner?"

"Like I said before, some guy looked like he was caught between the curb and his car. You know, like the car slid into the guy's foot and pinned him against the curb. I told Matt Grueber all of that."

"Grueber isn't on the case anymore, kid." Mickey still leaning against the table bent over to put his head between Brawley and Charlie. "So what's the answer again? We want to know about this alleged guy in trouble. We think you're trying to pull our leg kiddo. We think there was no guy but the guy in your imagination."

Charlie's bowels made sounds of a plunger on a pipe.

"A little loose in there, kid?" Mickey made a motion as if to push Charlie's stomach with his big scarred hand, "how's about I push some of that shit out of your head so you can give us the right stuff."

The enveloping depression weighed on Charlie like a terminal disease. He suddenly felt the dam in his butt about to burst, "Got-to-go-right-now." He jumped up and started for the door.

Mickey grabbed Charlie's collar and forced him back into the hard wooden chair.

"Better let the kid hit the toilet, Mickey."

"Too late, the kid shit his pants. Haw."

"I'm sorry, I'm sick to my stomach."

"Christ, Mickey. See what you've done now. The place stinks worse than usual."

Charlie bent over in pain. He reached into his back pocket for the bloody handkerchief. While he fidgeted with the cloth, he noticed Brawley grinning at Mickey who again stood behind Charlie. Charlie saw Mickey, in the mirror, pinching his nose closed.

Brawley resumed his even demeanor. "Charlie, let me get you something to clean that up with." He looked at his partner. "Say, Mickey, why don't you see if you can rustle up a wet rag or some towels? We can't let the kid sit here in his own stink. Better yet, why don't you escort him to the toilet and let him clean up."

"Let's go, kid." Mickey almost toppled Charlie as he pulled his chair back.

They went into the hall where Vince hovered like a raven looking for carrion. He spotted Charlie and Mickey. He saw something was wrong.

"Now what the hell is going on? What did you do to my son?"

"Nothing, Mr. Bonarelli," Brawley came out of the interrogation room. "The boy got sick. We're just letting him use the men's room before we ask him any more questions."

"Sorry, Dad, Aunt Theresa's breakfast I guess."

"Why don't you take your son to the toilet?" Mickey pointed to the men's room.

Matt Grueber came down the hall while Vince and Charlie went to the restroom.

"What's going on here?" He pointed to Vince and Charlie.

Mickey grunted, "Lt. Grueber, you've got no business here. This is our investigation now."

"Come over here you two." Grueber motioned to the two detectives. "I've got some news for you."

"Oh, yeah," Mickey smirked, "and what could that be?"

12

Witness

"What?" Charlie and Vince turned back as Brawley hollered again, "What?" They watched Mickey rock back and forth on the balls of his feet. "Haw, you got a witness? At eight-o'clock on a dark night?"

"Who's the witness?" Brawley squared off with Grueber.

Grueber motioned the two detectives to follow him into the recently vacated interrogation room. He suddenly turned back out of the room. "Jesus, this place stinks. Let's find someplace else."

Charlie and his father looked back down the hall at Grueber. "Vince, you can take Charlie home now. I'll talk to you later." Then he motioned for Brawley and Mickey to walk down the hall with him.

Charlie went to the toilet, and tried to clean up, but it was hopeless. He would have to go home and shower.

When he left the men's room, Charlie and Vince watched the three men in the hall. Mickey's arms and hands flailed like a wounded gooney bird. Brawley faced Grueber, with his hands on his hips like an umpire about to eject the batter.

"Haw," Mickey slapped a wall and almost doubled over with laughter, what? You gotta be kidding, Lt. Grueber, a blind guy? What the hell are you talking about?"

Vince put a finger to his lips, and grinned as they caught pieces of the conversation from the loud-mouth Mickey. "A guy, out for a walk with his dog, and the guy is blind -- right? You've got be shitting us."

Charlie and Vince moved within better listening range, to the three detectives who paid no attention to them.

Grueber talked, "Yes, it was a guy who lives in a home for the blind across from the park. Blind people have acute senses that compensate for their sight. Anyway, he says that he heard a conversation, mostly from a boy or young man. He says the voice asked about helping the motorist, something about a foot caught under the car. Then he heard a different voice, probably the motorist. Then the boy said that he'd have to get help.

"The witness said after the boy left he could hear some shuffling or scraping. Then he heard a man's voice and a grunt, like he was trying to push or pull something. But, before that, he was sure he heard a different voice."

Vince put a finger to his lips again as he and Charlie tried to catch the conversation.

Feeling weak, Charlie leaned his head against the cool wall. He heard Matt Grueber.

"The blind guy found the car and the motorist. He asked what was wrong and if he could help. The man didn't answer, but the blind man heard something scrape and then a car door open. He heard a different voice say, 'C'mon, let's get the hell out of here. Back it off the damn jack.' He also heard the car start, and a noise of metal falling. Someone picking up something, maybe the jack, and then a strange sound before the car took off.

"A uniform found a piece of the jack this morning, but not where it should have been in the street. The piece was in the park behind a tree. We don't know why the jack would be in the street and a piece behind a tree. The lab is checking the parts right now."

Charlie whispered to his father. "Someone must have repositioned that jack after I went for help. I hope that guy Mickey pees his pants. He's one rough bastard."

Mickey wasn't happy. "Lieutenant, what kind of crap is this? The D.A. is going to kick your butt for a story like that. Blind man my ass."

"It's already gone to the D.A. He's got his office following up on it."

"What?" Mickey turned red. "Who the hell took it to the D.A.? It's our case. Besides you don't even have a suspect now do you?"

Charlie was hoping to hear the rest of the story. Vince pulled on his left arm and motioned for them to leave. Charlie held up his hand to stall Vince. He wanted to hear Grueber and hoped that Grueber would get all over the two jerks who brought him in. He was rewarded for his patience.

"You two are handling this investigation like rookies. Since when do you bring in a witness and treat him like a suspect? The Bonarelli boy checked out. There was a bloody tissue by the girl's body. It was Bonarelli's, but it's consistent with the rest of his story; that he dropped it when he bent down to help the girl. Besides, I had the hospital examine him for anything suspicious -- nothing."

Reminded of that night, Charlie still wasn't appreciative that his privates were examined, and the reason for the exam. He felt his Dad pulling his arm again.

"Come on, Charlie, we've got to get you home before you have another accident."

They left to see a sputtering Mickey. "But, Bonarelli's the focus here. I can't buy the blind man shit."

Charlie saw Brawley hold up his hands to his partner. "Mickey, the Lieutenant is right. We are leaning on the kid. Let's go talk to the blind man."

Anyone within earshot of the three detectives in the hall would have heard Mickey's protest.

"Who me -- leaning on the kid?" Mickey turned to Grueber, "We're doing our job. I'm not convinced yet that the Bonarelli kid wasn't involved someway. I'm thinking that the kid isn't telling everything. Like maybe he's holding back. Maybe he saw something else, or somebody else, and he's not telling us."

Matt Grueber held up a hand for silence. "Charlie said there were probably two people at the crime scene, but he can't identify them. Did you forget about that?"

Brawley scratched his chin, "Shadows, playing tricks, maybe?"

"Haw, a mirage maybe." Mickey turned in time to see Charlie and Vince exiting the station. "We'll see how this plays out."

Charlie stared blankly out of the car window as Vince drove home. He wondered if he should tell the police he suspected Ralph Jay and Joe Birch as the two he saw in the park, but he still had no proof.

"I hate this, Dad. I'm living in a vise; people looking at me like I've done something. All I did was find that girl in the park. The car, it sure looks like Mr. Truwet's, but I'm not positive."

"Charlie, let the cops handle it. You tell them what you think and let them follow up. Those two you saw, do you know who they are yet?"

"Maybe some guys from school, but I can't prove it."

Vince looked at his son. "Who do you think it is?"

"I can't say yet. If I'm wrong, then those two guys would be in the same hot seat that I'm in."

"Friends of yours?"

"Not a snowball's chance in hell."

Vince was interested now. "How're you going to find out if it's the two guys you're thinking about?"

"I'm not sure. Maybe just confront them. You know, ask them."

"It's not that simple though is it, Charlie?" They're not going to tell you anything. Better let the police handle it."

"Dad you've got to be kidding, those two -- Mickey and Brawley?

"Look, Dad, I know this is a bad time for you, for the kids, and the family, but I've got to get some stuff straight."

"Okay, Charlie, now's as good a time as any – shoot."

"Maybe I'm whining, Dad, but this pressure is making me crazy."

"Lay it out."

"Okay, it's like this, I've hurt my shoulder, cut my hand and I find a dead girl for my trouble. Mom's sick, Karin is leaving, this is my last year of high-school, and I've got no prospects except the draft. Worse, I think the cops still believe that I had something to do with that dead girl."

Charlie saw a look of relief on Vince's face. "What?"

Vince couldn't contain his joy. "The neighbor girl, the woman with the kid, she's leaving? Where's she going?"

"She's moving with her folks to Arizona."

"Arizona. That's good. She's way out of your league right now. You couldn't support her, and you're too young to be taking on a family at eighteen," Vince smiled.

"Yeah, but I really care for her."

"Right, you care for her. You think your mom and I are fools? That babe has hot pants and you're jumping her. Don't give me that shit."

"I'm going to puke."

Vince pulled over to the curb. "Go ahead and throw up, outside the car please."

Charlie got out of the car. He spotted someone's old spilled milkshake on the pavement near the curb and got the dry heaves.

"C'mon, Son, you're empty. We're almost home; you'll feel better soon enough. I've got to get back to your Mom."

Charlie wiped a clammy hand over his mouth. "Yeah, I'm okay now. "Dad, the guy with the car . . . it's got to be Mr. Truwet. Same car, he's got a bum leg. He's lying. He didn't fall off of a ladder. He probably molested that girl and got himself in trouble with the car. Everything points to him and Matt Grueber knows about Truwet. I think he's dropped the ball with that creepy teach."

As he spoke, he couldn't help but think of Jay and Birch. *But why would Jay kill the girl? Maybe he was following Becky, but so what.*

Maybe, just maybe, he and Birch found the girl before I did. Jay was probably stalking Becky anyway. Or maybe, Jay and Birch did kill the girl?

"Hey, Son, we're home. Better get cleaned up. I don't suppose you want to go to school today. Anyway, you'll be late."

"I want to go to school. You can write me a note."

* * *

Charlie walked out of the school office with an official excuse for his teachers. A hand reached out as he passed a row of lockers. The hand grabbed hard and fast to Charlie's leather jacket, and pulled him into an alcove.

"Shit." Charlie lost his footing and stared into the face of Ralph Jay.

"You fucking with me, Bonarelli, you following me, you calling me and then hanging up?"

Charlie shot a left at Jay's nose, but Jay averted the punch and caught Charlie's wrist. Charlie thought Jay described the same things that were happening to him.

"Fuck you, Jay. Who wants to follow you unless it's somebody that wants to crack your fucking skull? Then concrete isn't easy to break. Let go, and I'll give it a try."

Jay, clutching Charlie's jacket with his right hand, still clasping Charlie's right wrist pushed him into a corner. "Listen, butt-wipe, you've been bugging me. I know it's you."

Charlie stared into Jay's face and the gray eyes. He thought, just like that cop, Mickey. "Who wants to follow a limp-dick like you anyway?"

Jay pressed Charlie further into the corner. Charlie worked his right hand free, made a fist and gave Jay a sharp blow in the ribs.

Jay gasped. Charlie followed through with a hard left punch into Jay's solar plexus but Jay was tough from months of brutal rehabilitation.

Being Bonarelli

Jay recovered and gave Charlie a gut punch.

Charlie doubled over in the alcove. He sucked air. His vision clouded, and he fought to stand. He grabbed Jay's jacket and head-butted the taller Jay in his chin. Jay's head hit the wall, stunning him. Still sucking air, Charlie held onto Jay's jacket like a sloth.

The two hung together trying to catch breath. Charlie recovered first and kicked Jay in his best leg. He threw a feeble left but his fist glanced off of Jay's shoulder and hit the wall.

A teacher intervened. "Stop this immediately, you two." She was smaller than both Charlie and Ralph, and twenty-five pounds lighter than either one. She pushed herself between some students who had gathered near the commotion.

"You two, now stop – stop!" The tiny women wedged herself between Charlie and Ralph Jay. She grabbed both boys by their shirt collars.

Her face was red, and Charlie, still sucking air almost laughed. Okay, you're off to see Mr. Greyer." She tugged on both of them as she scolded. "Puppies, no, big dogs, like big dogs you two, and it's probably just as well that you are leaving this school. The Army wants guys like you." She breathed hard, "The school doesn't."

She ran out of breath, but held on to the two boys like a crab. Charlie and Ralph tried to pull away from her; she held on as she was levitated between them. Determined to remain in control, the teacher clamped her hands tighter on the boys' shirt collars and tip-toed them to the school office.

Mr. Greyer came out of the office just as the three of them lurched up to the door. "Again?" He appeared unhappy but not surprised. "Okay, Mrs. Black, I'll take these two rascals into my office."

Mrs. Black released the boys and jammed her hands into the pockets of her dress. She rushed off, "Ruffians, just plain ruffians."

Mr. Greyer motioned with his head. "Come on you boys. Sit over there on the bench. I'll be right back."

The two boys sat like obedient beagles with hanging heads and sad eyes. They intentionally didn't look at each other.

As Mr. Greyer walked away, Charlie noticed he still had a slight limp.

The Assistant Principal returned in a few minutes. He motioned to the two to follow him into his office. "Okay boys, what's going on?" He looked them over critically. "Charlie, you've scraped a knuckle or two. You've got a big bump growing on the back or your head, Ralph." Mr. Greyer seemed more amused than concerned.

"Charlie, this is the second time that I've seen you in two days. We got a problem here? What about you, Ralph, what's going on?"

Charlie and Ralph remained silent.

"Well, what are your answers?"

Charlie contemplated his bleeding knuckles. He took out a handkerchief and wrapped it around his left hand. *I'm going through handkerchiefs like crazy. I may as well carry a roll of bandages.*

Ralph, barely audible, "Nothing's going on, Sir."

"What? I can't understand you, Ralph."

"Sir, nothing is going on. Just a little disagreement that's all."

Charlie watched absently through the street-side window at the cars passing. He turned to Mr. Greyer.

"Did you hurt your leg, Mr. Greyer?"

"What, my leg?" The unexpected question startled Mr. Greyer.

Charlie felt relieved the focus suddenly turned to Mr. Greyer. He pursued the question. "Yeah, I saw you limping a little yesterday, and then today. Like you hurt your leg maybe?"

The Assistant Principal reddened, "Just a little accident, and I'm asking the questions here. You were saying, a disagreement, Ralph, about what?" He stared at Ralph.

"Uh, I forgot now, wasn't important anyway."

"Well, we can't have senior boys scuffling in our school halls. It's bad for the rest of the student body to see graduating seniors acting like hooligans. You're both graduating in the spring aren't you?"

Charlie had a feeling about Mr. Greyer. He wasn't going to let it go. "So how did you hurt your leg, Mr. Greyer?"

Mr. Greyer reddened and thought for a moment. He wasn't going to lose control to a couple of feisty eighteen-year old boys. "It's not important. I'll be fine in a couple of days."

Charlie wondered what the man was hiding.

Mr. Greyer took charge again. "Here's what I'm going to do. I'm calling your parents to discuss this problem you seem to have with each other. The scramble in the hall isn't the first time you two have come to my attention. Some of the teachers have seen you in confrontations before. This is the first time we've seen fighting between you two. Have you been fighting elsewhere? This isn't healthy.

"You boys go to the lavatory and clean up. No, better yet, Ralph you go to the school nurse and have her look at your head. I want you back in here in fifteen minutes. Charlie, stay a minute.

*   *   *

"Charlie, you can wash up that hand in the lavatory. Before you go, I have a question. I saw you leave the school office a few minutes ago with an excuse in your hand? Oh, and what's your Dad's work number?"

Charlie knew Mr. Greyer didn't know about his mother. His father would go to the office for only a few minutes before he went back to the hospital.

"Charlie, what's going on with you and Ralph? Is it over that poor girl in the park? What's Ralph Jay got to do with it?"

That question put Charlie on his guard. He thought it unusual that Mr. Greyer would connect the girl in the park with Ralph and himself. What did he know?

Charlie ignored the question.

Mr. Greyer waited, but no answer from Charlie.

"Okay, let's try this. Why were you late this morning? Sit down, Charlie."

Charlie sat in front of the man's desk. "The cops took me down to the station for an interview. I got sick. My Dad took me home until I felt better. My mother's in the hospital. Dad went back to St. Anthony's. You won't reach him for a while."

"What's going on with your mother?"

Charlie thought a moment. "She's really ill, probably the cancer coming back."

Mr. Greyer remained silent for a few seconds. "Go take care of that hand, then go ahead back to your classes. I'll deal with you later, after I've had a chance to talk to your father. Oh, Charlie, I'm sorry about your mother."

Charlie walked out of the school office towards his class room.

"Where're you going?" Charlie turned to see Ralph Jay.

"Nurse's office is closed for now. So why aren't you waiting in the office?"

Charlie smelled cafeteria food odors. His empty stomach grumbled and he was hungry despite the early episode. He didn't answer the question. Instead he had a question of his own. "How come you came on to me with those accusations? I'm pretty sure that I saw you and what's-his-name in the park two nights ago. You found the girl first didn't you? You asked me yesterday if I whacked her. Maybe you killed her yourself.

"And, who's called who and hanging up? Who's putting stuff about the girl around my house late at night? I'm thinking it's you doing all of that crap."

"Not me – not me at all. I don't know what you're talking about. So maybe I saw the girl, but she wasn't moving. I mean I almost stepped on her, but I didn't hurt her. Did you tell the cops that you saw me?"

Charlie didn't answer Ralph Jay. He asked instead, "What were you doing in the park? Why didn't you come forward to the cops that you found the girl?"

"None of your business, Bonarelli. Anyway, we . . . I never touched that girl. She was on the ground."

"So, asshole, I'm making it my business. Did you try to help her? You don't care if the cops try to hang me with the girl, right? You're a real standup guy, Jay. I'm telling the cops what I saw, and that's it." Charlie walked past Jay. "Wait, Bonarelli."

Charlie flipped him off and headed to his class. He would tell his Dad later that Ralph Jay found the girl first. His Dad would then call Matt Grueber. He thought that this would be the end of it.

He just made the end of his class before the bell rang for lunch period. No one waited outside the class to go to lunch. He looked around for Bobo and Zel but they weren't there. He hung around for a few seconds as the hall emptied.

Charlie felt a sudden loneliness as he walked the hall, a familiar voice from behind.

"Charlie, wait up."

13

That's Heavy

"Going my way?"

Charlie looked back to see Becky catching up with him, "Hey, Becky, how you doing? I'm on my way to lunch."

"Where've you been, Charlie? I missed you this morning."

"I was late. Everything should be okay now."

"Charlie, you've hurt your other hand? What's it this time, I mean every day . . . a new bandage? Geez, school's barely started."

He laughed and examined the fresh gauze Mr. Greyer had given him. "I'll make it." He held up the recently damaged left hand. "I had a little accident awhile ago."

Becky made a face, "Oh, a little accident? I heard you and Ralph Jay had a fight and that Ralph has a plum-size lump on his head. Was that the little accident?"

He shrugged off the question. "So, Becky, what's going on with you?"

They walked to the cafeteria as Becky caught Charlie up on their classes and that she thought it was "cool," that they were in History and Biology together. "Oh, and did you hear about those escapees from the state mental hospital in Pueblo?" she asked.

"Escapees, oh yeah, I saw something in the headlines a few days ago. I've been so wrapped up with the girl in the park and my mother's illness that I forgot about those guys. What was it, four, five -- I don't remember."

"Yeah, five guys. Anyway the thing that's weird is that Mr. Greyer's son was one of the guys who got away. He's still missing. Anyway, Charlie, how's your Mom?"

Charlie stopped with a sudden revelation. "What?"

"Your mother, how is she?"

"Yeah, Mom, we're not sure. She's in a lot of pain. I'll be getting back to the hospital after school." He faded into thought.

"Charlie, catch up."

Charlie stopped in his tracks. "Becky, did you say Mr. Greyer's son was one of the escapees? Where did you learn that?"

He could tell by her expression she wasn't supposed to know. "Ruthie told me. She was in the school office picking up some stuff to deliver to classrooms. She said that she heard a couple of teachers talking about the guys who got away. Anyway, she said that a teacher mentioned that four escapees made it to Denver and one was Mr. Greyer's son by his first wife."

"Mr. Greyer, a son, first wife -- what are you talking about?"

Becky was a chatter-box and Charlie made no effort to stop her.

"You don't know about Mr. Greyer's son? Mr. Greyer was married to a real nutty woman. Becky told me. Anyway, he divorced her years ago and the son, Willie, who doesn't use his Dad's last name, goes by Burris or Burnis, something like that."

"So what else did Ruthie hear?" He listened for anything that might provide a clue to his situation.

"Ruthie said that about a year ago, Mr. Greyer's son, Willie, and his girlfriend robbed some guy and took his car. They drove the car to California but they were caught by the authorities. Anyway, Willie pleaded insanity and ended up in Pueblo."

"That's heavy, Becky. I mean, just like that," Charlie snapped his fingers, "this Willie gets an insanity conviction. He must have had a good attorney. Are you sure about that?"

"Oh yeah, Ruthie got all of the facts – I think. Charlie, where're you going?" Becky pulled on Charlie's sleeve as he went another direction.

"I'll see you after school Becky. Are you going to be with Ruthie?" He didn't wait for the answer and quick-stepped down the hall towards the school library.

* * *

In the school library, newspapers hung like limp flags on a wooden rack. Charlie looked for the morning paper, but it was gone. He went to the librarian's counter.

The librarian didn't look up but sensed Charlie leaning on her counter. She backed off a bit like she got a whiff of yesterday's garlic. "Yes, what can I do for you?"

Charlie, watching the librarian, was reminded of two nights before. "The morning paper, I'm looking for the *Rocky Mountain News*.

The librarian looked past Charlie and pointed to a girl at a table looking over an open paper. "There, it's in use. I let her work the crosswords during lunch hour.

"I'll check it out. Thanks." Charlie watched the girl leaning over the paper as she put a pencil up to her brow in thought.

Charlie thought she looked different, studious maybe, far out or a nerd. He didn't recognize her. He thought she must be a sophomore or a junior maybe. He smiled at her. "Hi."

The girl looked up dumfounded.

Charlie tried again. "Hi, mind if we share the paper?"

She stared at him. No response.

He thought he had cleaned up okay after the morning with the cops. Maybe he still stunk. He looked at the half of her he saw above the table. She appeared to be slender; an almost boyish-looking girl. She wore big horn rimmed glasses over an inquisitive look. Her blue eyes sparkled in her plain face. She wore no makeup, and her hair was secured to each side of her head in rubber bands. He was reminded of a ventriloquist's dummy. "I see you like crosswords. How's it going?"

He sat down next to the girl and acted interested. "Listen, I think there is a story in the news this morning about some state hospital escapees."

"Huh?"

"I'm Charlie. What's your name?"

"Uh, oh I'm sorry, I'm J."

"Jay? You mean like the bird? Like Blue-Jay?"

The girl looked Charlie over, "No, like the letter J."

"That's pretty short isn't it?" He smiled again at J. "How did you end up with a name like J?"

"J's not my full name. I don't use my full name. It's Jewell. With two lls."

"Your name's Jewell?" Charlie thought she was rather plain for a jewel.

"Yes, but everyone calls me J. I know who you are. You're Charlie Bonarelli, yes?"

"How would you know me?"

She turned red in the face. "I've seen you around with the other seniors. Anyway, you found that murdered girl in the park two nights ago, right? It's all over the school, and I read about it in the paper."

"Okay, yeah, I guess that's about right."

Jewell stared at Charlie like a cop. It made him uncomfortable and he fidgeted in his chair.

"How come you need the paper? Is there something in here" Jewell tapped the paper, "that has your interest? There's just a small article about the girl in park and that there are no suspects yet."

"No, I'm not looking for the article about the girl, but I'll read it anyway." Charlie reached for the paper, but Jewell put her forearms over the spread-out paper and clenched her fists.

Charlie pulled his hand back.

The librarian passed nearby, "Quiet, please."

They sat quietly until the librarian went to another part of the room.

Under his breath, "Look, I'm interested in the escapees from the state hospital in Pueblo. Do you mind if I read the article?"

Jewell lifted her arms. "Sure go ahead," she whispered, "have at it."

A sheepish Charlie whispered his thanks. He pulled the paper slowly towards himself and flipped the paper back to the front page. In his haste to get to the hospital that morning he hadn't opened the paper to read: *Area Scoured for Four Hospital Escapees*. He skimmed the story and followed it to an inside page. There were four photos under the forwarded headline. Charlie studied a picture of twenty-year-old Willie Burris. He saw the resemblance of the escapee to the Assistant Principal, Mr. Greyer.

Jewell looked at the story and back at Charlie. "So what's so interesting about the story?"

Trying to talk in a low voice, Charlie said "This guy," he pointed to the first photo in a line of four, "he's Mr. Greyer's son. At least that's what B . . . a friend told me a few minutes ago."

"Mr. Greyer?" Jewell's eyes widened, "the Assistant Principal, you sure?" How would your friend know that? The guy," she put a finger under the photo, "Burris, doesn't have the same name."

Charlie answered, "Mr. Greyer is divorced from Burris's mother. The mother is some kind of a fruitcake."

"Haw." The girl started to laugh but remembered she was in the library and put her hand over her mouth.

Charlie heard the, "haw" and grimaced. That asshole cop, Mickey, laughs like that, he thought.

"So Jewell, uh, J, what's your last name?"

The school bell rang, and the girl jumped up. "Gotta go, see-ya around."

Charlie watched the tall slender girl walk toward the front of the library. He thought, nice walk, sexy even. He focused on her hips and her small butt. She wore a tight skirt like Becky. Charlie thought, must be a new trend.

"Nice ass." He mouthed the words and almost whistled. He looked around the room wondering if he had just made a big noise that everyone in the library heard. The room had cleared out.

The librarian lifted her head and gave Charlie a questioning look. She pointed at a clock and asked, "Class?"

He shook his head. He had a free period before his next class, and he had lost his appetite. He studied the front page of the newspaper and the account of four state hospital inmates. The authorities were searching for them in Denver. A fifth escapee was already caught.

Charlie had a sudden thought, he did see something else. *That's it. I didn't tell the cops that there was something in the back seat of that guy's car.* It was a lump with a blanket over it.

He thought about the story and the connection to finding the body in the park. Was it Mr. Greyer in the park and not Mr. Truwet? Was that lump in the car Mr. Greyer's son, Willie Burris?

Charlie studied the inside page and the four photos again. He fixated on Burris's photo. Burris, under big glasses, looked like Mr. Greyer. Charlie flipped through the pages until he located the automobile advertisements. He found what he looked for, an advertisement with a picture of a *1956 Oldsmobile, 2-Tone Hard Top.* Was that a 1956 and not a 1957 car? Mr. Truwet had a brand new 57, probably bought on a year-end closeout. Truwet's 1957 car would be a little longer than the 56.

Maybe the shadows from the trees and poor light made the car look different. He wondered what Mr. Greyer drove?

Charlie jumped up from the table. "I'm taking a look," he blurted to no one. He walked quickly out of the library and ran down the stairway two steps at a time.

Banging out of the door to the faculty parking, he ran up and down the string of cars until he saw Mr. Truwet's car and stopped. Slowly he walked around it then walked carefully down the rows of cars.

A teacher getting out of her car saw him. "Young man, what are you doing? Are you looking for something?"

"Uh, no . . . I mean, uh . . . yeah, Mr. Greyer asked me to check something on his car, but I don't remember which one it is."

The teacher made a critical assessment of Charlie. "You're all beat up. What happened to you?" She examined the bandages around his hands, an abrasion on his forehead and a fresh cut on his ear.

"Uh, accident. Yeah, I'm accident prone, but I'm cool."

The teacher looked around the lot and pointed towards the door Charlie had just run out from. In his haste, he ran by the cars closest to the door. "Mr. Greyer parks near the school door – there." She pointed to a gray 1956 Oldsmobile hard top.

He was almost speechless. How could he have missed it? "Yeah, right, the Olds."

"Yes, young man, the gray car over there."

"Right. Well thanks, Mum." Despite his Italian heritage he sometimes slipped into his mother's English expressions.

"Mum?" Amused, the teacher walked towards the school. She shook her head. "These kids," Charlie heard her laugh.

Charlie fought to remain calm until the teacher went through the door. Once she was gone, he ran back to where she had pointed out the gray Olds.

"That's it. Mr. Greyer's car is a two-tone gray 1956 Oldsmobile. It wasn't Mr. Truwet's car that I saw. I'll bet it was this one."

He walked around the car five times before he heard the nearby door to the school open and suddenly close. He looked at the door but saw no one. He went back to inspecting the car. He ran his fingers along the front bumper and felt scratched chrome near the passenger side. He knelt down and looked at the scratch. "That could be made by a jack."

The school bell rang. He had to go to class, but he was convinced that this was the car he saw that night. He looked into the car interior and saw an old army blanket in the backseat.

"Yeah, the guy could have hidden under that blanket."

Charlie ran back into the school. Lost in thought, he didn't see anyone watching from under a stairwell as he passed by.

"Charlie." Someone stepped from the shadows. "Can I talk to you?"

14

Charlie stopped in his tracks, "Mr. Greyer?"

"Charlie, let's go to my office. I need to talk with you."

Charlie thought Mr. Greyer caught him inspecting his car. He had already convinced himself that it had to be Mr. Greyer's car, and not Truwet's car he saw at the park the night he found the girl's body. He thought now the form in the back seat may have been Mr. Greyer's son, the escapee, Willie Burris. Mr. Greyer was probably hiding him.

Charlie also thought the son might have had something to do with the girl in the park. He had to tell his Dad and Matt Grueber. He guessed Mr. Greyer would try to prevent Charlie from telling the police who he thought was involved with the dead girl.

Mr. Greyer led Charlie into his office. "Sit down, Charlie." He looked Charlie over as if assessing the physical damage. "I'm sorry to have to tell you this on top of your *current problems.*"

What problems? Maybe I have a few scratches. He probably saw me looking over his car . . . figured out that I'm on to him and his lunatic son, Burris. He's going to cause me some problems alright.

"Charlie, your father is sending someone to pick you up. He wants you to go to the hospital. I'm sorry Charlie, but I think your mother's condition is serious."

"What?"

"I'm terribly sorry, Charlie. I'll make sure your teachers know you will be out for the rest of the day. Someone in each of your classes will get your assignments to you."

"Who's picking me up?"

"Your aunt, I believe. Theresa? She should be here any time now. It took me awhile to find you."

"Oh."

There was a knock on the door. A school secretary stuck her head in. "Excuse me, Mr. Greyer, there's a Theresa Bonarelli here."

Charlie jumped up from his chair.

"Thank you, Emily. We are just coming out."

Mr. Greyer held the door for Charlie. He saw Theresa and reached out to shake her hand. "Miss Bonarelli, I'm Richard Greyer, the Assistant Principal."

Theresa looked at Charlie with sad eyes. She let go of Mr. Greyer's hand and put an arm around her nephew. "We've got to go to the hospital, Charlie."

"What about Jody and Sam? I'm supposed to watch them after school."

"Mama and Papa will take care of them when they get home from school. I've double parked so we've got to hurry." Theresa led Charlie down the hall and out of the school door.

"What's going on, Theresa?"

"Bea is serious. The doctors think she is fading. They're pretty sure she's going into a final coma."

"A final coma?" Charlie understood now his mother was never coming home again. It all seemed so sudden. He knew she had been sick, but he never thought she was so serious that she might die. Tears ran down his cheeks.

Theresa cried. "Vince needs us. Let's try to bear up." She took a handkerchief from the sleeve of her sweater to wipe her eyes.

*   *   *

110

At the hospital, they found Vince waiting outside Bea's hospital room.

Vince spoke in a low tone. "The doctors and nurses are attending to her now."

Theresa put her arms around her brother. "I'm so sorry, Vincent." She cried on his shoulder.

Vince sobbed, "My poor Bea."

Charlie had never seen his father so emotional or heartbroken.

A nurse came out of Bea's room. "You can go in now."

A doctor stood at Bea's bedside. He held her hand and patted her arm. He turned to the family.

"Mr. Bonarelli, I'm sorry about your wife. It won't be long now. She's comfortable. Sit with her as long as you like."

Vince nodded and thanked the doctor. Theresa's eyes ran tears. Charlie wiped his tears on the sleeves of his jacket.

A Catholic priest came into the room, "Mr. Bonarelli, I'm Father Miller, the hospital Chaplain. I'm very sorry about your wife. Would you like me to administer the Last Rites?"

"Yes, Father, thank you."

The priest went to Bea's bedside and took out the items to perform the Sacred Rites.

Charlie knew that this act by the Catholic Priest was the anointing of a sick or dying person. *Big fucking deal. What's oil and words going to do to help my mother who has no idea what is going on? She's out of it.* Charlie wasn't so out of it that he couldn't swear at God, the dirty son-of-a-bitch, for allowing his mom to die.

After the priest left, the three of them stood together at her bedside.

Theresa wept and dabbed at her eyes with a soggy handkerchief. Vince put his arms around Theresa while Charlie stood by Bea's bed, unbelieving, immobile. *What can I do?* He felt his father and aunt next to him. They put their arms around each other.

Vince took his wife's hand; he tried to control his grief as he leaned over and whispered his love to his dying wife.

The three stood silent, watching the woman in the bed. After a few minutes Bea mumbled something unintelligible, took two sharp breaths and passed.

"That fast?" Charlie looked at his father and aunt. "She's gone? Is she gone?" He didn't need an answer as he walked out of the room and stood like a lost dog looking for direction but seeing nothing that he recognized. His mind went blank. He turned and leaned against the wall and buried his head into his right arm.

Hospital staff went in and out of Bea's room. A nurse touched Charlie's shoulder. "We will be moving your mother now. You can say a final goodbye if you wish."

Charlie couldn't believe this, a final goodbye? He thought he was dreaming. He couldn't believe that his mother was gone. Jody and Sam, they don't get the final goodbye, whatever that is. We'll never see our mother again. We'll never have our beautiful mother again with her charming British accent.

Numb, Charlie walked back into the room. Two attendants disconnected a monitor and the oxygen. They placed Bea on a gurney and wrapped a sheet over her.

Theresa leaned on Vince's shoulder while the attendants wheeled the gurney through the door and down a hallway.

A Catholic nun entered the room. She spoke to Vince and Theresa about the disposition of "Bea," and said they could call a funeral home as soon as the death certificate was signed.

Vince nodded his head; Theresa took in the information without a sound.

Charlie stood in the doorway and smoldered, a slow-burning fuse. "This is bullshit. Mom can't be gone. Why couldn't the doctors help her, Dad? Why couldn't he help her? He was mad at the doctors and mad at God, and he was mad at the cops. It was all he could do to remain calm, and then a bomb went off in his head.

He lost control of himself as he slammed his left fist, the one he had hurt that morning into the wall. The pain brought him back to his senses. "Oh shit."

Vince and Theresa looked at him. Theresa put her hand to her mouth.

Vince couldn't move. "What?"

The nun walked calmly over to Charlie and took the hand. She gently felt the bone structure. "Broken; at least two fingers. Let's take him down to the emergency room. He'll need x-rays."

"What the hell did you do, Charlie?" Vince didn't know what to think now.

"I don't know. I don't know why I did that, it just happened. Geez, I don't know."

The nun led Charlie gently down the hall. "Let's get you downstairs."

*   *   *

In the emergency room the nun spoke to an admitting nurse who then came over to the Bonarellis. "I'm sorry for your loss. We better get the boy in and look at the hand. Are you sure it's just a hand?" The nurse looked Charlie up and down.

The cut ear had coagulated but still looked ugly. The bandage on the cut right hand needed changing. Charlie felt like he'd been through a battle.

"Yeah, just the hand." Charlie held up his injured left hand, now throbbing with pain. The earlier bandaging had frayed.

He sat on the edge of an emergency room table. He thought what have I done to myself God-damn-it? I keep beating the shit out of myself. He looked over to the side of the room where he saw his father and aunt both lost in their own thoughts.

Theresa sniffled occasionally. Vince sat drained of emotion. An attendant with a clip board made a slight knock. She needed some admitting information.

The wait seemed long to Charlie, though the day's events went fast. Too clumsily fast he thought it was probably the worst day of his life.

A doctor came into the room, made a quick assessment, and ordered an x-ray of Charlie's hand.

While Charlie waited for the x-ray, he sat silent listening to his father and aunt.

Theresa got up from her chair. "I'll call Mama and Papa. I guess they'll have to tell the kids."

"No." Vince surprised them. "It's okay, you call Mama and Papa, but I'll tell the kids. Make sure Mama and Papa know that. Ask them to put Jody and Sam to bed.

"Sure, I understand." Theresa knew Papa Bonarelli could be abrupt. He spoke with a heavy Italian accent that sometimes left Jody and Sam perplexed.

Vince said, "I'll have to wire Bea's family in England."

"Yes, of course, the Strikers," Theresa said.

Vince took out a pocket secretary and found an empty page. I'll write it out and call Western Union."

An x-ray technician came into the room; she looked at Charlie sitting on the edge of the table. She checked a chart in her hand. "Charlie, I'm going to take you to x-ray. It'll only take five minutes and we're back here.

"You folks," looking at Vince and Theresa, the technician said, "can stay here or get yourselves some coffee. We'll be here after the x-rays."

Theresa got up, "Where is the phone please?"

"You can use that one." The technician pointed out the door towards a nearby desk.

Theresa left the room as Vince composed his message to his wife's English relatives. He left to make the call.

114

* * *

Charlie was already back in the room when Vince and Theresa returned.

A doctor came in with the film of Charlie's hand. He put it up against a lighted box on the wall. "Here and here." He pointed. "Fractures in the *proximal phalanx* on two fingers, some trauma to the *capitate*, and it looks like a hairline in the *lunate*."

Charlie asked, "What's that mean in English, Doctor? It hurts like hell."

"It means you broke the fourth bones in the middle and left index fingers of the left hand and that you hurt the knuckle bone in the middle index, right here. Also, you will experience pain in the wrist." The doctor touched a sensitive area on Charlie's damaged hand.

"We'll splint and tape the fingers together. We can wrap the wrist but it isn't necessary. It'll hurt like the devil for awhile. It'll take six weeks to heal properly. No batting practice or heavy work with that hand for several days. You get crazy with the hand, and we'll have to cast it. Take aspirin for the pain. Oh, and we may try a sling.

"Next time you feel overcome, try a punching bag – it helps, and you won't have to see me again. I'm truly sorry for your loss, and this." The doctor pointed at Charlie's left hand as a nurse came into the room. She was carrying bandages and splints for Charlie. "The nurse will fix the dressing on both of your hands."

* * *

The three Bonarellis left the hospital late into a dark and cold night.

"No moon." Charlie looked at the cloud cover. The darkness overcame his whole being as they walked silently to the parking lot.

On the drive home, Charlie thought about telling Vince about his fight with Ralph Jay and what Jay had revealed. He dozed off before he could open his mouth.

15

Where's Mom?

"What?"

"Charlie, wake up." It was late. Lights were on in the Bonarelli house. Theresa had parked in front and was already in the kitchen with Nonna and Papa Bonarelli when Vince and Charlie came up the back stairs from the garage.

Nonna cried and held out her arms to them.

Papa Bonarelli stood with his hands to his sides like a statue. He adored his daughter-in-law, Bea. He was mad. The former soldier had barely survived the World War One in the Italian army and had a vengeful hatred of death.

"The sono-fa-beetch, *il diavolo*, he come again, the sono-fa-beetch. I keel-im-the-sono-fa-beetch."

Nonna Bonarelli wept and waved a hand at Papa to shut up.

"The kids -- Jody and Sam," Vince asked, "asleep I hope."

"Yes, yes, we put them to bed." Nonna wiped tears with her apron.

"I'll tell them in the morning." Vince choked.

Everyone sat around the kitchen table staring at the designs on the tablecloth while Nonna warmed soup and bread from the evening meal.

"You must eat. Here Vincenzo, you sit down and eat. Carlo, Theresa, I made *minestra, mangiare*."

They ate while Nonna chattered about funeral arrangements. "We have to call everybody. What should we dress her in; what were her favorite songs? Who would be the pallbearers?"

Theresa, normally very cool, threw up her hands. "Mama, Mama, please. We'll talk about this tomorrow. Vince and Charlie, and I, we need some rest. I'll help you clean up the kitchen then we need to get some rest. We'll call people in the morning, okay?"

* * *

They all slept uneasily. Vince, not wanting to sleep in his and Bea's bed, dozed in a living room chair. Theresa was in Jody's room and Nonna slept in Sam's room. Papa Bonarelli slept in Charlie's room. Charlie lay on the couch half awake.

"Nonna snores." Sam came into the living room as the early morning sunlight peeked through the front blinds. "How come Nonna is still here?"

Charlie lay still for a few seconds. He felt sore all over. "Huh, oh, Sam." He saw Vince rub his face with his hands and yawn.

"I've got to clean up." Vince yawned again. "Look, Sam, I'll tell you what's going on after we've cleaned up and have breakfast."

"Dad, how come you and Charlie are sleeping in the living room?"

"We'll all talk later, Sam." Vince got up and stretched.

Charlie was stiff. It hurt to move. His right hand hurt, but his left hand raged with pain. "Oh." He tried to move. "Sammy, help me up please."

Sam obliged by pulling on his brother's left arm. "What happened to your hand, Charlie? Where's Mom, is she still in the hospital?"

Jody came into the room trailing a threadbare Raggedy Ann doll and wiping the sleep from her eyes. Yawning, she said, "Auntie slept with me last night."

The phone rang.

Charlie looked at his watch. "Jesus, it's not even seven in the morning." Oh, God, my hand is throbbing. I need aspirin." He hobbled to the kitchen hallway and picked up the phone.

"Hello . . . Yeah, just a minute please. Dad, it's for you. Someone from the funer . . . uh." He remembered Jody and Sam hadn't been told yet.

Charlie put the phone down and took the stairs to his room. Papa Bonarelli was just getting up from Charlie's bed. He swore oaths in Italian.

"*Bon Giorno*, Carlo, you gonna be okay?"

"Yeah, Papa, I'll be okay, you want to use the bathroom?"

"Shoo-shoo," he mumbled.

Charlie sat staring at a wall while Papa Bonarelli was in the bathroom. His mind flip-flopped from the past to the future. What would life be like without his mother? How will Mom's absence affect his brother and sister? What about Dad?

He thought hard about his mother and about his future after high school. These and other thoughts ricocheted through his mind. Then suddenly his mind went blank, exhausted.

"Carlo," Papa Bonarelli touched Charlie on his shoulder.

"Huh?"

"I'm-a-done." He left the room.

Charlie leaned back in the chair staring at his school books stacked on a corner of the desk. "How am I going to keep up?" He picked up his history book, and absent-mindedly leafed through the pages.

An illustration depicting Christopher Columbus and his three ships caught his attention. Charlie thought aloud, "Man that must have been some voyage. Columbus didn't know what he was facing. He had no idea what was out there. Hostile Indians, bad weather, sick crew, and I'm worried?" He read in the book for a few minutes to clear his mind. He turned on the radio listening for the early morning news. He learned that one of the escapees from the Pueblo State Mental Hospital was captured in Denver.

"Which one, which one?" He spoke to the radio and turned up the volume. "A name, give me a name." He wanted it to be Willie Burris, but the announcer didn't have the name yet. He announced the three other escapees remained at large.

"Need to take a shower."

* * *

Charlie cleaned up as well as he could while trying to hold his left hand away from the water. Later he went up to the kitchen, crowded with his family and the odors of coffee and cooking bacon.

Theresa hugged Charlie. "I'm sorry you got sick yesterday. I think you must have got a bad sausage or something. Come on now, eat some breakfast."

"I can wait. I'll get the paper."

Charlie went out to the front yard and picked up the *Rocky Mountain News*. He didn't see anything on the front page about the escapees. For the first time in three days there was no further coverage about the murdered girl. There was something about the escapees on page two. He thought the news was stale, but the authorities had caught only two out of the five so far. He studied the paper on the way into the house.

Vince wasn't around but Charlie heard water running in the main bathroom.

"Where's Mommy?" Jody cried.

Sam joined in. "Yeah, when's Mom coming home?"

The bathroom door opened and Vince came out in his underwear and went into his bedroom to dress. He reappeared in the kitchen. "Sam, Jody, I have something to tell you. Charlie, can you come in, too? We'll go to the front room."

Papa Bonarelli sat at the kitchen table slurping his coffee. He set his cup down and put his head into his hands. Nonna wiped her eyes with her apron.

"You need me, Vince?" Theresa got up from the kitchen table.

"No, I think I can do this, Charlie's here, too."

Jody sat silently on the couch.

Charlie watched his smaller brother. He wasn't sure what he was supposed to do or say. He didn't take his mother's death any better than he expected Sam and Jody to understand it.

"Mom's not coming home is she?" Sam clenched his seat cushion. "She's really sick . . . or?"

Jody started crying again. "What's the matter with Mommy?"

Vince put an arm around Sam. Charlie picked up Jody and sat her on his lap.

Vince did most of the talking. He told Sam and Jody, as gently as he knew how, about their mother and that she was in heaven now.

Jody stiffened, "Heaven, Mommy's in heaven?"

Sam didn't know what to say. He sat still and introspective. He shrugged his Aunt Theresa off.

Jody handled their mother's death better than Charlie would have imagined. "Who's going to take care of Daddy, Charlie and Sam?"

Nonna heard Jody and cried. "Oh *Madonna mia*, my little baby, she's such a big girl now," she sobbed.

"Mama, Mama." Vince went to his mother. "It's going to be alright. We'll get through this."

Sam went to his room and closed the door. Charlie followed and opened the door. "Hey, Sammy you going to be okay?"

Sam sat immobile on his bed.

The phone rang.

Theresa called, "Charlie it's for you."

Charlie closed the door to Sam's room. "Dad, you'd better look in on Sam." He went to the phone.

"Hello." He listened to his cousin Bobo on the other end. "Yeah, Bobo, last night, how'd you know already?"

"Is that Bobo?" Theresa asked.

Charlie nodded.

"I called Aunt Mary, last night. She's probably called everyone in the country by now."

Charlie spoke, "Bobo, I'm not going to school, probably for a few days. Yeah, I'll see you later."

The phone rang most of the morning as people called with condolences. By late morning, friends and relatives had flooded the house with food and sympathy.

Theresa took charge of traffic while Nonna took care of the food. Papa Bonarelli sat at the table and drummed his fingers between sips of coffee laced with brandy from the bottle on the table.

Vince called his office to instruct his new secretary how to handle the business for the next few days. She was just hired to replace the secretary who had been with him for years. He tried to be patient, but Charlie heard the worry in his father's voice.

Sam stayed in his room while Jody walked about like a little mother. She watched everything and everybody as people came and went. She put on a brave face, but Charlie knew that she would cry herself to sleep this night.

Later in the day, Charlie went with Vince and Theresa to the funeral home to make Bea's final arrangements. Charlie dreaded the funeral home, but felt he needed to do this with his family.

The funeral director made it as comfortable as possible and they got through the ordeal soon enough Charlie thought. He was relieved when they left the funeral home.

*   *   *

Papa Bonarelli met them at the front door as they returned to the house. "The *Inglese*, they called."

Vince looked at his father as he came up the steps. "What, Papa?"

"The *Inglese*, Striker, you know, *il cognato, Bernardo*."

"Oh, my brother-in-law, Bernard Striker, about the telegram I sent last night."

"*Si*, yes" Papa Bonarelli nodded his head. "He's coming to here you know . . . he's bringing the mama, e *l'amico*."

Vince smiled at Theresa. "Bernie is bringing Bea's mother and her boyfriend?"

Papa Bonarelli motioned with his hands, "*Si*, yes that's it. Bernardo wants you to call him on the island."

Theresa laughed. "Is this a new boyfriend or the old one from last time?"

Charlie grinned as he thought about Uncle Bernard and his English Grandmother, Mildred Striker. They had not seen his mother's family for three years. The last time they visited, Grandmother Striker had a proper Englishman with her. Grandpa Striker, Bea's father, was killed during World War Two, while the son, Bernard barely survived the Royal Air Force.

Vince looked at his watch. "I'll call them in the morning. It must be 11:00P.M. in London now."

Papa Bonarelli waved his hands and shook his head. "No, he wants you to call him when you get back. He wants to make the travel, you know the *aeroplano*."

"Okay, then I better do it now."

"Where are Jody and Sam?" Vince asked his father.

"With your mama. Sammy, he's-a-not-doing so good."

Theresa brushed past them. "I'll help. Vince you better make that call; I'll check on Jody. Charlie, please see to Sammy."

Charlie found his brother and sister with Nonna Bonarelli in Sam's room. Sam sat between Nonna and Jody. Nonna hugged Sam.

Jody stroked her brother's head. "It's going to be better, Sammy."

Theresa stood by wiping the tears from her eyes as Sam cried.

Charlie's broken fingers throbbed with pain. He went to the bathroom for aspirin. He came out with the pills and headed for the kitchen for a glass. Charlie saw his Dad cradling the phone waiting for a connection to Bernard Striker.

"This'll cost an arm and a leg."

"What, Dad?"

"Nothing," he waved for Charlie to be quiet. "Yes, operator, I'm here."

"Bernie, yes it's Vince. Yes, thank you. We're okay. Yes, she passed last night . . . peacefully. Yes, we just came back from the funeral home. Okay, three days from now. You want to try and make it in two days? That's pushing it. Can you do it . . . I mean it's an expensive trip and all?"

Charlie imagined his Uncle Bernie, animated, on the other end. Mom always said that her brother talked like an Italian with his hands.

Vince continued to listen to his brother-in-law. "Okay, Mildred has a friend, he is? He's coming, too? Okay. We may have to put you up in a hotel downtown. Do you mind? What?"

Charlie saw the surprised look on his father's face.

Vince answered. "He did?"

He put his hand over the receiver. "Your Grandmother Striker's boyfriend is in the hotel business. He's made arrangements for them to stay at the Brown Palace downtown."

Charlie left Vince to finish his conversation. As he reached in the cabinet for a glass, he looked out the back window onto the driveway as if he saw a mirage, "Mom?"

She was standing on a sunlit driveway looking towards the house, shading her eyes. "But you're gone," then she was. Charlie couldn't move. He expected her to reappear. Tears streamed down his face. Then he suddenly thought of Karin. His mother had warned him about getting involved with Karin just a few days ago, "What's the connection?"

"Everything okay, Charlie?" He felt his aunt's arms around him.

16

Mickey Split

"Daydreaming," his mother called it when Charlie stood for long moments staring out the back window at nothing. The vision of his mother pulled on him as he thought about Karin. He stared into the neighborhood beyond the alley at Karin's roof. He hadn't seen her in two days. She probably didn't know about his mother. *I'll call her, maybe? I know things don't look so good between us right now anyway.* His thoughts drifted to the girl, Jewell or J, who he had met in the library the day before, and the newspaper story about the escapees.

Escapees, death, cops, the physical and mental beatings are ruining my life. I could use some rest, Charlie thought as he watched a car drive slowly up the alley. He couldn't see the driver, but he noticed a spotlight on the side of the car and a radio antenna -- cops.

The cops are checking on me here? Did he forget to tell Vince about Mr. Greyer's car and his son, Willie Burris, oh and, Ralph Jay? He couldn't remember. Charlie watched through the window but didn't see the car again. His Dad's voice startled him.

"Charlie, I just spoke with England. Uncle Bernie, Grandmother Striker, and her friend, Roland, are on the way to the U.S. They'll be in New York tomorrow afternoon. They should be here in a couple of days. Your grandmother's boyfriend has some connections in the hotel business. They're staying at the Brown Palace, and . . . ."

"Dad, you mentioned it a minute ago. I've got something to tell you. I think I know who was involved with that girl's body in the park. Mr. Greyer's son is an escapee from the state mental hospital. There may have been another person in that car hiding under a blanket. Anyway, I went to the school parking lot and found Mr. Greyer's car. I saw a blanket in the backseat. I think it was the car I saw that night, and not Mr. Truwet's car. Mr. Greyer hurt his right foot, too. He got really defensive when I asked him about it. It makes sense.

"Maybe Mr. Greyer helped his son escape or maybe he didn't even know about the girl. Oh, and another thing I didn't mention to Matt Grueber – 1t was Ralph Jay and his pal who were near the picnic table that night."

Vince lit a cigarette. His face was as hot as the match. "So how come you didn't tell Matt this when he first talked to you? What a goddamn mess this is turning out to be."

"Dad, I wasn't sure. It happened so fast that I wasn't sure it was Jay. I asked Jay about it, you know, after the fight."

"Fight, what fight?" Vince exhaled a billow of smoke. Charlie's mother had frowned on his father's smoking in the house, but it didn't take Vince long to forget that.

"Oh, didn't Mr. Greyer call you? Ralph Jay and I had a little disagreement at school after I got back from that crap with the cops."

"No, I didn't hear from Mr. Greyer. We haven't had a chance to talk about anything except Bea. The house has been in an uproar with the arrangements and friends. Now her family is going to be here. I'm sorry, I haven't been paying attention. I saw that little scrape on your left hand before you broke the fingers. I forgot to ask about it. Anyway, how's the right hand, the cut? I saw you taking aspirin; do you have pain in both hands?"

"I'll be okay, except I just saw a detective's car cruising up the alley."

Vince went to the window above the sink to look out at the alley. He turned on the tap and put the newly lit cigarette out. Charlie thought his father remembered Bea's disapproval of smoking in the house.

"The cops aren't going to leave you alone. I'll call Matt right now."

The phone rang before Vince could make the call. He picked up the phone and spoke a few seconds then he called for Theresa. He tried to lower his voice, but Charlie could still hear him. "This is the funeral home. They want us to come back over to make some additional arrangements. It'll only take a few minutes." He called into the kitchen, "Charlie, I'll call Matt later."

"I'll call him myself, Dad."

Vince came back into the kitchen. "No, I'll do this. I know him well and he's not supposed to be on the case now anyway."

"What's going on?" Theresa came into the kitchen. She saw the tension in Vince's face, but she didn't wait for an answer. "Jody's going to be alright, but I'm not sure about Sam. Charlie, can you talk to Sammy? I'll go with Vince. Oh, and Mama and Papa will be here soon."

Charlie went into Sam's room. He felt awkward as he and Sam both stared at the walls.

"Sam, want to watch a little TV? I think there's some postseason baseball stuff on now. A sportscaster is interviewing Mickey Mantle. Mantle hit thirty-four home runs this year. That's pretty incredible, huh?"

Sam was unimpressed. "Roy Sievers hit forty-two, and Ted Williams hit thirty-eight." He clammed up again.

Charlie wasn't going to move Sam, the statistics nerd, with his limited knowledge.

"So, Sam, Grandma Striker is going to be here tomorrow. She's got a new boyfriend. His name's Roland. They're staying downtown at the Brown Palace. Pretty cool, huh?"

Sam brightened some. "Uncle Bernie, he's coming, too, right?"

"Yeah, sure, Sam, Uncle Bernie is coming, too."

Sam smiled, "He's funny. You know, the way he talks, like Mom but a little wacky, too."

"Yeah, that's it. He's a little crazy, but that's what makes him so interesting, Sammy. Maybe we'll get to go to England sometime to visit. They always come here."

"It's been two or three years, Charlie, but I remember him." Sam's voice trailed off. He stared at the wall again.

"Look, Sammy, let's . . . ," the phone rang.

Papa Bonarelli, who had just come in with Nonna, hollered from the hallway, "Carlo, its-a-fo-you."

Charlie left Sam who was staring at his bed. He went to the phone. "Hello, hey, Zel, how you doing? Yeah, you've got my school assignments? Thanks. No . . . come on over. I still have to do school work. Okay, I'll see you in a few."

Charlie hung up. "Zellie's coming over with my class work." He said it loud enough for anyone in earshot to hear. "Nonna, we got anything to eat? You know how Zel likes to *gnosh*."

Nonna Bonarelli called into the kitchen. "What's that, *gnosh*?

"You know *mangiare*."

Nonna, who used a powerful banter of Italian and English interchangeably, answered, "So okay, *mangiare*, how come you don't use English in the first place?

"Carlo, do we have anything, you crazy? The people, they bring – look at all of this food." She opened the refrigerator. "It's all Betty Crocker in there. Nobody cooks from scratch anymore. You gotta have biscuit dough and casserole. No sausage, no polenta, no gnocchi. What's the matter with this world?"

Charlie left the kitchen as Nonna made the sign of the cross and talked on about the world going to *il diavolo* in poodle skirts and girls in Capri pants, "*Madonna Mia*."

Charlie went downstairs to the family room and his drum set. He picked up one of Jody's dolls and set it on a chair. He tripped and almost fell on one of Sam's baseballs and glove. "Mom's going to be upset that this ball's in the house . . . oh hell."

The drum set was Charlie's sanctuary from the world of shit coming down. He picked up a pair of drum brushes and stroked a slow scrape around the snare drum with his left hand. It was almost impossible to position the brush in his broken fingers without pain. He winced, but kept the stroke. His left foot worked the high-hat-cymbals in a slow steady beat. He kept a mechanical cadence on the ride cymbal as well as he could with his bandaged right hand. It felt to Charlie like trying to maneuver a board as he concentrated on a Philly Joe Jones lick.

"Nice for a gimp."

Charlie jumped up and almost knocked over the snare drum.

Zellie stood in the doorway of the room. He chewed a celery stick. "I love celery stuffed with cream cheese like this." He grinned, showing Charlie a mouthful of green celery and cheese smeared across his lips and teeth.

"Hey, Zel, you made it quick." Charlie put the brushes down and left the drum set.

Zellie continued chewing like a cow. He lived in a Jewish enclave across the lake from Charlie's neighborhood "Well it's not like I'm from across the city."

Parts of Zel's neighborhood reminded Charlie of photos of shops in New York's Hester Street he had seen, less the push carts. On Friday nights Charlie could see the Orthodox Jews, lucky enough to live in the big houses by the lake, through their big picture windows observing the *Shabbats* meal. Once, Charlie passed the neighborhood saw the lady of the house light the candles for the blessing.

Zellie was supposed to be Orthodox, but that depended on what side of the lake he was on at any given time. "Sorry again about your Mom. She was a real cool lady."

"Thanks, Zel, and, thanks for bringing my class stuff over."

Zellie nodded. "I've got my father's car for a few minutes. Where's your Dad?"

"Dad and Theresa had to make some last minute arrangements. They're at the funeral home. The services are the day after tomorrow. My Mom's family will be here from England."

Zellie's analytical mind went into gear. "Oy, from England already," he swallowed and made a low whistle. "They must be taking the big Lockheed-Starliner, the Super Constellation." He stuck the celery stick in one side of his mouth and spoke like a used car salesman chewing a cigar.

"It's brand new this year. TWA calls it, *Jetstream*. Four huge supercharged engines, 350 miles per hour at 22,000 feet." Zellie planed around the room with his arms spread like wings. He almost dropped Charlie's papers, still clutched in one hand.

"Zel, come back to earth man. That's pretty cool the way you suck up the minutia of current events and science to run in a droll stream of conscious."

"Huh? Where'd you get that shit?" Zellie put the papers on a table.

"From you, man, you're always cramming that stuff into your skull and sometimes a little leaks out to us small-fry."

"Uh, okay. Anyway here's your stuff. Looks like some math and English, but you don't have a history assignment due until next week. The math teacher said there's a test on Friday, but if you need some extra time it's okay. Oh, and you've got a paper due for comp next Wednesday. Hey, and Becky told me she's got your biology stuff. She said that you're dissecting a frog next week."

"Ouch, and I'm not talking about my hands. I'll handle it. Oh, hey, I've got to call my boss again at the market. I hope he can get by without me. Let's go upstairs while I make the call."

Zellie sat at the kitchen table with Papa Bonarelli. He got a kick out of listening to Papa murder English. It reminded Zellie of his own grandfather who spoke mostly Yiddish at home.

Charlie made the call. He didn't like the results.

"Carlo, what's the-face-a-fo?" Papa Bonarelli asked.

"My boss at the market is going to let me go. He says he's sorry about Mom, but that he needs somebody right now and he's already hired another guy. I've only been gone a few nights. I'm thinking that me finding the girl in the park, the newspaper stuff, and the cops aren't helping my employment situation. It's about the girl; I'm sure of it."

There was a knock on the door.

"I'll get it," Jody hollered from the front room.

"*Madonna,*" Nonna Bonarelli crossed herself, "it's probably more mourners. Zellie, *non siate timidi.*"

Zellie smiled at Nonna's admonition, "Don't be shy." She opened the refrigerator. "*Mangiare,*" she reached into the frig to rummage for food.

Charlie put his left hand in a more comfortable position while Papa Bonarelli slurped his coffee, and watched as Zellie looked into the refrigerator. Zellie was done for.

"That's all *treyf*, not a bit of it kosher. Better give me a plate."

Nonna beamed. She loved to watch Zellie eat. "That's my boy."

"I never get this at home, Nonna; you better say a novena for me."

"*Si, si,* you're forgiven if God asks."

Jody came into the kitchen. Detective Mickey followed. "Charlie, it's a big guy, I think he's a cop," she made a questioning shrug.

Papa Bonarelli put his coffee down as Nonna got into Detective Mickey's face. "You can't come in here. We are in mourning."

The detective walked into the kitchen. "I've got some questions kid." He looked at Charlie and ignored the others.

"*La impudenza*, you've got some nerve coming into this house now. You make my grandson sick and he's lost his Mama. I'm calling the police."

"Nonna," Charlie put out his right arm to keep her from accosting Mickey, "he is the police, it's okay." Charlie got up and Detective Mickey followed him back into the living room.

"So now what?" Charlie motioned Mickey to take a chair.

Mickey seemed sheepish.

"You supposed to be here, Detective?"

"Look, Bonarelli, I'm sorry about your mother – really. And maybe we got off to a bad start the other morning. I think that you're holding back. You saw something else in that park didn't you?"

Charlie wasn't sure how he should respond. His father hadn't called Matt Grueber yet. Mickey was going to be all over him until the case was solved. "You working with Matt Grueber on this?"

Mickey turned a blotchy red like a weathered bandana.

Charlie felt trapped, but was determined not to let the pressure rattle him. "So where's your partner?" he stalled.

Mickey ignored the question. "Look kid, I'm playing this hunch, you're protecting somebody."

Charlie wasn't going to let Mickey get under his skin, but he felt caught between the authorities and his father who was going to call Matt Grueber himself. "I'm not protecting anyone. I saw someone else, but I didn't know who it was. A couple of things have come up and my Dad was going to call Matt Grueber. He was called away to the funeral home before he could talk to Grueber."

Charlie saw by the look on Mickey's face that he was flying solo. He wasn't supposed to be here.

"Look kid, Charlie, this is my . . . uh our case downtown. Lieutenant Grueber is out of it as far as we're concerned. If you're holding something back, this is going to go against you."

What should I do about this cop? Charlie asked himself. I need to talk to my father before I tell this guy anything. "Come into the kitchen. You can wait a few minutes can't you?"

Charlie got up and went to the kitchen with Mickey following.

Papa Bonarelli slurped his coffee while giving Mickey the evil eye. Nonna was poised to hit him with the wooden spoon in her hand. She wasn't sure if she should offer Mickey something or smack him on the side of the head.

"You want something to eat? Here, have a cup of coffee." Nonna didn't wait for an answer. She handed a cup to Mickey with one hand while she pointed at the table with the wooden spoon in the other hand, "sit."

Charlie played with the opportunity to slip a laxative into *il bastardo's* coffee.

Zellie sensed Charlie's uneasiness. He scooted his chair closer to eye the big detective like examining an amoeba under a microscope. Jody and Sam came in from other rooms and stared at Mickey.

This bastard is on Bonarelli turf Charlie thought and he can squirm with all this attention.

"I'm Mickey, Detective Mickey." The big man sat at the table and tried to smile but nobody bought it.

Zellie chewed a mouth full of food and stared at the detective. Charlie wondered how a guy like Mickey could be made more uncomfortable than having this ravenous Zel-creature chewing his carnage in Mickey's ear.

Mickey covered his coffee cup with his hand in case Zel erupted.

The back door opened.

Finally, Charlie thought.

Vince and Theresa came in. Theresa wiped her eyes with a hanky.

"What's this?" Vince saw Detective Mickey sitting at the table. "Charlie saw you already. Is there something else? Damn, I haven't called Matt Grueber yet."

Mickey bristled. "Lieutenant Grueber is off this case, but not before he screwed us up with the D.A. Now, I need some more information, and your son Charlie is telling me he saw somebody else in the park the night he found the girl. Now the kid explains everything or I haul him back down to the station and we work it out. Got it?"

"I'm calling Grueber. Where's your partner, the other guy, you doing this on your own maybe?"

Inwardly elated, Charlie thought, Bingo, Dad, you read him the same as I did.

"Okay, wait a minute." Mickey held up his hands. "Let me call Grueber. We're going to have to go down to the station anyway. Maybe Charlie here can identify some photos."

Vince wasn't having it. "That's a pretense. Charlie told you that he couldn't identify anyone because it was dark. He thinks maybe there was someone else in that car, you know, the driver that Charlie tried to help. He thinks maybe it was somebody from his school trying to help somebody else."

Mickey held up his hands again. "Look, I'll call the Lieutenant. Can I use your phone?"

17

Joey Waves Goodbye

Fifteen minutes later a pissed-off Detective Lieutenant Matt Grueber showed up at the Bonarelli house. "What are you doing here, Mickey? Can't you even let these people alone in their bereavement? Where's your partner, Brawley?"

Mickey put up his hands. "I had a hunch, and it was a good one. The kid saw somebody else in the park the night he found the girl."

Vince stood between Grueber and Mickey. "Okay, so now you think that Charlie just found the girl, therefore, he had nothing to do with her death so he's no longer a suspect, right?"

Charlie thought, yeah, Dad, kick ass. The kitchen was crowded with the family, and Zellie.

Vince raised his voice above the din.

"Wait." Matt Grueber cautioned him. "I'm sorry Vince, but we'll have to go to the station and get this down on paper. Vince and Charlie, you can ride with me."

Vince exploded. "Matt, we're bushed. You know, Bea's death, and the thing with the girl. We haven't slept, we can't work, Charlie's under a lot of pressure at school, this can wait."

Charlie watched Nonna as she threatened to wade into these troubled waters armed with her wooden spoon.

Vince put his hand up as if to hold her back, "It's okay, Mama."

Matt Grueber watched Nonna through the corner of his eye expecting a whack with the spoon. "I'm sorry, Vince. It's a murder investigation. We can't wait, but we'll try to expedite the interview. C'mon, let's go get this done, okay?"

Mickey grinned. "I'll meet you downtown."

Matt grabbed Mickey's shoulder. "Mickey, again, where's your partner, Brawley?"

Mickey mumbled an answer.

"You're working this on your own aren't you? I guess we'll talk about this later with the Captain."

Mickey fumed out, "I'll see you at the station."

*   *   *

Two hours later, Matt Grueber brought Charlie and Vince home. "Vince, I'm sorry for the trouble. Things just go this way sometimes, but Charlie's new information helps. Charlie, I understand now why you didn't come forward right away. I probably would have reacted the same way, but if you hear anything else you call me, okay?"

Charlie nodded, "I'm going to bed," he headed for his basement room.

Vince called after him. "Don't forget that Grandmother Striker and your Uncle Bernie will be here tomorrow."

Charlie felt the exhaustion. He thought when is this going to end? I'll have to get up early to do my homework. Damn it, my hands are hurting like hell. He found the aspirin in his bathroom cabinet and chugged two down as he swallowed water directly from the bathroom faucet.

"Can't you use a glass?" Vince had come down from upstairs.

He didn't wait for the answer. "Mama and Papa have gone home. They'll be back early tomorrow morning."

Charlie wiped his mouth. "See you in the morning, Dad, goodnight."

In his room, he dropped his clothes and fell into bed. He fell asleep and dreamed of the girl in the park. She had Karin's face.

Charlie woke with a start. He had to pee, and remembered because his mouth tasted like week-old pizza that he hadn't brushed his teeth before falling into bed.

He turned on his bedside lamp. A note he hadn't seen before lay on his lamp table. He picked it up but put it down without reading it. It could wait until morning, he thought, probably more homework.

*   *   *

Charlie woke early, and turned on the table lamp. He saw and remembered the note. He read it, threw it back on the table and lay back on his pillow. He pulled the covers around his neck contemplating Karin's words. He couldn't go back to sleep.

He groaned out of bed and felt the cold on his injuries. "I'll take a hot shower. Christ, pain all over," Charlie hop-skipped to his bathroom. He wrapped his bandaged left forearm with a towel and held it out of the water. The hot water invigorated him, but the contents of the note weighed on his mind, *she's leaving for sure.*

There was a knock on the bathroom door. "Charlie, breakfast," Theresa called from the other side of the door.

"Okay, I'll be up in five minutes."

Charlie couldn't get Karin out of his mind. She's leaving? Why? What about us? What about me? He padded to his bedroom and dressed as well as he could with the hurting arm.

Upstairs, he wolfed down his breakfast.

"Charlie, take it slower." Theresa watched him across the table, "You'll choke."

Vince came into the kitchen yawning.

"You both look beat," Theresa admonished. "I've got to go home for awhile. I'll be back in a few hours."

"What about work, T?" Vince scratched his face. "You've missed a couple of days already."

"It's okay. I'm taking some vacation time."

"Vacation time, weren't you planning a trip to Italy for spring? How're you going to do that now?"

"It's okay, I'll work something out."

Charlie left the table. "I gotta go out for awhile."

Vince yawned, "What for? Where're you going? Theresa has to go home, I've got to check into the office, and the family from England will be here this afternoon. We got a telegram this morning with the time and flight info. Mama and Papa won't be here for awhile. Somebody has to watch Jody and Sam."

Theresa intervened. "I think he wants to see someone. It's okay. I can stay a little longer."

Charlie knew then that his aunt had read the note.

"She left the note with me last night, Charlie. I peeked. Sorry?"

"Who left what note? Who's she?" Vince asked Theresa.

"Charlie's got a girlfriend, Vince. Didn't you know?"

"Huh, a girlfriend, somebody from school?"

"You better let Charlie tell you, Vince."

"Okay, so tell me, Charlie."

"It's Karin, Dad. I want to talk to her."

"Oh yeah, the neighbor, the woman around the corner; the one with the kid. What are you doing fooling around with a woman with a baby?"

"Look, Dad, we discussed this two days ago. Did you forget? She's a friend."

"A friend, right, with a baby. She's a good-looking woman, not a girl, and I know she's more than just a friend. I thought you said she was leaving."

"Take it easy, Vince." Theresa shook her head at her brother. "She is leaving."

"Where's she going? Out of the city, I hope."

Charlie felt the heat in his cheeks. His hands hurt again. "I don't know for sure where she's going. That's why I want to talk with her."

Vince wasn't convinced. He looked at Theresa. "He's got something going with a woman who has a baby, and he's not even out of high school. Is that some kind of crazy? He better not bring home a wife and a kid already, and him barely eighteen. Jesus Christ, he's not even dry behind the ears yet. Jesus Christ."

"Calm down, Vince." Theresa put a hand on her brother's shoulder. "It's just kid stuff. And, besides she's leaving – remember?"

They heard a whine. "Who's leaving? Sam came into the kitchen with Jody not far behind, "Somebody going somewhere? When are Uncle Bernie and Grandmother Striker going to be here? So who's leaving?"

"Are we going somewhere?" Jody came into the kitchen. "I don't want to go nowhere. Are we going to school today? I'm hungry. What's for breakfast?"

Charlie said, "Gotta go – be back in a few minutes." He scooted down the back steps to his bathroom to brush his teeth. He saw a red-faced, red-eyed, droopy-lidded halfwit in the mirror. "Dig this, man, vampire eyes. I need to get some sleep. What's Karin up to? She's got no money and she has Joey."

Charlie grabbed his jacket, ran up the stairs and out the back door. He had left the arm sling in his room. It was colder this morning prompting him to scrunch his shoulders and jam his hands in his pocket. "Ouch." The pockets pressed on his mangled hands. He pulled them out of his pockets and let them swing which made them hurt in a different way.

"Ouch, damn it." He hit a trash can with his right hand. The can lid hit the ground with a clatter. Dogs barked as he cut across the construction site, and headed to Karin's house.

"Cripes." He saw the Delaney's garage door opening. Karin's parents were still home. He would wait until the parents left for work. He found a large tree and stood behind it, out of sight of Karin's house.

"Charlie, is that you?"

Oh hell, busted. Charlie turned.

Mr. Costello, in his bathrobe with a girth larger than the tree, was behind Charlie. He carried the morning paper.

"What are you doing here this early? Are you hiding behind a tree?"

"Huh, oh yeah, Mr. Costello, it's me, uh no, Mr. C., I'm just hanging out, uh waiting for someone."

"Sorry about your mother, Charlie."

"Right, uh thanks, Mr. C."

Charlie looked around the tree. He saw Karin's parent's car turn at the corner.

"Uh, gotta go now, Mr. Costello. I'll see you around."

"Okay, Charlie." Mr. Costello opened his paper, "Hmm, caught another one."

Charlie looked over his shoulder to make sure that Mr. Costello wasn't watching after him as he crossed over to the Delaney's house. Karin let him in after the second knock.

"Charlie, you got my note. I'm really sorry about your mother. Gosh, I knew she had been sick but I had no idea that she was so ill. I'm so sorry, baby."

"Uh thanks, Karin. But what about you, you're leaving? Where are you going?"

"Hang on, Charlie, I've got to check on Joey."

He saw boxes stacked in one corner. Some items wrapped in newspaper lay on the floor by a drawer from an end table. He looked into the dining room and saw the table covered with stacks of dishes and serving pieces.

Karin startled Charlie, "Joey's still sleeping. He's such a little doll."

"You're already packing to move? Where are you going?"

"My Dad's been transferred to Arizona. He got a promotion. Mom gave up her job. I'm finishing my semester downtown, but I'm going to be living across town with an aunt and uncle. Thing is, we have to be out of here before the end of the month. Dad has to be in Arizona before Thanksgiving."

Charlie asked, "What about Joey?"

"They're taking Joey to Arizona with them. This semester is over in two months. I've already applied and have been accepted to a university in Arizona. I don't like leaving Joey for two months, but I'm excited."

"You knew about this, right? You didn't tell me before? Yeah, right, that's cool, but what about us?"

"Charlie, baby, there is no us. I mean, I really like you, but I'm going to finish my education, and I'm going to go to law school. I can do it for sure now. It'll be tough, with Joey and all, but I'll do it. Besides, Arizona should be a good place to raise Joey. My mother wants to take care of him while I go to school fulltime."

Charlie felt hurt but relieved at the same time, "But what about me?"

"Charlie, we've been good together, but I'm going to have a career. What are you going to do when you get out of high school? Do you have any plans? What about the draft, aren't you eligible for the Army? I mean you can't get a deferment or anything unless you're going to college, right?"

Charlie didn't know if he was sad or glad about Karin. Everything seemed to cave in around him, his mother's death, family obligations, troubles at school, nagging depression, the cops, and fired from the only steady job he knew. And now, he thought, Karin is dropping me.

"Uh, maybe I'll be a musician. You know -- the band."

He saw the doubt in her eyes.

Karin smiled. "This isn't meant to insult you, baby, but that band needs practice and you need steady work to make a living as a drummer. C'mon, Charlie, get real."

There was a noise from a bedroom. Karin turned, "Oh-oh, sounds liked Joey is waking up and wanting breakfast. Hang on a minute. Oh, help yourself to coffee, it's fresh."

Charlie sat on the couch and stewed. *She's right. I've got nothing going for me and I'll sure as hell get drafted. Maybe that's what I want, I don't know.*

Joey waved hello to Charlie as Karin came back into the room holding her son. The toddler continued to wave his hand.

"Hi, Joey."

Karin hugged her son. "I'm sorry, Charlie, I've got to get going. My mother will be back from taking Daddy to work. Joey has a doctor's appointment at ten-o-clock." She went to Charlie, and put her free hand around his neck. She gave him a long kiss. Joey drooled on Charlie.

Karin leaned back. "I hope to see you before we leave, Charlie."

He wasn't easily put off. "But you'll still be here for two months for school."

"I'm going to be busy at school and my aunt and uncle work out of their house – Tupperware. I won't be having any boys around while I'm living with relatives. Sorry, Charlie."

There was a noise from the back door from the garage.

"It's my Mom."

Karin's mother came into the house. "Who's this?"

"Oh, this is Charlie Bonarelli. You know, our neighbor. He came by to say goodbye and wish us good luck."

"Oh sure, I heard about your mother, Charlie. I'm very sorry."

Charlie thanked her and said that he should be getting back to his house.

"Okay then," Mrs. Delaney put her purse down to remove her coat. "I guess we better start packing again. I'll take Joey. I'd like you to use the step ladder and get stuff down from the kitchen cupboards." She took Joey and faced Charlie. "Nice to see you again, Charlie." She took Karin's son and left the room. Joey waved goodbye to Charlie.

Charlie said goodbye to Karin and left the house as another door closed in his life.

18

The Strikers

Charlie spent the morning sitting at his desk thinking about his mother and Karin. His mind, a gray funk; homework lay forgotten in front of him. He dozed with his head in his hands unaware that Nonna Bonarelli had come into the room.

"Carlo, what's going on with you?"

He came out of his chair, almost tipping it over. "It's nothing Nonna, I'm just thinking about things."

"*Si, si, capisco.*"

Nonna put her arms around him. He needed that.

"This is a bad time, but it will get better. I lost my Mama when I was fourteen, the influenza. It was very bad. I never forget Mama, but she's with God and the saints."

"You think Mom is with the saints? I think she's dead. Dead is dead and there aren't any saints. It's all crap."

"*Madonna Mia*, don't talk this way, it's a sacrilege." Nonna Bonarelli made the sign of the cross. She put a gentle hand over Charlie's mouth as if to keep his thoughts from escaping out of his head.

"God is watching. He's taking care of your Mama." Nonna pulled a hanky from her apron to wipe away her tears. "Come up now. The kids are eating lunch. You need to eat.

"Your father called from his office. He's going to the airport to pick up the *Inglese*, the Strikers, after he leaves his office. I don't think he will be home for dinner. I think he will take your Grandmother Striker, Uncle Bernie and *il conte* to the hotel."

Instinctively, Charlie understood Nonna's disapproval of his maternal grandmother traveling with a boyfriend. "I think Grandmother's friend is a businessman. I'm not sure that he's royalty. And, anyway, Uncle Bernie will keep them from making-out in public."

"Carlo, you have such a tongue, the making-out you call it. It is disgraceful that you talk about the *Inglese* that way. *Dio Mio*, that, Bernie I remember, he's the crazy one, always talking with his hands like my father, everything with the hands. You remember the last time your Uncle Bernie was here, the house went crazy for the entire week. Oh, but he is *pazzo*, and those teeth."

Charlie couldn't help but laugh at Nonna's assessment of Uncle Bernie as crazy. He remembered Bernard, "Bernie," Striker as tall, boyish, handsome except for a gap in his front teeth. "Papa Bonarelli says that Uncle Bernie can suck spaghetti through that gap."

Nonna laughed. "Yes, Bernie, he's the funny one alright. Come on up, time to eat -- *mangia*."

* * *

At the table, Charlie watched Jody and Sam pick at their food. He didn't feel like eating either.

"I miss Mama." Jody pouted.

"Me, too," Sam slammed his fork on the table, "this isn't fair. I want Mama."

Papa Bonarelli put his head down so he couldn't see Jody and Sam's pain. Charlie watched him stare at his coffee and sigh. He wiped tears from his eyes with a shirt sleeve.

Nonna put her soup spoon down and fretted under her breath that there would be no rosary ceremony the night before Bea's funeral. Bea was a convert and didn't like, "all of that bead-rattling affair."

"I have all of your clothes pressed and ready for the services to-morrow. Carlo, you have a dark tie?"

"Yeah, somewhere, I'll find it."

Nonna Bonarelli waved her wooden spoon. "You got something on your suit, but I think I got it out with cleaning fluid." She pinched her nose and made a face.

Charlie nodded his head. "Oh yeah, I forgot to take it to the cleaners. It was frosting from that wedding cake. You know, two weeks ago when the band played the wedding down at Potenza Hall."

"I remember," Sam gleamed, "frosting? Sure, you were drunk and puked on yourself."

"Inebriated," Jody corrected Sam. "That's a Scrabble word that Mama used a couple of weeks ago. She said that she remembered the word because Charlie came home 'inebriated' from that wedding. She was mad at Charlie."

"Somebody slipped whiskey into my cola."

"Some-a-body slipa the whole bottle, I thinka." Glad for the diversion, Papa Bonarelli put his cup down. *"Si, Carlo – ebbro pari il asino."*

"Yeah, Papa, drunk like a jackass." Jody made braying sounds.

Papa Bonarelli joined in, then Sam.

Everyone but Charlie laughed.

Charlie waved Jody's comment aside. "Okay, I get the picture. I got a little sick, that's all."

"Jody, you're one smart little girl." Nonna grabbed Jody and hugged her. "God bless my little angel."

Charlie got up from the table. "I gotta do some homework."

"Oh no," Nonna pointed at Charlie's unfinished lunch with her wooden spoon. She wasn't going to let him leave the table without eating.

"I'll take it with me." Charlie picked up his plate and walked downstairs to his room. He put the plate on his night stand and went to his desk where he tried to lose himself in an algebra problem.

Instead of concentrating on algebra, he thought about his own troubles. I'm a senior in high school, and I'm just taking algebra now. I should be doing calculus like Zel. Even Bobo, whose brain's got to be damaged, took geometry. If I didn't have to take this crap to graduate I wouldn't even care. I don't understand it anyway.

He stared at the book willing a solution to all that was bothering him then. He picked at a problem, went back and read the example and worked it out.

"Yeah, I think I can do this stuff. It's a pain in the ass and I'll probably never use it."

He finished the problems and took up his history book. He always saved the best until all the other work was completed. He was in familiar territory, something that created pictures in his mind. He opened the book and made notes as he read.

Charlie thought he would try to get to the library before his paper was due. I wonder if I better stay away from libraries, they seem to get me into trouble.

He thought again about the girl in the park and about the other girl in the school library. "Jewell, I wonder who she is?" He didn't know her last name but thought it didn't matter since he probably would never see her again.

"Knock, knock." Bobo stood in the bedroom doorway.

"Hey, Bobo, you out of school already?"

"You get lost, daddy-o? It's almost five-o'clock. My parents and Grandma are visiting upstairs. You can't hear the *dagos* carrying on up there?" Bobo pointed towards the upstairs.

"Yeah, now that you mention it, I was reading."

"Hey man, you going to eat this?" Bobo pointed at Charlie's lunch plate on the nightstand.

"No, go ahead."

Bobo finished the lunch in two bites.

"Bobo, you're going to choke to death eating like that."

Charlie's cousin gulped and burped. "You got anything to drink?"

"Yeah, go back in the laundry room. There's the extra fridge back there. Probably got some pop in it."

"Okay. I'll be right back."

Charlie heard the refrigerator door and the rattling of bottles.

Bobo came back to Charlie's room, "What's this? Okay if I eat some? There's a note on it." He held a big refrigerator cake in his hands.

Charlie got up from his desk to look at the note.

Bobo licked his lips. "It's got your name on it. 'Condolences,' and it's signed 'Jewell.' Who's Jewell?"

"Huh? Oh, just someone I met at school a couple of days ago. Like, I don't even really know her. I saw her in the library. I didn't tell her anything about Mom. We hardly spoke."

"Well she remembered you. Let's go upstairs and get a fork. I love this stuff."

Charlie followed Bobo and the cake upstairs. His Aunt Mary, Uncle Ralph and Bobo's grandma gave him their condolences again.

Nonna Bonarelli saw the cake. "Oh, Carlo, I'm sorry. I forgot to tell you that this little girl brought this for you when you and Vincenzo were at the police. She's different, kind of cute though. Who is she . . . Diamond?"

"Jewell. Her name's Jewell. I don't know her last name. I just met her. I don't know how she found out about Mom. Oh, yeah, she reads the paper, likes to do the crossword puzzles. She must have seen the notice. I guess she reads the obituaries, too."

Nonna took the cake. "Oh, and another girl, Becky, she called you when you were out." Nonna cut the cake and served Bobo. "You got girls hanging around you all the time, Carlo." She shook her head.

"Uh-humnn," Bobo hummed through a mouth full of cake.

Charlie could have hit him.

"Charlie's a stallion," Sam said as a matter of fact.

The room went silent.

Bobo laughed and dropped his fork. Charlie kicked him under the table.

Sam continued. "It's on television. They call big male horses stallions."

"*Stallone*," Papa Bonarelli smiled at Charlie.

The kitchen erupted in laughter.

Charlie felt the heat in his cheeks. "C'mon, Bobo, let's go back downstairs."

In his room Charlie slumped in his desk chair. "Hey thanks, man."

"Oh, that's okay, *Stallone*. I like that, Zel is going to love it."

"Don't tell him that. He doesn't know what it means anyway."

"Oh, heck no, the smartest guy in school and he doesn't know anything about your diddling ways."

"Hey, smart-ass, you got nothing better to do than bug me about girls? Why don't you go punch a bag or kick a wall? You know, get in shape for that Golden Gloves bout in a couple of weeks. Better wear a bucket on your head. I understand that Rudi Gomez is a kick-butt boxer."

"Yeah, yeah, he's got a reputation but I can handle him. I'll waste him."

Charlie rolled his eyes. "Sure, like you wasted that last guy. He was kind of a pussy, too. Isn't that what you said before you got in the ring with him?"

Bobo colored at Charlie's reminder that he was soundly beaten by a skinny black boxer who looked like a noodle and talked with a lisp. "He got lucky. I wasn't feeling so good that night anyway."

"Yeah, you were feeling a lot worse when the officials picked your ass up off the mat."

"Okay, I get it. Let's talk about something else, like Karin."

"Let's not talk about Karin. She's leaving, moving to Arizona after this semester at college."

"No shit? How come? Oh I know. You got caught nailing her, didn't you? *Stall . . . .*"

"Now you're pissing me off, Bobo. Hey, you brought another piece of cake -- *Tu sono il porco*."

Bobo put a piece of cake in his mouth and grinned, extruding whipped cream like a frothing dog.

"Bobo, let's go." Bob's father Ralph called down the stairwell, "We gotta get Grandma home."

Bobo swallowed a big mouthful of cake. "See you tomorrow at the funeral. Sorry again about Aunt Bea."

"Okay, thanks, see you tomorrow." Charlie walked up the stairs with Bobo to say goodbye to his family.

He started back downstairs when the phone rang. "Hi, Becky. Thanks . . . yeah everything is okay . . . that's okay . . . I understand . . . I wasn't expecting kids from school anyway."

Charlie listened to Becky for a few more seconds. "It's going to be a short service. I'll be back in school in a couple of days. Okay, see you later."

He went back to his room to concentrate on his studies. Nonna Bonarelli called him for supper. He ate quickly and went back downstairs to the family room. He put one of his favorite jazz albums on the player and sat at the drum set. He played along with the quirky rhythms of Monk, as well as he could with the broken wrist and nagging pain.

The music and the drumming did little to mask the noise coming from upstairs and a heavy footstep on the stairs.

"Charlie, you rascal," a tall well-dressed man entered the room. The gap in his upper teeth made Bernard Striker's handsome smile almost comical. He looked like Terry Thomas.

"Uncle Bernie? I thought we wouldn't see you until tomorrow morning."

"Well old man, look at you. You sound like a professional down here, playing along with Thelonious Monk, I'm impressed. I was sure that you were an Elvis Presley fan. Smashing, absolutely smashing. What's that contraption on your hand?"

Without waiting for an answer, Bernard moved his hands as if he was drumming. "It is just great to see you, old man."

Charlie's recollection of his uncle was reinforced when he saw older British movies on TV. The dialogue always reminded Charlie of his Uncle Bernie with his high-class British accent and the stereotypical expressions.

"Come on up with the family. Your Grandmother is keen to see you, and you must meet Roland, Millie's new tea cozy." Bernard laughed at his own joke.

Charlie thought it irreverent that Uncle Bernie called his own mother by her first name. He remembered his pretty and stately Grandmother Mildred, "Millie," from her last visit.

He followed his uncle upstairs and found Grandmother Striker equally as attractive as if she hadn't changed at all over the few years when he last saw her, tall, silver-haired, fair-skinned, poised, quick-eyed and quick-tongued. Her husband, Charlie's Grandfather Striker, was killed during the bombing of London by the Germans during the war. He knew that his grandmother Mildred scandalized both her English and Italian-American families with her amorous affairs.

"Dear, Grandson." Mildred Striker held out her arms to Charlie, "Just look at you, you beautiful boy. Roland, look at my beautiful American family. Have you ever seen more wonderful looking people?"

A tall distinguished man, dressed in what Charlie guessed was a Seville Row business suit, and carrying a bowler, held out his hand to Charlie. "Good to meet you, Charles."

"It's really, Carlo, but you can call me, Charlie."

"Charlie, yes of course, do call me Roland."

Vince interrupted the conversation. "Sorry to intrude, but I should be taking you down to your hotel. It's getting late and I am sure you need some rest before tomorrow. There is a viewing at 10:00am and the service starts at 11:00."

There was a knock and the front door opened. Theresa walked into the living room. "*Bona Sera.*" She smiled as she saw the Strikers and Roland.

"My word, this has to be, Theresa." Bernard held out his hand. "I'm Bernard, call me Bernie." We never met last time. You were away, at university, I believe."

Theresa blushed as Bernie held on to her hand. He stared unabashedly at the tall and beautiful Theresa Bonarelli. "Will you show me, I mean us, around Denver whilst we are here? Oh, but of course you probably have a commitment, how rude of me."

Charlie was amused as Nonna Bonarelli scrutinized the big Englishman and said, "Yes, she's working in the big attorney's office downtown. Our children make us proud."

"Now, Bernard, don't be such a wolf," Grandmother Mildred put her arm around Theresa's shoulder. "You were just a girl when we last met. You are a beautiful woman now, aren't you? Oh and this is, Roland le Gerrier."

"Charmed," Roland held out his hand.

Nonna Bonarelli couldn't help but ogle the big gold ring on le Gerrier's hand. She turned to Charlie. "Carlo, come to the kitchen and help me with coffee and cake." She clasped Charlie's sore shoulder.

"Ouch, Nonna, that's still a little tender there."

In the kitchen he asked, "Nonna, I thought they were leaving."

"*Si, Dio, che razza del anello*, Carlo?"

"Yeah, Nonna, I saw the ring. What about it?"

"What about it?" Like the Pope. A crest, old and the name le Gerrier, *dello regio*?"

"You think royalty, Nonna, really? He looks like a regular London stiff to me."

"Your manners, you watch your manners. He's a gentleman, I'm sure."

"Yeah, right, Nonna. Let me help you with the coffee."

Vince was about set to drive the Strikers to their hotel. He frowned when Nonna and Charlie appeared with a serving tray heaped with coffee and Italian pastry.

"Coffee, how lovely. Thank you, Mrs. Bonarelli." Mildred sat on the couch with Jody and Sam to either side of her.

Sam reached for a pastry and got a rebuke from Nonna Bonarelli. He quickly redrew his hand.

Charlie watched as Roland le Gerrier sat stiffly on a chair and Bernie lionized Theresa who stood, more or less, pinioned against a wall.

Grandmother Striker was tired from her trip and obviously annoyed by Bernard's flirting. "Bernard, do come and sit down."

Nonna looked around for Vince. "Vincenzo," she called.

Charlie excused himself and went through the kitchen still cluttered with the supper dishes. He looked in the hall where the phone was. His father was on the phone soothing a customer.

"What's going on, Dad?"

Vince motioned to Charlie to stop talking so that he could hear the customer.

Charlie whispered, "You're supposed to take Grandma Striker to the hotel."

Vince answered the customer. "Okay, George, I'll take care of this in the morning. I'll have my secretary straighten this out tomorrow . . . sorry for the inconvenience. No, I'll be out all day tomorrow. Look, George, I'm sorry about the problem, but we'll take care of it. Okay, I'll follow up later."

Vince hung up the phone. Charlie followed him into the living room. "Sorry folks, I had to help a customer. We better get you to your hotel. I'll pick you up early for the viewing. Oh, and thanks again for coming all the way from England for this. Poor Bea, she always talked about England and the family." Vince turned so that the Strikers couldn't see his grief.

Bernard went silent.

Theresa broke the awkward silence. "Vince, why don't I drive the family downtown? It's not out of the way, and you need some rest. I'll bet you haven't eaten yet."

"Yes, do let Theresa take us to our hotel." Bernie smiled. "I'll transfer the lot from your car into Theresa's auto. Can you show me, Theresa?"

Grandmother Striker got up from the couch. "Yes, dear boy, do get some food and rest. We appreciate what you have done. Please, if it is not an inconvenience, Theresa will be ever so helpful."

Charlie watched as Roland stood up and adjusted his bowler. He looked around the room. "Where's Papa Bonarelli?

19

Papa's Down

Charlie called into the basement, "Papa, where are you?" He saw the back door was cracked open, and went out thinking that he would see Papa Bonarelli smoking his pipe. Faint light emitted from the garage side door. Charlie heard noise and walked in.

"Papa, are you in here?" Charlie walked further into the garage. He saw Papa Bonarelli slumped over the workbench; his pipe lay on the floor with some tools.

"Papa, what's happened here?"

There was blood on the back of Papa Bonarelli's head, but he was conscious. "Carlo, I-think-a-somebody-a-smack-me-in-*l'testa.*"

"Here, let me help you. Let's get you inside." Charlie put his arm around Papa Bonarelli and walked him toward the door. He noticed garden tools that normally stood against a wall had fallen to the garage floor or against the cars. "Papa, are you going to be okay to walk into the house?"

He grunted, "Shu."

Charlie guided his grandfather into the back door of the house, and called up the stairs. "Papa's been hurt, we need some help here."

Theresa appeared at the top of the stairs. "Oh my God, what's happened?"

Charlie looked up at his father and Nonna as Theresa came down the stairs. "Theresa, grab his arms, I'll support him. He thinks somebody hit him on his head."

155

Vince said, "What the hell? Here, Theresa let me do this." He grabbed his father who was light enough that he could have picked him up.

They moved Papa Bonarelli up to the kitchen and into a chair.

Vince glared at Charlie and then nodded at his father. "I think we better call an ambulance and the cops."

Papa shook his head, "no wagon, Vincenzo. I'm a-going-to-be-okay."

Vince looked around at the rest of the family. "He must have surprised somebody in the garage when he went out to smoke his pipe."

"Good Lord, what's happened to Mr. Bonarelli -- poor man?" Mildred Striker came into the kitchen.

Charlie tried to calm Nonna who cursed in Italian while repeating the sign of the cross.

Bernard Striker peered into the kitchen at the activity. "Good Lord."

Mildred took charge. "I've said that, Bernard. Do make yourself useful. Someone please get ice out of the frig and something to wrap it in. The poor man is bleeding."

Everyone chattered like parrots while Mildred patched Papa Bonarelli. Nonna gave him a cup of coffee and poured some whiskey into the hot liquid.

"You drink this now, Papa." Nonna turned to Vince. "Vincenzo, you call the police. Somebody tried to kill my Pietro."

Theresa inserted herself into the confusion. "This room is a little crowded. Let's go into the living room. We'll make sure that Papa is okay. Don't you think we better take him to the hospital?"

"I think he is shaken, surly, but his eyes are not dilated. The head wound appears superficial, Theresa."

"Thank you Mrs. Striker, thank you for helping with Papa. You think he'll be okay?"

"I say, what is going on here?" Everyone looked at Roland who had not spoken since the introductions. "This is troublesome. I observe that young Charlie here is damaged, and now Mr. Bonarelli is attacked at the family home? Suspicious, what?"

Mildred Striker gave Roland a hard stare and put her right index finger towards her lips. "Shush, Roland, let's not make a fuss. I'm sure that the Bonarelli's will sort this all out. We should go."

She looked past Roland, "Theresa, thank you for the offer to take us to our hotel. I think that is a good idea. I believe that Mr. Bonarelli will have a fine mend. I have seen serious head trauma, keep that ice on his head. I believe the bleeding has stopped."

Vince called the police.

Nonna cried in her apron. "Too much going on here, Carlo, Beatrice, then Papa . . . *Madonna Mia*, our world is falling apart."

"A skulker, a bloody brigand?" Bernard Striker asked. "Why would someone be lurking in your gah-rajh. Suspicious?"

"Quite so," Roland put his hands behind his back. He watched Charlie, then spotted Jody and Sam as they fidgeted on the couch. "You are a couple of quiet ones for all of this going on?"

Jody cried.

Sam put his arm around his sister, "It's okay, Jody. Daddy will fix it."

Theresa flipped her long black hair over her coat collar as she prepared to leave. "We should go. The police will be here and there is nothing we can do this evening." She looked at Mildred Striker. "I'll fill you in with the details of the last few days. There may be a connection between those events and the attack on Papa."

Theresa walked into the kitchen. "Is everything okay in here? Did the bleeding stop, Papa?" She kissed him lightly. "Poor, Papa. The police will get that *brigante*."

"Il bastardo, I'm-agoing-to-kill-him-son-a-fa-beech."

Vince examined his father, "You sure that you're going to be okay, Papa?"

Papa Bonarelli nodded his head, "Si."

Vince continued assessing his father's head, "Yes, we'll get whoever hit you. The police should arrive soon. I'll say goodbye to the Strikers and Roland."

Vince walked his in-laws to the front door. "I'm sorry about all of this. Theresa will give you some background about what's been going on around here. It all started when Charlie found a young lady, murdered the police think, in a park."

"Oh!" Mildred put a hand to her cheek. "Ghastly."

Jody had stopped crying and giggled.

"Oh, you think that Grandmother Striker is a hoot with her funny English speech. We will see if I can cheer you up. Now give us a kiss goodbye." She gathered up Jody and Sam to give them a hug.

A knock on the front door brought a silence.

Vince opened the front door, "That was fast."

"Are you, Mr. Bonarelli -- you call us?" A youngish policeman looked through the glass storm door at everyone inside.

Vince opened the storm door, "Yes someone hit my father while he was out in the garage."

"Hit your father? Is he injured? Do we need to get him to a hospital? What was he doing in the garage? Why would someone want to hit him? Can we come in?"

Vince opened the door wider to let two policemen in.

The first cop, asking the questions, continued, "Who are all of these people? Where are they going? How come so many of you are here? Where's the garage?"

A tired Vince said, "Let me answer your first four questions."

"Oh, sure," the cop, hesitated.

The second cop, about Vince's age asked, "Can we see the victim please? He looked at his young partner. "Let's do this one at a time, Burke."

Vince responded, "First, my in-laws are here from England, for my wife's funeral. They were just leaving for their hotel. We were visiting when the incident happened. Is it okay if they leave?"

Officer Burke blurted, "I don't know. We'll need to see the victim first."

The second officer intervened. "Yeah, it's probably okay if they were in here when the incident happened. We'll want to be able to contact them later though." The older cop took Burke aside to tell him something. He turned back to the family. "Let's see the victim, is he in here? Oh, and our condolences about your wife."

"Thank you." Vince looked at the Strikers, "I'll pick you up at your hotel in the morning, at nine-o-clock. We'll meet a limo at the funeral home. Thank you again for coming across the ocean."

Vince addressed the two officers as the Strikers left. "My father, Pietro Bonarelli, is in the kitchen." He pointed the way.

The two officers went into the kitchen where they saw Papa Bonarelli with a wet cloth full of ice tied on his head. He sipped his whiskey-laced coffee.

The older officer took charge. "Sir, I'm Officer Jenowitcz and this is my partner, Officer Burke. We are sorry about your trouble here. Can you tell us what happened?"

"I'm-dona-know. I'm-a-smoking . . . pipa-and-smack-ona-l'testa."

Burk, perplexed, "Ya know ya just can't understand these eeytalins."

"My mother is Italian, and I understood Mr. Bonarelli perfectly. He says that he was smoking his pipe when someone hit him on the head."

Burke reddened. "Okay. Maybe I could go look around in the garage, how's the light out there?"

Vince took charge. "Charlie, since you found Papa, why don't you show Officer Burke and I.

"Papa, why don't you tell Officer Jenowitcz what happened while we go out to the garage."

Jenowitcz sat at the table and smiled at Papa Bonarelli, "How're you feeling, Mr. Bonarelli? Would you like us to take you down to the emergency hospital?"

Papa Bonarelli shook his head no and waved a hand over his coffee.

Office Jenowitcz pulled out a small notepad. Nonna automatically put a cup of coffee in front of him. She held up the whiskey bottle with a questioning look. He grinned and shook his head no.

* * *

The garage was a refrigerator.

"Why does your father come out here to smoke his pipe?" Burke shuddered with the chill.

"He likes to putter around the garage when he's smoking." Vince pointed to the workbench. "He thinks that he's *Mastro Gepetto*, you know, the woodcarver."

"Sure, Pinocchio, I know. Walt Disney, right?" Was he eeytalin, too?"

"Something like that," Vince looked at Charlie and rolled his eyes. He mouthed a word, "*stupido.*"

"Well lookee-here." Officer Burke held up a two-foot long piece of hardwood. "This is like a club. Must be hickory or some other hardwood, there's blood and hair on it. The old man, uh, your father probably got hit with this." Burke carelessly took hold of the piece.

"That's a child's baseball bat, Officer Burke." Vince responded. "My father carved it for the kids. What about fingerprints? You're just adding your own prints or destroying what may have been there."

Vince called to his son who was looking around the garage, "Charlie, anything missing?"

Burke put the bat down on the work bench, "I'll look around, too. The light's not too good." Anyway, I have a good light. Here," he handed a long handled flashlight to Charlie. "You probably know what you're looking for."

Charlie took the light. He moved carefully over the area between the cars. "I think my baseball bat is gone. Dad, you know the bat that I used for the *Old Timers*? It's missing."

160

"You played with the *Old Timers*? Me, too," Officer Burke grinned, "boy, I loved that. I was a few years before you."

Charlie realized that Burke was trying to smooth his shaky start. "Cool. Our team was O'Rourke's Bar and Grill. You know, downtown."

Burke brightened, "Yeah that's right. I remember that joint. We were Mickey's Tavern over on Federal. Not too far from my high school."

Charlie looked around the rest of the garage looking for anything else missing. "North, that's close to Mickey's."

"Right, kiddo, Class of 1953," Burke smiled. Those were great days . . . anyway what did you find?"

Charlie mumbled, "yeah, North High . . . great days alright, if you can live through them. I'll be out next year."

Burke had another flashlight that he found on the work bench. He looked under the cars. "Lucky you; all you have to do now is get into college or get drafted into the army. You got your draft card yet?" He looked at the overhead door latches. "Let's open the main door. Maybe we'll be able to look around better." He pulled a rope to open the two end latches on the door.

The door rolled up. A piece of cardboard fell into the garage.

"What's this?" Burke picked up the cardboard. "Some writing -- this for you?" He handed the cardboard to Charlie.

C.B. quit snooping around or I'm going to hammer your ass.

Burke shined his light on the message. "Not exactly a fan message for, C.B. That you?" He asked Charlie.

"Yeah, I'm that daddy-o. More shit for the fan."

Vince looked at the cardboard. "God-damn-it, Charlie, you stir crap up all over the place. What the hell is this now? 'Snooping around,' what the hell does that mean?"

Burke scrutinized the message. "That's a threat. Somebody you know maybe? A little smudged -- red crayon maybe? Better we leave this be. We'll go in and call the detectives. Okay if I use your phone?"

20

Gelido

A new set of detectives came and went. They checked the garage for fingerprints and anything that looked suspicious. There was nothing missing except the bat. The detectives took the piece of cardboard with the threatening words.

Charlie didn't get to bed until midnight where he lay awake and questioned how his family got caught up in something that evolved from a simple Samaritan act. Finding the body in the park came with complications, and his personal troubles grew along with his ambivalence over Karin. Did he love her enough to pursue her? He agonized over his troubles with Ralph Jay, and his suspicions about who may or may not be involved in the girl's death.

Charlie recognized the girl but really didn't know her. But the nature of her death affected him. Maybe she was mentally haywire, but she was a human being. He thought that she was probably lonely, had no one, and was in the wrong place at the wrong time. He had seen her a few times hanging around the park, a skinny and weird chick whose head shook like a bobble-head doll when she walked. Why would anyone kill her?

Charlie couldn't sleep. He got up early, showered, shaved, and dressed for his mother's funeral. He went up to the kitchen. Vince was already there. Theresa bustled through the front door with an armload of fresh Italian bread.

"*Bon Giorno*, I stopped at the bakery on the way over, we'll need these for later. How are you holding up this morning?"

"We'll get through it." Vince straightened his tie. "You got the Strikers to the hotel okay?"

"*Madonna Mia*, the Strikers. Certainly the most polite and re-served people I have ever met; nonetheless, relentless in their ques-tions after I mentioned Charlie's troubles, *sono implacabile.*"

Vince grinned, "Yes, Bernie in particular. His father was a high-ranking British intelligence officer. He introduced Bernie into British Intelligence where I met him at the beginning of the war. That's how I met Bea too. Bernie is very skilled at extracting information with-out appearing to do so. The cops could learn some techniques from him."

Theresa smiled, "Oh yeah, *il stregare?*"

Dad smiled at Theresa, "Bernard, charming yes, but not devious. Did he tell you what he's doing for a living now? You were in school the last time he visited here. He's never married, but he was once engaged. Lovely girl, I met her a few times during the 'row' as Bernie calls the war."

"Yes," Theresa smiled, "to answer your first question, Bernie's in the music producing business, something about British rhythm and blues bands. Can you imagine? Is there a future in that? What about the girl he was to marry, what happened?"

"She was an air combat controller; perished from a direct hit by a German bomb."

"*Dio*, the Strikers carry themselves well for people who have suf-fered much."

"Watch out for Bernie, he'll charm you right into the sack, T."

Theresa colored. "Don't worry about it."

This was an interesting exchange, Charlie thought as he studied them over his cup of coffee. He hadn't thought about his beautiful Aunt Theresa in lust like he thought about every other female, but he saw the way men looked at her. Intrigued, he listened to his father and aunt playfully chide each other. This was good he thought. His family used dialogue and sometimes off-color storytelling to defuse problems and sadness.

Charlie would miss his mother's British wit that topped anything the ribald Italian side cooked up. Humor, he understood, was the way he fought his own nagging depression and lonely introspection.

He felt as if he was privy to something adult and sexual. When he was thirteen he once heard noise coming from over his head from his parent's bedroom. This confirmed his suspicions that his parents must have sex.

"What are you thinking, Charlie?" Theresa's voice and an amused look interrupted his thoughts.

"Just thinking -- nothing important."

"Hmm, everything is important today." Theresa removed her coat and put it over the back of a kitchen chair. "I'll get Jody and Sam up. Mama and Papa will be here in a little while."

"So how is Papa this morning?" Vince asked. "I tried to call just a couple of minutes ago."

Theresa answered. "Papa's okay, head hurts, but he's okay. They're on their way. I called them just as they were leaving. I asked to pick them up but Papa thought the walk would clear his head. You know Papa when he makes up his mind about something, *testardo*." She feigned knocking on her head.

Vince grinned. "Yes, he's stubborn. Sounds like someone else I know. That's why you're a good lawyer in a sea of men. How come you haven't snagged one of those big law partners yet?"

Theresa touched the end of her tongue to her top front teeth. "If you've got to know, they're all wind and no fire except in court. No *passione* off of the playing field."

Anticipating another remark from her brother Theresa protested, "*Basta,* enough. I've got to get the kids up. I hope that they got some sleep. They have an arduous day ahead."

"Oh, she knows how to use the words hum, Charlie?" Vince smiled as he sipped his coffee.

A noise as the front door opened. "It's Mama and Papa." Vince got up from the table.

The senior Bonarelli's walked into the kitchen. "*Rinfrescare*," Papa Bonarelli slapped is arms around his shoulders.

"*Gelido*, like a popsicle," Nonna Bonarelli swore under her breath in Italian about Papa Bonarelli dragging her six blocks in cold weather, "*Caffe*."

Vince poured two cups of hot coffee. "The limo will be here in an hour. The mortuary called, they'll pick up the Strikers at the Brown. I talked to Bernie and gave him the message. The rest of the family will meet us at the church. The service will take less than an hour and then we'll go out to Mount Olivet. We'll come back here after the internment. Aunt Dorina arranged with the church to help with the food here. The family will bring food, too."

"*Si, si*, I talked to Dorina, God bless her," Nonna Bonarelli removed her coat. She was dressed in the dreary black of the old country Italians. Vince took his mother's coat and put his arms around her as she wept.

"It's going to be all right, Mama, we'll get through this."

"Jody and Sam, *i ragazzi*," Nonna cried, my poor babies. Charlie saw the tears in Papa Bonarelli's eyes as he picked up the coats and walked out of the kitchen. He thought, God help us get through this day.

The doorbell rang, and Charlie answered it. Bobo's parents, Aunt Mary and Uncle Anthony were on the porch. Bobo was behind, helping his grandmother.

Aunt Mary's eyes ran. "We thought we better stop by here early before we go to the church. She carried a huge roaster that smelled of peppers and sausage.

Uncle Ralph lugged onion sacks full of groceries. He asked, "How's Papa Bonarelli today."

Theresa answered. "He's going to be okay. Mama and Papa walked here this morning from their home -- can you believe it?"

Aunt Mary scowled, "This morning? *Gelido*, it's like a Popsicle out there. What's that man doing walking in this cold with a split head, and Mama?"

Charlie shrugged. "You know, she's mad as hell, but Dad put a little whiskey in her coffee."

Bobo had settled his grandmother in the living room. "Hey, Charlie, you okay?" He put his arm around his cousin's shoulder. "Zellie called me. He'll be at the service. He wanted to know if he should wear his yammakak. I said sure, that's cool, so what's that?"

Charlie held a laugh. "You mean *yarmulke*, the little beanie cap on the back of the head. You know, like *the yeshiva bokhers*_wear when they don't have the big hat on." He took his cousin aside from the babbling adults.

Bobo had a questioning look on his face.

"You know, cuz, you see those serious looking guys walking on West Colfax when you are over there sniffing after that little knish. Zellie will figure out soon enough that men don't wear head covers in the Catholic Church except *gli maggiornete*."

"Huh?" Bobo was confused. "Oh, right, the boogiemen, right?"

"C'mon, Bobo, we'll go downstairs and talk a little before we have to leave. Take something to eat?"

"Yeah. Hey, what's this about Papa Bonarelli gets whacked on the head?" Bobo grabbed a roll and coffee on the way downstairs to Charlie's room.

"I don't know what's going on. Somebody hit him when he went out to smoke his pipe. Whoever it was left a message on a piece of cardboard, a threat to get me."

Bobo took a huge bite out a roll, chewed twice and swallowed with a gulp, "You think it's Ralph Jay maybe?"

Charlie marveled at his cousin's ability to eat, talk and not choke to death. "That doesn't make any sense. I thought we worked out our differences when we cooled our asses in Mr. Greyer's office a couple of days ago, Bobo.

"Then there's Mr. Greyer. Maybe that's the connection. I'm sure now that somebody was in the back of the car that I tried to help the night I found the girl. Dig this: I think the car was Mr. Greyer's. I'm thinking that he's the cat who was stuck, not Mr. Truwet. I'm thinking what I saw in the back of the car was Mr. Greyer's son under a blanket maybe."

Bobo spoke through a mouthful of roll. "Not Mr. Truwet, the bad leg? Mr. Greyer's son? Yeah right, the son. Mr. Greyer's kid escaping from the state hospital. Man that's some heavy shit -- you sure about that? Wow. You tell the fuzz?"

Charlie ducked a piece of roll launched from his cousin's mouth. "The night of the big interview, but I'm not sure that the cops have figured it out yet. That one cop, Mickey, I think still likes me for the death of the girl. So much has been going down that I haven't been able to work the puzzle. The cops haven't put anybody in jail yet. Matt Grueber's off of the case and the Mickey Spillane types are bungling it now. They keep questioning me like I hurt that girl. We were at it again the night before last. Now I've got somebody that wants to 'hammer my ass.'"

Charlie saw Bobo lost in thought. He playfully tapped his cousin's forehead. "What's going on in there, Bobo?"

"Charlie, what about Mr. Greyer's son, he's still on the loose right?"

"Yeah, as far as I know. Why would he want to threaten me? I can't even be sure he saw me. He was covered with a blanket, I think, in the back of the car. I wasn't there that long."

Bobo rolled his eyes. "Man, that's heavy shit for sure. The guy escaped from the state hospital. Don't you think that this guy is nuts enough to take you out if he thought you could finger him?"

"Finger him, you reading the pulps again, Bobo? You mean he might think that I really did see him, and maybe he whacked the girl, and I can tie him into the girl's murder, right?"

"Right, daddyo; that cat is *pazzo*."

Jody came downstairs. "Auntie says that you guys better come up and get something to eat before we leave. The limo will be here in thirty minutes."

"Hey, Jody, how's my favorite girlfriend?" Bobo picked Jody up and gave her a hug.

"Bobo, you're funny. I know you got a girlfriend. Charlie says she lives on the West Side."

"Oh yeah, well Charlie's full of cheese, like a ravioli. You are definitely the babe for me."

"C'mon, Bobo, we better split," Charlie tugged on Bobo's suit jacket.

"Okay." Bobo carried Jody and followed Charlie up the stairs.

"So what are you going to do, Charlie?" Bobo asked.

21

The Quiet

Charlie tried to remember the service held for his mother that morning, but everything was a blur. It seemed after the internment that everyone that knew the family came to the house and paid their respects. After the mourners left the house, he looked at the guest book to remember who was there.

Nonna studied the book to see who wasn't there. "Angelina Petriano, she was your mother's hair dresser. The Clemens family, where were they? The grocer, George Pietra?" Nonna Bonarelli put a thumb nail to her front teeth and snapped a click, her ultimate rebuke.

"Next time you see those people it will be the evil eye, *il malocchio*, huh, Nonna," Charlie chuckled.

He watched as Grandmother Striker studied Nonna.

"Mrs. Bonarelli, a good turnout for Beatrice, don't you think?"

"Hum." Nonna alternated between smiles and tears as she studied the book of mourners who attended the services. "*Madonna Mia*, I think everyone loved our Bea, *che belleza.*"

"Yes, of course. She was a comely and proper girl. I remember when she was just eleven . . . ." Mildred Striker wiped a tear from her right eye with a lace hanky. She was unable to continue the story.

While the family cleaned up the house, Grandmother Mildred, and Nonna sat at the kitchen table speaking of the departed Beatrice. Mildred dabbed her eyes, while Nonna Bonarelli cried openly.

171

Charlie and Bobo helped as Vince, Theresa and Mary straightened furniture and washed dishes. Sam and Jody watched TV. They saw the picture only, fuzzy and poor at best, as Roland ran a noisy vacuum in the same room.

"I insist," was all that he said as he took the vacuum from Aunt Mary.

An amused Mildred watched as Roland expertly vacuumed the front room. "He hasn't always been a hotel magnate. He started as a bellhop and worked his way up from doorman to management. He's made his way through shrewd real property dealings after the war. He's quite good you know."

"Where are Bernie and Papa Bonarelli?" Vince asked.

Theresa, up to her elbows in dishwater, nodded towards the back kitchen window. "I think they went out to the garage. Papa wanted to smoke his pipe. Bernie was asking him questions about last night."

"Yeah, he's interested in whoever hit Papa." Charlie wiped a plate. "He asked me a bunch of questions a little while ago. He wanted to know all about the thing in the park and what kind of stuff the police asked me. Then, just as intensely, he wanted to know what I thought of Elvis Presley. The guy is a real hit in England, too, I guess."

True to form, Aunt Mary spoke to Nonna in Italian about Bernie's obvious attention to Theresa.

Vince looked at his sister Theresa and shook his head. He mouthed an "Oh-oh."

"No, no, *di impossible*," Nonna ventured.

Vince sensed that Theresa knew the way that the conversation was headed with the redundant question, 'Theresa when are you ever going to get married?'

Theresa saw from Grandmother Mildred's smile that she understood. "Speak English, you two, we have guests."

"Oh girls, don't stop your dialogue on my account, *e il coure che fa circolare il sangue.*

Dumbstruck Mary dropped the cup she was putting away.

Theresa laughed, "Yes, literally, it is the heart that keeps the blood flowing, and . . . ." She looked at Nonna and Aunt Mary, "and the mouth that gets ahead of the brain."

Aunt Mary turned red as Nonna sat at the table with her hands over her mouth.

Mary choked out, "You speak Italian?"

"Oh, *si con molto gusto*. I'm sorry. You may recall, Mrs. Bonarelli, as luck would have it, I was at university in Rome when The Great War broke out. That is World War I. I stayed on as a field hospital nurse where I met Reginald, my late husband. But of course, Mrs. Bonarelli, we haven't seen each other for years, and it was so long ago.

"Oh, I was just a girl then, everything was so brilliant, *Che magnificenza*. The city of Rome *la cita vibrante; il sangue* indeed, the history, the art, the food, but then Mussolini, *il duce*. He was just a young upstart then. I watched the political weather change, the whole atmosphere of Europe changed after the first war, and yet we never thought it would become the disaster that it did.

"Oh, and Roland, that dear boy, he's been such a godsend. You know he has interest in a hotel near the Vatican. We will be traveling there next spring."

"Sir Roland isn't it?" Theresa asked.

All eyes were on Mildred Striker now. The vacuum ran in a back room.

"Well, yes, but he prefers Roland. Please do not call him Sir Roland. He likes to fit into what you yanks call, 'the scene.'"

Bobo put a hand on his mother's shoulder, "It's cool, Mom."

Mary remained dumbfounded and quiet for at least four minutes.

Mildred continued, "I suppose that I should have mentioned some things. You understand; the absolute quickness of all of this. Roland dislikes pretense, not his show. I do apologize."

Vince took a dishtowel out of his sister's hand. "Here Mary, you've worked a long day, thank you. Let me take over with this. You should get Anthony and his mama. She's probably exhausted.

Mary removed her apron and put it on the back of a chair. "Yes, we should be going, Vince. Bobo, find your father and gather up you Grandmother Marcantonio, she's in Jody's room taking a nap. You have school tomorrow. Charlie, are you going back to school tomorrow"?

Charlie answered, "I don't know, I think I should stay home a day or two. Jody and Sam need some help getting stuff ready for school, too. He now felt the loss of his mother in real terms. Who was going to make the meals, wash the clothes, do the ironing, do the shopping, make the lunches, take Jody and Sam to school and doctor appointments?"

"Geez, Dad." Charlie gave an astonished look. A pain in his ribs flared, "Mom did everything."

Vince understood immediately what bothered his son. "She kept the family together didn't she?" It occurred to Vince, too; they would have to fill the void left by Bea's death.

"You need to go to school, Son. Life has to go on, and your mother would have insisted on it."

Mary and Theresa sensing the dilemma parroted, "We'll help out."

Theresa asked Mary to stay a few minutes while they made arrangements to help at the house for the next few days until Vince and Charlie became adjusted to the situation.

Nonna Bonarelli stood and threw up her hands. "Not to worry, Nonna is here to help. We can all help, *si la famiglia*."

Charlie saw the strain in his Grandmother Mildred's face.

"Distance," Mildred looked crushed. "We have to go back to England. But, we'll do our part."

There were voices at the back door as Bernie and Papa Bonarelli came up the stairs into the kitchen.

Papa Bonarelli rubbed the back of his head. "*Aspirina, l'testa,* she still hurts."

Nonna went to a kitchen cabinet where Bea had kept the aspirin. She took a bottle down and handed two tablets to her husband.

"Pietro, we are going to help tomorrow morning with Jody and Sam," she poured a glass of water for Papa Bonarelli.

Papa looked confused as he took his aspirin, "Oh, shu." He realized that he would be helping with his son's family now. "Shu-shu-every-ting's okay."

The vacuuming noise stopped, and Roland stood at the kitchen entrance from the living room with Bernard.

Mildred looked at her son, "Bernard, we are going to invite Jody and Sam to visit us in London come summertime, aren't we."

"Absolutely, old girl," Bernie's grin accentuated the gap in his teeth. Charlie stifled a laugh.

Vince blanched and Charlie knew that his father was thinking how he could possibly afford to send his two grade-school-aged children on a trip to England by themselves.

"Uh, Mildred, we need to talk about this."

"Pooh, pooh, they are my grandchildren and if I want to send the airfare, those two can get to England. Roland will arrange for a hotel in New York for the overnight, and someone will be with them at all times. Charlie, you are invited as well, of course, but I understand there is the military obligation perhaps?"

Charlie didn't need any reminder that he had registered for the draft after his eighteenth birthday.

Mildred brightened, "Bernard will make the arrangements." She looked at Vince, "There's a good boy, it's all settled."

Everyone in the room understood that Mildred Striker's edict was not a request.

A red-faced Vince spoke. "Yes, thank you Mildred, but I think that we should discuss this later."

Aunt Mary said, "Well, here are Anthony and Mama. I guess we had better go."

Vince thanked everyone. "I'll drive Mama and Papa home. Theresa, can you take Mildred, Bernie and Roland back to the hotel? Oh and are you going into your office in the morning?"

"Yes and yes. I'm helping a partner prepare for a big trial coming up in a couple of weeks. I'll come over here tomorrow evening. Charlie, can you get our coats please?"

Charlie left the kitchen and went to his parent's bedroom where all of the coats had been piled. He heard the buzz of conversation from the kitchen. He looked at a clock on his mother's nightstand. Depression covered him like a blanket.

It struck him that, from now on, his father would be by himself in this room at nights.

He was tired but still had things to do before he went to his room. He picked up an armload of coats and walked into the living room. He called to the kitchen, "Coats here. Dad, when you get back, I need to talk to you about something."

Vince came into the room followed by the Strikers. "Can it wait until morning? You look like you could use some rest. Tell you what, if you're still awake when I return we'll talk. See that Jody and Sam get to bed okay. I shouldn't be too long."

Everyone said their goodbyes. The house emptied except for Charlie, Jody and Sam.

It was late and Charlie wanted to beg off reading to Jody before she fell asleep. He didn't have to worry, both his brother and sister dropped off to sleep before he switched off their bedroom lights.

The house was silent except for a short humming from the refrigerator. Charlie thought of turning on the radio but lost interest as he dozed at the kitchen table.

"Charlie, I'm back." Vince shook his shoulder. "Better get to bed now. I think you should go to school in the morning."

"Geez, my neck," Charlie rubbed a crick in his shoulder and neck muscles. "Right," he got up from the table but was thinking he still had unfinished homework but it would wait until morning. He went to his room, threw his clothes on a chair; plodded to his bathroom and back. He barely lay down before he slept.

Charlie dreamed. He saw his mother at the end of the bed and woke with a start; someone or something was in his room. His heart pounded. He couldn't see or hear anything, but he felt a presence.

"What?" The sound of his voice startled him. He groped for the nightstand light and switched it on. He saw movement as his eyes adjusted to the light, "Nothing." His ribs hurt and his skin crawled with chill as he stared at the opposite wall. He saw only a shadow from some furniture, held up a hand and another shadow, like a silhouette puppet, appeared on the wall, "Oh."

The clock on his nightstand showed three-thirty. "I may as well get up and do some homework."

He searched for the clothes he had draped on the chair from the night before. He got up and switched on the overhead light. The clothes were gone. "What the heck?"

"Oh well." He sat in his underwear at his desk wrapped in a blanket. His algebra book was open to the assignment that he needed to study before the next class.

"Hmm," he remembered he hadn't left his book open to where it was now. "I didn't leave the book open?" He hunched over the book and switched on the radio to low volume while he pondered the introduction in front of his eyes. He heard a squeak and turned around to face the door, nothing. "Damn it's cold in here."

Charlie chucked the blanket and went to his closet for a robe. He found his clothes from the night before hung neatly on hangers. He stood staring, perplexed then pulled his robe from a hanger and went back to the desk.

An unfamiliar radio show played on the Zenith *Transoceanic*, which took up much of the top of his desk. He adjusted the dial for a better signal. "It's Daddy-O-Dewey Phillips, *Red, and White & Blue*, coming to y'all from radio WHBZ in Memphis . . . and now for some Bo-Diddley. Let's roll them Rhythm'n'Blues."

The voice of the southern screamer disc-jockey sang along with *Who Do You Love?*

Charlie visualized a wacky DJ jumping up and down in his chair, spinning black rhythm and blues through the late night. He tried to concentrate on algebra, but his thoughts were *Red, White and Blue.*

He wondered if he could play the beat coming out of the Zenith and tapped his desk with a pencil.

22

Grief Grows

Charlie couldn't get the sounds of those early morning blues out of his mind.

"And here it is ya'll," the voice of DJ Dewey Phillips brought Charlie out of a half sleep, half funk, as he stared blindly at an algebra problem.

"The original genuine (genu-iiiine) *Rock Around The Clock*. This here it is the granddaddy of rock-a-billy-rock-n-roll – let's dig it right (raht) now."

"Damn, that's some great stuff." Charlie awoke out of his comatose state to tap the rhythm on his algebra book. He closed his eyes and swayed with the music.

"Charlie."

Startled, Charlie turned to see Vince in the doorway. He looked beat.

"What the hell are you doing up this early? What's that shit you're listening to?"

"Huh? How come you're up, Dad? I didn't wake you did I?"

"Christ, kiddo, it's really early. You reading that book or just beating the hell out of it? I couldn't sleep either." Vince sat down on the bed. "I don't know, Charlie . . . ."

Charlie turned the radio off. The grief on his father's tired face left him unsure of what to say, if he should say anything. He guessed that his father's mind was in turmoil of what to do; how to cope with the loss of a beloved wife and mother.

"Your mother would want us to go on with our lives. She suffered the German blitz when people were bombed out of their homes and killed in the street. It was brutal and the Strikers like so many other families got through it, God only knows how.

"When I met, Bea, I was a green Ensign. I had volunteered for the U.S. Navy. The U.S. wasn't in the war yet, but I was part of the Lend Lease deal. I had a couple of years of college, spoke Italian and of course, Italy was in it with the Germans by then.

"It was rough on the family here, too. First generation Germans, Italians, and the Japanese were all suspect. We were lucky though, we didn't get put into camps like the Japs. Roosevelt said that, 'Italians where just a bunch of opera singers.' There were some attempts of internment camps for us, but that didn't last, I don't think.

"Nevertheless, people looked at Papa and Mama, old country Italians like they were the enemy, at first. Mama and Papa moved out to the country with our relatives until after the war. Papa is a good vegetable farmer and Mama made cheese and sausage. They sold vegetables and cheese from the back of the car to the city and factory workers. That's how Papa eventually got into that fruit and vegetable business that Uncle Anthony is running now.

"So the point is, we still have those old country roots, and some things are just understood. You know, like a period of mourning, walking around like the world just came to an end. Maybe it did for us, but we'll get through it. Your mother was the real strength of the family. She's gone, and I'm having a hell of a time with the business right now, but I think things will get better.

"Anyway, we've got to keep going, set an example for Jody and Sam. Mary and Theresa will help. Papa and Mama are great, but it's a little tough for Papa to get around with the old injury from his mining days; his arthritis is getting to his back, too. You probably noticed that your Nonna's hands aren't as strong as they used to be."

"Yeah, I saw her slicing bread yesterday. I could see the pain in her face from the pressure of the knife."

"Pressure, yeah right, Mama's hurting and we all have our own pressures to deal with but we keep going. Things have changed though. No more widows weeds and black arm bands. The war, and then Korea, really exposed death for what it is – it's shit, but the living move on."

Charlie understood his father's dam of emotion.

"Black clothes and dour attitudes don't cut it anymore. The wailing and the gnashing of teeth aren't going to help the business or your and the kids' futures. Jody and Sam have to grow up a little too fast but kids throughout the centuries have lost parents to worst circumstances."

Vince wiped his eyes. "Umm, I'll go upstairs and put the coffee on. The paper will be here pretty soon. Maybe there's good news to cheer us up. I want you to go to school so that you don't get behind.

"I'll drive you this morning. I'm going to the office. I can sit there as well as here and I have some things that need attending. Theresa will stop by on her way to her office. Mary is coming over this morning to help with the kids. I can start packing their lunches. You want a lunch too?"

"No thanks, I'll grab something out of the frig before I go. It's loaded from yesterday."

"Okay." Vince got up. "Don't let me bend your ear too much about things."

"Not to worry, Dad. Oh, and thanks for hanging up my clothes from last night."

Vince looked confused. "Your clothes, I didn't hang them?" He turned and went out of the room.

A perplexed Charlie wondered about the clothes, but thought too about his father talking to him like he had. He felt like he had just had something, incomprehensible yet, thrown at him. Vince talked to him more as an equal than as a young son.

Charlie thought of his Dad as one to show less emotion that the rest of his Italian family who came apart at the slightest upset.

Too, Charlie felt reluctant to discuss certain things, emotions and goals with his Dad. Vince was always absorbed in business or with things Charlie didn't understand yet. He understood now that his father and mother had kept her physical problems to themselves.

Charlie also knew now why his Dad never seemed to be around when he wanted to take part in school events like sports. He thought back to the time he tried the swim team, but he was too slow. He knew that he wasn't driven. Nobody cared enough, not even him.

It was a joke on Charlie when he tried wrestling. He found out quickly that this was not a good sport for him. He became so weak from trying to lose weight overnight for a match that a one-armed wrestler from the "B" squad pinned him in less than a minute.

There was no support from home except Sam who thought it was "really cool" that his brother was a wrestler. Whenever an event came up Vince was busy trying to make ends meet and Bea had to take care of the kids.

Now he knew that Jody and Sam where going to be partly his responsibility. He thought that he needed to find a part time job, too.

When he went up for breakfast, Vince asked, "Charlie, can you be home when Jody and Sam get out of school? Your Aunt Mary's got to take Anthony's mother to the doctor today at 4:00. Bobo's training for a Golden Gloves bout in a couple of weeks. Is he any good?"

Vince didn't wait for an answer. The front door opened. Aunt Mary was already there. She carried the morning paper. "*Buono Giorno, il giornale di interresante.*" She handed the paper to Charlie. "The authorities have caught all of the escapees from the hospital but one, the son of your school Dean I think."

Charlie read intently. He turned each page looking for anything related to the girl in the park and the escapees.

There was a small article that the girl had finally been identified. Charlie couldn't connect her name, Dorothy something, with anybody. Her body was still at the Coroner's pending the autopsy report."

"Jesus, you'd think the cops would have arrested that crazy guy by now. They know that it is Mr. Greyer's son, and it doesn't take half a brain to figure out that Mr. Greyer is probably protecting the guy. Look at this." Charlie pointed out the story to Vince. "They still haven't caught Mr. Greyer's son. You told Matt Grueber about what I found out – right?"

"Yeah, sure, I'm sure I told him. I think that I told him."

"Oh-oh, Dad, you didn't tell him did you?" I mean after all the crap coming down you probably forgot to tell your pal Matt. He wasn't at Mom's service either. He knew Mom, how come?"

"He called. He had to go to court on some other case the same time as your Mother's service. Nevertheless, we will probably see him soon enough. He wants to see your Uncle Bernie. We all worked in the same office during the war. You know, Grueber, the German expert or so the military thought.

"I need to get going, Charlie. You'll be a little early but you've got a place to go, right?" Vince turned to call down the hall towards the back bedrooms, "Mary, you have Jody and Sam up already?"

Jody came into the kitchen rubbing her eyes. "Hey, where's M . . . oh." The television was on in the living room.

"Sam's up," Vince said as he left the kitchen to talk with his youngest son.

Mary came into the kitchen, "Where's Vince?"

Charlie nodded towards the living room, "With Sam, we're leaving."

"Okay. Theresa will stop by soon on her way to her office. Mama and Papa will be here too." She left the room looking for Vince.

"Charlie, can I have some orange juice?" Jody tugged on Charlie's shirt.

"Sure, sweet face." Charlie got up from the table and went to the refrigerator. He grabbed the juice and looked for something to take for lunch. He spotted a small piece of refrigerator cake left from two days before. "Jewell."

"What jewel?" Vince was back in the kitchen wearing his over-coat and holding his hat.

Charlie held up the morsel of cake. "Nonna saved this sliver. Jewell from school, she brought this a couple of days ago. I surprised Bobo didn't vacuum it in."

"Oh, okay, let's get going. Are you ready to go?"

"I'll get my jacket, brush my teeth; meet you at the car."

Mary came back into the kitchen. "It's cold out there this morning, better bundle up. Good morning, Jody, how's my little pumpkin? *Belleza*," she squeezed Jody's cheeks.

"Ouch," Jody winced.

Charlie grimaced in sympathy. "Oh that makes you pucker, huh, Sis? See you later. Hey, Aunt Mary, where's Bobo this morning?"

"He running, 'roadwork' he calls it."

Sam walked into the kitchen, "He'll get pounded." Charlie laughed, "Okay, see you guys this afternoon."

* * *

Charlie stared out the car window in silence. Vince didn't say much as he watched the streets.

"It's cold. Look at the car exhausts puffing this morning."

"Yeah, right." Charlie thought that he had better find the girl named Jewell, "J", and thank her for the cake. He didn't know where to find her except the library, but it was too early, she might not be there yet.

Vince dropped him off in front of the school. He saw a group of kids that he didn't known except that they looked like they might be juniors.

"Hey, how you doing?" Charlie approached a group of four kids. They looked at Charlie as an anomaly. Upperclassmen never spoke to them unless "the big shots" wanted something that only the lower class had.

"What's up?" The boldest of the four students asked?

"Yeah, well, I'm looking for Jewell."

The group looked puzzled.

A girl giggled, "Try a jewelry store."

"Jewell, a girl, I think she's a junior. You know her? You guys are juniors aren't you?"

"Yeah," the students chimed."

"So who's, Jewell?" one of the group asked.

Charlie remembered that the girl he was looking for used "J" and not Jewell.

"J, she calls herself J."

"Oh, yeah, J," The girl giggled again, "She's probably at the cafeteria. That's where she eats her breakfast. She likes to read when nobody is around. Try there, but school's going to start pretty soon anyway."

Charlie walked towards the building. He heard the girl giggle again. "Thanks," he waved back at them, "goofy broad. I wonder if I should bother anyway. I could send a note but I don't know her address. Oh well what the hell."

23

What Kind of Jewel Are You?

Charlie walked into school and headed for the cafeteria in the west basement. To Charlie the green painted room seemed like a dreary place to start the day. There were a few students; some ate while others read in the early morning study-hall. One of the gym teachers sipped coffee and monitored the students. He raised his eyes when he saw Charlie then went back to reading a newspaper.

As Charlie looked for Jewell, he thought that no one would think of looking for anybody in here this time of the morning. He spotted her a corner table by herself. He sat down across the table from Jewell who concentrated on a textbook, "So serious already?"

"Oh, it's you," Jewell blushed, "I'm sorry about your Mom . . . . uh."

Charlie said, "Thanks, and thanks for the desert cake. My family scarfed it up. You like to make food?"

She blushed again. "One of those simple things you learn in junior high home-economics, simple, easy to remember, tasty."

"Right, tasty." He noticed she was sharper-looking than when he saw her for the first time in the library. Her black hair was down and neatly combed. She took off her glasses and smiled.

"You've got a little brother and sister. I saw them when I delivered the cake. They said you were with your Dad somewhere. Not that it's any of my business."

"Yeah, I was back with the cops, getting grilled again. I think maybe they might even believe me now that I didn't molest that girl.

That damn Mickey, S.O.B., is a hard guy to convince though. I finally found out this morning who the girl is."

"Mickey?" Jewell went blood red.

"Yeah, Detective Mickey, he's the guy on the case, and his partner. "Hey, you okay?"

The school bell rang.

"I have to go. I'm glad you liked the cake." Jewell jumped up like a rabbit out of a box.

"Hey, Jewell, I still don't know your last name."

"Goodbye." She waved.

Charlie got up and mouthed to no one in particular. "Well what the hell now?" He picked up his books and went out of the back entrance of the cafeteria. He saw Becky and Ruthie as he ascended the stairs to the main floor.

Becky grabbed his elbow. "Oh, Charlie, I'm so sorry about your mother."

Ruthie put a hand on his shoulder. "Charlie, that's really sad about your Mom, I'm sorry, too."

"How are your brother and sister, Charlie?" Becky asked.

"We'll work it out. Guess we'd better get to class." He spotted Zellie and Bobo. Bobo ran to his locker, deposited some books and ran towards them.

Zellie asked, "Bobo, you look pumped up this morning. What's up?"

Bobo ran in place and shadow boxed. "I'm working out again, trying to get my wind up for the bout in a couple of weeks."

Charlie rolled his eyes at Zellie who gave Bobo a serious look.

"I understand that guy you are matched with is hell-on-wheels."

"Yeah, Zel, I'll box his ass off." Bobo jabbed the air.

Charlie waved Bobo off. "C'mon you guys, we'll be late for home-room, let's split man." Bobo picked up the pace as all five ran to their respective classrooms.

Charlie and Becky got to home-room just as Mr. Bleeker, the senior class advisor, went to the blackboard.

Mr. Bleeker looked at his class. He spotted Charlie, "Mr. Bonarelli," he nodded, Mr. Bleeker insisted on formality in his classroom. "Getting you ready for adulthood," he instructed his charges. "If you act like adults now you'll do fine when you get out of here. He turned to Charlie. "Mr. Bonarelli, please accept our condolences about your mother."

The class looked at Charlie for a few moments. He felt like a freak. He lowered his eyes and mumbled, "Thanks." He willed the attention to go away. Things would be different here, too.

Mr. Bleeker turned back to the blackboard. "Here's a list of things you will need before you graduate next spring. Write this down in your notebooks."

The class wrote down requirements and things to do before graduation several months away. There were a few groans and comments.

The counselor turned around to face his class. He peered over his glasses with a questioning look, "Problem?"

No one answered, and Mr. Bleeker turned to face the board again.

Becky passed a note to Charlie. *Meet me after school in front of the school office. I have some information. I couldn't tell you this morning.*

Mr. Bleeker turned. "Don't forget Career Day for seniors next week. Career Day will be held in the gym all day and will consist of representatives from local companies like Mountain Bell, Public Service, Samsonite, Gates Rubber Company, and the military will be here, too."

Someone in the classroom asked, "Why the military?"

"You boys who aren't eighteen yet will probably reach draft age before you leave school. You know about the draft and all eligible boys eighteen and over are subject to draft or deferment. Some of you might like the choice of branches of service before the Army arbitrarily drafts you." Mr. Bleeker wrote on the board. *Army, Navy, Air Force, Marines, Coast Guard.*

Some boys talked among themselves.

"I'm going to college."

"I'm for the Marines."

"I've got a medical problem, flat feet I think."

Charlie sat silent, questioning himself for his ambivalence, his indecisiveness about his future.

What would my mother think? He asked himself. What was he going to do with rest of his life? Could he go to college? Should he find a trade, or should he just drift into something? Can I make a living as a musician he wondered? What was he going to do? How was his dad going to get along without him?

Christ, where's my ambition? What do I want? He squirmed in his chair as he listened to his classmates discussing their options.

Mr. Bleeker brought order back to the room, "Ladies and gentlemen, set goals for yourselves. The job fair is a chance to find options and what's out there for you. You've got the rest of your life to look forward to. The last twelve years of school have prepared you. Now it's up to you to do your best, to contribute back to the world.

"There are many ways you can contribute. Just look around your own families. What do they do? Maybe you want to follow in your parent's footsteps. Who do you admire? What occupations appeal to you?"

Charlie couldn't imagine himself in his Dad's machinery sales business. He had seen his father at work beating his brains out over budgets, deals, where to get the money for inventory, the market always fluctuating. He hated his Dad's business and resented that his father never had enough time for the family. He was always working to stay ahead.

"What about you, Charlie?" A classmate tapped his shoulder.

Uncomfortable with his lack of decision, Charlie hadn't thought about what his options for the next month were let alone the rest of his life. "I never really thought about it before, the draft maybe. Maybe I'll just get a job until I'm called into the Army."

Mr. Bleeker picked up on Charlie's words. "Okay ladies and gentlemen. Let's talk again about how we set goals and work to achieve them."

Charlie daydreamed. When he didn't know what to do he always fell into a reverie of pretense and emotion. He visualized himself climbing a mountain, defusing enemy mines in rough beach-landing operations; riding a horse into the sunset with his best girl, *I gotta go to work and make a living.*

His system reacted like gum on a hot sidewalk. Emotion spread through his body as if administered through a syringe. He thought I'm just a fucking stupid bastard with no skills, no talent, no future, and no possibilities. What's a stupid fuck like me supposed to do?

* * *

After home-room, Charlie went into the lavatory. He stood staring at himself in the mirror.

"Feeling sorry for yourself, Bonarelli? You look a little teary-eyed."

Charlie looked around. He didn't see who spoke.

A door banged. "Lay off asshole, you're pushing it, man. Who the fuck are you anyway?" Bobo said as he and Zel walked into the boy's room.

"What?" Charlie looked around the porcelain room. He saw someone at a urinal who he didn't recognize. The person was unkempt and older. "Who are you? You don't go to school here do you?"

Mr. Greyer appeared out of nowhere. "What are you doing here?" He grabbed the boy at the urinal by his shoulders and pushed him out the door as the young man zipped up his pants.

"I had to piss." He shook Mr. Greyer off.

"Are you crazy –- coming into my school like this? The police are looking for you. They just left. How did they miss you?"

"Jesus Christ, that fuck-stick is Mr. Greyer's son, the one the cops are looking for." Bobo ran out of the door to follow.

Zel looked puzzled. "Hey, Charlie, you think that *mumzer* is talking you? Maybe he's the one leaving the notes behind your house. Maybe he's the one who gave your *zayde* such a *zetz.*

191

"Huh? That's Mr. Greyer's son? You think maybe that he's the guy who hit Papa Bonarelli in the head? What the fuck is he doing here?"

Charlie and Zel went through the door in late pursuit. They ran into a puzzled Bobo.

"The guy just disappeared, like he's gone, man." A red-faced Bobo, "God damn it. That son-of-a-bitch split like a fucking ghost."

Zel pondered, "You know what? I've got a theory, but let's talk about it at lunch. We're going to be late for class. Charlie, you better call the cops or maybe your Dad about this. I'm thinking if the cops haven't found Mr. Greyer's son by now that somebody's hiding him."

The three of them sang like the choir, "Mr. Greyer."

"Shit. Okay, I'll see you at lunch. I'm going to call Dad. He'll call Matt Grueber. I don't trust those other two prick cops."

Charlie walked toward a pay phone booth in the front hall. "Dad . . . yeah I'm okay, but listen . . . yeah, I've got my lunch, anyway . . . , Dad listen to me, this is important. We're thinking that Mr. Greyer's son is hiding in this school. Yeah Bobo, Zel and me see this moron in the boy's room between classes. The guy said something to me. He knows who I am. Before I could get . . . no Dad, don't take your other phone, I've got to talk to you.

"Fuck." Charlie knew his father had put the phone down. "God damn it, Dad where'd you go?" He could hear Vince talking on another phone. Someone picked up the phone. "Dad, you're making a fucking deal, but you could give a shit that Mr. Greyer's son is here, in school for Christ's sake, you don't give a shit about anything but your fucking deals . . . ."

"Charlie, it's Vince's secretary."

He heard the unfamiliar female voice on the other end of the phone. He felt himself reddening, "Fuck," he mouthed.

"Vince had to take a call from Mexico."

Charlie apologized to the secretary. "Please tell Dad to call Matt Grueber. Mr. Greyer's son, the guy that escaped from the state mental hospital, he's here at school. I think he's after me."

The bell rang.

"Gotta go."

24

Closet Caper

At lunch Charlie asked Zellie, "Bobo's out running during the lunch hour. You think he's going to do okay in two weeks, Zel?"

Zellie scrunched his shoulders, grimaced at Charlie and drew a finger across his throat.

Charlie laughed, "You think it's that bad, huh?"

Zel slowly nodded his head. "The other guy is dedicated and damn good from what I've read in the sports pages. Hey, and what about you, are you going to be able to go to the bout? You've got *tsuris* with the cops, and that schmuck in the boys' room?"

"Things are crazy now, but the family thinks we all need to keep up our routine. Everyone is taking Mom's death hard. Dad says sitting around doesn't make things better. I'll probably go unless I have to watch Jody and Sam. It doesn't help that I'm still not completely cleared in that girl's death. The cops are looking at me for something; I don't know what. They're around when I don't need them, and vaporize when I do.

"Like this morning. If that guy is Mr. Greyer's son, then I gotta talk to Mr. Greyer. He knows that I'm in the soup, and I don't like it when the soup has an alligator in it, and for what?

"What if his son, Burris, killed that girl? And, what if he thinks that I saw him do it? I mean that's stupid. If anybody saw something it was Ralph Jay and his asshole buddy Joe Birch. I think that

Detectives Mickey and Brawley are trying to connect me to the girl in the park just so they can put the blame on somebody."

"Hi guys." Becky waved.

Becky and Ruthie sat down at the table.

"Hey, Becky, hi Ruthie, what's up?" Zellie grinned.

Becky looked upset. "Charlie, that guy's here, he's here in school, I saw him, you know, Mr. Greyer's son, Willie Burris."

"Willie Burris, yeah I think that must be the guy that was in the boy's room this morning. He said something to me and Mr. Greyer walks in and snatches the guy. Bobo tried to find him but the guy, and Mr. Greyer disappeared." Charlie got up from the table. "I'm going to talk to Mr. Greyer right now."

Ruthie grabbed his arm. "Mr. Greyer left school just before lunch, Charlie. He's going to be gone all day. I was in the office when he rushed in and rushed out again. Oh, and some police detectives were in the office, too, looking for Mr. Greyer. What's going on?"

Becky said, "Charlie. I think this Willie Burris guy is hiding in the school. I saw him this morning, just before home room. That's what the note that I gave you is about. I didn't have time to write the details because I had to leave early for a doctor's appointment.

"Anyway, I'm sure I saw that guy, Burris, running into the janitor's closet on the first floor. I peeked in but there was nobody there? Where do you suppose he went?"

"Closet," Charlie asked, "he ran into a closet? You looked, and you couldn't find him? That was taking a risk, don't you think?"

"Yeah maybe, but all I saw were mops, buckets, toilet paper, but no Willie Burris?" Becky got up. I'll show you. C'mon, we have some time."

Zellie got up and excused himself. "Let me know what's up. I'm meeting with the physics teacher before class. See you later, Okay? Besides, if the guy was in there, he'd of split by now if he knows someone is snooping. Maybe Mr. Greyer rushed him out of school."

*   *   *

The janitor's closet was located near the boys' restroom where Charlie saw Willie Burris earlier that morning. A few students passed by but no one paid attention as Charlie and the girls stood by the janitor's closet door.

"He must be hiding in the school, and his father, Mr. Greyer, is probably helping his boy." Becky opened the closet door, "See, nowhere to go."

Charlie went into the closet and looked through an accumulation of mops, buckets and paper goods. A void through some mops in the back of the closet caught his eye. He picked up a broom to probe, but was interrupted by one of the janitors.

"Hey, what are you guys doing in here? Get out of there now. C'mon, I said, get out of there. You kids go find somewhere else to fool around. How'd you get in here anyhow? We keep this door locked."

Becky was puzzled, "Locked?" Charlie and Ruthie followed Becky as she walked away from the janitor's closet. "It wasn't locked this morning when I saw that Burris guy?"

Charlie had an idea, "Maybe there's an inside lock, and just maybe there's a space behind the mops and the crap where Burris is hiding. Where are the cops? They should be turning the school upside down looking for that pri . . . uh, guy."

Becky grabbed Charlie's left arm. "Charlie, let's look after school. There's got to be a way for us to get into the closet."

"Yeah, Becky, I think you're right. But, I have to get home for Jody and Sam this afternoon." Charlie thought for a few seconds. "Okay, maybe just a few minutes. I'll meet you in front of that closet after the last bell. The teachers and janitors are about the only ones left in that hallway after classes are out."

*   *   *

After the last bell, Charlie met Becky and Ruthie. "So how are we getting in?"

Becky grinned, "Ruthie, show Charlie."

Ruthie produced a key for the closet.

"If we're spotted, Ruthie can say something like she is finishing up some work for the school office and we are waiting for her, okay?"

Charlie looked at the key. "You're a devious girl, Ruthie." Something gnawed on Charlie about her. "Where'd you get that key, Ruthie?" Charlie thought that Ruthie was always in the middle of things, always too clever. She knew about his visits to the school psychologist. She had probably read his files.

Ruthie smiled as she held up the key. "It hangs on the keyboard in the main office; spares for all of the doors in the school. I'll return it before the office knows it's missing."

"Let's try it." Charlie held out his hand for the key then retracted his hand. "Wait," he tried the closet doorknob, the door was unlocked.

"This is crazy," Becky blurted. "We know that the janitor locked it when he saw us this morning."

Charlie pulled on the door. "Maybe he's been working out of the closet since then." He opened the door and stepped in. "Wet mops smell really bad."

The fading afternoon light added a mysterious element to the stinking mops and cleaning product odors. Charlie looked for a light. "Man, I can't see, can you open the door a little more?"

"Somebody's coming." Ruthie grabbed Becky, pulled her into the closet and closed the door. The three stood quietly in the stinking vacuum-like blackness.

"Becky breathed hard, "I've got to get out of here, I'm claustrophobic."

"It's really dark in here isn't it?" Ruthie wanted out, too.

Becky, almost breathless, "Charlie, I can't stay in here, let's go."

Charlie didn't answer but he thought he found something.

"Charlie, where are you? Ruthie?"

Ruthie didn't answer either. There was the rattle of a bucket.

"C'mon you two this isn't funny. I'm looking for you."

Brooms fell and mops moved as Becky groped in the dark. She fought to stifle a scream.

Charlie felt for Becky in the dark. The door clicked. Charlie grabbed her and pulled backward through some mops.

"Oh!"

"It's okay, Becky, it's me." Charlie whispered. "Be quiet now."

The door opened. "What the heck, the door is unlocked again."

They heard the rattling of a bucket and the door closing again, a click as the janitor locked the door.

"What's going on?" Becky whimpered.

Charlie stood in back of her. He put his left arm around her left shoulder; his mouth close to her face and gently breathed into her ear, "Quiet."

Becky relaxed some. She whispered, "What're you doing, Charlie?"

Ruthie coughed. "Quit that now, I know what you're doing, Charlie, you filthy beast."

Becky forgot about her claustrophobia as long as Charlie held on to her. "We are in a space behind the janitors stuff." He took his arm away and took her right hand. "Ruthie, hold onto Becky.

"This is no good. There's no light. Let's get out of here. I'll find a flash light and come back. I'll bet Burris is using this as a hiding place."

Becky held tight to Charlie. "Let's get out of here right now. What if he's in here?"

A devilish, throaty, laugh caused Becky to scream. Charlie pulled her towards the door.

"I'm sorry, guys I get a little giddy when I'm frightened." Ruthie said, "Let's get the heck out of here."

Becky screamed again as Charlie found an inside latch and pulled the girls through the open door into the hall light.

"What's wrong now, Becky?" He laughed at the sight of the pretty blonde with a wet rag hanging over her face."

Ruthie giggled as she pulled the wet rag from her friend's head.

"Oh yuck," Becky's face colored, "I've got to go to the girls room."

Ruthie balked, "Not now, Becky. I've got to get this key back into the school office before they lock us in school for the night."

"Don't worry, the janitors work late," Charlie said, "We'll be okay. But, I've got to find a flashlight."

"I thought that you had to get home, Charlie." Becky wiped her wet hair with a hanky.

"Yeah, I do, but I think we're on to something. I want to see what's behind the janitors stuff. I wonder why there'd be a room behind the mops?"

Ruthie fast walked towards the office. "There's a flashlight in the office. I'll get it."

Charlie asked Becky, "Is Ruthie a little light-handed or what?"

Becky continued to wipe at her wet hair. "What do you mean?"

"I mean, she gets the key to the janitor's closet, and then she's in the office lifting a flashlight. Oh, and did you ever wonder why she is always a step ahead of everyone else. She knows what's going down before anyone does."

"She is handy isn't she?" Becky giggled. "She got us into my car last night when I locked the keys inside. She found a hanger and jimmied the lock."

Ruthie hurried back. "Here's the flashlight. I'll stay outside while you two go in and check out the closet."

"Uh, Ruthie," Becky stopped walking. "I think that you better go in with Charlie. I'll stay outside. That closet gives me the creeps."

Ruthie still had the closet key. She unlocked the door and pulled it open.

Charlie walked into the dark closet. "Okay, Becky, keep a sharp eye." He turned on the flashlight. Before Ruthie and Charlie could get into the void they discovered earlier, a wild looking creature burst through the mops and the brooms.

"Burris, it's Willie Burris," Becky hollered as the hospital escapee rushed for the door.

Willie Burris, about five-foot-eight-inches, 165 pounds, brown hair sticking to one side of his head and the other side like a butt-shot turkey, knocked Becky to the floor in his rush to get out.

"Take care of Becky," Charlie called to Ruthie as he ran after the fleeing Burris, "I'll get him."

He caught up with Burris and grabbed the back of his collar. Burris pulled away and exited an outside door. Charlie caught up with him again.

Burris turned suddenly, he clutched something. Charlie recognized the bat stolen out of his Dad's garage the night Papa Bonarelli was hurt.

"Son-of-a-bitch, Burris, you hurt my Papa." Charlie lunged just as Burris swung the bat into Charlie's midsection. He went to the ground like a stunned animal sucking air. A pain in his ribs made it difficult to breath.

Becky was out of the door and her hollering stopped a swing from the bat to Charlie's head. "Don't you hit him again you bastard." She ran at Burris shoving him away from the prone Charlie.

"Hey, what's going on out here?" A janitor called from the school door. He ran towards the disabled Charlie.

Charlie fought for breath. Lying on the concrete walk, all he saw was a step and Ruthie's legs as the door opened again.

Burris ran.

Becky hollered, "I see a cop car. I'll bet they're after that guy. I think he ran down the street – the other way though. The cops are going the wrong way!"

The girls and the janitor helped Charlie to his feet. He was still fighting for breath, unable stand on his own.

"We better call the police." The janitor lifted Charlie up.

Ruthie pointed to the street. "That was the police. I'm sure that was a detective's car that just went past us. I think they're chasing Willie Burris."

Charlie's eyes filled with tears as he fought the pain in his ribs.

Becky put an arm around Charlie's waist for support. "God, I'm so sorry, Charlie. You've been hit again. Poor, Charlie."

"I've got him, little lady. Let's get him inside." The janitor picked Charlie up and carried him into the school and down the hall. "We'll go into the office. I'm calling the cops anyway."

Becky and Ruthie followed into the office.

The janitor sat Charlie in a chair. "He's breathing okay." He saw Charlie's bandages and the hands from previous injuries. "He looks kind of beat up though. Is this kid having some problems?" He didn't wait for an answer. "You girls watch him while I phone the cops."

The janitor went behind the school office counter to use the phone.

Ruthie whispered to Becky, "I've got to get the key and the flashlight back before somebody finds them missing. You watch Charlie, okay?"

Becky had an arm around Charlie and cradled his head on her shoulder. "Poor, Charlie, my poor little, Charlie."

"Yeah, I think he'll be okay," the janitor said into the phone.

Charlie's breath came easier, but his ribs were on fire. He saw Ruthie sneak around the school office counter and the janitor while she put the key and flashlight back in their places.

"The cops are on their way." The janitor came back to where Charlie sat in the chair. "You think you're going to be okay?" Do we need to take you to the hospital?"

"I'm okay," Charlie forced an answer, "A little short of breath. Maybe you can call my Dad please." He told the janitor the phone number between labored breaths, and sank back into the chair.

The janitor wrote down the number. "So what's going on here?"

25

Matt Gets An Earful

"What the hell is going on now, Charlie?" Vince's irritation increased when he saw the police. Charlie and his father sat in the school office while two cops fumbled through a cursory report. They were anxious to go.

Charlie hung into the chair with the pain in his ribs nagging at him.

One police officer approached Vince, "You the father? He looks okay, huh?"

"Yes, I'm Vincent Bonarelli. Is that your professional diagnosis? How do you know he's okay? His ribs are probably broken."

The cop pushed his hat back. "Right, Mr. Bonarelli. Well the kid looks okay. He's breathing. Maybe give him some aspirin, huh?"

"Maybe get him to the hospital, huh?" Vince stood up. He was taller than the cop.

Charlie waved off his Dad's notion. "No more damn hospitals."

The cop turned from Vince and motioned for his partner to go. "We've got to try and find the guy. These kids think he's hanging around this school."

Vince glared at the two police officers as they left the school office. He said, "Charlie, through the police department's eyes, you're trouble more than troubled. You're walking around under a gray cloud like Al Capp's comic character what's his name?"

"Joe Btfspik," Ruthie gleamed. "He's always walking around un-der a dark cloud. It's always raining over his head."

"Uh, Dad, this is Ruthie and Becky. You may have met them before."

"Right, hello girls, I'll get Charlie home. Thanks for hanging around. I think I'd better drive Charlie to the hospital. You need a ride home?"

"No hospital, no way."

Becky answered, "I have a car, Mr. Bonarelli, thanks for the offer." She looked at Charlie. "Will you be okay, Charlie? I wonder? You should wrap your ribs when you get home. She took a head-to-toe look at him and shook her head. "Can I call you later?"

Charlie nodded.

Vince smiled, "Becky, he'll be fine. I'll get him home. His Nonna will fix him up."

Charlie blanched; he shook his head and mouthed, "NO!" to his father.

They drove in silence until Vince collected his thoughts. "Charlie, what have you gotten yourself into?"

Charlie wheezed, "What's going on is that Mr. Greyer's son," he paused for breath, "is one of the escapees from the state mental hos-pital. I think Mr. Greyer was hiding him in our school."

"Nah, Charlie. That would cost him his job. It's not logical."

"Yeah, not logical but another thing is this guy, Willie Burris, wants to pound me for some reason. He's probably the guy that hit Papa Bonarelli. He had my bat, that's what he hit me with.

"I can't figure what Willie Burris thinks about me. I don't even know the guy." Charlie sat still for a few seconds collecting his breath. "You know that Burris cat has his wiring all shorted out. I'm thinking maybe he whacked that girl in the park and he thinks that I saw him do it.

"Truth is I already told the police about those two guys from school. I think I saw when I found the girl, maybe they did it or they know who did."

"Who's that?"

Charlie looked at Vince as if seeing him for the first time. "Ralph Jay, and Joe Birch," he breathed in short breaths, "I already told you. You haven't forgotten have you? I think maybe the cops have."

"Okay, right." Vince stopped for a traffic signal and looked around at Charlie. "Who're they and how come you didn't tell me before?"

"I told you and the cops a few nights ago. You weren't listening, you know, Mom and all. I told the cops, too. What's going on? Nobody's listening to me."

In the waning daylight Charlie watched Vince's red face about to explode.

"God damn it," Vince hit the steering wheel, "it's not like there's nothing going on. Look, I'm sorry, Son. There's just too much crap that I'm trying to get through, and I've been hoping you might pick up the slack. I'm depending on you to help us through this." Vince thought a moment. "This thing with Burris has me wondering."

"The light's green, Dad, wondering what?"

Vince accelerated the car while he thought another moment, "I wonder why the cops haven't caught this Burris. If Mr. Greyer is hiding him in your school, he's endangering the kids and the staff. Is this Mr. Greyer crazy or something?

"I'll call Matt Grueber as soon as we get home. We've got to get our lives back in order. Hey, I understand that Bobo is boxing in a couple of weeks. You'll probably want to go. Maybe I'll go, too. Papa and Mama will probably watch Jody and Sam."

"I was thinking of staying home, Dad. I've lost my part time job, the band doesn't have any gigs coming up, and I can't handle the sticks with this anyway." Charlie held up his cast. His breathing was labored again as he felt the pain back in his ribs.

"The way I'm feeling now, I couldn't begin to sit through a fight with a bunch of noisy people. I can use the time to study."

Vince nodded his head. "Yeah, I suppose that's a good idea. Don't forget that your Uncle Bernie is still here for a while. Bernie asked Theresa to show him around the city before he leaves."

Charlie fought the worsening pain in his ribs to ask, "What's up with Uncle Bernie?"

Vince replied, "Bernie's staying in the States for a few weeks, traveling out to California then south and back through New York." Vince pulled into the alley to the garage. "I'm not entirely clear, but it has something to do with promoting his brand of Brit blues music. Bernie is a music nut. He's been bitten by the black rhythm and blues stuff. Maybe the same music I heard on your radio the morning you couldn't sleep."

"No kidding?" Charlie winced in pain. "Very cool . . . I'll ask him about it."

Vince stopped outside of the garage. "Can you get the door?"

"Sure." Charlie opened the car door to get out but stopped with a sharp yelp."

"What's wrong?"

"My ribs, there's a pain." Charlie could barely take a breath. "Burris must have cracked a couple of my ribs. I'm feeling it now."

Vince shut the engine. "Hang on I'm coming around to help you out."

Charlie's eyes were wet with the pain in his ribs, "Ouch."

Jody and Sam rushed to the top of the stairs as Vince helped Charlie up to the kitchen.

"What's wrong, Charlie?" Jody asked as Sam looked over her shoulder.

Vince grumbled, "Charlie got beat up again. This time he may have hurt ribs."

Mamma Bonarelli appeared behind the children. "What's going on?"

"Charlie may have a cracked rib or two."

Nonna called into the kitchen to Papa Bonarelli who wasn't there, then down the stairs and into the kitchen again. Dialect hit the airwaves as Nonna Bonarelli went into a bi-lingual tirade. "Where's Papa when I need him?"

"He took the bus to the market, Nonna, remember?" Sam shrugged his shoulders.

"It's okay, Mama, it's okay," Vince called up to his mother, "Charlie's walking and talking."

Nonna took charge, "I'll make a mustard plaster and wrap him. Carlo, you get in here right now and let me see the damage. *Madonna mia* everything is going to the devil around here."

Charlie walked gingerly up the back stairs helped by Vince. "Wow, there's some pain there."

Jody asked. "Where's it hurting, Charlie?"

He took his sister's hand and placed it where the pain was the sharpest.

Jody gently felt Charlie's ribs cage. "Fifth rib, right under the sternum, probably a crack then."

Charlie took a shallow breath. He winced from his sister's gentle touch but would have laughed if the pain were not so sharp. "You a doctor now, how'd you know that stuff?"

Nonna put her hands up in wonder. "Did you hear that, my little angel? That Jody, she's so smart." She squeezed her granddaughter's cheek, "*Bellezza*!"

"Ouch, Nonna," Jody rubbed her cheeks but continued on. "I saw this book with skeletons, *Gray's Anatomy*, in the public library. The librarian made me put it up when I got to the sexy parts."

"*Madonna*," Nonna Bonarelli crossed herself, "my baby looking at naked skeletons, *Madonna*."

Charlie cried with pain and laughter. He held on to the stair rail to keep from falling.

"*Buona sera*," Theresa walked into the kitchen, "*Che cosa* -- what?"

Bernie came in with a "Good evening everyone," but stopped short when he saw Charlie.

Nonna waved everyone away from the kitchen table as she led Charlie to a chair. She wiped her eyes, "*il sinistrato*, my poor Carlo."

"The sufferer, what's happened here?" Theresa stood shocked by her nephew's appearance, "Charlie, dear God."

Nonna sat Charlie down and helped him remove his shirt gently from around all of his previous damage.

"Nephew, what have we got here? My God, man, you're a bloody bag of bones. Do cut the garment from him, Mrs. Bonarelli, whilst we prepare some bandaging."

Bernie took his brother-in-law aside, "Vince, what's happening here? The poor boy isn't going to make it through next week at this rate."

Vince said, "Listen up, please." He told everyone about Willie Burris. "For some reason, Burris is targeting Charlie. I'll call Matt Grueber."

"Grueber?" Bernie grinned. "Matthias Grueber, that young Lieutenant from the war? The German linguist, special officer, righto, he's a Denver boy isn't he? I had forgotten that both of you came from the same city in the States. He's with the coppers?"

"That's right," Vince answered. "Matt wasn't at the funeral because he was in court. You'll see him soon enough." He walked into the hallway to phone Grueber. He had difficulty listening to the detective through the cacophony in the kitchen. The clatter of dishes, coffee pot, voices, and an occasional "ouch," from Charlie rose and fell as Nonna Bonarelli wrapped her grandson's ribs.

The room went silent when Papa Bonarelli came into the house after a day helping at the market. He carried a cabbage and some peppers in a net bag.

"Oh, oh," Theresa went to her father and explained quickly, in Italian, what was going on.

Papa Bonarelli listened to his daughter while looking past her at his grandson Carlo. He stood in the kitchen entry, the bag of vegetables hanging in one hand, his wide brimmed hat in the other hand; his unlit pipe hung from one side of his mouth.

Tears streamed from Theresa as she saw Papa Bonarelli's bewilderment. His hurt and forlorn look embodied the feelings of the entire Bonarelli family that night.

Theresa hugged and held on to her father for some time before she took the sack from his hands. "Papa, sit down at the table, we'll get your coffee and a little whiskey.

"Here, Mama, let me finish that." Theresa took the bandages out of her mother's hand. *Dio*, but that mustard plaster is repugnant."

Nonna let her daughter finish wrapping Charlie. "I'll get Papa's coffee and make some *minestra* with all of the leftovers."

Vince walked back into the kitchen. "Hi, Papa, here I'll help you. Let me take your hat and overcoat."

Papa Bonarelli held up a hand, "*Aspettare,*" he searched in his overcoat pocket to take out his tobacco pouch.

Bernie reached for Papa Bonarelli's hat, "Here, Vince, let me help your father."

"*Grazie,*" Papa Bonarelli gave Bernie his hat and let him help him with the coat.

Bernie smiled. "Think nothing of it." He looked at Vince. "Oh, by the way, Vince, did you find Matt Grueber?"

"He's on his way over, unofficially. The case is supposed to be out of his hands, but he intervenes on our behalf."

"Splendid, I'm keen to see him again." Bernie made his gap-toothed approval.

Uncharacteristically, the family ate in silence with an occasional "ump" of discomfort from Charlie.

The doorbell rang.

"I'll get it. It's probably Matt." Vince got up from the table and went through the living room to answer the door.

The family heard Vince, "C'mon in, Matt. Here, let me take your coat and hat. How about a cup of coffee? You eat yet?"

Matt Grueber walked into the kitchen with Vince, "Hello everyone."

Bernie got out of his chair, "Grueber, you old dog."

They shook hands.

"Captain Striker -- Bernie." Grueber gave a wide smile. "I knew that you came for Bea's service, but I thought I'd missed you -- so terrible about Bea. It's great to see you again though despite the circumstances."

Bernie put his arms around both Vince and Matt,"The Three Musketeers. Jolly chaps we were then, right?"

Vince laughed for the first time in days. "Oh yeah, it's a good thing that Command looked the other way a few times."

"It was more than a few times," Matt grinned. "We got away with a lot more than anyone should have."

Bernie roared, "Right, bloody stretched it, but we got our job done and a nice batch of medals to boot."

Charlie winced with pain to stifle a laugh at the thought that Bernie could probably whistle a happy tune through the gap in his toothy smile.

Nonna Bonarelli smiled at Matt Grueber and made a place for him at the table.

"Thank you Mrs. Bonarelli, but I've just finished dinner with my family, I'll take the coffee though."

"Look, Matt. Sorry to call you out tonight, but Charlie had the hell beat out of him by this escapee Willie Burris. And, Papa was hit in the head in our own garage. We think that it was this Burris guy. Burris's father, Charlie's assistant principal, is probably protecting Burris. Burris is the assistant principal's kid from a failed marriage."

Grueber didn't appear surprised, but watched the family over his coffee cup as he listened.

"Charlie saw Burris in school today. He thinks that Mr. Greyer, Burris's father, is hiding his son in the school for Christ's sake."

Nonna Bonarelli "shush-shushed" and made the sign of the cross as she rolled her eyes to heaven.

Grueber put his coffee down. "It's okay, Mrs. Bonarelli, we'll catch this Burris guy. It turns out that Willie Burris should have been named Wiley. He's that good at evading us. Uh, don't let that information get out of here.

"We're very interested in Burris. We think maybe that he's working his father, Mr. Greyer. Maybe Burris thinks he has something on his father that keeps the man protecting him.

"We've talked to Mr. Greyer, and he swears that he doesn't know where Burris is, although he did say that Burris showed up at school today. Burris is out of the school now. The two detectives, Mickey and his partner have searched . . . ."

Charlie interrupted, each breath cutting like a knife, "Did they check the janitor's closet on the first floor by the boys lavatory?"

Grueber looked closely at Charlie. "I think maybe you need to go to the emergency room and have those ribs X-rayed, Charlie."

Charlie wheezed, "I've had enough of emergency rooms, doctors, nurses, helpful folks," he fought to catch another breath, "authorities and cops." Oh that hurt to say, but I better get it out. "I'm the victim now and I just figured out where I place in this whole scene."

Everyone stared at Charlie.

Nonna wrung her hands, "*Basta*, enough, they're beating my beautiful grandson to pieces. He's under the *malocchio*. The devil has him in his eyes. I'm going to take him to see *il stregone*."

"Wait, Mama, please," Vince held up his hand, "Charlie what were you going to say?"

"Bait," Charlie breathed out, "I'm the bait."

"Precisely!" Bernie looked at Charlie and panned the room. "He's the pegged hare to attract the fox."

Grueber turned red in the face.

Vince looked at Grueber, "Don't choke on your coffee, Matt. Is this true? Is Charlie being used? Are the police trying to track this guy, Burris, through Charlie?" Vince glared at his friend.

"I don't know." Grueber wanted to evade the question. He knew that Charlie was being followed by the detectives because Willie Burris seemed close to wherever Charlie was. "I never considered it that way, but it has that appearance doesn't it?"

"You're damn right it has the appearance." Vince got up from the table, "I want you to catch this guy. Charlie is sure that the driver that he tried to help in the park, that night the girl was killed, was hiding Burris in the back seat of the car covered with a blanket. But, then he told the other detectives that."

Charlie spoke slowly, "It was like the questions from the other detectives were more accusations than questions. Remember I got sick the first time, but later, I mentioned that Willie Burris might be involved, but I wasn't sure then."

"Are you sure now?" Grueber asked.

"After today," Charlie leaned over the table to catch his breath, "I'd bet that Willie Burris is convinced that I can do him some harm. It was probably Mr. Greyer and Burris in the park that night."

Matt sipped his coffee, "Where's the evidence?"

Charlie, hurt, mad and frustrated fought for breath. "There's no real evidence but me. Also I told you that Ralph Jay and Joe Birch were there, too. Jay admitted it to me during our little mix-up, but I can't prove anything. He'll probably deny it." A sharp pain made sweat bead on Charlie's forehead.

"Ralph Jay and Joe Birch." Grueber wrote the names in his note pad. "They're students, right? I'll check them out for sure."

"C'mon, I've given the cops that information before. Don't tell me, you guys haven't followed it through. You're too busy trying to nail Burris – yeah that's it, I'm bait."

"Nevertheless, it appears that someone is trying to lay the blame on you, old man." Bernie gave an accusatory look at Matt Grueber. "I think that you better find your man, Matt, before any more harm finds Charlie."

Matt set his cup down. "We're not sure it's a man that killed the girl."

All eyes were on Grueber now. "I can't give you the details because we don't know them yet. I can tell you that there was something inconsistent, with that woman, and sexual assaults. We are not sure this was a rape as we first surmised."

Theresa flared, "Well, you'd better damn well find out soon and the police better find Willie Burris before he finds Charlie again."

26

Pain Makes A Decision

The phone rang. Jody ran to get it.
"Charlie, it's for you. It's a girl, Becky."
He took the receiver and wheezed "Hi, Becky."
Becky asked, "Charlie, how're you doing?"
A whispered wheeze, "I'll live but I have a cracked rib or two. It hurts to breathe, to laugh, to talk, to blink my eyes."
"Oh Charlie, you poor guy, you want me to come over and administer to the wounded?"
He thought about Becky's nice boobs rubbing across his face as she patted the pillow behind his head but answered, "Uh, nooo-oh, thanks anyway . . . just need a couple of days . . . uh maybe I better take some more aspirin or something . . . see you in school tomorrow, thank you for calling."
Charlie hung up the phone and worked slowly down the stairs to his room. He felt the downward movement in his ribs. It hurt to lie on his bed. It hurt worse trying to get out of bed. He thought maybe he could wash up. He realized that he wouldn't be taking a shower while taped into a fuming mustard plaster.
He thought, damn! What the hell is this thing supposed to do? My skin is on fire; it hurts to breath. The stink from the plaster is enough to make me puke.
"Charlie," Vince called down the stairwell, "you going to be okay?"

215

Charlie pushed himself up again on the edge of the bed. He felt like his eyes were bleeding and it was increasingly difficult to move. He couldn't respond with any volume. The wrap and the pain combined made him reluctant to answer. He forced a shallow breath.

Vince came down the stairs, "What's the matter?"

"I can't breathe with this mustard plaster, the tape, it's too tight. I've got to get it off before I go up in flames."

They picked at the tape and pulled the mustard-plaster. The pain of pulling hair and skin from near the damaged ribs almost caused Charlie to faint. His skin was on fire.

"Son, I'm going to take you to the hospital. Maybe something else is going on in there."

Fighting for the breath to reply, "No I don't want to go back to the hospital." They both remembered the night Bea died and Charlie's subsequent trip to the emergency room to fix his hand.

"I'm going to be okay. It's not like I'm spitting blood or anything. Let's get this off before I suffocate."

Vince examined the skin where the mustard plaster had been. "It's pretty red there."

"It's just from the crap in that thing that Nonna put on. I think she put in her secret ingredient. Check the paint thinner can. Don't light any matches."

Vince couldn't help but laugh, "Yeah, I remember when we were kids; she concocted some awful stuff for us to drink or stick up our noses. It's a wonder that we lived."

"Ow, ow," Charlie stifled a laugh and cried with the pain.

"Look, kiddo, I'll help you lie back in the bed. You start feeling dizzy or need to vomit, you call me. We'll check on you."

Vince examined his son again. "You probably can't call me because of the pain just to breath. I'll come back down in a few minutes."

Charlie dozed but woke when he heard Jody call upstairs. "Charlie's sleeping now, Daddy. I turned off the light. He's still in his jeans though."

He was barely awake when he heard Vince come down the stairs.

"It's okay, Jody I don't think he wants to move his body anytime too soon. Your brother is really beat up and I've got to do something. I'll go to school tomorrow and talk with the principal. It seems that Charlie's assistant principal, Mr. Greyer, left school today and nobody knows where he went."

Charlie lay still, dreading to move. He fell between troubled sleep, strange dreams about his mother, and wakefulness. He worried about his father who was probably alone at the kitchen table now. Nonna and Papa Bonarelli had gone to their home, Theresa and Bernie, were gone. Jody and Sam were in bed. He knew because the TV set was turned so low that the floor above him wasn't reverberating.

He woke in the dark early morning to an eerily silent house. It was an effort for him to pull a blanket over his cold skin. He listened as a car passed through the alley. As the sky lighted he heard the stairs squeak. Jody came into the room.

"Charlie, you awake?"

"Yes," He choked out the words.

"Daddy's asleep at the table. He hasn't been in his bed all night."

"Here, Jody, help me up."

She flipped on the light switch to see her older brother with the blanket up to his chin. She helped him as well as a seven-year old could. They both struggled to get him upright on the bed.

Charlie fought to stand up.

"A little wobbly, Charlie."

"Please get me a hot wash rag. I'll waddle into the bathroom and wash my face. Then we can go upstairs and see about, Dad."

* * *

"Daddy," Jody gently shook Vince. "We've got to get ready for school."

Vince rubbed his eyes and stretched. "Wow, have I got a neck-ache. The table makes a lousy Mattress. I better check on, Charlie."

Charlie leaned in the kitchen doorway. "I'm here . . . I can hardly move. Maybe a little heat will help. Where's the heating pad?"

"I'll take care of him, Jody. You get Sam up and get ready for school. Christ, Charlie, you look terrible. Come and sit down. I'll find the heating pad."

"I know where it is," Jody nodded, "I'll get it. Oh, and Aunt Mary is coming over for a little while this morning. Maybe she can help with Charlie."

"Dad, I'm going back to my room. I didn't sleep well either. I'm not sure that I'll be able to make it to school today."

"Okay, Son. I'll be down to check on you in a little while and bring the heating pad."

Charlie worked his way, gingerly, down the stairs thinking he should have stayed in the front room on the couch. He managed to get his clothes off, from the day before. The clothing lay where dropped as he labored to use the bathroom.

"Geez, it even smells cold down here." He heard the hum of the refrigerator in the laundry room as he walked slowly to his bed. He couldn't lie down, but leaned against the headboard. He turned and carefully sat on the bed, "Oomph."

Vince came downstairs with the heating pad in one hand while he massaged the kink in his neck with his other hand.

"This room is cold, Charlie. You should have stayed upstairs."

"I just need help to sit up and maybe I can stand. I've got to go again."

"Okay, let's try this." Vince leaned towards him. "Put your good arm around my neck." Vince put a hand in back of Charlie's head and one around his waist. "Up we go."

"Jesus," Charlie yelped with pain.

"Sorry . . . you think that you can walk? How the hell did you make it up the stairs a few minutes ago?"

"I don't know . . . just pulled on the hand rail. Yeah, I think I can walk."

Jody came into the room with Aunt Mary.

"What's that odor?" Mary wrinkled her nose. She looked around and saw the remains of the mustard-plaster hanging over the edge of Charlie's wastebasket. "Oh, one of Mama's remedies, whew that smells awful."

"Wait, Daddy. You'll hurt yourself. Lift from the knees."

"Jody, how do you know all of this stuff?" Mary asked. Jody started crying. "Mama, she told me and showed me in a Red Cross first aid book one time."

"It's okay honey." Mary kneeled down and put her arms around Jody. "It will get better, it just takes time."

Charlie grunted like a pig as Vince helped him up from the bed. He guided his son out of the room and into the bathroom.

"I'm okay. You can shut the door, Dad. I'll walk it out. I think I just have to work out the pain. I'd like to wash up and shave."

Vince closed the bathroom door, and called through. "I'm phoning Dr. Lewis."

Charlie turned on the shower hoping the hot water would help relieve the discomfort. It hurt to adjust the faucets with one good hand. He cracked the door to let the hot shower steam escape and heard Aunt Mary.

"Vince, you think Charlie's hurt worse than cracked ribs?"

"I don't know. He's going to the doctor today. I'm not having any argument from him either."

"Charlie," Vince called through the crack in the bathroom door, "Pound on the wall or make some noise when you're done. I'll help you upstairs after you clean up."

As he toweled off he heard Vince on the phone to the family doctor. It was difficult to use the towel and he waited for most of the water to evaporate before he tried to put on clothes.

He managed to pull a button-front shirt from a hanger in his closet. He draped it around himself the best that he could and shuffled towards his bathroom again.

"Charlie, how are you doing?" Jody had come down again to check on her brother. She carried a handful of bandaging.

"Get me some shorts please, Jody." He held the tails of his shirt over his scrotum.

She came back into the bathroom with a pair of clean under shorts and went out again. "Let me know when I can come in."

Charlie took several minutes to work his shorts on with on one hand. "Okay, you can come in now."

"Hold still while I change the dressing -- over here." She had stepped on top of the toilet seat to reach her brother's head.

Charlie heard the creaking of the toilet seat as Jody unwound his head bandage. "Is that you making that noise or is my head coming off?"

After Jody changed Charlie's dressing he shuffled to the stairs. Tears pooled in his eyes from the pain of climbing up the stairs again.

Aunt Mary muttered, "*L'asino ostinato.* "You were supposed to ask Vince to help you."

"Don't swear, Auntie?" Jody scolded.

Sam laughed.

Mary grimaced, "Look at this boy . . . like a truck hit him. Hurt ribs, wrapped hand, a bandage on his head -- what next?"

Vince asserted, "Charlie, I called Dr. Lewis' office. He's going to come over here."

The odor of frying bacon caused Charlie to retch.

Mary cracked eggs one-handed as she turned the bacon with the other. "Dr. Lewis is coming over here? Can you believe it? He's a dying breed – *mangiare.*" Mary took the pan from the stove, grease popping, eggs sizzling and burning in the grease.

Vince sipped his coffee. "Yes, he's still making house calls, but he's going to retire this year. That'll be the end of it."

"Charlie, breakfast?" Aunt Mary poured a cup of coffee for him. "Bobo thought he could drive you to school today, but it doesn't look like you'll be going."

"Just the coffee, thanks."

Vince left the kitchen to answer the ringing phone.

He came back into the kitchen. "Matt Grueber called to see how Charlie is. He thinks the two detectives on the girl's case probably want to talk to him again. They'll probably come over here."

Vince diverted his attention as the doorbell rang. "I'll get it, that's probably Dr. Lewis."

The doctor came into the kitchen carrying a small medical bag.

"Thanks for coming, Dr. Lewis." Vince took Dr. Lewis's coat and hat.

"Hello, Charlie. I understand that you're having some trouble with villains. Let's take a look."

His shirt already open, Charlie cringed as the doctor probed and felt along the rib cage for damage.

Mary shooed Sam and Jody out of the room to get them ready for school.

"Stick out your tongue. Okay, try to breathe without hurting too much. Hold it. Okay exhale."

The doctor's probing and the cold stethoscope made Charlie flinch. "Are you spitting any blood, Charlie?"

Charlie shook his head, no.

"I think there are a couple of cracked ribs. We can send you the hospital for X-rays, but I doubt that they will prove any different than my diagnosis. I don't see any evidence of internal bleeding. Not much you can do with ribs. I'm not sure that wrapping the torso does anything either. You just have to take it easy and hope that the pain doesn't double you over. There may be a problem sitting in class all day.

"I can give you some pain killers but then you won't be able to function. Try aspirin and rest. Ribs take time to heal.

"We don't have a sure-fire way to treat rib injuries. You get any swelling, try an ice pack. But then, cold seems to make the hurt worse. I'm not sure that heat works too well either, but alternate the ice and the heat if it makes you comfortable."

Dr. Lewis left. Mary served breakfast to Vince and cleaned the kitchen. "It seems to me that Mama's mustard plaster probably would do as well as anything."

"No," Charlie pleaded, "I'll see stars."

Vince laughed. "Mama's mustard plaster almost killed Charlie last night. We'll do the aspirin."

"I want to go to school."

"What, you can barely walk or talk." Vince said, "You're crazy. You can't go to school in your condition."

"School's got to be better than sitting around waiting for the healing." He breathed the words. "I'm better standing up than sitting or lying down."

The front door opened, Bobo came in.

"Hey, Charlie, you still alive?" Bobo looked his cousin over. "I've come out better after seven rounds with the Tasmanian Devil, you're being used for a trampoline."

"Hush, Bobo," Mary squeezed her son's ears, "you talk too much. You help Charlie while I get Jody and Sam going.

"Vince, what do you want for dinner? I'll get something out of the freezer. There's still stuff left from Bea's funeral."

Vince said, "No, I think I'll just bring home a pizza from Carl's."

"Yeah, pizza, and we can watch TV and eat." Sam smiled happily for the first time since his mother's passing. "Get some pop, too, Dad."

"Get orange and some lime, too, Daddy," Jody pleaded.

"Well, if all it takes is pizza and pop to make you kids laugh we'll do it more often." He picked Jody up and rubbed his face against her smooth cheeks.

"Geez, Daddy, you need to shave."

"Okay, your right. Charlie, you want anything special tonight? Son, are you going to be okay?" Vince touched Charlie's shoulder.

"Huh?"

"You okay?"

"Yeah, I'm just thinking. I've decided that I shouldn't go to school today. I want to go away for a while."

Everyone looked at one another and made a collective, "What are you talking about?"

Charlie wheezed, "I'm talking about getting out of harm's way, at least until I start feeling better."

"Hey what about school?" Bobo made a circling motion with his finger around his right ear.

"I'm not crazy, just surviving."

"What have you got in mind?"

Someone asked, "Hey, Theresa, when did you come in?"

"During the commotion; sounds like magpies in here, *cantare del gallo.*"

"So what have you got in mind, Charlie?" Vince asked.

"The cabin."

The family shook their heads with a resounding negative.

Vince said, "No. You can't possibly be there alone with those ribs. Are you nuts?"

27

Cabin in the Sky

Vince looked at Charlie, "The cabin -- have you lost your marbles? It's colder than hell up there this time of year. Did you forget that we boarded the windows and shut the water off for winter? It'll take the spring thaw to make it comfortable even if the snow level isn't too bad."

"Can I intervene here?" Theresa asked.

"Maybe that's not such a bad idea. There are two good wood-burning stoves, lots of comforters and I understand that the snow isn't bad up there right now. The frigid cold isn't really on us yet. We cut up a huge amount of firewood last year. You remember the contest about who could cut more wood? My muscles have finally stopped cramping. Bernie wants to see the mountains. I'll ask him to drive Charlie up there and spend a few days. I think it will give Bernie and Charlie a chance to get to know one another."

Charlie reminded himself to give Theresa a big thank you later. The cabin near Central City, originally a low log shack built during the mining boom was on an 80-acre plot of pine trees and rock. This was the Bonarelli family's retreat. Vince had found the place during one of his mining deals. The mountains around the compound were dotted with abandoned mines and broken-down structures. It looked like a mining play right out of old photos and historical documents. The property had improved over years of additions. A new bunk house with a shower was added the previous summer.

Sam almost derailed the idea. "The British drive on the wrong side of the road; Uncle Bernie will crash them," he beamed. "I saw it on television."

"What's he going to drive?" Vince asked Theresa.

"What about Bea's car?" She asked.

"Bea's car? Oh, I forgot about her car." Vince pondered the question. "Yeah I guess Charlie could use a car anyway. He's got his license and he can help take Jody and Sam around when they need to go places. I hadn't thought about it."

Charlie brightened, "Yeah, Mom's car drives like a truck anyway, and it always took those hills around the cabin better than anything."

Theresa saw Charlie's pain. "This kid needs some time to mend. Let me ask Bernie if he's interested in driving Charlie to the property. It's not too far. Bernie wants to think through the details for his business deal before he finishes his trip through the U.S. and back home to England anyway."

Aunt Mary gave Theresa a knowing look. "You seem to know Bernie's schedule pretty well."

It was all Aunt Theresa could do from turning red. "Don't read anything into it. I've been taxiing Bernie around the city for the last few days. Besides, he really likes it here. I think he would like to help us take care of Charlie while he mends."

*   *   *

It was two days later when they got on the road to the cabin. Vince arranged with Charlie's school for an excused absence. Charlie had second thoughts about Bernie's driving and wasn't sure that his uncle was ready to drive in the mountains yet.

"Blasted, lorry drivers, can't they move over a bit."

The shooting pains in his ribs reminded Charlie not to laugh.

"Why can't you Americans drive on the correct side of the road? This is all backwards — really."

226

"Don't hit anything, Uncle B, we'll have groceries and gear around our ears." Charlie pointed to the over-loaded back seat of the old Chevrolet sedan.

"I can't even see out of the bloody mirror here." Bernie squinted at the rearview mirror obstructed by the load in the back seat. "The side mirrors are tricky as well."

They drove in silence as Bernard familiarized himself with the car. After several miles up Clear Creek canyon, he relaxed some.

"What can you tell me about this rugged scenery and the water coming through this canyon, although somewhat impaired by the frozen spots?"

"Clear Creek, it's polluted," Charlie answered.

"Spoiled you say? It looks pristine from where we are viewing it."

Charlie gave his uncle some local history in slow doses, "Mine tailings and drainage from the old gold and silver mines up here," The reverberation inside his ribs still grated like a washboard.

"Gregory Gulch . . . up that way." He pointed in the general direction between Blackhawk and Central City. Gold discovered by a guy named . . . . "

"Gregory." Bernard smiled a toothy grin.

"In 1859," Charlie replied. "Watch the road Uncle B."

Bernie made a quick correction just before they collided with the back end of a truck as they rounded a curve. The jerking caused Charlie to double over.

"Bloody hell, that was a near miss, I'll keep my eyes on the road. Sorry lad, but do go on."

"We'll be turning soon, at Blackhawk," Charlie wheezed. "The largest remaining mining towns around here, Blackhawk and Central City, are mostly tourist places now. You know, restaurants, cotton candy, bars, and there's the Central City Opera House."

"Intriguing," Bernie concentrated on his driving as he spoke to the windshield, "You say an opera house, up here in the wilds?"

"Damn, Uncle B, it hurts to laugh. Not exactly the wilds any-more. There're still lots of holes in the ground, mostly abandoned mines, old homes in need of repair, and the tourist stuff.

"The mines and the mills ooze chemicals like cyanide and iron oxide from the spent tailings. It eventually ends up in the river."

Bernie made a face, "Cyanide in the river?"

Charlie loved the drama of the place and the history. "Yeah, the stuff used to process the crushed ore. See?" he pointed along the sides of the river, "All of that red iron oxide discoloration is mine and tailings run-off."

"Do tell me about the opera house."

Charlie's pains had subsided some after the last mishap with the truck. He felt like talking again. "The opera house, it's been around for a long time. Central City was a real boom town and the people wanted entertainment. The opera house has light op-era, and legitimate opera, you know like Puccini's *Tosca,* just last summer."

"*Tosca,* a little on the heavy side for me," Bernard grinned.

"Oh they do Gilbert and Sullivan, too."

"Really?" It sounded like "rally."

"Yeah, sure, you know," Charlie explained. "Like two years ago a whole slew of that English stuff."

"That English stuff?" Bernard laughed.

"Yeah, like, *The Mikado, Yeoman of the Guard, HMS Pinafore.*"

"*Pinafore,* you don't say?"

Bernie sang, "*I am the Captain of the Pinafore; and a right good captain too! You're very-very good, and be it understood, I command a right good crew, we're very-very good, and be it understood, He com-mands a right good crew.*"

Charlie watched his Uncle's facial expressions as he sang both the lead and the chorus.

"Enough, Uncle B, I'm hurting, I wheeze like an old bus."

"Sorry my boy, I didn't mean to carry on. We're at a fork in the road."

Charlie pointed, "Turn up that highway."

"Is this the scenic route? If it is, I appreciate it, interesting country." Bernie looked at a curve in the road.

"We'll take another scenic route on the way back." Charlie said. "I was thinking of the stretch between Central City and over the 'Oh My God' road to Idaho Springs. We're still in the hills now." He felt a relief at the same time exhilaration came over him whenever he traveled into the mountains. "It's not too cold and there's hardly any snow. The cabin may be a different story. You'll love it."

Bernie observed, "There are mounds of derelict mining equipment and dilapidated buildings between the village of Blackhawk and the road to Central City. Tarnished but very interesting, isn't it?"

"You digging this Uncle, B, a beat up old mining district -- full of stories."

"Is any mining still alive here?"

"The road, Uncle B, we're wandering again."

"Oh right." Bernie corrected his steering as a passing car honked.

"Yeah, there are a couple of operations." Charlie looked in his side mirror and barely made out a car turning from the main highway. "There are some mines, but mostly small operations. There's a mill over there still doing some custom work." He pointed to a jumble of rustic buildings where water drained from a pipe and smoke belched from a stack in one of the buildings.

Bernie navigated between the road that skirted tailing piles and decrepit buildings. "I do wish that I could see a little better. You think we can stop? Maybe I can make a dent in that lot." Bernie pointed at the load in the back seat.

"Sure, there's a pull-off up there." Charlie pointed to a graveled place at the side of the road.

Bernie pulled the car over, stopped the engine, and got out. The car Charlie had seen in the mirror drove slowly past. The driver looked straight ahead, a big hat pushed to the right side of his head. It seemed odd to Charlie that someone would pass them on this road without looking or to see if they needed help.

Charlie got out of the car and opened the back door. "I think I can put a sack of groceries under my legs up front. We don't have too far to go now anyway. I can stand the lump on the floor board for a little while.

"Yes, that might work. At the least I'll have a peep hole for the mirror."

There was the noise of rustling bags and boxes as Bernie repositioned the load.

Bernie opened the trunk. "Not a bit more room in the boot. How the devil did we get all of that stuff in there anyway?"

"I'll drive for a while, Uncle B. I think I can handle it. Do you mind that sack of groceries under your legs?"

"Right, I'm due to take a break. By the by, is there a loo around here?"

"What's a loo?"

Bernie saw Charlie's confusion. "Right, Jody calls it a potty."

"There." Charlie pointed up a nearby hill.

Bernard raised his eyebrows, "A tree? Right, I'll be back directly."

Charlie waited by the car.

Another car was parked on the side of the road, far enough ahead that it was barely visible. Charlie only saw it because of a reflection of light from the sun on a chrome bumper. He didn't think anything of it then and looked the other direction down the road.

"Car coming, Uncle B, better hustle, man."

"Good, feeling much better. We brought a thermos . . . could each use a cup of coffee now."

Charlie reached inside the car. "Sure, I put it on the front seat when we stopped, I'll get it."

"We might as well get along, Charlie. You're driving then. I'll try to pour the coffee without spilling it."

Charlie got in behind the wheel. The car he saw parked earlier was gone.

* * *

Charlie drove without too much pain. "It hurts only when I make a sharp turn. We'll be following the road through Central City, past the Glory Hole, an old mine in the mountain, and up towards Nevadaville."

They turned into a steep incline surrounded by few pine trees and rock outcroppings.

"Careful my boy, I'll have the coffee down my trousers."

"Yeah, this old car does a bump-and-grind. You'll be better to get rid of the coffee while we climb this hill. It looks like very little snow. We won't have to get the guy with the snow plow from Central City to clear us out."

Charlie drove with a grinding of gears and crunching of gravel under the tires, up the uneven stone and dirt road. They went through the little cluster of buildings named Nevadaville, more of a derelict than a town.

Bernie held onto a strap while Charlie drove over an uneven road as the car crawled upward. They continued to climb and then Charlie grunted as he made the sharp turn into the access road to the family property.

"A bit rugged, we are on safari here." Bernie bounced in his seat.

Charlie gripped the wheel with his right hand. His bandaged and now splinted left hand was almost useless. He ground his teeth with the pain.

"Whew, there's the cabin. A little snow, but we can stomp through it. Lots of firewood so we'll get the place heated up soon enough. Anyway we'll get the cabin livable before it gets dark." Charlie pulled up to the cabin and stopped the engine, "Man that was a gas."

"You okay, Charlie."
"Whew, yeah I'm cool."
"Cool? You should require another jacket?"
"No, Uncle B, it means everything is jolly good."
Bernard laughed, "Right. I'll start unloading this lot."

28

The Deputy

"How are you keeping, Charlie?" Bernard called as they worked to loosen and remove the covering from the front windows.

"We'll do some more tomorrow, Uncle B. My ribs won't take anymore pulling shutters today. Anyway, we need to get the cabin cozy and think about grub."

Bernard gave Charlie the gap tooth smile. "Grub -- of course -- food. I could go for a 'snack' as you call it. We have a lot of things in that ice chest. By the way, the ice will melt in the next two days, don't you think?"

Charlie sat down on a big rock by the front of the main cabin to rest his ribs. "Yeah, we'll put some snow around the food once the ice is gone. We're bringing up a refrigerator next summer. If we have to we'll go to Central City and buy a block of ice. Right now though, I'm thinking about putting some ice on my right arm. I pulled a muscle moving the firewood. The pain in his left wrist peaked. "I'm feeling this," he said as he rubbed the pained wrist.

"I think you've overcompensated with that right arm, an easy thing to do with the damage. Say what about electrical power, running water, the amenities, old boy?"

Charlie studied his uncle's grin as he reveled in the freshness of the mountains. They watched the clouds scud over the tall pines like sailboats on a high mountain lake.

"We have one line of electricity. We'll have some lights, but we may want to supplement with a couple of lanterns. We'll draw the power down some if we thaw out the big water tank in the back. We don't need to unbutton the bunk house though. The indoor toilet pipes are drained. We'll have to use the outhouse for a couple of days."

Bernard studied the outhouse and the building several yards away from the main cabin, "The bunkhouse, like the western movies. Right, I like the look of that horseshoe hanging above the door there." He pointed at the bunkhouse and affected a western twang. "We'll be moseying around the bunk house, play 'n checkers, and singing ballads about the cows. I say, Charlie, did those cowpunchers, as you Yanks call them, have girl friends? They seem mighty close to them cows, pardner." Bernard's laughter shook him with a force that might split the side of an old steam boiler.

"I can hear the harmonica now, but we better get the rest of the stuff in the cabin. It gets dark here early, Uncle B."

"Right," Bernard went to unload the gear from the back of the car.

"I'll be behind the cabin working on the woodpile."

"What about that pain, Charlie?"

"It's okay now."

Charlie walked slowly back to the immense stock of wood the family had laid in the previous summer. He picked gingerly at the wood as twinges of pain shot through his side as he brushed off snow.

He plodded along but stopped a moment to listen to a distant grinding of gears from the main road below the cabin's access road. He picked up some wood and walked out to where Bernard was unloading the gear. "Shouldn't be too many people up here this time of year, but every once in a while you'll hear noises from the road below. Mostly you'll hear the breeze through the pine trees and on sunny days and Gray Jays chattering," Charlie said as he went to the front of the cabin with the firewood.

Bernard studied the trees like he was scoping for the *Luftwaffe*. "Gray Jays?"

"We call them camp robbers. They are of the same family as Steller's or Blue Jays. Despite cold and snow, we're relatively temperate. They hang around here most of the year. They're aggressive, and they'll be eating out of your hand if you give them the slightest encouragement."

Bernie, intent on the trees now voiced, "Really?"

"Yeah, the birds around here are normally shy until they get used to you. Then you can't keep them away if you're outside with food. You hold up a piece of cheese and they'll almost take a finger off to get it."

Bernie looked into the trees as he walked around the compound. "You seem knowledgeable about the wildlife up here, Nephew." He brushed some old snow off of a picnic table between the main cabin and the bunkhouse. "Maybe we can eat a bite out here tomorrow if we get warming sun. I'd like to see those birds you've mentioned."

"Sure. For now though, I'll get the stove going and turn the heater on the water tank. We've got this big old galvanized steel tank in back that Dad brought from his business. We put a heater in it and traced the pipes with an electric heat wire. We only keep the tank half full from summer in case of freeze expansion. We'll remember to drain the pipe again when we leave."

"Right, the business." Bernie knew that Vince worked hard to stay afloat. "How is the business going these days? Second hand mining machinery, isn't that it?"

"Yeah mining equipment and other stuff." Charlie walked back to the firewood pile with his Uncle Bernie tagging along. "The business is struggling a little right now, I think. Dad doesn't talk about it too much, but he seems to worry a lot. He had a business partner, but he got sick and he had to leave the business.

Bernard picked up some firewood. "He's got his hands full, Charlie. It's fortunate that you have such a big and helpful family. We can help too even though we are some distance away."

Charlie thought, some distance away, like half-way around the world.

"So how long are you thinking about staying, Uncle B?" Charlie was curious about his uncle's music business if for no other reason than to make small talk.

"Oh I've made some contacts on your west coast, and I have some interesting people to meet around Memphis and Nashville, Tennessee . . . probably another month."

"Tennessee? Man, that's far out."

"I'm keen to meet those people in Tennessee. That's where your Elvis Presley fellow got started. He seems to be getting along."

"Yeah, I'd say that cat is getting along. I'll bet he's making more than $50,000 a year. What are you going to do back in England?"

"Oh, plotting to sell our lads on the future of the Rhythm and Blues venue. We've got some talent on the way up you know. We'll be breaking into the U.S. market in no time at all."

Charlie quipped, "Sure, Uncle B, It's only a one-half of the distance around the world. How're you going to get this English stuff back to the U.S.?"

"Oh yes, the English stuff. Remember your Central City Opera, and the recent Gilbert and Sullivan? We'll manage, I'm sure."

"Yeah, you have a point."

Bernard looked beyond Charlie through the woods and toward the access road. His expression prompted Charlie to turn around and look. "I say, Charlie, looks like a visitor."

They watched an old Jeep crunching up the rocky road to the cabin. Charlie recognized the army surplus vehicle from the summer.

"Yeah, it's the county deputy sheriff."

The Jeep stopped in front of the cabin where Charlie had put down the firewood. Bernard studied the vehicle a few moments before he put down the wood he carried.

The deputy got out of the Jeep and put on a cowboy hat.

Uncle B. whispered. "I thought these western types never took their hats or boots off."

Charlie laughed and thought that it probably sent a wrong message to the deputy.

The deputy walked over to Charlie and his uncle. "Good afternoon. I thought I saw some fresh tire tracks off of the road as I was passing through, you the property owner?" The deputy looked past Charlie. He figured that the adult must be in charge. "I'm Deputy Barnes."

Charlie answered before his uncle could reply. "My family owns the property. I'm Charlie Bonarelli."

"Oh, Bonarelli, yeah, I think I've met a Mr. Bonarelli last summer. Italian ain't it?" The deputy looked away to address Bernard. "And, you're?"

"Bernard Striker." Bernard held out his hand. "A beautiful day, officer, don't you agree?"

"You ain't from around here are you?" The deputy shook hands with the Englishman"

He gave the deputy a wide grin. "Right you are, just visiting my brother-in-law who lost his wife, my sister, recently. My nephew, Charlie and I are taking a short holiday while the boy heals."

Deputy Barnes turned to Charlie. He stared at his bandaged hands. "Oh, sorry about your mother, I take it?" The deputy shifted his eyes to Charlie's face. "It takes some time, the grieving I mean."

Charlie faltered, "Uh, right, thanks."

The deputy looked Charlie over again from head to toe. "Looks, like you're bandaged in a couple of places, accident maybe?"

"Uh, right, accident."

The deputy asked Charlie, "So how long you reckon, you'll be up here?"

Charlie, lost in thought, envisioned that the deputy would pull out a toothpick and pick his teeth. That would have made a good stereotype for his uncle to talk about.

Without waiting for Charlie's answer, Deputy Barnes turned and walked back to his Jeep. "Well, just checking, making sure that the owners are up here. We've had some break-ins over the last two weeks . . . just making sure that everything is okay." Deputy Barnes got back into his rattletrap.

Bernard patted the hood of the jeep like it was a tired pony. "Right, officer, good of you to give us a look. We'll be staying a few days. Best get back to unloading the gear."

The deputy started his Jeep. "Okay, nice to meet you folks. I'll see you later." He looked Charlie over one more time. "Carlo, you take care now." The deputy drove slowly back down the cabin access road to the main road.

"You think he was just checking on the cabin?" He knew my name, Carlo. What do you think, just a deputy doing his duty?"

Bernard thought about it. "What do you think, Charlie?"

"That's a rhetorical question. He was sent. I introduced myself as Charlie not Carlo. He knew us before he got here. I think this guy could give a damn whether we are breaking into the place or not."

"Sent? Oh, I understand. Maybe your Denver police keeping an eye on you; checking your whereabouts?" Bernard watched the Jeep trundle down the property's road. "Perhaps you're right." He turned to the open trunk of the car. "I'll get the rest of this lot out straight-away." He stopped to think a moment. "Or maybe there are some break-ins, and he's legit. George Raft would say 'legit,' wouldn't he? Or I guess I should have said, genuine. Well that's jolly . . . I mean cool, yes?"

Charlie laughed until the pain was too great and brought on coughing, "Right, cool." He wasn't sure that Uncle Bernie was wrong about the deputy's visit. He walked around the property while his uncle finished unloading.

Inside the cabin the stove crackled emitting a bit of acrid smoke until Charlie adjusted the damper. Fire light danced through the grates of the old wood stove as the room warmed.

"We've got a little wood heating stove in the backroom by the two bedrooms. I'll fire it up." The cabin took on warmth as the musty, closed cabin, smell went away.

"We can use our sleeping bags on the bunks back there. The mattresses will warm some from the stove."

They made a dinner of canned chili and bacon. Charlie's ribs hurt again from the work of getting the cabin in shape. As he found aspirin and a glass of water, he felt that his uncle wanted to chat about his music business. Charlie wanted rest. "I'm turning in early, Uncle B."

Bernard looked through a stack of books on a shelf. "Right, Charlie. I'll be along directly."

Charlie put an extra blanket over his sleeping bag and crawled in. He thought about the deputy sheriff's visit and the pried boards that he had found on the back of the bunkhouse. He also wondered about the footprints in the snow. He had seen that the window wasn't forced or broken. *Maybe we surprised somebody before they got into the bunkhouse?* He fell asleep thinking about his mother, Bea.

29

The Ruckus

Charlie woke with a start as something stirred in the front of the cabin. He heard his Uncle Bernie shout, "Devil," accompanied by heavy thumping.

Struggling to move, Charlie painfully pulled himself up by the bottom of the top bunk-bed. The room smelled faintly of old smoke and dying embers. Cold shot through his feet from the freezing floor, and he fought shivers as he stuck his head out of the door to see what the noise was about.

"Devil-be-damned."

Bernard hopped around the table in the middle of the room on one foot. He had switched on the single light in the big room and he held an unlit lantern in one hand.

"Eh, what's up Doc?"

Bernie wasn't in the mood for Charlie's cartoon humor. The look on his face and his jumping about on one foot told Charlie that his uncle had stubbed a toe.

Bernard grimaced. "I didn't see the bloody table leg for the shadows. You really should get more light in this place don't you think?"

Charlie coughed with the pain in his ribs as he squelched a laugh. "Sorry about that, Uncle B."

Bernard set the lantern on the table and limped to a couch along one wall as he flapped his arms to warm himself.

"Sit there a few minutes, Uncle B. I'll find a blanket for you and then get the stoves going again." Charlie stumbled to put his jeans and shoes on before shivers and pain in his ribs overcame him. He found the blanket for his uncle, and goaded the stove embers with fresh firewood. If the room wasn't warm yet at least the flickering flames and crackling wood in both stoves gave the cabin a cozy look. Bernie shivered in the blanket as Charlie put a fresh pot of water on the main wood stove.

The wood crackled blue and red with the flames as Charlie went back to the bunk room to put on more clothes. It took him awhile, with his bandaged hands and sore ribs, to pull a sweater over his head. "Now I know how a victim, skinned alive by the inquisition felt. Wow, I need to use the outhouse.

"I'll be back in a few minutes, Uncle B." He walked out into an inch of fresh snow. The sun peaked through clouds and the compound took on a Christmas card glow. "Not too bad." The temperature wasn't as frigid as the scene appeared. Charlie thought that the snow might melt by the afternoon. Favoring his sore ribs, he walked gingerly to the outhouse with its squeaking door and damp human smell not even disguised in the cold weather.

"You'd think that this shit smell would at least be dead from the damn cold." He said to himself as he dropped his jeans and undershorts. The feel of cold wood on his ass made him groan.

He heard something heavy hit the wooden door, and a muffled voice. "You're talking to yourself, Bonarelli."

Charlie couldn't identify if it was a man's or a woman's voice. He froze and thought that his heart either stopped or skipped a few beats. "Who's that?" He jumped up from the outhouse bench and pulled up his jeans. "Oh, that hurts. Who's there?" No answer. "Hey, who's there?" He pushed on the door but nothing gave.

The whack-whack-whack sound of gunfire and a slight splintering of wood from the outhouse door caused Charlie to rock back against the rough outhouse wall. Charlie guessed that the gun was probably a small caliber. The outhouse was a solid two-boards-thick of pine and cedar that stopped the bullets from penetrating with force. He cringed as splintered wood burst into the outhouse. A splinter hit him under one eye.

His brain stopped operating and his mouth opened, "God-damn-the-son-of-a-bitch-who-put-me-into-this-making-brick-a-brack-of-my-bones-and-fucking-with-my-head-because-I-was-unlucky-enough-to-find-a-jacked-up-body-in-a-park-good-samaritan-shit."

Then he heard hollering. Something dropped near the outhouse, then scraping and the door of the outhouse flew open. Charlie put his arms up in anticipation of what may come next.

"Are you all right, Charlie? I heard gunfire." Bernard was bare-footed and dressed only in his underwear, but he looked surprisingly warm now despite the fact a few minutes earlier he shivered with the cold. "I chased the bugger off -- probably never find him now. He high stepped it into the forest there." Bernie pointed.

"Who was it?" Charlie asked.

"I'm sorry, old man. I couldn't see him for the fur parka he was wearing, and a sort of pullover skiing mask, as well."

They stood in the cold snow while following the footprints into the woods with their eyes. "Let's get inside before you get pneumonia, Uncle B."

"Right, good idea, I'll freeze my arse off out here. But what the devil is going on?"

"I'm not sure, but some fuck just tried to waste me while I was trying to take a crap. Let's get back into the cabin and warm up. We'll come back here in a few minutes to figure this out."

Bernie gave Charlie a searching look. "Lad, I think someone is trying to take you out of the picture or wishes to warn you away from something. Yes, that's it. Whoever is meddling in your life is trying to frighten you away, but from what? Whoever it is could have killed you by now, perish the thought. We will need to get your deputy sheriff up here again."

Charlie thought about it as they went back into the cabin to warm up in front of the stove. "Yeah, we'll have to drive down to Central City and tell the Sheriff what's going on. But, let's get breakfast and see where the shooter came from."

He tried to act cool, in control, but inside he boiled hot and ready to shoot it out with whoever tried to kill him or scare him. Whoever it was succeeded in the scare, but Charlie still had to use the outhouse.

This time, he took down the old hunting rifle the family kept in the cabin. He found a half-full box of high-powered rifle cartridges and remembered the last time that he fired the gun the recoil bruised his shoulder. Charlie loaded the magazine but left the bolt open. In the outhouse, he dropped his pants, but this time he propped the door wide open. He took his arm out of a makeshift sling and sat with the rifle pointed outside.

Charlie hollered out of the open outhouse door. "Come on you miserable son-of-a-bitch, this time I'll shoot your ass off."

He tested the rifle against his shoulder and shoved the bolt home and chambered a round with a snap. He mouthed, "bang-bang-bang and zingada-up-your-ass." In his enthusiasm Charlie squeezed the trigger. The blast from the gun inside the outhouse deafened him. The recoil kicked and slammed his head on the back wall.

Bernard came running out again, this time with a chunk of firewood swinging from his right hand.

"Good Gawd, Charlie, what the devil is it this time?"

Charlie sat up from the back of the outhouse still grasping the rifle he used to balance himself. The rifle's recoil caused him to kick his jeans out the front of the outhouse and into the snow around the little building.

"Ouch-god-damn-it, my shoulder took the recoil all the way into my damaged right hand. There's a bell ringing in my head and my ribs are bursting into flame. I'm a stupid shit if there ever was one."

Bernard frowned. "Well, Charlie, my boy, you did put cartridges in that piece before you trotted out here. Were you firing at something in particular or just wanting to hear the roar?"

"Would you hand me my jeans, please." He pointed to the crumpled pants as he stood up and pulled on his underwear that hadn't quite cleared the front door of the outhouse.

Bernard grinned at his nephew. "Say old boy, why don't you finish the job. Here give me the rifle. I'll stand sentinel outside this domicile of excretion whilst you go about the rest of the job unmolested and undamaged."

A quiet Charlie felt his face burning. "Okay, but close the door, please." He sat for a few minutes.

"Everything alright in there . . . you have not gone down the rabbit hole have you?"

Charlie finished the job and opened the door.

"Thanks, Uncle B."

"Right, then let's get on down to the city of Central –- a strange name for a Colorado mountain town."

They secured the cabin, brushed light snow from the car and drove the few miles to Central City.

"This is a city again?" Bernard took in Central City as they came down the mountain, with one short sweep. "Isn't this just a group of shanties, a few houses and shops to be sure and of course the opera house, but who lives here?"

Charlie drove the main street to the Gilpin County Sheriff's office, a store front stuck between shops. The deputy's Jeep moldered on the street. Inside the office, Charlie thought about miner's boots scraping and kicking up the bare wood into the fine dust that pervaded the air. Sunlight illuminated the particles like fools-gold in a streambed.

The deputy sat behind a wooden desk with a newspaper spread out before him. What was left of his breakfast lay beside the news where syrup dripped from the plate onto the corner of the paper.

Deputy Barnes looked up as he turned a page then showed a slight irritation as the stuck together pages adhered to the desk top.

"Well, lookee-here, it's the boys from up top the mountain. Bonarelli ain't it, and Bernard? Good to see you this morning. What's up? Oh, want some coffee." Deputy Barnes pointed at a big blue enameled coffee pot on an electric hot plate. "She's done dripping. Cups and stuff right next to the pot."

"Right, don't mind if I do. What about you, Charlie? Bernard showed the big gap in his teeth that almost cost Deputy Barnes his composure.

"You know you look like that English Actor —- Thomas ain't it?

"Right you are, deputy. That's Terry Thomas. He's not quite as good looking as I am."

"Sure, of course not," Deputy Barnes laughed.

Charlie saw a back hallway leading to what he thought were other offices or a holding cell. Wanted posters and official documents looked out from bulletin boards around the room. A few chairs lined the wall across from the deputy's desk.

"So, how can I help you?"

Bernard poured two cups of coffee and stirred in some cream for himself.

Charlie and his uncle sat in front of the desk.

"The lad is troubled. Someone tried to shoot him this morning, or maybe just put a scare into him."

"Really?" Barnes lost interest in the paper. "You're okay then." He looked Charlie over. "What happened?"

Charlie told him everything as he remembered it, but left out the detail about firing the hunting rifle through the open outhouse door.

Deputy Barnes got up from behind his desk. "I suppose last night's snow is melting by now, but we need to take a look. I'll follow you up. We'll need to file a report. Excuse me a minute."

Barnes went into the back hall and another room where a big man came out with a pistol stuck in his belt at the front of his waist. Barnes remained behind in a small office.

Uncle Bernie whispered to Charlie. "Not what one would expect from a western lawman. I fancy a big six-shooter slung at the side and tied to his leg with a lariat."

"I believe a lariat would strangle his leg, Uncle B, but he might use a piece of rawhide instead."

"Right, rawhide, pardner," Bernie got up out of his chair as the big man approached.

The man looked at Charlie.

"You're the Bonarelli boy? You must be the uncle," he said to Bernard. "I'm Sheriff Kelso. Deputy Barnes says you think that somebody has been shooting at you. You're okay though?" He looked back to Charlie.

"There's no thinking about it, Sheriff. This little scratch here, under my right eye is where a splinter of wood from the outhouse door hit me in the face."

"Stand up, boy. Let's have a look at you."

Charlie could hear Deputy Barnes talking in the back. He must have been on the phone because he only heard Barnes' voice.

Charlie got out of his chair where the Sheriff stood about five feet from giving him a good look over. He smelled the Sir Walter Raleigh pipe tobacco emitting from Kelso's clothes, the same stuff Papa Bonarelli smoked.

Sheriff Kelso saw the bandages, and scrutinized Charlie's left arm in the sling. "Boy, you got things falling off of you or what? You're all patched up here and there."

Deputy Barnes came back into the room. "I just got off the phone with the big city boys, they want to come up and take a look with us."

Bernard asked, "Who would you be talking about, deputy? Somebody else involved with the ruckus?"

"Ruckus?" Deputy Barnes smiled, and Sheriff Kelso chuckled as he reached inside a vest pocket for his pipe. "Well, yes, I suppose you'd call it a ruckus with the boy here getting shot at, looking worse for wear."

Deputy Barnes held up a hand. "Anyway the Denver Police have some interest and want to meet us up at the Bonarelli cabin."

"What for?" Charlie bleated like a lamb knowing that the light at the end of the tunnel was probably the gleam from a meat hook.

Sheriff Kelso tapped his pipe on his hand. "Seems that you're involved in something, and from what I've heard you've got yourself a tar-baby . . . it's not letting you loose."

"So who's coming up here?" Charlie knew the answer already.

Deputy Barnes took a piece of paper out of his shirt pocket and read "Mickey and his partner, Brawley."

"Let's go, Uncle B. I can't wait to see those two Mike Hammer types."

Sheriff Kelso stopped them. "Tell you what, Bonarelli and Uncle Bernard here, why don't we all meet at your place. The Denver detectives should be up here in two hours. We'll see you about noon. Oh, and don't be doing a lot of walking around until we've had a chance to follow footprints and look for clues." He turned to Barnes. "Better bring Orley, too."

"Okay, Sheriff, good idea," Barnes' wide grin exposed a gold canine tooth.

"Who's Orley?" Charlie asked.

Deputy Barnes said, "See you up there at your place."

Bernard studied Sheriff Kelso and Deputy Barnes.

As they left the office, "Mutt and Jeff, two of my favorite American comic characters, you think they're capable, old boy?"

30

Bernard shook his nephew. "Lad, wake up."
Charlie had stretched out on the picnic table in front of the cabin. The sun's warmth made him doze like a cat behind a window. He dreamed of Karin, and woke with a lazy self-assured feeling that his parts were still working as his erection pressed against his jeans.

"The authorities are arriving." Bernard nodded towards the access road.

They heard noise from two different vehicles and recognized the grinding of gears from Deputy Barnes's Jeep. Charlie got off the table to see the vehicles driving toward them.

A newer Willys Wagon, with three people inside pulled up, "Gilpin County Sheriff," and a star emblem marked the side of the vehicle. Deputy Barnes's Jeep followed the Sheriff's car but passed by. There was somebody or something beside the deputy in the passenger's side.

The sheriff left his vehicle in front of the cabin and got out. The back doors opened. Denver detectives Mickey and Brawley got out dressed in sports jackets, ties and Fedoras.

"Hey, Bonarelli, nice to see you, kid." Mickey stretched as he looked Charlie and Bernard over. "Neat place you've got here -- must be nice to be a landowner."

"My father's place, we're just here for a few days."

249

Charlie watched Deputy Barnes's Jeep as he drove around the circle road in the compound like he was scouting for a lead. The head of a mangy dog, half German-Shepherd and half Heinz hound, Charlie thought, poked its head out. "What kind of mutt is that?"

"That's Orley." Sheriff Kelso acted as if Charlie had insulted his wife. "That's the best tracking dog I've ever seen."

Deputy Barnes drove back around the compound and stopped his Jeep behind the Sheriff's vehicle. He got out and opened the passenger door.

"Tracking dog? How's that dog going to track anything with the snow almost melted?" Charlie asked.

"Don't need no footprints, kid." Sheriff Kelso hitched up his pants. "This ain't no big deal for Orley." The dog came up and nuzzled the Sheriff. "This here's the dog to take scent and sniff the buggers out. Best dog for all these damned abandoned mines around here. We've got to find some explorer or misguided rock hound at least twice a year. Orley's the best there is."

"Everybody knows everybody. Let's get going." Deputy Barnes took the lead with Orley beside him. Mickey laughed as the dog came up and nuzzled Charlie hard with a big sniffing snout right between his legs.

"She does like the young men," Deputy Barnes let out a whoop. "Let's go girl."

"Girl? Orley's a female?" Charlie rubbed his balls where the dog had given him a rough nuzzling hit."

"That's Suzie Orley. We just call her Orley. C'mon girl, let's go find the bad guy." Deputy Barnes pulled Orley toward the back of the cabin. "Orley's a girl dog, named after a favorite crib gal, but don't never-mind about that, she's the girl that gets the job done. Let's go now. You say the shooter hit the outhouse a couple of times?"

Detective Mickey, in his enthusiasm, worked his way to the front of the group. Everybody saw Orley jam her muzzle right up the detective's ass. "Son of a bitch." He jumped and almost stumbled.

Charlie held a laugh as Mickey's partner, Brawley, affected an effeminate lisping voice, "A bit goosey?"

Mickey glared back at his partner.

"Let's go boys." Sheriff Kelso emphasized "boys" as he watched the dog pick up scent.

They all watched as Deputy Barnes and the dog worked together. "Settle down, Orley." The deputy pulled back on Orley's leash. "She's anxious, knows she's on the hunt. Everybody back off a bit and I'll have her sniff around the building. Looks like there's some prints in the wet ground still visible. Are those yours maybe?"

"No," Bernard interjected. "We didn't go chasing after the culprit who shot at Charlie. I warned my nephew about the advantage of the shooter having the trees and the rocks for cover if he wanted to snipe away. He also had the advantage of a good start before we got our bearings. I think he was out to put a scare into us. The shooter could have had us both if he was really intent on killing us."

"Good point, Mr. Bernie." Sheriff Kelso wheezed up behind the group as they formed around the outhouse.

Mickey made what he thought was a joke, "Brothers and sisters, we are all gathered here this morning to find the shit-house shooter." Detective Brawley laughed at Mickey who then made a wry face and grinned as he pulled a pack of cigarettes from his shirt pocket.

Charlie thought, Fuck you, Mickey Mouse, you weren't the one getting his ass shot at. Uncomfortable with Mickey and Brawley being here, he thought them inept, at best, and he wanted those two moronic Schmoos out of his life.

Sheriff Kelso wasn't amused either. Charlie felt that the Sheriff didn't like city cops sticking their noses in his business.

"This here is serious business. We don't like folks shooting at us. And by the way, don't light that cigarette --forest fire danger and all of that." Sheriff Kelso sucked on the empty pipe that hung from his mouth.

Mickey looked around at the wet ground and the snow patches. "It's forty degrees out here and wet as a duck's ass."

"I'm the Sheriff here and I say, there's danger —- then there's danger. And, tobacco smoke puts the dog off."

That's when Charlie came to appreciate Sheriff Kelso in a friendlier way. He thought, Sheriff you know a wise-ass cop when you see one.

Sheriff Kelso pointed at Orley. "Let her off the leash to do her sniffing around the outhouse and see if she picks up a trail. Look over here. That's a mitten or a glove, ain't it?" He picked up a heavy ski mitten from a low tree near the outhouse.

"Here, girl," Sheriff Kelso held out the mitten for Orley to sniff. "The shooter probably took this off to fire his rifle. Here's some shell casings, too . . . 22-caliber, long rifle, looks like."

They all watched Orley sniff the mitten and the shell casings in Sheriff Kelso's hand. "Good girl. Find."

Everybody followed the dog, with her nose to the ground, as she scoured the trail and paced quickly into the woods. Orley picked up a good scent as she scurried through pine trees and rock outcroppings.

Charlie heard Mickey and Brawley huffing to keep up. His ribs pained sharply from the jarring through rough terrain.

They followed Orley for ten minutes. Charlie was thankful when Sheriff Kelso asked Deputy Barnes to put Orley on a leash before they lost her.

This gave them pause for about twenty-seconds. Bernard wiped his forehead. "Lad, this brisk walk does warm the body and stretch the lungs. Unaccustomed to this altitude, I wish to rest for a few minutes." Mickey and Brawley huffed up behind them and sat on a rock outcropping.

"This has got to be one strong guy if he's kicking through these mountains like a damned goat." Brawley took of his hat and fanned his face. "It's not even warm out here yet."

"Let's go, boys. Orley is hot to trot." Deputy Barnes took off as the dog tugged hard.

Charlie's ribs hurt like fire. He wasn't in any better shape than his uncle and he felt light-headed. They all went down a small incline. Charlie watched as a bird flew overhead. He wished he were that bird as Orley let out a bark.

Sheriff Kelso called back, "We still on your property, Bonarelli?"

"I'm sure we're out of our boundary, Sheriff. Some slashed trees back there, about one-hundred yards, is where our property ends. There's an open mine tunnel around here. We avoid it when we're hiking around in the summer."

"Sheriff, it looks like Orley found something." Deputy Barnes called from around a big rock formation. "We've got us an open tunnel here. Fresh footprints all around, whoever was here probably skedaddled. See those prints leading away from the tunnel. They look real fresh. Wait, Orley wants to go in. I've got a flashlight."

Sheriff Kelso called out, "I've got my flashlight, too. Tread real careful and don't go in any farther than the footprints lead. You make sure she's on the leash now. Don't want to be losing her down no shaft."

"We'll go in, too," Mickey said as he and Brawley came out of the woods and spotted the tunnel.

Sheriff Kelso held up a hand. The empty pipe danced up and down in his mouth. "Not a chance, detectives. Barnes knows what to do in there. We're looking for somebody already. We don't need no rescue effort for two bumbles that fell down a mine shaft today."

Charlie gloated as the sting of Sheriff Kelso's rebuke caused the faces of the two city detectives to color.

Bernard took Charlie aside. "Now there's an old dear, our Sheriff Kelso. Let's watch how the experts do this."

The four waited while the dog led Deputy Barnes and Sheriff Kelso into the abandoned mine shaft.

Charlie and his uncle stood while Mickey and Brawley sat on an old plank bench near the mine entrance.

"I say, detectives, what is your interest in all of this? You must think that whoever tried to shoot down the outbuilding has something to do with Charlie?"

A steamed Mickey didn't like the way his day was going. He didn't answer.

Bernard asked again. "Well, detectives, we would like to know what you are doing here?"

Brawley answered, "We knew you guys were headed up here. We asked the Sheriff to keep an eye on Charlie. We think this is the same guy that's chasing him around his high school, Greyer's boy, Willie Burris."

Charlie didn't like the answer. "Burris is still on the loose? I thought you would've caught him by now. What was all of that show at school the other day when the guy flew out of the janitor's closet and you cops chased him through the neighborhood? The other thing, why is Willie Burris so interested in me? Hey, you think that maybe he thinks that I had something to do with that girl's death? What's the girl to him?" Suddenly the light went on in his brain.

"That's it —- it's the girlfriend. The one he skipped the state with two years ago when they went on that shoot-em-up in, where was that -- California? Here all along, I'm thinking Burris was hiding in that car, and that maybe he killed the girl.

"Well, what is it? Or are you guys going to keep messing with me? I'm really tired of this shit and you two -- *detectives*? You're using me for bait." Charlie picked up rocks, pieces of wood, and any debris that he could hurl at Mickey and Brawley.

"Hold-it, Bonarelli." Brawley held up his hands and ducked the missiles the Charlie threw without any real purpose other than to vent his anger.

"Nasty-mother-fuckers-go-shit-up-a-tree." Charlie picked up a large stone and readied it to hurl at Mickey. His ribs screamed in pain and brought tears to his eyes.

Mickey pulled out his service revolver as Bernard stepped between the two of them and grabbed the rock. He took the rock out of Charlie's hand and dropped it.

"Lad, the copper wants to shoot you, and I'm afraid he would get away with self-defense." He turned to Mickey who still had the revolver pointed at Charlie. "Detective, put the revolver away before I come over and stick it up your arse."

Orley barked at the tunnel mouth.

"Hey, what the hell are you doing, Detective?" Sheriff Kelso held his gun, having kept it pointed ahead of him in the tunnel. He stopped and raised the pistol, pointing it towards the two detectives. "Bonarelli and the gentleman are unarmed. What the hell's going on here?"

Mickey stood like stone, his eyes bearing on Bernard and Charlie like a machine.

"Put it away, Detective. You're on my shooting range now." Orley barked and pulled, while Deputy Barnes held two hands on the dog's leash.

"Orley likes to bite threats. You want to put that piece away now?"

"Mickey," Brawley, caught in a decision to help Mickey or get out of the way, pleaded, "C'mon, Robert, put it away."

Charlie's life flashed through his mind before Mickey relaxed his stance. The detective lowered his gun, putting it back into a shoulder holster.

Sheriff Kelso, not so eager, slowly lowered his gun. "Okay, then, we'll sort this out later. The guy's gone. There's a road over there," he pointed his gun a trail. "Anybody investigate those tire tracks while we were inside the mine? Hell no, you guys just sat on your ass playing with the gun. Well, whoever was shooting at Bonarelli is long gone no doubt." Sheriff Kelso pushed his gun into the front of his belt. "Let's get back to the cabin."

Charlie's eruption brought the pain in his ribs to full heat. He barely breathed. "Uncle, B," he wheezed, "I need to rest for a few minutes."

"You men, you don't need us anymore. The lad needs to rest his ribs. Sheriff, you can sort out the problem here with Detectives Mickey and Brawley. We'll be at the cabin if you need to come back. I'm suggesting to my nephew that we go back to Denver in the morning. This isn't a safe haven either."

Sheriff Kelso thought on Bernard's proposal. "You know your way back. I think that the shooter left but we'll get my vehicle and come back around this way. This road leads to other mines. It's a popular 4-wheel drive area in summer. Yeah, I think we can do that. Anyway, I'll take the two city fellows back to my office and their car. I'll be back in about two hours. Don't leave without seeing me first."

31

"Oh My God"

They were almost packed by the time Sheriff Kelso stopped by the next morning. Bernard shuttered the front windows while Charlie took their extra gear to the bunkhouse.

"You boys about ready to leave, I see. Didn't find nothing but tire tracks when we went back up that road from yesterday morning; got the two detectives back on their way to Denver. You'll be seeing them again I'm sorry to say -- you coming back through Central City?"

Charlie had promised Bernard another scenic route back to Denver. "We're going over the top. I want to point out some historical sites to Uncle Bernie."

"You be careful there, Bonarelli. It ain't named 'Oh-My-God-Road,' for nothing. That road was closed for snow a while back. I think the county's fixed her since about two days ago. Still, be driving real close to the good side now. I'll be calling the Clear Creek County Sheriff over in Georgetown when I get back to the office. He should have a deputy in Idaho Springs by the time you get down. We'll want to know that you got down okay. When you leaving?"

"We'll be going in about thirty minutes. Uh, Sheriff, about yesterday morning, thanks."

Sheriff Kelso winked. "We're not too keen on them cops from Denver coming up here and making like they're taking over from us bumpkins. We manage. Like I said, Bonarelli, you be real careful driving down Virginia Canyon, she's tricky when dry and deadly when wet. Oh, and those tire tracks from that old mine site, they're headed your way, and out of our county. I suspect the guy is gone by now, but watch out."

Charlie drove them out of the family compound. "We're okay, Uncle Bernie. Now hold on to your seat. You're going to see some trees -- from the top down." He kept the car in second gear as they left the cabin access road and headed south between two mountains down toward the ghost town of Nevadaville and the Glory Hole mine before they made the turn to the graveled highway to Idaho Springs.

"Lad, what about some of these mines around here, any chance that I might take some snap shots?"

"At this time of year with the road barely open, Uncle B, we'll not be taking any detours. There are lots of mine access roads up here but you need a Jeep to get in during the best of times."

Snow was piled up on the high sides of the road making for one lane traffic in some spots. Over the edge they saw where the snow was intentionally plowed over to make room for more snow. Farther down in the valley, pine trees poked through snow and occasional clear spots in the terrain.

Charlie inched the car down the twisting decline through Virginia Canyon to Idaho Springs. He glanced at his uncle who stared through the side window. Once in a while Bernard averted his eyes to the windshield, and gripped the front seat with both hands. Charlie held tightly onto the steering wheel only letting go to change to a lower gear if he felt the car rolling too fast.

Bernard reacted to the scenery, "Yes, 'O-My-God', is quite appropriate."

"Don't worry, Uncle B . . ." Charlie didn't finish his thought. He looked through the rearview mirror as an old beater of a car rushed down the road they had just covered. *Madonna, il bastardo--pazzo?*"

"What is it, Charlie?"

Bernard turned his head and saw the car, too. "That bloody auto is out of control. Do you think we can find a spot to pull over before we impact?" He barely got the words out when they took a hit.

Charlie held onto the wheel. He forgot about the jarring pain in his ribs as the car behind them backed off and banged into them again. Their car fish-tailed over a wet patch of graveled road, Charlie fought for control as they headed for the edge of a steep decline. Adrenalin pumped through Charlie and beads of sweat felt cold on his face. The pain in his hands weakened his grip on the steering wheel.

"Bloody hell," Bernard seeing Charlie's trouble grabbed the wheel with his left hand and helped guide the car out of the soft snow at the edge.

The car behind them shot past and that was the end of it, they thought.

"Good God, Charlie. What possessed that devil to come charging pell-mell? At the first impact I thought maybe an auto out of control. The intentional second hit told me differently. Are we going to be all right? Can you drive? Can we turn back and go through Central City again?"

Charlie had stopped the car in the middle of the road. He started to shake but then got control by griping the steering wheel almost breaking it from the column.

"Easy, lad, we are going to be okay, I think. Let's take it very easy down the road. It appears there is no place to turn around and reverse our direction. Is this road much the same the rest of the way down?

"Yeah, and then some," Charlie concentrated.

Bernard gave another, "Bloody hell, I guess we are in it now. Can we slowly maneuver down this nightmare? Perhaps the bugger is gone and we may survive."

Wide-eyed and alert for the smallest movement or detail, Charlie sat for another minute then started down the twisting mountain road. He flinched when a sitting squirrel, on a nearby snow bank, flicked its tail.

"Would it be better if I drove?" The tone in Bernard's voice told Charlie that he had better stay behind the wheel.

"No, I'll manage. Look, there are tire tracks over the bank of the road." Fearing to let go of the wheel, he nodded to a fresh break in the piled snow at the edge of the road. Something went through and over the edge."

Bernard strained to see. "Right, there is a breach through that snow bank. Perhaps we should stop, may be something down there."

"Oh, yeah, there's something down there alright. If it's the car that tried to hit us I hope the driver broke his fucking neck." Reluctantly, Charlie slowed and then stopped.

Surprising himself, Charlie didn't wobble or go over the edge once he got out of the car. The brisk mountain air helped as he carefully walked to the breach. Uncle Bernie looked intently over the edge.

"I can't see a thing, Charlie. It looks like whatever it is an auto no doubt, went over and caused a snow slide, perhaps covering it."

"Yeah, like maybe a small avalanche. Killed the bastard, too, I hope."

"Really, Charlie, we don't know that it was the auto that tried to hit us now, do we?"

"Who else could it have possibly been? It's like a car comes out of nowhere and tries to push us over the edge. Then there's this fresh break and a snow slide, like just now. It wasn't Jesus on skis, Uncle B."

"Right, I suppose we better get down to the next town and inform the authorities. We are out of Sheriff Kelso's county, yes?"

"Yeah, we're in Clear Creek County now. The county seat's up in Georgetown, but I'm not driving up there to report this. We'll find somebody with a badge in Idaho Springs. Anyway, Sheriff Kelso said he was calling the Clear Creek County Sheriff for someone to meet us on the bottom.

Instead of somebody with a badge, they almost ran head on into a county snow plow. The snow plow driver stopped, backed up and pushed a clearing for the plow-truck to pull into for them to pass.

The driver got out, seeing that they weren't trying to get around him, but to talk to him. "You fellows really want to go down this road today. It's a little tricky down near that hairpin curve."

Charlie was glad, for once, to see some kind of authority. "Hey, somebody just tried to run us off the road. We think that whoever it was went over the edge up there about a mile back. We didn't see a car for the snow, but there's probably a car over the side up there." Charlie and his uncle relaxed now that someone else was on the road and they could talk to without the thought of being hijacked.

"Oh, oh, I knew something like this was going to happen at least once from the last storm. I'll call it in on my radio."

"Whoever it was tried to push us over. Better call the Sheriff, too."

The snow plow driver sat in his truck cab with the radio microphone in his hand, Charlie and Bernard listening.

"My boss got a hold of the Clear Creek County Sheriff. They're on their way up now. They want us to meet them where you say the car went over."

"Oh yeah, I'm going to back up a mile where the son-of-a-bitch tried to push us over?"

The snow plow driver said, "Never mind that. I'll back my plow up out of this spot and you pull your car into here. We'll all go up in the plow."

The driver, whose name was Parker, made room in the truck cab for them among a shovel, a lunch box and a big rock lying on the floor of the cab.

"Mr. Parker, you usually drive about the mountains with a rock as your companion?" Bernard smiled wide. The sight of big gap in his teeth almost made the driver lose control.

"Say, you're not that British actor are you?"

"Certainly not," Uncle Bernie said. "I'm the handsome one. He's just plain."

Parker wanted to talk. "Yeah, the wife and I, we're into those artsy movies; we like the Brit stuff. A big deal for us is to drive down to Denver and go to the movies and grab a burger. We saw "*Green Man*" a few months ago. The wife is up for seeing "*Blue Murder at St. Tinian's*," she loves Terry Thomas."

It's a rip," and Bernard gave Mr. Parker a short synopsis of Thomas's latest film, "I won't give the end away for Mr. Parker here."

Charlie interrupted, "There's the breakthrough." He pointed to the breach in the snow.

Parker stopped the plow truck. "The sheriffs in both counties will close off the approaches. We've done this before."

The three of them got out of the plow truck and walked to the edge where the car had disappeared.

"We'll try to get whoever is down there out, but we'll probably have to ask the alpine rescue team to go into that mess. That's a long way into a nook-and-cranny. If this is what I think it is, we probably won't find anything until the spring thaw."

"What's that Mr. Parker?" Bernard held onto a tree, and leaned close, too close Charlie thought, to the side hoping to get a good look.

Parker warned Bernard. "Be careful there, Mr. Striker or you'll disappear yourself. Once down there in that deep snow, you're stuck. Better wait for the guys with the ropes."

They heard the grinding of gears coming up the mountain road and a lower geared vehicle coming from up the top where they had driven from.

"It's the boys with the rescue gear." Mr. Parker got back into his truck. "You fellows can stand there while I make room for the others."

Parker started his truck to plow out several yards above the accident site. They caught a glimpse of Sheriff Kelso's vehicle coming down the road and pulling to a stop while Parker pushed out a space for them to park.

They watched as Sheriff Kelso, Deputy Barnes, and Orley walked down toward them.

Two more vehicles, marked as "Clear Creek County Sheriff" pulled to a stop down the hill from them. Several men got out and trudged up the road towards the breach. They also heard the low grinding of a large laboring truck down the road from where the Clear Creek County Sheriff had come from.

A big man with a big gun strapped to his side came up to Charlie and Bernard.

"Whew, that's a haul. Hey there's Kelso and Barnes from Gilpin. Looks like Orley, too. Hey, Orley." The dog came up panting and looking to have his ears scratched by the Clear Creek County Sheriff.

Charlie introduced himself and Bernard to the Sheriff. He pointed to where they thought a vehicle had gone over.

"Well damn. Looks like a job for the rescue people. We'll wait for the truck." The Sheriff took off a big hat and wiped his brow with the sleeve of his jacket. "Gets damn warm up here when the sun hits just right, okay boys, lets . . . ," He hadn't finished his thought when a big alpine rescue truck pulled up behind the other vehicles, and stopped.

They saw a shaggy, graying, red-headed driver. He hollered out of his window, "What's up, Sheriff?" Just then another truck marked U.S. Forest Serviced pulled up near the alpine rescue.

32

Rescue?

The ex-military 4x4 truck stopped on the incline behind the Clear Creek County Sheriff. Another man got out of the passenger side and came over to the group clustered around where the car had gone over the edge.

"Howdy, Sheriff, I understand there's a car over the side; you can't reach it from below?"

"Hey, Maxwell, right over the side here," he pointed, "According to these two witnesses, they didn't actually see the vehicle go over -- says someone tried to run them off of the road, probably the same vehicle. Couldn't correct and went right over the side."

Maxwell turned to the snow plow operator, "Been plowing up here quite a bit, have you, Mr. Parker?" The rescue worker seemed to know everybody.

"Sure, pushing snow for the last couple of days right over the edge. I imagine any vehicle that has gone over has got itself buried pretty good. From up here looks like a big slide followed the car down. She's buried alright."

Maxwell made some mental calculations. "We'll need some room here for the winch truck. Mr. Parker, can you plow out around here without pushing more snow down the mountain?"

Charlie and his uncle listened as Maxell instructed everyone to move their vehicles up and down the road so the plow could work. Mr. Parker took a couple of swipes with his plow truck and the rescue truck pulled

265

into position. The U.S. Forrest drove within ten-yards behind the other parked vehicles. The narrow and steep mountain road was cluttered with activity as the rescue workers prepared to make a way over the side.

The winch from the front of the rescue vehicle whined as cable played out. Maxwell and another rescue worker rigged up a small double-ended aluminum boat-like sled and prepared to go over the side. Maxwell got into the sled. "I'll go down first. No sense in putting us all down there. No room to work probably, and maybe even tip the sled in the snow. Give me one of those long bamboo poles off the back of the truck. Hand me the walkie-talkie." As Maxwell belted himself in the sled someone handed to him a big military walkie-talkie. "Okay, let her down—easy-now."

The group stood around the edge of the mountain road watching the winch cable dig into the snow as the device went over the side and down.

Charlie asked how stable the sled was. "You think he's going to keep that thing from tipping?"

The Clear Creek County Sheriff grunted. "It's tricky, but Maxwell will keep her going steady. Is anybody listening for that walkie-talkie?"

One of the rescue workers said as he watched the sled descend, "He's still in sight, Sheriff. He's signaling to be let down lower." He signaled to a man in the cab of the winch truck to keep it steady. "We're controlling the descent with the winch, otherwise he'd slide to the bottom. Okay, he's out of sight." The man clicked on his walkie-talkie, "Maxwell, you doing okay?"

Two audible clicks and arm signals from the rescue worker hanging over the edge trying to guide the now invisible Maxwell. Then the rescue worker signaled the man in the truck cab to slow the descent, and then a stop signal.

The walkie-talkie squelched. The rescue worker listened, and then motioned for the Clear Creek County Sheriff. Maxwell says he's found a car . . . mostly buried. He's probing with the pole."

The group stood around in silence. Sheriff Kelso puffed on his pipe as the dog, Orley, sat patiently by the sheriff then suddenly put its head in the air and let out a yelp.

"Orley's trying to tell us something." Sheriff Kelso watched closely as Orley sniffed the ground around the area where the vehicle had gone over. The dog sniffed and then worked its way back to the other side of the road, but stopped at a recently plowed snow bank.

Sheriff Kelso hollered. "Hey, you fellows see any footprints around the edge where the car went over . . . that is, before you people tracked up the place with your own prints?"

Bernard's face lit-up like a coal-oil lantern. "Good Lord, Charlie. Do you suppose the bugger bailed before the car went over the edge? I believe that is what our Sheriff Kelso is alluding to."

Before they could speculate, Sheriff Kelso and Orley had worked their way around the end of the plowed snow and partially up the side of the mountain.

"We've got prints here. I'll bet dimes to donuts that this is the guy we tried to find earlier up at Bonarelli's place. Orley still has that scent in her oily-factory."

Bernard grimaced, "'Oily factory?' Do you mean olfactory, Sheriff Kelso? You think the man's scent, from our earlier jaunt, is embedded?"

"Scent -- of course the scent, right there in Orley's nose brain." Sheriff Kelso tapped his own nose for emphasis. "Our driver is up here, not down the mountain. Get Maxwell back up, he's wasting his time. You can get that vehicle after the spring thaw."

Everyone except the rescue truck workers struggled through snow to assemble up the hill with Sheriff Kelso and Orley.

"Now looka-here, ya can't be stomp 'n all over the place and expect Orley to find our man. If the driver is to be found, my deputy and Orley will smell him out."

Orley strained at her leash and let out a yelp.

"C'mon, Orley."

"Now you wait a minute, Sheriff Kelso." The Clear Creek County Sheriff spoke. "This here's my jurisdiction. We appreciate your co-operation, the dog and all, but this here's our job now. You want to join in, fine, we can use your dog, but I'm leading the search here now. Uh, what are we looking for?"

Bernard took Charlie aside. "I sense some dissent between the officials."

"I hope the trail doesn't get cold while they argue over whose pine tree belongs to whom, Uncle B."

"Right. Charlie, didn't those two U.S. Forest Service chaps arrive in a truck?" The Englishman pointed at the two forest officers standing by the group arguing over who would follow Orley.

"Yeah, that's them, Uncle B."

"Then why do you suppose their vehicle is gone missing?"

Charlie looked down the road where the Forest Service parked their truck. It was gone. He caught the flash from the sun on glass, through the trees, of a vehicle moving down the road.

"I say, gentlemen." Bernard interrupted the conclave of officials. "Is anyone missing a vehicle?"

One of the forest rangers stared to where he had parked the truck. "Jack, you move the truck?"

"No."

"Son-a-fa-bitch."

The two U.S. Forest Service rangers stumbled from the side of the mountain down to the road and ran towards where their truck had been parked.

The rescue truck pulled the sled and Maxwell back from the edge. The loud grinding noise from the winch had probably masked any sound from the U.S. Forest Service truck. The winch stopped and Maxwell jumped out of the sled.

One of the forest rangers ran down the road while the other one ran back to the group motioning for them to come down from the mountain.

Bernard and Charlie already decided that trudging up a mountain in knee-deep snow was futile. The ranger ran up past them and hollered up the mountain.

"The truck is gone. Somebody has taken off with our truck. Can you radio down the mountain . . . you got a road block there or something keeping traffic out of here for now?"

Sheriff Kelso beamed. "See, it's like I told you, the guy got away. He's got the truck and skeeee-daddled. We're wasting our time here. C'mon Orley, let's get down this damn hill."

The group came down to the road. The Clear Creek County Sheriff radioed to his officers below to watch out for the U.S. Forest truck coming down, to stop it and hold the driver.

Sheriff Kelso refilled his pipe with tobacco. "Nice work fella's. Now we can all go back to the office with our tails between our legs."

Mr. Parker walked away. "Well I guess I better get going, got to finish before noon."

Charlie saw that Mr. Parker might choke on his laughter, but he composed himself and got into his truck.

"Guess you don't need us anymore." Maxwell smiled. "We'll secure and be getting back to our jobs. See you later."

"C'mon, Jack, you can ride with us back to town. We'll pick up your guy . . . find the truck at the bottom no doubt."

Just then, the Clear Creek County Sheriff's radio crackled and they heard a voice. "Sheriff, we hear the truck, and we're ready for him."

"Okay, 10-4, you catch that guy, we'll be right down."

The Clear Creek County Sheriff dropped Charlie and Bernard at their car. Charlie drove behind the sheriff's car down the mountain, but had to slow down. He wasn't as confident as the Sheriff who hurried down as fast as his vehicle could handle the road. By the time they caught up with the Sheriff's car the U.S. Forest truck was stopped and surrounded by the Sheriff and his deputies.

Charlie stopped the car a few yards back from the group. The Forest Service vehicle driver's door was open and the truck was empty.

Charlie and his uncle got out and walked near the group of men surrounding the truck, their weapons drawn.

"Where the hell's the driver?" The Sheriff fumed. "Are you telling me that the driver of this vehicle got away from you guys -- bunch of goddamned amateurs. Well, damn-it, find some footprints or something. The guy can't have gotten far for Christ's sake. Let's go."

"Sheriff Wickee." One of the deputies held something. "Found this, looks like a neck scarf or something."

This was the first time Charlie or his uncle had heard this Sheriff's name.

The Sheriff took the item and looked it over carefully. "scarp . . . pink?" Our guy was wearing a pink neck scarf? Where'd you find this . . . some kinda faggot stole the truck?"

"Charlie, I believe this is the first time that I've heard the Sheriff's name, 'Wickee' is it?"

"He's known as Wickee-Wackee around here. But, you didn't hear it from me." Maxwell stood behind them watching the Sheriff holding the pink scarf with his deputies looking on.

Bernard turned towards, Maxwell. "Looks like a circle of serious crime investigation to me."

Maxwell hollered towards the Sheriff. "Maybe we can get by you guys if it's okay with you. We need to get back to our jobs."

Sheriff, Wickee glared at Maxwell. "Hold your damn horses, Maxwell. We've got to get this thing off the road, but we're going to fingerprint the interior before we move this truck. If you can get around us, okay, otherwise you're stuck until we finish."

The Sheriff turned to one of his deputy's. Bobby, you've got the kit don't you? Better get on it. Take a couple of photos too. The rest of you guys fan out and find this person, we're wasting time."

33

Close-and-Personal

Bernard and Charlie talked about the morning's craziness, "Charlie, do you suppose Sheriff Wickee and his bunch can find the culprit?"

"That's a rhetorical question, Uncle B. If you really want an answer, I'd guess Sheriff Wickee couldn't find his ass with both of his hands."

"Quite, I can't but chuckle over my recollection of the two county sheriffs we had the good fortune to meet. A script writer who I know is dying for some color to add to his modern western. My friend is an Italian, living in London . . . never set foot in the States. He will simply love it when I tell him the story of Sheriffs Kelso and Wickee. Picture these modern frontier peace-officers purging the mountains of bad hombres.

Say, Charlie, you've become introspective all of a sudden?"

"Yeah, I'm thinking about that pink neck scarf. I only caught a glimpse of it in Sheriff Wickee's hand. I've seen one like it. I'm trying to place it . . . yeah; I think it was at school. Some girl I know, I think."

"A coincidence, Charlie?"

"Has to be, but why would a guy wear a pink scarf?"

"Unless it's not a guy?"

271

"Not a guy? Sure, it's got to be a guy, but the scarf? Anyway, we'll be back in Denver soon. Take a look at the city once we get over this hill, Uncle B., it's really cool."

Bernard made a wide gesture with his hands. "The Queen City of the Plains; I read that in the hotel brochure."

"Yeah, that's right, Uncle B. I hope that whoever is after me, doesn't make it back to see the Queen . . . you know, you may have something there . . . about the guy not being a guy but maybe a chick."

Bernard replied, "She would have to be rather rugged. I wouldn't want to meet a girl like that under dark circumstances. A regular killer no doubt or a person who wants to appear as scary?"

"Scary? Maybe that's it. Whoever it is probably wants to scare me. But, why? It's like the shooter could have whacked me when I was in the outhouse, opened the door as I sat there in the vapors, and murdered my ass."

"A terrible thought, Charlie, but I believe you are on to something. The question is why someone wants to harm you or scare you away from something?

"Let's take it in order." Bernard questioned as Charlie went through the series of events connecting Charlie to the girl in the park -- "and who or what was in the back seat of the car?"

Charlie replied, "I ask myself, why someone would be hiding in the back of the car? Why would the driver be so anxious to get away that he couldn't wait for help? Why, the next day does this substitute teacher, Mr. Truwet, have a damaged leg, scratched face and driving the same car I thought I had seen? Then it turns out that Mr. Greyer has a similar car, and that his son, Willie Burris had escaped from the state mental hospital and as far as we still know . . . ."

Bernard finished the sentence, "Has gone missing. Yet why does the fellow, Burris, keep turning up in your life?"

"I've got a theory about Willie Burris, Ralph Jay, and that pink scarf."

"What is it, Charlie?"

"I'm not sure, but I think I know who belongs to that scarf, and I think I know the connection between Jay and the park where the body was found, but I don't understand why, someone would kill that retarded girl."

"Motive," Bernard screwed up his face, "maybe jealousy, not murder, perhaps an accident? However, you did say she may have been sexually assaulted?"

"I'm not clear on that either. It appears she was raped, but the police never pursued that. Don't forget Matt Grueber mentioned she may not have been sexually assaulted. I am sure that a mention of rape was made or written after the first story appeared in the paper. Maybe the Coroner's autopsy found different."

"Charlie, you mean the authorities are uncertain? It does seem we should have heard more about the sexual assault."

"Yeah, well, I've been thinking about it. It's not like I've been able to concentrate on much else except for Mom. I'll probably fail my classes; haven't had more than one day to study four days of classwork.

"Geez, Uncle B, my life has gone to hell in a hand-basket and I'm not so sure that Dad's toleration level is very high either. He's been a little short-tempered with me the last few days."

"Yes, Charlie. I'm afraid your father has the world on his shoulders about now. But, he'll come around. He's no stranger to suffering and death, but his latest troubles are what you Yanks call, close-and-personal.

Personal? "That's it, Uncle B. Someone is trying to play me. I mean, what's with all of the stuff that's happened to me in the last few days? I'm thinking someone is trying to hang something on me to take the suspicion away from -- who?"

"Framed, I believe you Yanks like that term. Like an old American gangster movie, 'framed, you dirty rat'."

"There's a dirty rat for sure. I'm wondering though how it's connected to the pink scarf? If the scarf owner is who I think it is, why?"

"Who is it, Charlie? Who owns that scarf?"

"I know a girl at school who wears a scarf like that, and she knows what's going on between me, Jay, the school and the incident at the library. But, I don't want to say until I've had a chance to check it out.

"I'm going back to school in the morning. It's pointless for me to take off any more time, and it's all uphill to make up my class work."

* * *

The two returned to Denver, and Charlie's world went upside down.

Nonna Bonarelli came out of the back door as they started unloading the car. "Vincenzo was called by those two police detectives, Mickey Mouse, and what's-his-face."

Charlie was amused but cautious at the same time. He understood that Detectives Mickey and Brawley were offended by Sheriff Kelso, and he sure hadn't heard the end of it. Charlie anticipated the detectives would go out of their way to make his life even more miserable.

"What's going on, Nonna?"

"They say the little girl wasn't—uh—you know—uh."

"Raped," Charlie filled in the odious word for her. Nonna had difficulty believing such evil existed and that simple people were victims.

"The poor little thing."

Charlie gave Nonna his handkerchief to wipe the tears from her eyes.

"So what's going on, Nonna?"

"Your father is upset at *quelli investigatori*, those snoopers. They came around again before you and Bernard got back. They said that they want to talk to you, something about withholding . . . uh, I'm not sure, Carlo."

"Withholding? What could that mean? I told them everything that I could think of."

"They told your father you probably know who was there at the park that night, and that you are just protecting someone."

"Well that's a pile of horse s . . . I've already told them who I think may have been at the park. They have short memories."

"Carlo, you're mouth. That's what gets you into trouble with *l'polizia*. You must behave yourself before . . . ."

"That's right Bonarelli."

Charlie nearly jumped out of his skin. The two detectives, Mickey and Brawley, appeared on the sidewalk between the garage and the house.

"Now what, Detectives?"

"We're taking you in, Charlie boy. It's time you came up with some names and better information. The person who tried to wax you up there in frontier-land knows you, and I'll bet you know him. Whoever it is -- probably tied into our case. You're not cooperating, so I'm, uh, we're putting you under arrest as an accomplice."

Bernard intervened. "That makes no sense, Detectives. You're only trying to intimidate the boy, and you have no reason to arrest him because someone tried to shoot him. Oh, I remember, this is *The Keystone Cops* here. Isn't that correct?"

"We can take you in, too, Mr. Proper Brit. Be a wise guy and see what it gets you here in Denver."

"Shoot? Who's shooting -- someone shooting at my grandson? Nonna whipped out her wooden spoon from her apron and smacked Detective Mickey hard across the back of his neck with a sound that made everyone pause as if the world had stopped turning.

Mickey, with reddened face, was first to react. "Okay, lady, you're going in, too. Brawley, cuff her. I'll take care of Charlie boy myself." He took out his handcuffs and tightened them on Charlie's wrists before he could blink three times. The cuffs barely closing over the bandaged wrists.

"But, Mickey, this is their grandmother. She's only smacked you. We're cuffing her for that, and then what?"

"We haul them in."

Bernard intervened. "Are you two thinking at all?" This is ridiculous. The Nazi's are out of power — aren't they?"

"You want a ride downtown, too, buddy?"

"I'm not your buddy, and if you take Mrs. Bonarelli and her grandson in for a simple infraction, remember your *Alice Through The Looking Glass*. I'll wager that both of your heads roll."

"What the hell are you blowing about? Damn limey."

"Limey is it. I was covering your Yankee behind when you were probably peeling potatoes for some safe mess behind the lines, like New Jersey or somewhere in Iowa."

"What the hell is going on here?"

Vince came out of the back door of the house. He hadn't taken off his overcoat and hat yet.

He saw his mother with one handcuff on, resisting the not- too-confident, Brawley.

"Jesus Christ. You're handcuffing my mother, and my son, for what? You, take those goddamn cuffs of off them right now."

"Mickey made a wide toothy grin. "It ain't happening. You're mommy and sonny boy here are going down to the . . . ."

He didn't finish his sentence before Vince shot a quick left fist straight into the big man's face. Mickey's mouth bled where Vince's fist connected but the detective held his ground.

"Now you've done it," Brawley said as he restrained Nonna with the other cuff snapped to Charlie's car door handle. "You're all going downtown."

For once Bernard was speechless. Vince whispered to him and followed him with his eyes as he left the group and walked into the backdoor.

Mickey came back to his senses. "Where the hell do you think you're going?"

Bernard walked into the house and shut the door as if he hadn't heard anything while Nonna Bonarelli filled the air with Italian invective Charlie had never heard from her before or since.

34

The Bonarelli Mob

Theresa Bonarelli threaded through a gang of reporters and photographers as she met the paddy-wagon at Denver Police headquarters.

Through a back window of the van, Charlie saw a Denver Police Captain come out the front doors of the station into the crowd. A policeman opened the back doors. "Okay, one at a time. Watch your step."

Detectives Brawley and Mickey pulled up behind the paddy-wagon.

"What the hell is going on here?" The Captain asked before Mickey could get out of his side of the car.

Mickey rolled down his window. "Resisting arrest, assaulting a police officer with a weapon . . . ."

The captain inspected Charlie, Vince, and Nonna Bonarelli in her apron as they exited the vehicle.

"Weapon? What is it, a gun, a knife?"

Mickey held out Nonna's wooden spoon. "This, she's deadly with it."

"You two," the Captain shook his head, "just what we need is more silliness. And how did the press get wind of this?"

The reporters laughed and flashbulbs popped as they surged around the Bonarelli family. One reporter already knew their name.

"The Bonarelli mob," he laughed, "they look pretty dangerous to me."

Charlie saw the captain lift his right foot behind Detective Mickey as if to kick his backside.

"Get them inside, for Christ's sake, now."

A reporter hollered near Charlie's right ear. "Hold up the weapon so that we can all see. Detective Mickey, how do you spell your name?"

Mickey chuffed as he escorted the Bonarellis to the door. Brawley held back and tried to get lost in the crowd but the Captain saw him. "C'mon, Brawley, you're part of this too." He caught the skulking detective by the neck like he just nailed a little boy who had put a match to his mama's curtains.

Theresa stirred the pot in front of the duty Sergeant's desk. She chewed the Captain, the two detectives and anyone within earshot. "What are you doing with my family? This is ridiculous. Arresting my mother for brandishing a wooden spoon, take those handcuffs off of her, and my brother, and my nephew?

You two hard-case cops," shaking a finger at Mickey and Brawley, "have nothing better to do than harass the Bonarelli family while the victim and the trail get cold."

You're after a suspect, the man from the mental hospital, and yet you're continuing to harass our family. You can't even let us get over our own tragedies. The school year is about ruined for my nephew. You're dragging this family through the mire at a particularly painful time and these two, pointing her finger again, are blunderers of the first order."

"Here, here," Bernard Striker, had shown up, having alerted Bobo who had rushed over to the house and had driven Bernard, Papa Bonarelli and himself to the fray at police headquarters.

Theresa took the police captain aside and spoke in low tones. Charlie could hear but a few words, "Incompetent, the Mayor, lawsuit."

"Okay, everybody settle down." The Captain looked at the crowd. A flash bulb popped. "Get the press out of here. How'd you let them get in anyway? They know they are not allowed in here." The Captain glared at the duty Sergeant.

The Sergeant shooed the reporters out of the foyer and separated Charlie, Vince, and Nonna Bonarelli from the crowd to put them into an interrogation room. "Stay in here until we get sorted out. Brawley, come on in here and take the cuffs off these people, Good God," he shook his head in disbelief.

As the crowd disbursed, Charlie heard Theresa and Bernard outside the open interrogation room door speaking to each other.

"I'm sorry, Bernard, you must think your American family is a rowdy bunch. This is quite out of the ordinary. Things have really gotten out of hand and I intend to clear this up for good."

The captain came into the interrogation room. "I'm sorry about this mix up folks. Our detectives are under a strain to find the killer of this girl and pick up that last escapee from the mental hospital. There seems to be a connection."

Charlie steamed, "Look, Captain, I've been trying to get some information to your department. I think I saw two kids from my school that night in the park but I can't identify them for sure, except one of them told me he was there."

"Wait, Son. I'll get someone to record this."

Theresa came back into the room. "It's already recorded, Captain. Why don't you act on it? You're still focusing on Charlie, why?"

"Mrs. Bonarelli" he addressed Nonna and Vince, "Mr. Bonarelli," I apologize for this mix up. Those two detectives will hear from me. But, we need to talk with Charlie for a few minutes."

The captain left the room, but left the door open.

Nonna shook her head. She and Vince stuck around. "What's this, Charlie? Vince asked, "You saw someone else?"

"I've told you before. Grueber knows, Brawley and Mickey, they know about Ralph Jay, Joe Birch and Willie Burris. I didn't really see anyone, part of a jacket behind a tree, but it's the voices that I heard. Jay admitted to me that he was there. He didn't give me the details why they were in the park that night though."

"Matt?" Vince saw Detective Grueber. "What the hell is going on here?"

Grueber held up both of his hands. "I'm sorry that this investigation, about the girl, has come to this, Vince. Mrs. Bonarelli, I'm terribly sorry for this. You and Vince are free to go. "Vince," I need to talk to Charlie, alone. Hopefully this will take only a few minutes. You can wait outside."

Theresa walked into the room. "Matt, I'm not only Charlie's Aunt, I'm his attorney. I'm staying in the room with my client."

"Okay, Theresa, he's got the right to an attorney, but this isn't an interrogation, and he's not charged with anything. I just want to ask him about new information."

After the room cleared, Matt Grueber produced a tape recorder. Charlie had seen one like it before when Brawley and Mickey had him.

"Not an interrogation, my foot." Theresa pointed, "So what's the recorder for?"

Grueber ignored the questions. "Damn." Can't someone invent a smaller recorder?" He almost dropped it. "Wait a minute." He opened the door. "Emily, come on in here and operate the recorder please."

A uniformed woman came in. Charlie was surprised to see a Denver policewoman. He knew that the police department recruited women but he had never seen one before this in uniform.

"Can you operate this thing while I do the interview please? Careful you don't drop the damn thing. It feels like it weighs a ton."

The policewoman nodded and proceeded to set up the recorder with the microphone between Charlie and Matt Grueber.

"Okay? He looked at the policewoman.

She nodded to go ahead.

Grueber said his name, the time, the date, and Charlie's name, 'Carlo "Charlie" Bonarelli.' "Okay, Charlie. We've talked, before, about the voices in the park that night."

It was two guys from school, Ralph Jay and Joe Birch -- I've said it before, to you."

"Why do you think it was those two, Jay and Birch?" You know them well?"

"Well enough that we don't like each other. Jay is looking for any excuse to destroy me. We've mixed it up. No permanent damage though."

"Why doesn't Jay like you?"

"He's got the hots for a friend of mine and he acts like I'm coming between him -- like I'm stopping him from putting the moves on my friend."

"So this friend, a girl I presume, is of interest to Jay and he's jealous?"

"Yeah, like that."

"So how does the other guy, Birch," he looked at his notes "How does Joe Birch fit into the scheme?"

"He's Jay's shadow. He couldn't tie his shoes if Jay didn't show him how."

"So these guys, Jay and Birch, are in the park that night, you think?"

"The voices were Jay and Birch. I've heard them threaten and talk tough enough times that I have their voices imbedded; something to do with my musical ear.

"Musical ear? You're a musician then?"

"Yeah when my hands aren't broken or damaged and you and the rest of the world aren't dogging me."

"So your musical career is on hold, at least until you mend?"

"Yeah, something like that, and if I don't get killed first."

"How's that, if you don't get killed first?"

Charlie told Matt Grueber about the shooting at the cabin, about Mickey and Brawley showing up, and about the ride down the mountain when someone tried to push them off. "Don't you cops communicate with each other?"

Grueber took time to digest this. Charlie looked up, and for the first time he noticed the glass behind Matt's head. The policewoman stopped the recorder on Grueber's signal.

"Excuse me, Charlie. I need a glass of water. Can I bring you something, how about you, Theresa?"

She shook her head.

"Yeah," Charlie asked, "How's about a glass of water and a couple of aspirin please?"

"Okay, be right back."

The policewoman sat silent, looking at the opposite wall. Charlie stared at the mirrored glass on the wall. "What's with the mirror on the wall?"

The policewoman didn't answer.

"There's someone behind it watching us, Charlie." Theresa pointed an accusing finger at the glass.

The door opened and Matt Grueber came in with the Captain. "You've met Captain Willsey?"

The captain intervened, "Not formally. I'm the precinct captain here. We've sent your family home. Detective Grueber will drive you home when we're finished."

Theresa, ready to lambaste the police, spoke. "I'll drive him home, we'll be leaving soon."

Captain Willsey addressed Charlie, "So Charlie, what's this about someone trying to shoot you at your mountain cabin? And, then there's the incident when someone tried to push you and this uncle of yours, Bernard off a mountain. What happened?"

"Captain, haven't you read your detectives reports?" Theresa asked.

"There haven't been any reports yet. Brawley and Mickey haven't had time to write them."

Charlie gripped the table. The Captain knew. That explained the mirrored glass. Sure, now, Charlie felt for sure he was a public figure. Anybody interested, and maybe their friends and relatives knew him by now. He thought the whole world probably saw him sick on the first go-around a few days ago.

Charlie, embarrassed by the thought, couldn't speak like the mouthy teenager he usually portrayed. He wanted out of the room. He wanted to go home. He wanted his mother to be alive and he wanted her to hold him in her arms like when he was a child.

"So why's this person trying to kill you or appear like they want to kill you? Or maybe it's more than one person? Maybe it's these guys, Jay and Birch?" Matt asked the questions while the Captain listened.

Charlie concentrated on the revolving tape recorder reels. "Who's behind that window?"

The captain raised his eyebrows. "No one, we're all here."

Charlie didn't believe him. He was in the pot and the cooks controlled the heat. It never occurred to him during any of the earlier interviews that he should have an attorney, and now he watched his Aunt Theresa, the attorney, in action.

"This is going on too long. Didn't you say you wanted to calm my nephew down, maybe get a couple of names? This has turned out to be a full-blown interrogation, and you've been questioning him almost every-other-day or so since the incident. If you don't have it now, you'll never get it."

"It's okay, Theresa. It's not like we're going to charge him. He's got something to tell us."

Charlie quickly filled in the details about the shooting and the near miss in the mountains.

Theresa said. "Okay, Charlie, we're done here." She pointed her finger at Grueber. "You're treating Charlie like a felon and he's the one who's getting shot at and threatened. What incompetence, what impudence, what poor police work. Let's go, Charlie."

"Wait, Miss Bonarelli." Captain Willsey held up his hands in defeat, but with a begging question. "How can we protect your nephew if we don't have the details?"

"You've had the details, for days; you're impotent, without as much as a sting. Do your job. Okay, we're gone."

With that, Theresa opened the door and motioned Charlie to follow her. He didn't take the opportunity to mention the pink scarf.

He thought about it on the ride home, the pink scarf. It's as if a rainbow suddenly appeared over his head. His English Literature teacher liked to use the word "epiphany," to describe the protagonist's revelation. Charlie preferred the metaphor as being hit by a truck but coming out of it.

The pink scarf was the truck that jarred his thinking.

35

In the Pink

When Charlie returned to classes, he wasted no time tracing the possible pink scarf link. "Becky, Hi, where's Ruthie?"

Becky pouted, "Charlie, I haven't seen you in days and the first thing out of your mouth is, 'Where's Ruthie?' I'm hurt."

"I'm sorry; don't be insulted, it's important. Where is she?"

"Geez, I don't know exactly. I haven't seen her for days. Her dad takes her hunting with him every year."

"Hunting?"

"Yeah, she's bagged a few deer. I think it's awful. She showed me the animal she shot last year, hanging in her dad's garage. The poor little thing looked like a big dog. Becky took offense when I called her, 'Bambi killer.'"

"Where'd they go hunting?"

"I don't really know. Someplace above Idaho Springs, I think."

"Idaho Springs, like maybe even around Central City?"

"Yeah, I think closer to Central City, but it's pretty bare up there in some areas isn't it? You'd think they'd go hunting further up in the mountains, but her dad has a hobby mine up there, so they hunt nearby. She's an outdoorsy girl, likes to get her gun and shoot things. Frankly, that's one part of Ruthie I find kinda creepy.

"Why so interested in Ruthie now? I thought you liked me just a little bit."

"Of course I like you, and more than a little bit, but it's a coincidence that Ruthie is up in Central City about the same time me and Uncle Bernie were there."

"Yeah, maybe, but you wouldn't necessarily run into her. She never mentioned that she knew you had a cabin up there, and anyway, she's probably out shooting up the mountains."

"Shooting up the mountains? That's one way to put it. By the way, doesn't Ruthie wear a pink neck scarf? I've noticed that she's almost always got that loud pink scarf wrapped around her neck."

"Yeah, Charlie, she's got a pink neck scarf, her 'lucky scarf,' she calls it. Is that important?"

"I'll tell you later. When's Ruthie getting back?"

"Well, I think she's probably out for the rest of the week. Like, you know, there's only tomorrow before the weekend. She may as well stay out for a couple more days. I hope she doesn't want to show me her deer this year --- yuck."

"Let's talk later. I've got to see a teacher before class starts. I'll be lucky to catch up my school work this year, but I think I can do it if somebody doesn't take me out first."

"What does that mean, 'take you out?' You in some more trouble, Charlie?"

"Trouble -- who me? Nah, never happen. So maybe I'll see you during lunch."

She smiled and waved. Charlie watched her walk down the hall and thought, what a great chick. He thought about the two girls that meant the most in his life right now, at least the ones that he felt some physical attraction to. Karin Delaney, that beautiful woman now since her Joey. *I'll probably never see her again even though she'll still be around the city until the end of her college semester. Becky, she's a real doll, a genuine sweet and smart girl, but I'm not frothing at the mouth for her like I do over Karin. Then there's this new little cutie, Jewell, a real mystery. Under her façade is a hot looking babe – I think. But, she's really hard to figure out – yeah a real mystery.*

"Charlie, Hey you, I haven't see you around school for a few days."

Charlie turned to see Jewell. *Well, think of the . . . . I still don't know her last name.*

"So you got a minute?"

"Hi, Jewell, I'm trying to get to my first-period class before the bell rings and catch up on my assignments."

"Yeah, right. I heard you've been up in the mountains."

Jewell suddenly had a look on her face like she'd just revealed a state secret.

"How'd you know that?"

"Uh . . . oh I heard someone talking about it, like maybe something happened to you, but you look okay to me."

"Jewell, I don't even know your full name. You seem to know more about me than I do you, how come?"

She ignored his question. "Look, meet me in the library during your lunch hour. Better yet, why don't I meet you on the back steps by the smoking area right after the lunch bell, okay? I want to ask you something."

"Ask me something? Let me ask you, what's your last name?" She walked away leaving Charlie without an answer.

"What's going on here? I'm not in control of my life. I can't even get an answer to a simple question. I seem to have lost my life to the cops or whoever is trying to dismantle me. I think it has something to do with, Becky's friend, Ruthie."

Charlie never really paid much attention to Ruthie, except that she was always with Becky. He thought about it the rest of the morning. After his first three classes he found Bobo and Zel by their lockers.

"Hey you guys, you know anything odd about Becky's pal Ruthie?"

Bobo answered, "Not much, but I think she's a little weird."

"Weird in what way?"

"Well, for starters, she likes biology class way too much if you ask me. Ruthie likes to cut up frogs, and volunteers to bring in animals that she has shot to dissect. You know she's a shooter, don't you?"

"Yeah, I just learned that from Becky."

"So now you got the hots for Ruthie? I mean, man, she's really not your type." Bobo made a rude facial expression.

"I'm not interested in Ruthie that way. I'm wondering what makes her tick. Becky told me that she's deer hunting with her dad nea`r Idaho Springs, maybe even around the old mining claims where our cabin is."

Bobo looked like he had just discovered electricity. "Man, you don't think that she's the person who's trying to whack you? I mean, check it out, a babe with a deer rifle, that's a tough broad. But, why?"

"Hey, Zel, check it out man. Charlie's got Ruthie Grey hot on his trail with a high-powered rifle trying to smoke his ass."

Sunlight framed Zel's red frizzy hair with a golden halo. "Just a matter of time before one of those little girls beats up on our boy, *il stallone*."

"Oh yeah, that's it, you're the angel of death now. I treat my friends well, that's very cool of you. And, so what would Ruthie have against me anyway?"

Zel pushed his glasses back up his nose. "Let's analyze it."

Charlie runs to get help at the library on the same night that Becky and Ruthie are supposed to be studying together inside the library. Ruthie never shows up, but you know she's dogging the Animal, because she's got it bad for him. So maybe she spots Jay and Birch as she's coming through the park to meet Becky and she finds Jay."

Maybe Zel was on to something Charlie thought and asked him, "So, how does the girl in the park find her way into the picture? Was it Ralph Jay and Joe Birch who really hurt the girl?"

Zel answered, "I don't think so, what's the motive. I mean we know that he's a mean son-of-a-bitch, but why's he in the park in the first place?"

"Becky." Both Bobo and Charlie answered as one.

Zel brightened. "Becky, that's it, sure. He's hot for Becky so he's shadowing her from the park and maybe gets close when something happens. But what?"

"Yeah, how's the retard get in the picture?" Bobo made a face.

"Careful there, Bobo, try mentally challenged," Zel adjusted his glasses. "That's the new term for mentally deficient people."

"Mentally challenged, huh?" Bobo said, "I've seen her around the park and walking around the school. She could have been a real looker, but whoever takes care of her must dress her out of granny's closet. She walked, tall and scanky, but her head turns around like a robot when she passes you by. And she was always wearing a shit-eating grin." Bobo made a wide grin but couldn't come close to copying the dead girl.

"Was, and did," Zel emphasized, "she's one of Denver's statistics now."

Charlie interjected, "Geez, Zel, she's a person, was a person, now she's dead." Charlie paused, "And, I've got the police and the press still on my back. Now, somebody's trying to kill me."

Charlie filled in the details about the trip to the mountains and the second interview at the police station when the whole family was nearly arrested. For the first time in a long time both Bobo and Zel were at a loss for words.

The silence didn't last long before Bobo blurted. "Jesus Christ, Charlie, you better leave Dodge City or something huh?"

Zel, excited now, "Yeah, this is making sense."

"Think about this one Zellie. I'm on the crapper, the door is jammed shut and someone is making a sieve through the wood. That someone hollers my name and then a couple of bullets send flying splinters into the outhouse. Luckily my Uncle Bernie chased the person away."

"The person had a rifle, and you and your uncle are unarmed?" Zel questioned him. "So what prevented that person from just putting a few bullets into both of you?"

"The only reason we could think of shot is that the person only wanted to scare me. Probably the same person drove the car that tried to push us over the edge of the mountains, then the pink scarf thing. Ruthie wears a pink scarf all of the time."

"Yeah, I think she has her head tied on with it." Bobo made the crazy grin again.

"Makes no sense at all," Zel shook his head. "She wouldn't be calling attention to herself if she had killed the girl in the park. No, it's got to be something else. Maybe she's jealous, maybe she's just trying to scare you, then maybe not."

"Wait." Charlie held up a hand. "What if Jay put her up to it? You know, 'Show me you love me baby, shoot Bonarelli or wipe him out anyway you can.'"

"This is stupid. You're a high school student, and you were making a delivery, you tried to help someone in the park that night. It makes no sense." Zel was upset. "I'm off to physics. I'll think about this and see you after school."

*   *   *

Charlie never answered Jewell about meeting her, but she probably knew that she had his interest. He met her at the designated place behind the school where the students were allowed to smoke cigarettes on school grounds. This was a no-man's land for the rah-rahs. But he had seen varsity boys spying through a windowed passage over the area. He heard boys talk about any girls seen smoking as "fast." Anyone seen smoking here was soiled and a "greaser". Charlie smoked a cigarette here once in a while, but this was not an area where he usually hung out.

"Charlie, I thought we'd better meet here. Nobody we know is probably going to bother with this place."

"Why should we care if anybody knows us?"

Jewell colored. "I want to ask you something."

"No, first, I want to know your last name."

"Okay, that's fair enough, it's, uh, 'M.'"

"M? How do you spell it?"

"Uh, "M . . . . um, "M." You know like the letter "M."

"Sure, that makes a lot of sense now doesn't it? Your name is Jewell but you're also called, "J" like the letter "J."

Oh, and 'M,' that makes perfect sense." 'J.M?' C'mon, what's your full last name?"

"Charlie, the bell's going to ring pretty soon. I wanted to ask you if you would go with me to the Junior Class Sock Hop. We're organizing it like *American Bandstand*. It'll be really cool with a DJ, the latest records, refreshments, I'll buy the tickets –- you wanna go?"

Charlie was flattered, but caution left him speechless.

"Please think about it, okay, Charlie? I understand, it's really close to your mother's death, but you know, we don't always have to mourn a long time like our great-grandparents."

The bell rang and J.M ran into school.

"J.M? I doubt it. What's that going to look like on a driver's license or a legal document? There's something fishy here, and I'm going to find out what it is."

36

The Void

Charlie read the article Vince left open on the kitchen table.
Police have positively identified the young lady, found in Highland Park last week, as Dorothy "Dot" Wallick, age twenty. She lived at a home for the mentally disabled near the park. It was some time before the Coroner could make a positive identification because of a mix-up in procedure about informing the home, a quasi-state government facility, about the woman's identity.

He read on thinking that several kids around school had a story about Dorothy, and if they could embellish it they did. But no one knew her name or where she lived. They knew her by appearance, and referred to her as "Crazy Red". She was skinny, about 5'8", white female, with flaming red hair and a freckled face on a head that was in constant motion. She wore the same purple dress, white hose, and men's shoes any time that Charlie saw her walking around the park or school.

He came to a dead stop over the article then jumped up from his chair to make a bullish charge for the phone. The phone rang as he reached for the hand piece.

"Yeah, Bobo, yeah, I read it just now. Can you believe it? Man, it's making more sense now." Charlie went over the part in the article that had enlightened him:

Wallick had a connection to a Colorado State Mental Hospital escapee, Willie Burris, who has been missing for almost two weeks from the

Pueblo facility. The Denver Police have not made a public statement, but this newspaper has found that Wallick sustained a permanent head injury during a police chase two years ago when she was on the run with Burris.

The two were apprehended in California, after a California Highway Patrolman stopped Burris's car in the Mojave Desert. Burris tried to drive over the patrolman whose shot through the windshield of Burris's car angled through the frontal lobe in Wallick's head.

Apprehended later, Burris stopped to help Wallick who has since lost partial mental and physical function as a result of the shooting.

"Geez-Louise, Bobo, it had to be Willie Burris in the back of that car, Mr. Greyer's car, I'll bet, and who knows, maybe Burris whacked his own girlfriend.

"But, that doesn't explain why and if Ralph Jay and Joe Birch were there. And what's the deal with Ruthie and the rifle?"

"Bobo, I think that Ruthie wants to make it look like this Burris guy is after me while covering for Jay and Birch. And, if that is so, I think it's Ruthie who's touched in the head. So I'm guessing that Ruthie is putting the heat on me to make it look like Burris is after me, when all along it's probably Ruthie that's trying to make me the headliner."

Bobo answered, "Yeah, so how do you prove it? Hey, and maybe the cops can squeeze Jay and Birch. Birch would pop like a zit. So how're you going to get the cops to figure out Jay and Birch if those two aren't talking?"

"Look, Bobo, I've got some thinking to do. Can you pick me up for school? Uncle Bernie is using my car. By the way, Bernie is leaving today. He's invited me to visit in London, maybe learn the music business from him. Anyway, let's talk later. I've got a couple more problems to think about.

Bobo snorted, "Yeah, and one of them is a girl no doubt. See ya in a few."

* * *

A sullen kitchen with Vince, Jody, Sam, and Charlie trying to get themselves together on a morning when they all felt Bea's loss more than they had when the house was busy with relatives and friends. It was the four of them now, trying to fill in the holes that Bea always filled. Make lunches, fix breakfast, and make sure that they had clean clothes.

Charlie helped Jody and Sam get ready for school. Bobo's car horn alerted Charlie to get moving.

"Where's my cowboy shirt?" Sam came into the kitchen in a T-shirt, dirty jeans and no shoes or socks.

Vince put down a jar of peanut butter and stared at Sam. "Kiddo, you look like a goddamn street urchin. Find something clean to put on. Your mother is probably watching from somewhere right now and saying, 'Haven't I taught you anything?'"

Jody looked around as if expecting Bea to be shaking her head in disgust at Sam. She cried, "Mommy, I want, Mommy."

Vince put down a knife full of peanut butter and picked up Jody. "I'm sorry little pumpkin. It's going to be difficult for a while, but we'll get through it one-day-at-a-time." He looked at Charlie. "You better go. Bobo will wake up the neighborhood with that horn."

"Okay, I'm gone. See you as soon as I get home from school. Who's picking up the kids from school?"

"I'm going to ask my secretary to pick them up." Vince said. "Yeah, I'm glad you brought that up. Kids, Beverly Ann Mistletoe is picking you up at school. I'll call the school office and clear it. I'd pick you up, but I've got a customer coming in at the same time."

"Mistletoe? You mean like Christmas?" Sam laughed. "You've got to be kidding, huh, Dad?"

"Christmas," Jody wailed, "Mommy's not going to be here for Christmas."

"Mistletoe? Where'd you find her?" Charlie asked.

"Look, she's temporary until my regular lady gets back from the hospital, get the hell out of here. I don't want to hear . . . damn it,

Bobo's horn again. Move your butt, Beverly Ann will stay with the kids until you get home, now move."

* * *

"Geez, Charlie, what took you so long?"

"We haven't figured things out yet. Mom had a routine and we just kind of followed her directions. Right now, we're fish out of water. Anyway, let's get to school. I want to have a conversation with Jay and Birch."

Bobo looked at Charlie like he had just made friends with the hangman. "C'mon, what're you trying to prove? This time Jay may be hyped enough to pound you into the ground like a tent peg."

"I'm going to tell them, I'm going to nail them. It was Jay and that puke friend of his in the park. They want me to get stuck with the girl's murder."

"I'm thinking that he'll beat the crap out of you. Let the cops handle it. Put that jerk Detective Mickey on him. They're made for each other."

For some reason, at that moment, Charlie thought of Jewell. "Hey, you know that little girl from the junior class? Her name's Jewell. Likes to be called 'J,' and when I asked her last name she tells me it's 'M.'"

Bobo grinned, "Yeah, it's just like I said, there's a chick involved. Man, let it alone. Somebody's going to cut off your magic-twanger. You won't be able to write your name in the snow anymore."

"So what kind of name is J.M.? That doesn't make any sense, J.M.? So what about her? She got great tits probably or a fine behind — right?"

"Bobo, you've got me all wrong. I'm not after this girl. She's cute, but I barely know her."

Bobo rolled his eyes. "So lay it on me, Daddy-O, why should she be a problem if you hardly know her?"

"She's asked me to the Junior Sock Hop . . . says it's a real cool thing with a DJ and it's supposed to be like *American Bandstand*."

"C'mon, that's cool. So if you go, and Becky finds out, it's the ice-box for you. You don't really have anything going with Becky anyway. She gives you a ride once in a while. Hey that's it. You're riding Karin and Becky both. You nasty bastard, you're supposed to tell your old cuz these things. I mean, man, we're blood, you dig?"

"Here, Bobo." Charlie pulled a toothpick out of his jacket pocket and handed it to him.

"What's that for? I brushed my teeth."

"You'd never know it, cuz. The toothpick's to pick the crap out of your shit-eating grin."

"Charlie, I'm the guy who should be getting the girls. You know, handsome, a boxer, smooth, I'm the real deal. And you, look at you, you're all beat up, probably have parts falling off, and you're a revolving door with the babes. I can't figure it, man."

"Don't try to figure it. Karin is splitting, Becky is sharp, but I'm not really that tight with her. This girl, Jewell, well that's just a coincidence. She's cute, maybe even pretty in a tantalizing way."

"Tantalizing way -- what's that?"

"She likes crossword puzzles. That was one of her words. I like it."

"Oh, so now you're playing word games with the chick. That's a new approach. Tell me how that works."

"It works like this. I met her when I went to the school library to read a story in the newspaper. She had the paper, was doing crosswords, we struck up a conversation, then there was the thing when she brought the cake over for Mom's funeral . . . you know, you ate half of it yourself."

"Oh, that Jewell."

"No man, like I know a dozen girls named Jewell."

"Okay, so now that Jewell wants you to go to a dance with her. Pretty fast, don't you think?"

"We'll, I've known her now for a few days. That's not so fast is it?"

"Speaking of fast, what does your Dad say about mourning? You know, you're Nonna will wear black for a year and Papa Bonarelli will wear the black arm band until your Nonna tells him to remove it."

"Mom wouldn't have any of that. She told my Dad one time that people must go on with their lives and that we should live life full and colorful. Be like the Brits old man, chin up."

"That's a little odd for our family," Bobo said. Man, you know, we love black, the gnashing of teeth, falling apart at the casket, making the sign of the cross if somebody farts. I wondered how the Strikers held their composure at the services."

"They're kind of like Stoics, you know, keep a cool profile."

"Stoics?" There you go again with the words. That Jewell Chick is ruining your speech."

"Hey wise guy, I happen to enjoy the written word as much as you like punching people in the snout."

"Hey, cuz, do you think you can come to the match Saturday night? This one's important. I'd like you in my corner."

"Let me talk to Dad. He's got his hands full with Jody and Sam. Jody's like a little mother, but Sam's not taking Mom's death well at all. He's demanding, and only Jody or Nonna can handle him."

"Yeah, I dig, but see if you can make it. Oh, by the way, I'm going to confession Saturday afternoon. Maybe you should come along," Bobo raised his eyebrows as the all-knowing seeker of truth.

"Chuck it, Bobo, I'll take it under consideration. Meanwhile, I want to catch Jay and Birch before I lose my cool."

"Screw your cool, you've got me."

Don't worry about it, Bobo. I'm a little shorter than that big sucker Jay but a hard kick to the shins will bring him down to my size."

They went into the school, and Charlie waited by his locker, with Bobo and Zel, knowing that Jay and Birch would be plowing through the student filled hall any minute.

"There's Moses now." Zel pointed.

37

"Jay, I want to ask you something."

Ralph Jay grabbed Joe Birch who jumped in front of Jay like a scrappy puppy.

Jay pushed Birch aside, "What's up, Charlie boy?"

Birch jumped in front of Jay again. "Maybe he wants you to break his other hand."

Bobo slapped Birch across the top of his head, "Back-off, Birch."

Charlie pointed at Joe Birch, "You know what I think, and I've said it before, but now I'm convinced that you and pea-brain here were in the park that night when . . . ."

Birch blurted, "You're full of shit, Bonarelli, we wasn't there, huh, Ralphie."

"'Ralphie,' Isn't that sweet," Bobo taunted Birch.

"I recognized your voices even if I didn't get a full view. Squeaky here," Charlie pointed at Birch, "has a distinct pitch, like a wire pulled through a hole in a tin can. You can hear him a block away."

Birch plowed into Charlie, but Bobo easily pushed him away as Jay came to a defensive position. The damage was done. Charlie's sore ribs were just at the point where the pain wasn't so severe. He felt sweat break out on his forehead, but held his tongue. He didn't want either Jay or Birch to know that he was hurting.

"Okay, big-mouth, Bonarelli, suppose you think you have some-thing maybe, prove it. I can tell you that we didn't do anything to the redhead. And, for your information the cops have talked to us. We gave them nothing."

Birch gushed again, "So maybe we saw her but we gave them cops nothing."

Jay put a hand over Birch's mouth and whispered something in his ear.

"Okay, okay, sorry."

"You were saying, Charlie boy?"

Jay wasn't about to help Charlie one way or the other. It was better to bait Birch but he also guessed that Jay's whispered message to him was a death threat or worse, the promise of a beating.

The school bell rang.

"Gee, gotta go now. See me in about a month, Bonarelli."

Birch yapped, "Yeah, we'll visit you in jail."

Jay pushed Birch down the hall by his neck.

Charlie winced with the aggravated pain in his side but coughed out, "Well I'll just lay this on the cops again if you don't want to tell me."

Jay didn't acknowledge the threat.

Zel put his hand on Charlie's shoulder. "Charlie, maybe it's not such a good idea to make a public threat."

"Oh hell, not to worry," Bobo chimed, "he's probably going to kill Charlie anyway."

"I feel reassured, Bobo."

Zel said, "We've got to get to class, but the connection to the dead girl, Dorothy, Jay, and Birch are probably like you suspected. She was in the park maybe to meet the escapee, Willie Burris, when either she surprises Jay and Birch or they surprised her."

Bobo added, "Yeah and you know what a nasty piece of work that Birch is. He's only tolerated by Jay because nobody else likes him. I'm guessing that Birch came on to the redhead because he figured she's an easy piece, but maybe she puts up a fight and Birch does something to her."

Charlie asked, "So why just, Birch? He's attached to his master. Jay controls the guy like he's on a leash. Maybe Jay had a part in it, too."

Zel answered "Maybe, Charlie, but as much of a bully that the guy is I've never seen him get mean with the chicks. He's just the opposite. Look at him tagging after Becky. And, Ruthie is forever after Jay."

"I think that Birch hangs on to Jay just so he can get courage once in awhile to talk to a girl."

Bobo interrupted, "Yeah, plus Birch likes to intimidate everybody by using Jay as his front man. Otherwise Birch would shrivel up like the worm that he is."

"Think about it, Charlie." Zel said, "I'm off to class, probably see you guys at lunch. Oh, Bobo, are you coming over to the West Side after school?"

"I'm thinking about it."

"Let me know, I could use a ride home."

"Okay, see you later."

"Bobo," Charlie asked, "Have you still got something going with what's-her-name, the little Jewish dish?"

"Giselle? Yeah maybe. She got mad at me for something so we split for awhile. So maybe I'll let her make up to me. We'll see. Let's get to class."

Charlie thought Bobo and Zellie's analysis rang true, but how could he prove it. It wasn't up to him to do the police work, but it didn't look like the police were getting close to solving anything about Dorothy Wallick's death.

Later that afternoon, Bobo drove Zel and Charlie to the Bonarelli house. Charlie had to be there when Jody and Sam returned from school.

"C'mon in for a few minutes."

Bobo and Charlie waited in the living room, watching cartoons on TV while Zel scavenged the refrigerator.

"Hey, Zel bring me a pop, Orange Crush, okay?"

Zellie came into the living room, chewing on something that he found appetizing.

Sometimes Charlie wondered about the stuff Zel ate when he came into the Bonarelli home. It was good food, but Zel was supposed to keep kosher.

"Here." He handed a small bottle of Grapette to Bobo. "Man, that's not Orange Crush. They always have Orange Crush in the fridge."

"Nope, not this time. Grapette or 7up; you hate 7Up."

Bobo grabbed the pop from, Zel, "I hate 7Up."

Charlie wondered what Zel had found to eat. "What are you chewing on?"

"I don't know. It looked good; tastes interesting."

Bobo looked at Zel. "Your parents would kill you if they knew what you ate over here and at school. Man, I don't even eat half of the crap that you do, and I'm not Jewish."

Zel studied something in his hand and jammed it into his mouth. He chewed and swallowed. "Look, we're so kosher that we keep separate dishes for *trayf.*"

Bobo choked on his grape pop. "I know what that is, forbidden food. C'mon, your parents are so straight that they'd give you ten demerits or whatever you get when you eat stuff that's not kosher. Isn't that like a mortal sin or something?"

"Hey, that reminds me, Charlie, you gotta go to confession with me Saturday. We'll do that, then Saturday afternoon Mass, and I'm all set for the match Saturday night –– pretty cool huh?"

"Ten Hail Mary's are not going to save you from destruction, Bobo, and I'm not telling that crazy priest anything."

Bobo shook Charlie's protest off.

"You're going with me. Hey and where's your confidence? This kid here is hot, hot, hot! I'm going to kick the guy's butt." Bobo was on his feet punching the air.

"Watch the pop, Grapette stains things."

They all looked around to see Jody shaking a finger at, Bobo.

Sam walked in the door with a striking blond woman.

She looked at Charlie, "Hi, you must be, Charlie. I'm Beverly Ann Mistletoe."

Bobo jumped up, "I'm, Bobo," he stumbled over a coffee table as if to devour Little Red Riding Hood, "Beverly Ann Mistletoe?"

"Just call me 'Bev.'" She flashed Bobo a smile that probably stopped his heart for a couple of seconds.

Zel's jaw dropped with a mouth full of food. For once he was speechless.

"That's, Zellie." Charlie pointed out the slack-jawed carrot-top to his father's temporary secretary.

"We'll, I'll be getting back to, Vince, uh your dad's office. It was nice to meet you all," she flashed another killer smile. "I hope to see you again, Jody and Sam. Bye." She waved and went out the front door.

Bobo pushed on his chin with the heel of his right hand then threw a kiss to the door shutting behind Beverly Ann.

Jody gave Bobo a disgusting look and turned her glare to Zel. "Close your mouth, Zellie, you're dribbling food." She turned and went into the kitchen.

"I want to watch something else." Sam was already plopped down in front of the TV.

"Did you get a load of her?" Bobo made as many lewd gestures as he could before Sam turned and caught him.

"You're nasty, Bobo. I'm watching *Fred and Fay*." Sam switched the TV channel.

Bobo grimaced and mouthed, "Busted."

"Nice looking woman." Zel came back to his senses.

Bobo almost hollered, "Like where have you been man? Yeah, just a little bit. I swear to God that's Marilyn Monroe disguised as Beverly Ann Mistletoe. Man, I want to get under the Mistletoe, now. I can't wait for Christmas."

Charlie had bad thoughts going through his mind and they weren't erotic or lust-filled daydreams.

"Where did Uncle Vince find her?" Bobo asked.

"That's what I'm wondering, too."

Charlie saw the light go on in Zel's eyes."

"Don't even think that way, Charlie."

"She's temporary." Jody came back into the room with a glass of milk. "Here, Sam, and don't spill it either."

"Bev is nice," Sam slurped his milk.

Bobo wanted to change the subject. "Charlie, come on over to the West Side with us."

Jody called from the kitchen. "He's got to watch us, Bobo, and he's got to do his homework."

"Look, it's just for a few minutes, J-O-D-Y M-A-M-A, you and Sam can come with us. We'll go to Groban's, they've got a nice soda fountain."

"I'm watching TV," Sam protested.

Bobo turned to Sam, "C'mon Sam, I'll buy you a chocolate phosphate."

"Root-Beer-Float and it's a deal."

"Okay, a float."

"We've got homework," Jody protested.

"We'll be back in forty minutes."

Jody thought a few seconds. "Okay, but only forty minutes, and you better not be fibbing, Bobo. Charlie, leave a note just in case."

* * *

The Bonarelli's lived on the north side of Sloan's Lake. By some convoluted logic, the housing and business area on the south side of the lake was called, "The West Side."

Jody sat on Charlie's lap in the front seat with Bobo behind the wheel. The other three scrunched up in the backseat of Bobo's coupe.

"Give the kids the tour, Zel," Bobo laughed at his cleverness. He knew Zellie would give his best encyclopedic version of everything he knew about the west side.

"You want the long or the short version?"

"Better be quick, Groban's is coming up on the right." Charlie said.

"We are entering the West Side *Eruv*. The boundary of the Jewish Sabbath, and here is the heart and soul of the Denver Jewish community: "Bounded on the north by West 17th Avenue, on the east by Osceola Street, on the south by West 14th Avenue and on the west by Sheridan Boulevard.

"We are now traveling down the backbone of the Jewish commercial district, West Colfax Avenue. Here you can buy groceries, kosher goods, a nice *challah* from Forman's Bakery, and of course, Groban's Drugstore. Then looking way down to the left we can see the grade school. The Jewish Community Center is behind the school, close to the hospital and further . . . ."

"Hey, what about the Root-Beer-Float?"

"Hush, Sammy. Zel's talking," Jody grinned at Charlie.

Sam mimicked Jody, "Hush, Sammy."

"We're here." Bobo parked, and they unloaded like a circus car full of clowns.

"Hey, Zel, you forgot the Catholic connection." Bobo said.

"Oh yeah, St. Anthony's Hospital slipped in the corner of our Jewish community, a slight oversight."

Bobo laughed all the way into Groban's where he searched out and found his girlfriend, Giselle.

"Gisey, baby, how's my little knish?"

"Shut up, Bobo, will you please. I have to live here." She stared at Zel. "You had to bring this *meshugener* here?"

Bobo laughed, and gave Giselle a bear hug. "Let's get a soda. Hey, I brought my cousins. You know, Charlie. This is Jody and Sam.

38

Attitude

Giselle made a tight-mouthed hello to Jody and Sam then trained her ire on Bobo.

"You've got nerve coming over here. I've just about had enough of you, Bobo. You're chasing anything female. I've seen you do it, don't try to deny it."

"Uh, why don't I meet you guys at the soda fountain in a couple of minutes," Bobo guided Giselle away from his family and Zel who was already halfway across the store heading for the fountain. Jody and Charlie followed.

Sam stood adamant. "You're going to buy me a root-beer-float, Bobo."

"Okay, here's a dollar, you guys have what you want." Bobo fumbled in his jeans pocket while he held Giselle's attention. "Here."

He handed the money to Sam who said, "Thanks," and ran to catch up with Zel and Jody.

Despite the distance they could hear Bobo back-peddling with Giselle.

"But, sweetie, I'm your guy, I'm just friendly. Those other girls don't mean a thing to me. Besides, I need my girl to be in my corner Saturday night."

"Saturday night? You're boxing Saturday night?" I can't go until after sundown, it's *Shabbat* and then I'm sure that my parents won't let me go to the fights."

"You're old man loves the fights. The orthodox Sabbath is over after sunset on Saturday. I've see him at Golden Gloves. Just ask him to go along."

Charlie sat at the corner of the soda fountain with Zel and the kids.

The druggist manned the soda fountain, "Okay, what'll it be young lady? "How'd you like to try a Cherry Phosphate?"

Jody screwed up her nose, "Chocolate, I want something with chocolate."

"Maybe a chocolate Sundae?" Mr. Groban asked.

"No, that's too much ice cream before dinner. No, I'll have lime-ade please. We've got chocolate at home. That'll be after dinner."

"Good choice, young lady."

"Mr. Groban, how come you're soda-jerking today?" Zel looked over the counter for any condiment he might snatch, "Cherries?"

"I put the cherries back here," Mr. Groban pointed, "too many kids depleting the supply when the soda-jerk's back is turned.

"Once in a while I have to do the counter here before the school kid comes in, you know Jerry, he's sick today. His mother came in for a prescription. I hope the kid's going to be okay. Anyway I'm working the fountain and the pharmacy until I can get some temporary help."

"I can help!" Charlie jumped in with the hope of getting an after school job. "I'm good after 3:30PM to about 6:00PM."

"What about us, Charlie?" Jody tugged on Charlie's sleeve.

"I think maybe Nonna can stay with you until Dad gets home. I'm thinking maybe, since I'm driving Mom's car now, that I can pick you up at school, drive by for Nonna, or you could even stay with her and Papa Bonarelli until Dad picks you up."

"They don't have a TV. I'll miss my afternoon programs," Sam winced.

"Let me save you the trouble," Mr. Groban smiled. "First of all, kid, you're bandaged. I think a soda-jerk should have two hands free and bandages are unsanitary. Second, you have the look in your eyes of someone in pain, like maybe there's structural damage. Am I right?"

Charlie was still hurting from Joe Birch's crashing into him that morning.

"Look, kid, I like your spirit. I'm not a hasty man. Leave me your phone number, you never know. What'll you have?"

Charlie ordered a cola.

"It's on me, kid. I think you're okay."

Charlie thanked him and handed him a scrap of paper with his name and phone number.

"Carlo Bonarelli?" The druggist took the paper scrap. "I knew a, Vince Bonarelli, any relation?"

"I go by, Charlie, and yes, Vince is my Father."

Charlie thought this may have been the druggist's way of letting him know he also knew about Charlie's connection to the dead girl in the park.

Mr. Groban smiled again, "I met your Dad. He helped me with a little manufacturing deal that I'm involved in. We make some hair care products at another place. He helped find the equipment for me, nice guy. Did I read that Vince's wife, your mother, recently passed?"

"A couple of weeks ago."

Jody put her head on Charlie's arm and averted her eyes.

Mr. Groban took one of Jody's hands. "She was your mother too, huh little thing. I'm terribly sorry."

"Mr. Groban," a lady called from an aisle, "where's the Epson Salts, please?

"I'll be right with you, Mrs. Schwartz."

Mr. Groban finished everybody's order and left the soda fountain.

Bobo, holding hands with Giselle, walked to where his family sat, "So what'd you guys get?"

Sam turned his stool and slurped the root beer and suds before sticking his spoon in to finish the ice cream.

Zel had left the counter and was at the magazine rack studying *Popular Science.*

Jody was almost done with her limeade, "We got to get back, Bobo."

Charlie affirmed, "Yeah, got to split, man."

Giselle was disappointed they had to leave so soon, but Bobo soothed his girlfriend. "I'll call you later. Don't worry about the fight, I'll be okay."

Bobo dropped them off at home. They got inside just in time to meet Vince coming in the back door from the garage.

"Where've you been?"

"Bobo took us around the lake to Groban's Drugstore for a soda."

"Groban's? I remember Mr. Groban, the druggist."

"Yeah, I asked him for a part-time job; he said he'll think about it."

"A job? Hey, Jody and Sam, everything went okay with Bev, huh?"

Charlie jumped on this opening. "So, Beverly Ann Mistletoe, where'd you find her?"

Vince was visibly irritated by the tone in Charlie's voice. "She's from a temporary agency. She's worked for me before when the regular girl was out. She's probably going to be full time because my regular secretary is moving out of Denver, something about her health -- any problem with that?"

Charlie wondered why his father even asked him if there was a problem with that. It was Vince's office and his business. He replied, "No," but the subject ground on him.

Sam broke the ice. "Hey, Uncle Bernie is leaving on the train for Los Angeles tonight. Are we going to get to see him before he leaves?"

"Yes, he's bringing your mother's car back, Charlie's car now. Theresa is going to pick him up here and take him to Union Station."

A knock and the front door opened. Theresa came in. "Hey you guys, I brought some Chinese food. How about dinner? Bernard should be driving up the alley now. Somebody let him in the back door please? Jody, maybe you can help me with the table. Let's try the chopsticks, but better put forks down anyway."

Charlie went to the back door just as Bernard drove into the driveway. Charlie motioned him to wait while he opened the garage door for him. He drove the car in and shut the engine.

"Hi, Charlie."

"Need any help with bags, Uncle B?"

"No, thank you, I have already placed my luggage in Theresa's auto. Here are your keys. I finally got the hang of it, and now I'm on my way out. Have you been thinking about my offer?"

"Sure. Sounds great, and I'm definitely interested, except . . . ."

"Your military obligation is my guess."

"Good guess, Uncle B. I'm registered for the draft, and they're just waiting for me to leave high school with no education deferment."

"Right, I quite understand. Don't forget that the offer stands if you don't have to go into the service. Also, the offer is still out there when your service obligation is fulfilled."

* * *

They all sat around the table eating Chinese food, laughing at each other as they tried the chopsticks. Uncle Bernie was proficient and before the end of the meal he had trained Jody in the proper use of the bamboo implements.

"Good show, Jody, you've got the hang of it. Give it a try, Sam."

Sam couldn't be bothered. "I'm hungry. Stuff doesn't stick to those things like a fork." He took on food like a fireman shoveling coal into a locomotive.

Dad, appalled at the show, grabbed Sam's fork hand. "Slow down, Son. You're going to choke. I know, you think that the faster you eat the faster you'll get to the TV. I've got some news, kiddo."

"What?" Sam asked through a mouth full of rice.

"Homework. Finish that round and get to it. You, too, Miss Jody. How's your schoolwork, Charlie?"

Sam whined, "But, Dad."

Charlie had to think awhile before he figured out how far he was behind.

"Look, Charlie," Vince said, "I know that you want to earn some money, but you've got to get caught up. It's been tough, but you need to take care of school first."

Theresa intervened. "You've got the whole weekend to put your nose to the grindstone, Charlie. Start early, Saturday morning and stick to it. You'll be amazed how some quiet time and good attitude will speed you through the work."

"Attitude?" Charlie had attitude to burn but the wrong brand. He wanted all of the pressure and frustration to end and he was about to blow like a boiler. He sat and steamed as he nodded his head all the while contriving the destruction he should heap upon his enemies.

Maybe, he thought, that he could blow Ralph Jay and Joe Birch sky-high in a spectacular blast, innards and heads flying. He reasoned that he didn't have any explosives. Besides he remembered he once burnt his hands with fireworks. He thought he was clumsy enough to blow himself up. No, he'd have to do something less hazardous and more enjoyable, something that he could witness, maybe rat poison? Except that he couldn't bear to kill a little rat much less a human being with poison. *I couldn't shoot them. That would be a waste of good bullets.*

Finally, he gave up the idea of death and destruction. But maybe he could hurt them a little. Maybe he could accidentally, on purpose, drop a brick-laden trash can on Jay's head from the steps at school. If he were lucky maybe he could get both Jay and Birch with the same can. Nope, too many potential witnesses, and it would take more bricks in the can to do the job than he could lift.

Charlie enjoyed plotting his enemy's destruction, but in the end, he figured that he would just have to put up with the bastards until the end of school, murder wasn't his style. His Mother wouldn't approve and he knew that she was watching him, probably pointing "the finger" at him and shaking her head. But, this didn't rule out vengeance.

Then he thought about, Ruthie. Why would she be after me? Bobo and Zel, no doubt, were right when they said she was covering for Ralph Jay. Charlie mumbled to himself, "So Ruthie, you think that Jay even cares about your languishing love? Hell no, he only cares about his own skin."

"Charlie, are you with us?" Theresa stared at him.

"Uh, what, sure I'm here."

Jody chimed, "There's a phone call for you, Charlie. It's that girl."

Charlie, preoccupied with plotting against antagonists, didn't hear the phone ring."

"What girl?"

"You know, Jewell," Jody grinned.

"Hello." Charlie listened to Jewell ask him again if he could go to the dance with her.

"Uh, I'll check with the family. I'll see you at school tomorrow. Okay, see you, bye."

He worried about the proper time for mourning. The family was ambivalent about how much time, if any, was a proper mourning period. Nevertheless, Charlie felt that there was some protocol. His Mother was a person who lived life daily to the fullest. Most of the family felt that she would have wanted them to go on as if nothing out of the ordinary had happened.

Nonna and Papa Bonarelli came from a completely different culture where mourning was a sign of respect and required a certain period of time.

Bernard got up, "Thanks ever so much for everything. I hope to see you all in London someday soon, Cheerio."

Charlie, tell Bobo that I'm sorry to miss his bout. Let me know how he fares."

After the hugs and kisses from the family, Theresa and Bernie left. Charlie sulked at the table.

"It's okay, Charlie. I'll handle Mama and Papa. We can't live in the dungeon of grief for a year. Your mother would insist that you get out of this funk."

39

The Confessional

Saturday morning Charlie hit the books early. He was two hours into his studies when Jody brought him a cup of coffee and a piece of toast. As he sipped the coffee he remembered that Bobo wanted him to go to confession with him that afternoon. Charlie pushed his sinful existence out of his head with four hours of catch-up algebra. He liked writing and he could combine his history assignment with an English writing exercise.

His right hand still bothered him, and he nagged internally about his inability to use his drumsticks properly.

"I'm thinking seriously about the harmonica," He told Bobo later that afternoon when his cousin came to pick him up.

"The only thing you're going to blow is hot air in some sweet chick's ear, *stallone.*"

"Cool it, Bobo, I'm having a hard enough time thinking how I'm going to lay my stuff out on the priest in the confessional. Man, what do I tell him?"

"Self-abuse," Bobo chuckled. "I always use that one -- sounds better than, 'I've been playing with myself, Father.' Oh, kind of skip through the adultery part, ya-know-with-Karin-and-all. It helps to mumble. Those priests hear so much crap that they just want to get through it, I'm thinking."

"Thinking huh, sounds like conniving. Self-abuse? Man, that's bad for a boxer's legs isn't it? I thought you were an aspiring professional. Now I know that you're a perspiring pervert."

"Not me, man, Giselle. She likes to play, but no screwing. I mean how else do you tell a priest about playing with your girlfriend's privates?"

"Christ, Bobo, 'privates?' You make it sound like a clinical exam, try 'petting.' It has style. Besides what does a priest know from petting? Be careful how you lay that down in Italian, he'll think you're a goat-banging farmer."

Bobo grinned. "Petting, man, we're talking heavy petting and panting. Giselle breathes like a puppy when I've got my hand up her skirt."

"Yeah, and I'll bet that you're real cool yourself, Bobo. Like, you're probably barking at the moon. I've got it. Tell Father that you're rutting. He'll get your drift."

On the drive to Our Lady of Mount Carmel Church they continued to strategize on how to confess their sins without causing spontaneous combustion in the confessional.

They no sooner walked into North Denver's "Italian Church," when a crone in a babushka walked up to Charlie. The skinny, wrinkled pickle of a lady two head's shorter than him, pointed a bony finger straight at his face and hissed, "You're a sinner."

Charlie froze as if the desiccated woman punched a knife through his soul. Her stare burnt through him like the glowing red votive candles that flickered in a nearby stand. His heart lost two beats at the sound of coins dropping into the votive box and the odor of burning candle wax made him think of hell.

"Jesus." He turned back to leave the way he had come in.

Bobo grabbed him. "Hold on." He whispered under his breath. "We're in this together. You're going into the booth and tell all -- it'll be a kick."

"Kick my ass." Charlie tried to keep his voice down. "I figured it out; I'm just here for your moral support because you think that you need absolution before that guy kills you in the ring tonight."

Bobo had Charlie's arm and pushed him up one of the aisles to a line of people waiting for confession. People dressed as if they were going to a funeral, mostly old Italians in black, prayed the rosary as they shuffled to the dark wood booth.

As they got closer, Charlie listened to the little doors in the confessional slide open and shut. Bobo went in. Charlie heard a man's voice raise then lower. Bobo came out of the chamber in two minutes. Piously, Bobo strutted by, and winked. "See you later."

Somebody behind Charlie caused him to jump, "Your turn, kid." Charlie hesitated but went into the booth and waited. He kneeled in the dark and heard low voices from the other side of the confessional. A sickening perfume pervaded the booth as he waited.

The little door between Charlie and the priest slid open and the priest said something.

Charlie started his rehearsed dialogue in faltering Italian. The priest answered back in Italian. *Terrific, I'll act like I don't understand him very well. I can fake a limited knowledge of Italian.*

"Uh, *perdono mi, padre, io avere con peccato . . .* ah." Charlie mixed articles, nouns and verbs incorrectly. He faltered until he heard the priest, "*Dio, si bambino . . . ignorante . . . .*"

Boldly Charlie slipped back into English, like he couldn't say it in Italian. He figured that he would tell God's own emissary the truth even if he couldn't understand it. "I've been having sex with an un-married mother."

"*Si-si,*" and then silence, grunting, more silence.

Charlie smelled smoke coming from the other side, brimstone?

"How old are you?" perfect English.

Charlie's heart sunk. He was going to hell, never to see his home, his family, and absolutely and finally -- no Karin.

Five minutes later he exited the booth feeling the stares of people in line probably wondering what took him so long. He walked to the back of the church where Bobo, finished with his penance, probably five Hail Mary's and one Our Father.

"What took you so long?"

"I was in the fires of hell, wishing some kind soul to pour cold water on my hot sinful body. He wanted details."

"What's the matter with you? You're supposed to do the Italian slip-and-slide, man. Oh, I know, you got smart and figured if you confessed in English that the Father wouldn't understand. Man, the guy's from Denver, not like the rest of these priests from Italy. Didn't you see that it was Father Lorienti giving confessions today? Man, have you lost your cool, probably nailed you good, too. How many Hail Mary's?"

"Five Rosaries. He reduced it from ten. I made a good Act of Contrition."

"You better find some beads and start praying. You should be about half done when it's time for Mass and Communion."

The priest exited the confessional and went to the vestry to ready for the late afternoon Mass. At Mass, the priest looked hot and Charlie thanked God that Father's sermon didn't dwell on the sins of man or the impinged souls of adolescent boys.

"See, that wasn't so bad." Bobo gleamed as they left the Church.

"My mouth is dry," Charlie choked. "I need something to drink. Let's go over to the creamery and get a soda."

They walked across the street to Sally-Ann Creamery and took a seat at the soda fountain. Charlie looked at the mirror in back of the fountain. He saw a tense reflection over the jars of *Briocci*, candy, and the boxes of little Italian cheroots. He felt a kinship to those nasty, black, twisted cigars.

"What'll it be kids? Just coming from Mass, huh? How's about some nice ice cream?"

"Just a soda today, Sam." Bobo's got a bout tonight. I think he's got to eat a raw steak and a dozen eggs or something like that."

"Oh sure, the Golden Gloves. Too bad, I'm staying in the store tonight." Sam yelled to the back of the store, "Hey, Tommy-Nick, you going to the Golden Gloves tonight? Bobo here is fighting. "Who you matched up with, kid?"

"Some skinny Mexican, I'll cream him."

"Better watch that Mexican, Bobo." The owner's son came from behind a store shelf with a case of tomato paste. "I've been watching this guy. He's mentored by Rudolpho 'Corky' Gonzalez who was the Golden Gloves champion a few years back."

The street-side screen door slammed and a bell tinkled as a girl came into the store.

Bobo waved his hands, "No big deal, I'm in great shape. My conscience is clear, my mind is sharp; he's mine," Bobo thumped his chest.

Tommy-Nick placed small cans of tomato paste on a shelf. "Your opponent has a left jab that's constantly in a guy's face. His right hook is pretty effective, too. I'll be there, Bobo, good luck."

They finished their sodas and headed back to the Bonarelli home.

"Hey, Charlie, you want to ride with Dad and me? I'll have to go down a little early . . . ."

"No, I'll see you down there. Dad wants to go, too, if he can get someone to take care of Jody and Sam for a couple of hours."

"Okay, see you later."

Charlie went into the house to find Nonna Bonarelli cooking dinner. Papa Bonarelli sat at the table with his coffee, speaking Italian with Jody.

"Carlo, *che avete?*"

"Nothing, Papa." Charlie must have been wearing a long face. He thought maybe Papa Bonarelli could see into his nasty heart, too. *Geez, that old lady scared the crap out of me. It's like she's been following me around. She was probably riding on my back when I was banging Karin.*

Nonna turned from the stove where she had a big pot of soup boiling. "Chicken Soup, *molto saporito*. You look a little sick, Carlo, you okay? Come here and give your Nonna a kiss." She almost hit him with her wooden spoon as she embraced her grandson.

"Hi, Son," Vince came into the kitchen, "Mama and Papa will stay with the kids while we go down to the Elks and watch Bobo.

I think he'll do okay. That other kid has a terrific left jab though. You know how Bobo gets when someone is peppering his head. You think he's prepared for that?"

"Yeah, he says he's tuned as fine as a jaguar. Let's hope that his timing is as good as he thinks it is."

"Hey, Dad, how come I can't go to the fights with you and, Charlie?"

"That place isn't for little kids, Sammy. Besides, you'll choke to death from the cigar smoke. I'm not too happy about that part of it myself. You can go with us when you're sixteen, maybe. Let's eat, smells good."

Nonna beamed at her son, "Vincenzo, you bring the bagels from Forman's?"

"Sure, Mama, we'll have a good kosher meal tonight."

"Oh, Charlie, by-the-way, Mr. Groban wants you to call him. We had a nice chat on the phone. He thinks maybe you can stock shelves and clean up around the drugstore. He's not too sure yet about you working at the soda fountain with the bandages. Anyway, call him Monday morning from school if you get a chance."

* * *

Vince and Charlie parked near the Denver Elks Lodge and went into a crowded auditorium. Charlie looked around at the faces of teenagers, adults, and wise guys that looked like gamblers more than sports nuts.

The Golden Gloves amateur bouts were sponsored in Denver by the Elks Lodge; it was the best boxing event to fill the void between occasional organized professional bouts.

Charlie saw few females in the audience as he panned the crowd in the dank wood auditorium. A plaque on a balcony read, "William, 'Buffalo Bill' Cody's Funeral Was Held Here June 3, 1917."

Despite the dark hole of a cigar-stinking venue, one face stood out like a neon sign. Jewell M. Charlie didn't expect to see her here, and felt betrayed when he saw her sitting next to Detective Mickey.

Charlie stared at the girl. He thought, Jewell M? Jewell Mickey is more like it. No wonder she doesn't want me to know her name. All this J. M. stuff is just crap. Maybe he's using her to find out something from me – what crap.

The bouts came and went. Charlie paid little attention as he sat, stewed, glared, fidgeted and squirmed in his seat. "That little snitch, she's playing me just so she can give Daddy the dirt on me. Some chance meeting in the library I'll bet."

"What, Charlie?" Vince concentrated on a finishing round.

"Nothing, Dad."

Bobo's bout came up. Charlie tried to get into the cheering and hooting as Bobo, weaved, bobbed and took repeated jabs in his face from the opponent.

Bobo got mad. Unable to fend off the continuous jabbing and poking, he came in swinging wildly. He hit his nemesis a couple of good punches but they were wide and he opened himself up for a couple of quick gut punches.

"Ouch." Vince and Bobo's father, Anthony, said simultaneously.

Anthony called, "Bobo, cover your guts, you're wide open."

Jab-jab-jab, and a wet "woof" as moisture flew from Bobo's head. For every jab that Bobo took Charlie felt a corresponding pain.

He stared across the ring at Jewell.

She saw Charlie and tried to slump down in her chair to no purpose. She was embarrassed, and tried to avert her head. Detective Mickey, Charlie knew now that he was Jewell's father who seemed to relish that Bobo took hit after hit.

Bobo landed a lucky hook in the third round and finished the startled Mexican off with two well-placed shots in the head and another in the solar plexus. Bobo steamed like a kettle but settled down in his corner while the count went down over his opponent. Then Bobo did something so nuts that the match was forfeited.

"God damn it." Anthony jumped out of his seat. "The little pepper-head will be suspended. That's it," Bobo's father jumped out of his seat shaking his fists and screamed, "Bobo, *babbuino -- stupido*."

40

Disqualified

Bobo removed his mouth piece and trash talked the prone Mexican. He picked up his water bucket and ran to the groggy fighter where he emptied the bucket on his defeated opponent. "Get up goddamn-it I'm not through kicking your ass."

The ring filled with attendants and officials. A whistle shrilled; the referee grabbed Bobo and shoved him away into the arms of his trainer shouting, "Disqualified – disqualified!"

Bobo's father, Anthony, jumped up and down like a grinder's monkey hollering, "*Impudenza, il becco, stupido – bastardoooooo!*" He threw his folding chair into the ring barely missing one of the officials.

Charlie understood why his cousin Bobo acted like the he-goat Anthony swore about.

Detective Mickey grabbed Anthony by the shoulder, "I can arrest you for that. That your dumb kid — huh? You dago's are all alike, a bunch of hot heads."

Anthony poised to take a swing at Mickey's face. "If I didn't think it would improve your looks, I'd paste you one wise guy."

"Settle down, Anthony," Vince pulled his brother-in-law back into the crowd. "C'mon, that cop is looking for any excuse to get into our faces. Let's go find, Bobo. He should be getting a real ass chewing about now. He can probably kiss his fight career goodbye."

Charlie saw Jewell, and got close enough to pull her away from her father who was cajoling Bobo with the rest of the crowd.

Teary eyed, Jewell, froze.

"J.M., Jewell M? Try Jewell Mickey you little snitch broad. You've been screwing me around for Daddy"

She sobbed, "Charlie, I'm really sorry. I knew that my Dad was working on your case but I swear I didn't tell him about you. If he even thought that I liked you, he'd send me away to Catholic school in Nebraska -- I'd be exiled."

"Bonarelli, get away from my Daughter," Detective Mickey snatched Jewell into the jeering crowd quicker than sand down a sink hole.

"C'mon, Charlie," Vince shoved Anthony out of the crowd, "let's wait for your cousin. We'll meet him outside the locker room."

* * *

The three of them waited until most of the boxers and officials had gone. A sheepish Bobo came out of the locker room door.

Anthony went after Bobo, "Crazy bastard -- what the hell were you thinking? I suppose you're suspended for good."

Bobo shrugged, "Yeah, I suppose you're right, Pop. 'Temporary suspension,' they said they will review it, but I think I'm done boxing. Sorry, I guess I lost my cool when that little Mex kept connecting with those head shots. I could use a cold drink."

"Shit. We'll that's it kid. Let's go down to Duffy's, I feel like getting drunk."

Charlie thought that his Uncle Anthony took Bobo's probable suspension worse than Bobo did. Anthony fumed as Vince drove the three of them the few blocks to Duffy's Bar and Grill. Bobo, not wanting to talk with his father, followed in his car.

Bobo and Charlie ordered colas. Anthony, true to his word, ordered a double-bourbon with a beer chaser.

"Have a shot or two to go with your beer, Vince," Anthony lifted his shot glass. Charlie can drive you home if you get shit-faced."

Vince said, "Take it easy, Anthony, alright?"

Anthony threw back the double and swigged on his beer.

Bobo studied a business card in his hand.

"What'aya looking at kid," Anthony asked, "what's that?" He reached for the business card out of Bobo's hand.

"'Perry Promotions, Bobby Perry,' so what's this about?"

"That's why it took me awhile to get out of the locker room. This guy practically cornered me in the showers. I thought he was some kind of fruit, but then he starts telling me that he liked my attitude and maybe I should consider professional wrestling."

Anthony gave Bobo a dubious look over his beer, "Professional wrestling, this guy's a wrestling promoter?" The booze hit Anthony. "Hell kid, you're not even out of high school. He's exploiting you -- professional wrestling huh?"

Anthony thought about it for a minute and took a pull on his beer, "You've never wrestled before."

"He said they'd teach me. He likes the way I'm built and he says that I've got the juice to stir a crowd." Bobo perked up a little. "He said that the bucket deal was cool."

"What about college, Bobo?" Charlie asked. "You want to be a social worker someday, right?"

"I don't know it's not looking too good right now."

Anthony blushed, "Let's talk about it later, we better go."

Charlie gave Bobo a questioning look as they exited the tavern.

Bobo whispered, "I'll tell you about it later."

*   *   *

The following morning Charlie woke feeling physically much better. He sensed his body healing though his mind was in a funk over Jewell Mickey.

Jewell Mickey, He thought, I should have figured it out a long time ago with those Mickey Mouse explanations about who she was. "That's a joke, Bonarelli, Mickey Mouse – get it – hah and you are *shtuped* and stupid to boot."

"Charlie, you're spouting Yiddish, we're Italian, remember?"

Charlie hadn't heard his cousin Bobo come down the stairs to his room.

"Bobo, what're you doing here so early?"

"I needed to get out of the house. The shit hit the fan when Dad told Mom and the family what happened at the bout last night. Let's split, man and I'll tell you all about it. Hey you got something to tell me, too, about the little Jewell babe? C'mon, it's Sunday, Uncle Vince will take care of things around here. Let's go out for a cup of coffee, away from home."

Bobo drove them to a café on 38th Avenue where the meaning of greasy-spoon belched through the cigarette smoke and the food odors.

"This joint smells like breakfast, from last week, Bobo. You like it here?"

"Sure, it smells like home, doesn't it?"

"No, man, not my home, and don't give me that. Your house smells like peppers, sausage, garlic and anise just like my house."

"Okay, okay, so it stinks, but breakfast is cheap and free refills on the coffee."

"So what's on your mind, Bobo?"

Charlie's cousin studied his menu, but they both new that he would have a double order of bacon and eggs, wheat toast and orange juice.

"Come on, Bobo, out with it, you already know what you're having." They waited for the waitress to take their order and Bobo leaned over the worn Formica topped table. "It's like this, cuz, I'm probably not going to get to go to college next year. That means I'll be drafted, like you, if I can't get a deferment."

"Is that what pissed you off last night?"

"Dad told me before the bout that he's having trouble making ends meet with the business. He says all of the stores are buying better produce direct from California, and they're even bringing the stuff in from Mexico now –- can you believe it?"

"So why doesn't he sell the produce from California, too?"

"Well he does, and for Christ sakes, Bananas and grapefruit don't grow in Welby. He sells those doesn't he? I'm telling you, Charlie, something else is going on and he's not letting anybody in on it. The California thing is just an excuse."

"Did you know about this before?"

"I'm not sure but he's been acting really strange lately. People have been calling us, won't leave names if Dad's not there. My Mom suspects something, but she's not sure what it is. She's really buzzing his ears. He's getting edgy as hell to the point that we don't even want to be around him sometimes."

"Bobo, what do you think is wrong, any ideas?"

The waitress brought their food.

"How come you're not eating? What's with a piece of toast and that little-bitty glass of juice?"

"This isn't food in here, Bobo, it's a grease storm."

Bobo stoked the eggs and bacon in his oven door-like mouth.

"Jesus, Bobo, slow down for air."

"I can breathe through my nose," he choked the words out through a mouth full of food.

"You're not even enjoying yourself, just stuffing the pig."

Charlie dipped his toast in his coffee and ate the soggy bread, savoring the butter and coffee flavors together.

"Man, that's sick, who dunks toast in coffee?"

"Okay, Bobo, what is it? I mean, Uncle Anthony?"

"He's gambling the fucking money away. He and his pals at the market play *i dadi*. It used to be after the market closed, but now there's a game going on all the time. I caught them at it a couple of times when I drove down to the market. *Il Barboto,* the beard, that nasty game of dice that we learned as kids on the street. Except some kids get big, have families; still fuck with the dice and the cards, and the dogs, and the horses and . . . ."

"The fights." Charlie finished the sentence because he knew that some people at the Golden Gloves and the regular bouts were laying down bets with the bookies who might be the barber or the counterman or the auto repair man. Nobody thought about it as illegal, it was just a game. If the game got too serious and you lost money, and you didn't pay your bookie or your loan shark, some discomfort might befall you.

"So you think that you know that Uncle Anthony, that good man, is throwing the money away. I thought he already had you set for college. You were going to Regis, right?"

"Yeah right but now I'm going to be looking for a job and I hope that I can get into school part time."

"Look, Bobo, kids work their way through school. You can go to the C.U. campus downtown. Hey, and the draft is two years unless you join as a regular for four years. You've heard of the G.I. Bill, you can stand a couple of years, that'll help you with school when you get out. So what's a couple of years? We don't have any hot wars happening right now."

Bobo swallowed his food, "The Cold War, that's what they call it. Who knows when some of those jackasses might turn up the heat? Hey, I'm not afraid of the Army, but I wanted to finish school first. Maybe go in later as an officer."

"Hey, *cugino,* it'll work out, don't get in a sweat. By-the-way, I'm seriously considering the U.S. Naval Reserves. They meet at the Federal Center and I only have to drill one-night a week, boot camp and a two week cruise, two years active duty, probably somewhere exotic."

"Yeah, exotic," Bobo twirled a finger around his right ear, "you're more likely to end up at Great Lakes Naval Training Center, maybe in December."

"I'm thinking San Diego, California, Bobo."

"So you're really looking into it?"

"Yeah, as soon as I'm better, I'll be checking it out."

"You mean as soon as you can pass the physical without all of your bandages and broken bones showing."

"Something like that. Anyway, I don't have much going here. I'm not ready for more school yet, our band is not working, and I'm shit out of luck with the chicks."

Bobo chewed more food and was on his third cup of coffee, "Yeah, the chicks. You said something about that Jewell girl."

"Her old man is Detective Robert Mickey –– that putz of a policeman in plain clothes."

"You're shitting me."

"Nope, I saw her at the fights last night with Mickey. It turns out that she's his daughter."

"God, that's terrible, like a spy, huh?"

"That's what I'm thinking, but she says no-way."

"You believe her? I mean her old man has been out to screw you over for the last few weeks. Is that a coincidence or what?"

Bobo's question troubled Charlie, and he wasn't sure of the answer.

41

Cloaca Pink

Charlie lay in bed thinking about the pain in his ribs and won-dering if he should take the bandages off of his right hand. *Day Sixteen: Mom's been gone only sixteen days and it feels to me like a lifetime.* He could hear the bustle of breakfast preparations and his siblings getting ready for school. *It's Monday, Uncle B is gone, the mountains didn't kill us last week and my homework is just about caught up. But, then there's Ruthie Grey; she'll be back in school. I've got to confront her about the gunshots, the car thing and the pink scarf.*

Jody called down the stairwell, "Charlie, Aunt Theresa's making lunches, how's about a nice meatball sandwich?"

Charlie remembered that he and his lab partner Becky were dis-secting a frog in biology – before lunch. *I'll probably puke and a meatball sandwich with red sauce isn't what I'll want for lunch.*

"Charlie," Jody called again, "what about the meatball sandwich."

"No thanks, I'll try the cafeteria today."

* * *

Charlie was able to call Mr. Groban who told Charlie that he could come in tomorrow after school to discuss the part-time job. He was thinking of the job when Becky interrupted his thoughts.

"Careful, Charlie, you'll cut yourself."

"It's okay, Becky, I got it under control." Charlie wasn't thoroughly convinced that he was going to finish the dissection of the frog.

Becky spread-eagled and pinned the frog to a board while the teacher explained how to make the incisions; how to peel the skin and muscle.

"Jesus."

"Watch your language in here." Becky whispered at him.

"The fucking stench —- we get a rotten frog or something?"

Becky giggled as Charlie almost up-chucked and held his breath.

"Here, silly, let me do it." Becky took the scalpel out of his hand and made the cuts.

All of a sudden the outside color of the green frog went pink, purple, blue and shit-colored as Becky opened the frog up. Instead of barfing up breakfast, Charlie studied the intestines and an idea hit him.

"That's it, that's what I've got to do."

Becky gave him a puzzled look. "What do you have to do, Charlie?"

"Turn it inside out."

"What are you talking about? We just did." Becky held the scalpel and peeled tissue from the frog.

"No, I mean, the girl's murder —- if it was murder."

Becky put the scalpel down on the table. "Here, start sketching and naming the parts. Let's do the frog, and you let the police handle that unfortunate girl."

"The cops? They're dumbfounded. Nay, they're cuckolds."

"Charlie, where did you get that one? You know what that means? Oh, I get it, that's your poor attempt at a Shakespearean metaphor for what has been going on between you and the police."

"Yeah something like that, like somebody is screwing their wives and they have no clue."

"Charlie, that's disgusting."

"Excuse me, Becky, these cops and Mr. Greyer are messing with me. Cutting up this frog has given me an idea. It's like we can see the liver, the gallbladder, pancreas, spleen, intestines and right out the ass."

"The cloaca," Becky corrected.

"Yeah, that too, but we can't study the nervous system unless we pull the guts." He put his fingers into the frog, "So we gut the little bugger."

"Damn it, Charlie. We're supposed to take our time and diagram all of this." Becky was close to tears, "What a mess."

"Exactly, this is how I feel. I'm being dissected by the cops, the school, my friends, and my family."

"So what can you do about it?"

"I can get to the nervous system, the stuff you can't see right away, the stuff the cops don't give a thought to. They went for the guts on this one. I'm the obvious choice because I was there, I was visible, and that's all the cops want -- somebody to blame, to make them look good."

Tears ran down Becky's face, "Charlie, all of this is too much." She ran out of the room.

"Becky, where are you going?" The Biology teacher called out.

Becky didn't answer.

The teacher asked "Charlie, where's Becky going?"

He shrugged his shoulders, "Probably to the girl's lav."

He slowed down to diagram the frog's intestines for the report. When Becky returned, she looked composed, but Charlie knew that she simmered inside.

"Damn you, Charlie," she whispered, "now you've got me all upset. I can't finish this." She pointed at the frog. "Oh," she saw his sketches and notes, "that's pretty good."

"Feel better?" Charlie saw Becky relax a little. "Buy you a root-beer later at the Barrel. Oh, and ask Ruthie to meet us."

"Ruthie?" Becky looked hurt again.

"Yeah, and don't get your nose out of joint. I want to ask her some questions away from school. Don't let on, just say that we are meeting at the Barrel after school"

"Sure, Charlie, care to tell me why?"

"I'm working on something, and I think Miss Ruthie Grey is the key."

"Wow, wait until I see her. You think that she knows something?"

"Becky, keep it cool. I don't want Ruthie to split before I talk to her. You've got to act as if nothing is up. Do you understand?"

"Yeah, I think so."

"Okay, I'll take care of the rest of these notes. We've got a couple of days, and I'll finish this up. Meet you after school."

At lunch, Bobo and Zellie were already at a table when Charlie came out of the cafeteria line.

"So, Bobo," Charlie asked, "What's happening with the Golden Gloves? They dump you?"

"Yeah, I've had it. No more boxing for me. I'm thinking about Ju-Jitsu. Some cop has a place where he teaches downtown. I'm looking into it."

"What for -- some little Japanese guy will just hurl your ass against a wall. Anyway, I read somewhere that those Asian martial arts guys practice self-control. You threw your self-control out in that bucket of water that you poured on your last boxing opponent."

Bobo turned red while Zel, still chewing food, nodded in agreement.

"Okay, I can work on that. Anyways I'm reading about the sport. Martial arts are going to be a big deal someday. Maybe I'll even be in the movies or something."

"Oh right." Charlie said. "So let's talk about something realistic, like who killed that girl in the park."

Zellie swallowed his food. "You think that Jay, Birch, Burris, Mr. Greyer are all tied in with this girl don't you?"

"Yeah, and this girl, Dorothy or Dot was a twenty-year-old women. She was Willie Burris's girlfriend."

"Where're you getting your information?" Bobo asked, clearly very interested. "You have some secret source."

"Yeah, the newspapers, I showed you the story last week. But, the big deal is that Ruthie Grey has something to do with it, too. I'm sure of it now, but I'll let you know late tonight or in the morning.

"I'm meeting Becky at the Barrel after school and I asked her to bring Ruthie. I think she's involved."

"What the hell are you talking about? Ruthie, she's a psycho ding-bat."

"You think so, huh, Bobo? I guarantee that she's certifiable if my hunch is right, and I plan to find out after school."

"So let's all go to the Barrel together," Bobo blurted.

"Nope," Charlie held up his right hand, "I've got to do this alone. I'll call you later, and keep this to yourselves or Ruthie will split and we will never see her again." Charlie got up from the table without touching his lunch, "I'll see you later."

*   *   *

After school Charlie drove himself to the Barrel Drive-in and parked. As he ordered, Becky and Ruthie pulled in next to his passenger side, they waved. Just as Charlie was about to get out of his car and go to Becky's car, Bobo and Zel pulled up. Bobo parked on the other side of Becky.

Charlie's hand motions and facial expression as much as said, "Damn it, Bobo what are you doing here?" He should have known better than tell his cousin and Zel about meeting Becky here.

Becky called, "Charlie, come on in here."

He sat in the back just behind Ruthie, and leaned over the seat.

"Hey, Charlie," Ruthie turned awkwardly towards him. "Becky says you wanted to talk to me. How come here?"

Bobo and Zel stared at them. Becky waved at them as Charlie concentrated on Ruthie.

He fingered a bright pink scarf around Ruthie's neck.

"You always wear this, don't you, Ruthie? This one looks brand new though."

Ruthie cleared her throat, "Yeah, I like it."

"So what happened to the last one, Ruthie? I mean, that scarf goes with you everywhere? This one is new. Oh and by the way, how'd the deer hunting go? Did you shoot anything?"

"What're you talking about?" Ruthie whispered.

She turned her head back towards the dash. She wouldn't turn to face him again. Becky stared at Charlie, stared back at Ruthie, and back at Charlie again as if an explosion just went off in her head, "Oh!"

Bobo and Zellie had come around to the passenger side and pressed their faces against Ruthie's half-open window.

"I'm talking about you, Ruthie. You tried to shoot me, in the outhouse."

Bobo and Zel knew about the shooting at the cabin but Charlie had only speculated on the scarf that the Clear Creek County Sheriff found or his suspicions that Ruthie really was the shooter. He was grateful that Bobo and Zellie had kept what they already knew to themselves.

Becky sat stunned in her seat. "Ruthie? Ruthie, is that true? You were hunting with your father the same time that Charlie and his Uncle Bernard were at their cabin, and in the same area. Isn't that so? And, you came back without the pink neck scarf that you always wear. I mean, it's like a talisman or something. Even if you're not wearing the scarf it's always tucked in your purse or your coat."

"I, uh, I, uh, the scarf's right here." Ruthie fingered the bright pink cloth around her neck. What're you talking about? I've got it right here."

Charlie pressed Ruthie, "The new one, Ruthie. You lost the old one in the Forest Service officer's truck that you stole from 'Oh My God Road,' after you tried to push me and my Uncle Bernie over the side of the mountain. You bought that scarf new, just after you got back from the mountains. That's a brand new scarf, the edges aren't even worn like your old one, and the pink is brilliant. The old scarf had sweat marks, makeup and faded spots on it."

"Get out of my way." Ruthie tried to open the passenger side door, but Bobo blocked it and he wasn't about to let her out. "Get the hell out of my way, Bobo." She quickly opened the window; shoved her huge handbag through the opening and into Bobo's face. The bag caught him heavy in an eye that had been recently damaged during his last Golden Gloves bout.

"Shit, Goddamn, right in my bad eye." Bobo reeled away from the car door allowing Ruthie to get out. Zellie made a futile grab for Ruthie and ended up catching Ruthie's purse, swung in an upward bowling ball fashion, between his legs.

"Strike! Oh shit that's got to hurt!" Charlie hollered as Zel went over like a 10-pin.

"Holly-Shit, Ruthie?" Becky screamed.

Until today, Charlie had never heard Becky use any real off-color language. Her outburst would have made him laugh if he wasn't concentrating on getting his hands on Ruthie, to wring the truth out of her if he had to.

But he was still on the mend and not so quick. The doors between Becky's car and Bobo's were open, and in the confusion of Bobo nursing his eye; Zel doubled up grunting in pain, and Charlie lost Ruthie.

By now kids were getting out of their cars, horns honked and some joker howled like a wolf.

Charlie broke through the onlookers to see Ruthie running across Speer Boulevard. Car horns on the heavily trafficked street warned the girl wearing a pink scarf dodging and in an out of oncoming cars.

Charlie pulled a newly arrived tray with a foaming root beer from his driver's side window and thrust it at a bystander. He got in his car and hollered to Bobo and Zel, "Let's go. She ran into the neighborhood behind Hammonds Candy."

He backed out of the parking space as Bobo, with Zel barely moving behind him, hobbled to Bobo's car. He fell into the passenger seat.

Bobo followed Charlie out of the drive-in's parking lot. He held a handkerchief over the damaged eye and drove, one-handed behind his cousin.

Charlie looked back and saw Becky following Bobo then he accelerated across the street, barely avoiding cars from both directions. Bobo and Becky's cars had to wait. Charlie lost sight of them as he cruised the neighborhood where he had seen Ruthie run.

She was gone. Charlie stopped the car. Bobo and Becky's cars pulled up behind him.

"What's going on? Did you see her again?" Bobo called out the window of his car.

Charlie hollered back. "She's hiding somewhere. Maybe in an alley or a doorway or a bush for all we know. Let's drive around. Honk three times if you spot her."

The three cars drove the neighborhood for thirty minutes then met again on a side street.

"Looks like we lost her; where could she go?" Bobo asked Charlie.

"She's split, man. We should just go home. We'll talk later on the phone." Charlie waved to Becky. "We're giving up the search. She'll turn up sooner or later. I'll talk to you in a couple of hours."

Charlie drove home. "Yeah, Ruthie Grey, I'll talk to you later, too." He already knew what to do.

42

The Cousin Connection

Ruthie Grey had to be found. Charlie called Matt Grueber from a pay phone before he drove home from chasing around the neighborhood without spotting Ruthie. He explained the whole story to Matt and how he thought about Ruthie as a suspect, but a suspect for what? He asked Matt. "Why would she want to shoot me or push our car off of the road into a steep snow bank?"

"That doesn't make any sense, Charlie. What's the motive?" Matt asked. "Maybe she's upset with you but that's extreme. The scarf and the girl running — circumstantial, it doesn't prove anything. But you're right, why would she, if it is her, do these things? That takes planning and it's hard to believe that a seventeen-year-old girl would contrive to kill you and Bernie.

"And, by the way, you're still supposed to be giving any information you think is relevant to Mickey and his partner. They're still the lead investigators on this case. Mickey and Brawley went up there, in the mountains, with the Gilpin Sheriff, and they found nothing right?"

"Look, Matt, I'm not comfortable with your detectives. They think I'm a snoot-nose and a wiseass."

"Well . . . what gives them that impression?"

Charlie heard the chiding tone in Matt Grueber's voice and thought, Up yours, too.

"Charlie, we still have to follow procedure. I'll be the buffer between you and the two detectives, but it's their case again. I'll pass the information along and check out the girl, Ruthie Grey, with an 'e' and not an 'a,' right?"

Charlie sat in the phone both and struggled with his emotions. What was Matt going to do with the information? For all Charlie knew, Mickey and his partner would sit on it like they sat on their butts most of the day when they weren't dogging him.

*   *   *

When he got home, Charlie dialed Becky. "Becky, has Ruthie shown up at home or called you?"

"No, I think you really scared her. I hope she's okay. But, it makes no sense that she would do those things to you. She's just a girl."

"Just a girl, huh? So was Bonnie Parker when she and Clyde Barrow were whacked after their robbing and killing spree. Ruthie's not the only female to use a gun. Isn't she on the girl's rifle team at school?"

"Oh, God, that's right, Charlie. She's good, too. If she really wanted to kill you, if it was her, don't you think she could have? God, this is terrible."

"Now, don't cry, Becky. I've told the cops what I suspect; they'll find her. But, what do you know about her? What's her background, where's she from?"

Becky cried on the other end of the line as she tried to compose herself and answer Charlie's questions. "You, know, I don't know that much about her. I've met her mother and father. They seem like nice folks, but Ruthie's always been a little strange."

"She likes to fool around with psychology and guns." Charlie interjected, "That's a combination I find more than a little strange."

"She's always been very nice to me, Charlie. She treats me like I'm her big sister. She likes to hang out with me and you know she gets between me and Ralph Jay. She likes that creep Ralph, and I can't stand him. God, I think sometimes he's looking in my bedroom window when I'm getting ready for bed at night."

"Tree jumper, I knew it, mother . . ."

"Charlie, your language is deplorable. I can't believe I even like you with that mouth. You better clean it up, kiddo. Why do you think that you're always in trouble with those cops and Ralph and anybody else that makes you mad -- your mouth."

Charlie thought, she said she likes me, and what's wrong with my fucking mouth?

"Oh--okay, Becky, I'll work on it. Anyway, can you get me a little more information on Ruthie? Her habits, quirks, family background -- you know, the works. I'll talk to you later. Oh, and I'll work on my mouth, really." He hung up. "Really?" He thought about his attitude, his language; his future. Maybe I better change my game plan a little, he thought, but just a little.

* * *

After five days, Ruthie Grey was still missing. Charlie had a part-time job now at the drug store on the West Side. Mr. Groban, a decent employer, encouraged him to work a little slower until his hands and arms became completely functional. His hours were flexible, and he got in at least two hours after school stocking shelves or straightening the merchandise.

"Okay, Charlie, that's looking pretty good." Mr. Groban came from behind the pharmacy counter to check out the store and wait on customers. "Maybe you could help Mrs. Berstein over there. She's got her hands full of heavy soda bottles. I think she's giving a party for her mahjong girls."

Mr. Groban called out, "So Mrs. Berstein, you having your girl-friends over tonight?"

"We're going to have a blast while the hubbies are away in Vegas. Mrs. Goldberg is bringing her cream-cheese rolls."

Charlie looked at the stuff in her sacks as he took them out of her arms. The weight of the sack pressed on his one good arm. His stomach made noises when he thought of cream-cheese rolls covered in chocolate bonbons, washed down with strawberry soda.

"What's the matter young man? You look ill. You okay?"

Charlie didn't answer but stared at the person walking into the store. "I'll take these to your car, Mrs. Berstein." He hid his face behind the tall sack of heavy pop bottles.

"Okay, sonny, are you going to be alright?"

He nodded.

"Please follow me."

He lingered in the parking lot, arranging Mrs. Berstein's packages in the trunk of her Cadillac.

"Here you go, sonny," she handed him a quarter and got into her car. "What's your name?"

"Charlie."

"Well, Charlie, you're a cute boy, thank you."

He thanked her and walked into the store to the shelves he was stocking.

"Charlie."

He acted as if he hadn't heard.

"Charlie, you know your name don't you?"

Jewell Mickey stood in the aisle by the boxes of products that he had to price-mark and stock. "You're avoiding me on purpose."

"I've been busy; I'm working here now after school. How'd you find me? Aren't you out of your neighborhood?"

"I live on the east side of the lake near the junior high school. I come over here often enough. I found out from a friend who knows your cousin Bobo that you're working here. Anyway, I'm really sorry about the thing with my Father."

"What thing with your Father? The last time we saw each other, at the fights, you said that you don't discuss me with your Father. Now, what's this thing -- like you know something?"

"I know what I read in the papers. Anyway, I think that my dad and his partner . . . ."

Charlie finished her sentence, "Brawley, the other heavy-handed sleuth on the team."

"Okay, so maybe my Father's a little crude sometimes, but he treats his family well and he is my Dad."

"Good, it's nice to have parents, I have to work, see you around."

"Look, you," she pointed a finger at him, "I'm not giving up so easy. You think I like caring about a boy who my Dad thinks is the world's biggest wiseass?"

"Charlie, can you help at the soda fountain? Wrap that bandaged hand with Saran Wrap or a clean towel. Joey's behind and I've got prescriptions to fill."

"Sure, Mr. Groban."

"Saved, by the bell, huh? I'll see you at the soda fountain."

Charlie quick stepped to the soda fountain *Jewell Mickey is going to be a pain in the ass. She's a mouthy chick. What does she mean, 'caring about a boy?'*

He busied himself helping the regular soda-jerk. Jewell sat on the stool where he worked behind the counter. She stared at him and leaned over the counter.

"Well, are you going to the dance with me? You never answered me the last time I asked."

The people sitting at the counter all turned to Charlie. A boy asked, "So don't be a *nudnik*, you going or not?"

He grumbled and thought, so now, I'm the boring pest? She's got what my boss calls, *chutzpah*. If she were a man, she'd have balls.

"It's not like you have to come to the house to pick me up or any-thing. I'll meet you somewhere."

"Let's talk later. I'm working."

She occupied the stool until Joey said, "Okay, Charlie, I can han-dle it now, thanks."

Jewell followed him as he finished stocking shelves.

"Are you going to let my Dad scare you away?"

"Your old-man would love it if he ever found out we were dating, wouldn't he?" He busied himself with the shelves.

"He's not going to find out. Besides it's one dance already. I've bought the tickets and I want you to go with me -- please?"

"You're not too forward." Secretly Charlie liked being pursued by a girl whose father he was anxious to piss off a little more. "So, when's this dance again?"

Jewell brightened. "It's next Friday night, in the school gym. The class is serving refreshments. It's casual, a sock-hop. There's going to be a DJ spinning the latest songs. It's going to be great -- so, you'll come?"

"I'll think about it. Maybe I'll see you at school tomorrow."

*   *   *

After a few minutes, Charlie cleaned up the boxes and told Mr. Groban that he would be back tomorrow after school. Charlie had the car now on a regular basis. As he left the parking lot he saw Jewell walking east.

Charlie could have turned west, towards home, but he turned east instead. He slowed the car and got the bandaged right hand positioned on the window knob. He rolled down the passenger side window. "Need a ride?"

In the car, Jewell gave him directions to her neighborhood. "This is out of your way. Why so interested in taking me home now?"

"I'll swing around the lake after I drop you off. Anyway, you shouldn't be walking by yourself after dark."

"I don't have a problem. My Dad showed me a couple of things if anybody causes trouble."

"Yeah, like what?"

"Like, turn left at the next street please. Drop me off on a corner, about two blocks from Colfax."

"You don't want me to take you all the way to your house?"

"No, I'll get out over there." Jewell pointed out a cross street. "It wouldn't go well with my Dad if he saw us together."

"No shit? You think Daddy Detective Mickey might blow his cool?"

"No shit, Charlie."

"Jewell, you talk like me. Better watch that mouth. Daddy will give you . . . ."

She finished his sentence. "Such a *patsh*."

"Yeah, he might smack you. He's wanted to hit me a couple of times. How come you know a little Yiddish?"

"I live in this neighborhood. My mother is Jewish."

"And, your Father's a Mick?"

Jewell grinned as she exited the car, "My Father's a mutt. Thanks for the ride. See you tomorrow?"

He watched her walk up the street and turn at the corner. "That's weird. That car turned behind me, pulled over and now it's behind me again."

The incident on the mountain, with his Uncle Bernie, cautioned Charlie when out on the road. He was alert for strangers who seemed to have more than a passing interest.

He wondered why the cops had not picked up Willie Burris by now. He heard from Matt Grueber that Burris might have left the state, but Charlie didn't believe it. It's going on five-weeks since that son-of-a-bitch escaped.

The car he thought might be following him turned away as he reached 26th Avenue, north of the lake. *Nothing, my imagination.* He drove home thinking about Jewell.

At home he was welcomed by a plate of food from the oven.

Theresa supervised Jody and Sam at the kitchen table with their homework. Charlie took his food and went to his room to start his own homework. He was catching up but had a few more papers to write. The phone rang upstairs.

Theresa called down, "The phone's for you, Charlie. A girl, I think it's Jewell?"

He took two steps at a time. Theresa liked to listen on the phone, until he got to it.

"What are you doing?" he whispered as he reached for the phone.

She put her hand over the mouthpiece. "I listen to your girl-friends' breath, and if they say something while they're waiting for you, I can tell what kind of babe is calling you."

"Babe, huh?"

"Yeah, like, Karin. She's a heavy breather, throaty, sexy. Becky, she's high-toned and stylish; this other girl that called before, she's dynamic, knows what she wants."

"She called before?" Charlie took the phone and covered the mouthpiece.

"The other day, oh darn, I forgot to tell you. I had to leave before I wrote it down. Sorry."

"Hello."

"Charlie, it's me."

"Jewell?"

"My Dad's steaming mad at something. He's muttering about 'That Bonarelli kid.' He's been glaring at me since he got home. He came in about five minutes after I did."

"A car followed us from Groban's."

"Shit, it was Dad. It was him, I'm sure of it, shit."

"So why doesn't he beat you or something?"

Charlie detected invective venom under Jewell's breath. "He did that once before –- followed me, and I caught him. I got so mad, and my mother almost chewed his ears off. He promised he would never do that again."

Charlie relished the knowledge that he got under Mickey's skin, but he didn't like his daughter taking the heat.

"Jewell, maybe we better not go to the dance. Why get yourself in a jam with your Dad if it's going to be a hassle?"

"So you're seriously thinking about going to the dance with me? Great. Oh-oh, I'll see you tomorrow." Jewell hung up.

"What the hell?"

"She hung up, huh, Charlie?" Jody stood in the kitchen doorway shaking her head.

* * *

Charlie was on his way to lunch when he heard, "Hey, Charlie, you working at Groban's tonight?" It was Jewell.

"Uh, no, I'm not working tonight. Mr. Groban called me this morning, he doesn't need me today."

"So how about meeting for a soda somewhere, later?"

"Uh, can't tonight. I've got something to do. But, I'll call you later."

"Charlie, we're on for the dance?"

"The dance, yeah, right. How do you plan to handle Daddy Detective Mickey?"

Jewell rolled her eyes. "He took off like a passenger jet. He wouldn't stop bugging me about 'that Bonarelli punk.' What have you done to make him so mad anyway?"

"He's pushy, overbearing and a big pain in my butt. I gave him the finger when he leaned on me at the hospital the day before my Mother died. He and that Brawley jerk hauled me in and grilled me like I was a mad-dog killer. I got sick in the interrogation room."

Jewell laughed, "Oh, that's why he calls you, 'little shit-pants."

Charlie colored, "Little shit-pants." He thought about it and laughed, too, "I cleared out the room and it saved me from taking more abuse from those two gumshoes."

"Detectives, Charlie," Jewell corrected him and laughed "Mother smacked him with a rolled up newspaper, like hitting a dog that just peed on the floor. 'Following your daughter again, anyway, the Bonarelli boy is cleared of that homicide in the park, that's what you said.' She rolled over him like a truck. I'll meet you somewhere before the dance anyway. I don't want to cause more trouble with Dad."

"Well, don't look for a lot of jive dancing from me. I'm still sore in couple of places."

"So, work out the kinks, Mr. Cool. Tell you what, the dance starts at 8:00PM in the gym. I've asked one of my friends to meet up with me at my house, she's got a car. She's meeting her boyfriend here, too. As far as Dad knows, I'm going with my friend and I'll be home by eleven okay?"

"Okay, I'll meet you in front of the gym, Friday night, eight-o'clock."

The bell rang. "I've got to go; I'm meeting my pals for lunch. You're probably going to the library, right?"

Jewell looked a little upset that he didn't ask to sit with her during lunch. Man, he thought, he wasn't going to do that — that was serious. He couldn't be seen sitting with a new girl. Becky would find out sure thing, and he'd be dead in the water for any future help. Anyway, he reasoned, he wasn't sure if Jewell was serious stuff, just a dance date, and then he'd split.

* * *

"Hey, Mr. Cool." Bobo called to Charlie as he entered the lunch room. He and Zellie sat together. Zel pulverized a mouth full of food.

"Where're you getting the 'Mr. Cool' stuff?"

"Oh, I saw you in the hall with the Jewell chick. She called you, Mr. Cool."

Zellie took another bite of food, "Mr. Cool." Zellie grinned but it came out through his mouth full of food as "Miffer Drool."

"Miffer Drool.   Oh I like that."   Bobo slapped the table. "Remember that, Charlie, when you have your nose in the air or your head up your ass, Miffer Drool."

43

Game Changer

That night Charlie wondered about Ruthie Grey when Aunt Mary called downstairs. "Bobo and Anthony will be here any minute. We're all having dinner together. Better wash up and come upstairs, Vince just drove into the garage."

As he washed, Charlie heard the back door and his Dad's step up the stairs. He had gone to take off his coat and hat. Charlie heard him say, "I'll wash up and see you all at the table."

Bobo and Charlie's Uncle Anthony came through the front door. "Hey, Mom, what's for dinner?" Bobo headed to the stove to smell the aroma of cooking stew, "We got some bread, too?"

Anthony brought in a sack of fresh fruit and vegetables. "Here's some Florida grapefruit and some tomatoes from California."

"Hey, everybody," Vince came into the kitchen. He had taken off his suit coat and pulled his tie off. "Let's eat, I'm famished. Jody, Sam," he called into the front room, "It's time for dinner -- *mangiare*."

They all gathered at the table.

"Wait, Bobo," Aunt Mary smacked Bobo's reaching hand with a table knife, "we're saying Grace first. Vince, you want to say the prayer?"

Vince reddened, "Grace, for what? We procreate, we raise a family, we die, we try to live through the tragedies and the crap keeps coming down. Thanks, for what?"

Nobody said anything, but Charlie saw the pain on his Aunt Mary's face and the tears in her eyes as she tried to make things better. She wiped her eyes with a corner of her apron, "Just a little prayer?"

"I'll say Grace." Jody made the sign of the cross. Everyone looked at her and followed her direction as she made the simple "Bless us, Oh Lord, for these thy gifts which, we are about to receive . . . ."

They ate in silence, trying to avoid each other's eyes. Charlie wondered about his big family, who could fork a meatball in one cheek, go for the bread with their other hand while carrying on a normal conversation, all of a sudden a bunch of clams.

"I talked to Matt Grueber today."

Vince put down his fork and stared, "About what, Charlie?"

"Ruthie Grey," Bobo blurted.

"So who's Ruthie Grey?" Vince asked.

"You've met her, she's Becky's friend," Charlie answered.

"Oh, that Ruthie Grey, what about her?"

"She's the shooter."

"The shooter?" Vince asked.

Bobo nodded his head. "That crazy broad shot at Charlie in the crapper."

"What the hell are you talking about?" Vince asked.

"Charlie thinks she's the person who tried to shoot his ass up at the cabin and then tried to push him and Bernie off of the Oh-My-God-Road."

"Bobo, your language," Mary thwacked her son on the back of his fork hand with the flat of her knife.

"Ouch. That fuc . . . uh, that hurts, damn, that hurts."

She froze her son with a glance. "Shut up, and let Charlie talk."

Vince sat, uncomprehending. "What did you just say? Did you say that one of your school chums was the mystery person at our cabin?"

"I'm not sure she wants to kill me, maybe frighten me, but I'm certain that it was Ruthie Grey. She was supposed to hunt in the area with her father, and shoots through the door of the outhouse, small caliber gun, probably knew she'd take a few chips out of the wooden door in front of me to scare me."

"Scare you, what's that all about?"

The family erupted in questions, gestures, *Madonna Mia, Dio, My God, Jesus, Charlie,*" then went silent when the phone rang.

Mary said, "I'll get it," and went to answer the phone. "Charlie, it's Matt Grueber, he wants to talk to you."

"I'll take it." Vince got up before Charlie could react.

"Yeah, Matt, it's Vince, uh, yeah sure, okay."

Vince held out the phone to his son. He had a perplexed look on his face, "What's going on?"

Charlie took the phone. "Hello," he listened. "Yeah, thanks."

"Well, what did he say?" Vince asked.

"Yeah, what did he say" Jody chimed.

"Ruthie Grey is Mr. Greyer's niece. Mr. Greyer's brother, Frank Greyer, changed his family name to Grey. Willie Burris, the guy who is maybe after me, maybe not, I'm not sure now, is Ruthie Grey's first cousin."

A fork clattered onto Vince's plate.

Charlie continued, "Matt's theory is that somebody is trying to hurt somebody, scare someone, avenge someone, about who and what, he doesn't know. He passed the information on to Detectives Mickey and Brawley. I'll probably be hearing from them again."

Charlie no sooner got the sentence out of his mouth when there was a loud knock.

"Wait," Vince held up his hands, "I'll see who this is. Finish your dinner please."

*   *   *

"Wait in here please, I'll get him."

Vince called into the kitchen, "Charlie, it's the two detectives."

Charlie got up and motioned for everyone else to sit still. "Try to be quiet if you want to hear what's going on."

Detectives Mickey and Brawley sat on the couch in the front room. They kept their coats on, but both were holding their hats in their hands. They looked less menacing and maybe even a little contrite when Charlie walked into the room.

"Charlie." Not "Bonarelli, punk, kid, you little shit- pants," but Charlie. Detective Mickey started the conversation. "Uh, maybe, uh just maybe," he stopped, lost for words.

"Maybe, we were a little rough on you, Charlie," Brawley intervened. "It seems that there is some kind of conspiracy against you. The Grey girl, the Burris guy, and it appears like your counselor, this Mr. Greyer, the boy's father and the girl's uncle, is protecting them. We don't know why. Grueber is on his way to Greyer's home to question him. He may haul him in."

"We're on our way over to Ruthie Grey's house. Maybe the parents know where Ruthie is. She may have skipped though." Mickey gave Charlie a sheepish look. "We stopped by to offer an uh . . . uh, an uh . . . ."

"Apology," Brawley said, "We're sorry for the inconvenience kid."

Vince seethed, "Inconvenience? Charlie's in pieces because you guys were hounding him. This Burris guy is trying to wreck him; one of his classmates was trying to beat him up, Mr. Greyer is hitting foul balls and you think it's an inconvenience? Jesus Christ, where'd you guys come from?"

Charlie stood up, "Mr. Mickey."

Mickey looked up, "Yes."

"I want to take Jewell to the dance Friday night at school."

The room went silent. Vince gave Charlie a questioning look.

"I want to take your daughter, Jewell, to the school dance Friday night."

"Huh, my daughter . . . uh . . . um . . . oh . . . Jewell?"

"Yes, you know we've been introduced; a twist of fate, but we know each other. She's asked me to take her to the Junior Class Dance. I would like to come by your house and pick her up."

Without saying it everybody in the room, and now everybody from the dinner table appeared through the kitchen opening like people looking to buy a ticket on the last train from tragedy.

Everyone knew and understood that Charlie was apologizing, but for what? He wasn't really sure himself. For his attitude, for his grief, for his intolerance, for his mouth and demeanor; he didn't quite understand either. He knew that he was flipping out.

He thought that maybe he was being honest. Maybe he was out of line, he didn't know why but, it felt right. A silent family stared at Charlie like a herd of cattle in the headlights of a speeding truck.

Vince, stunned, threw up his hands and looked at Charlie, "What are you talking about?"

Mickey and Brawley sensed what he was talking about.

Charlie expected resistance from Mickey. He knew that the big detective didn't like him, he was sure of it.

"Sure Kid, c'mon by, I'll tell her."

"Thank you, Mr. Mickey, but I'd like to tell her tomorrow at school.

Detective Mickey, a little unsure of what had just happened answered him. "Yeah, that's good, Charlie, okay. Thanks for asking. Uh, you'll need police protection until this thing goes away. We still haven't caught Willie Burris."

"Yeah, Charlie," Brawley chimed, "we'll cover your backside until the thing blows over and we understand what the heck is going on with Mr. Greyer and his family."

"No thanks," Charlie answered, "I'll take care of myself, and I've got, Bobo."

"Yeah, I'll watch out for *il cugino mio*," Bobo grinned big.

By now, meal forgotten, the family had crowded into the front room.

Jody intervened. "Charlie, you're going to take a girl to a dance on Friday. Wow, that's really nice."

Mickey and Brawley, particularly Mickey, argued in favor of the police.

Mickey put a hand on Charlie's shoulder. "Look, Charlie, we're going to have to stake out your house now. You were right when you said once that you're bait. I'm sorry, kid, but it's turned out that way whether we planned it or not. Somebody's out to make an example out of you, and we can only guess that maybe Ruthie Grey and Willie Burris know or think something that you did, that you said, whatever. You're going to have to be watched. If we don't catch Burris by Friday, I'm thinking it's not a good idea to be escorting my daughter to the dance. We'll talk about it. You know, maybe I better tell Jewell so that I can work out the logistics."

The phone rang. Anthony called from the kitchen, "Detective Mickey, it's for you."

Mickey went to take the phone. Charlie sat perplexed and questioning now if he had done the right thing about asking Mickey about Jewell and the dance.

Mickey came back into the room. "Lt. Grueber has Mr. Greyer. We're to meet him at the station. We'll talk to you later, Charlie. In the meantime, Lt. Grueber is setting up a stakeout of this house. Don't worry if you see a car parked out front, and back, with a couple of people in them.

Charlie protested.

"It's routine, Charlie, we've got to do it." Mickey stuck out his hand to shake his hand, Brawley did the same.

"We'll let you know what's going on, Charlie." Brawley looked around the room at the family. Vince sat, silent, in his chair.

"It's okay, Dad, I'll be fine."

There were tears in Vince's eyes.

44

Spilled Oil

A sound like tires squealing, "C-h-a-r-l-i-e-e-e-e!"
Jewell waited in the school doorway for Charlie to come in.
Bobo reacted like Ike's bodyguard, but not quick enough.

She put an arm around Charlie and looked at him with her beautiful green eyes. She was crying, her nose ran. "You're picking me up at my house on Friday night. Oh, Charlie, you asked my Dad. You really made up with my Dad? Really? Oh I'm so happy that you did that." Jewell smiled and hugged him.

"Geez, Jewell, don't break something else. Ouch, Jewell. I just wanted to be upfront about it. I don't like sneaking around . . . uh."

Bobo whispered in his ear. "Oh not you, and not with Karin or anything, you sneaky bastard."

"You remember my cousin, Bobo, right?" Charlie asked Jewell.

"Oh, yes, the boxer. Are you going to the dance, too?"

"Nah, I hadn't thought about it. I don't have a date anyway."

Jewell squealed again. "Sure you do, I'll ask my girlfriend, Friday, who was supposed to ride with me to the dance. Her date got the mumps and had to cancel."

"Nah, I don't think so. It's too late to ask someone and who's going to want to go now? Who's Friday?"

"You'll meet her. I'll bring her to lunch and we'll talk then."

The first bell rang. "Gotta go. Oh, Charlie, I'm so happy." She saw somebody she knew, "Hey, Friday, wait up, we'll go to homeroom together, I want to talk to you." She ran. "See you guy's later."

As Jewell caught up with whomever she was trying to hail, a pert little thing with long blonde hair turned around to smile at Jewell.

Jewell grabbed the girl and they both looked back at Charlie and Bobo. Jewell waved and then turned to walk to class.

Bobo became a burbling statue, "Did you get a load of that girl, she's Friday? What a dish. Man, I've never seen her before. I can't wait until lunch; I want it to be Friday now." He broke his statuesque stance and was ready to bolt.

Charlie grabbed him. "Damn, cut it out, it still hurts to laugh. You'll meet her at lunch. You're in trouble, Bobo. What about the little babe on the West Side? Hey, there's Zel."

Zellie Goldfarb caught up to Charlie and Bobo. "It's the girl." He almost hollered it.

"Well, good morning to you, too, Zel," Charlie said. "What're you talking about? What do you mean, it's the girl."

"Dorothy Wallick. The chick you were talking about before. You know, you reminded me about her and Willie Burris. He thinks you scored on the girl and then maybe killed her. He saw you in the park and thinks you did that to his girlfriend. So now he's going to take you out. You better explain this to the police. Man, you're in danger."

"Oh you don't know the half of it, man." Bobo had lost sight of the little blonde. "Charlie, tell Zel about Ruthie Grey and who she is. Oh and don't leave out any details. And by the way, Zel, the cops escorted Charlie and me to school this morning, and they're shadowing us after school."

"What about Ruthie?" Zel asked, "and what are you talking about? You got a ride from the cops? You're not holding out on old Zel are you?"

"Let's get to class before the bell rings. We'll talk about it later."

*   *   *

"Pay attention to this, ladies and gentlemen." Charlie's homeroom teacher wrote something about Career Day and some possible contacts for college tuition money on the blackboard as he talked.

The teacher turned to the blackboard and Becky passed a note through a couple of other students before it reached Charlie. One of the student's, held the note on the pretense of reading it. Becky motioned to him to give the note to Charlie. He saw a, "You better not cross me," look in her eyes as she directed the smart guy with her finger.

Charlie read the note: *The police are talking to Mr. Greyer in his office.*

Charlie knew that Ruthie Grey was the key to all of the mess going on in his life. Charlie and Becky collided like neutrons after the bell rang.

"Charlie. Ruthie is still gone. I talked to her Mom this morning. The police went to Ruthie's house last night thinking she may have returned home –– she didn't. Do you know what's going on?

Charlie told her about the police and what he suspected. "Geez, Charlie, geeeeeez."

"She's that escapee's cousin? You think she's helping him? You think Mr. Greyer is in on it? I mean he's the guy's Dad. What a mess, Charlie, geeeeez."

"We've got to get to class. We'll talk about it later -- See you at lunch." Charlie walked away to his class. *Oh shit. Jewell's bringing the little blonde girl, Friday, to meet me and Bobo during lunch. What the hell am I going to do?*

"Damn it."

"What's wrong, man? Bobo grabbed Charlie by his good shoulder.

"Jewell, Friday, that's what's wrong."

"Yeah, Friday," Bobo grinned, "What a sweet-looking piece . . . ."

"Cool it, Bobo. I just told Becky that I'd see her during lunch. How's that going to look with a couple of junior girls and us sitting together when Becky walks in?"

"Oh, oh, protocol."
They turned to see Zellie following them.
"You're cooked, both of you."
"What do you mean, Zel?" Bobo asked.
"The little babe over on the West Side may go to a different school, but she's got intelligence agents all over North. She knows what you're up to, Bobo, before you get home at night. She's deadly with informants."
Bobo weighed his options. "It's okay. Things are a little tense between us right now. I begged off doing anything with her on Saturday night, so she's pissed off."
"Okay," Charlie said, "may as well piss her off some more. She'll find out if you take the little blonde to the dance and it's . . . ."
"*Gehenna* for you, Bobo. She'll *klop* and she'll *klop* and then," Zellie ran a finger across his throat. "At least you'll die kosher."
"What the hell are you talking about?" Bobo asked, "Speaka-da-English."
Zel grinned, "Her Uncle is the *shoykhet* down at your girlfriend's Dad's kosher beef plant. She'll probably use his knife, but it'll be quick. We'll say *Kaddish* for you. See you later, I've got a physics exam."
"Yeah, well that shit your talking sounds like Exlax to me, too," Bobo called after Zellie.
"What the fuck is he talking about anyway, Charlie?"
"Never mind, we're going to be late for class. But, you'd better watch your back."
"What the fuck. Hey wait up."
Ralph Jay walked by as Bobo and Charlie were going into the classroom. "Talk to you later, Charlie?" It sounded like a plea.
"Now what? He sees me trussed up like dried salami and wants to cause more damage? Oh what the heck, I've got one good arm left."
"What do you suppose he wants?"
"Beats me?"

"That's it -- he wants to finish the job. Never mind, I'll take care of him when the time comes."

*   *   *

They were in class fifteen minutes when a hall monitor entered the classroom with a message for the teacher.

"Charlie Bonarelli, you too, Bobo Marcantonio, to the office now, please."

Charlie and Bobo picked up their books.

Bobo asked, "Charlie, what the hell, the office? Must have something to do with the police, you think so?"

As they walked into the school office, a clerk scrunched her face and pointed to Mr. Greyer's office, "In there."

The Assistant Principal's office space was tight as they joined Mr. Greyer, Detectives Mickey and Brawley, Ralph Jay and Joe Birch.

"Come on in, boys," Detective Brawley motioned.

Detective Mickey leaned against a wall.

Brawley sat on the edge of Mr. Greyer's desk, Jay and Birch sat, glumly, in wooden chairs, Charlie and Bobo stood up. All of them looked at Mr. Greyer trying to remain calm behind his desk.

Brawley started the conversation. "Okay, here are the rules: Nobody speaks until spoken to. This is informal, but we can all do down to the station and sort this out if we have to."

"You, two boys, Ralph Jay, and Joe Birch," Brawley looked at a small notepad in his left hand. Where were you two the night that . . . ." He looked at the book and gave a date and time and place. "The park, behind Woodbury Library, you two were there."

"Who says we were there? Bonarelli, you stoolie," Birch spouted. "You've already asked us once and we said we didn't know nothin."

An irritated Brawley said, "Quiet, kid, I said I'll do the talking for now. Let me finish,"

"So you two guys where there, at least we've got a witness."

361

"Witness? He didn't see us." Birch turned red in the face as he pointed at Charlie.

Ralph put a hand on the back of Birch's neck and squeezed. "Please shut the . . . just shut it, and let the man talk."

"Okay, this is what we think went down." Brawley got off of Mr. Greyer's desk and stretched with a big yawn.

"See, Charlie here goes around the park on his way back from making a delivery at the Barrel. He stops to help a stranded motorist, no big deal, being a Samaritan and all that.

"But what he doesn't know at the time is that somebody was hiding in the backseat of the car. Charlie is unable to help the driver, Mr. Greyer, here." Brawley made an expansive gesture towards the counselor.

Mr. Greyer winced and put his head down avoiding the stares from everyone in the room.

"So, it went like this." Brawley continued. "Charlie can't help the motorist, Mr. Greyer, because the man's foot is stuck between the curb and the car. You'd think the son, Willie boy, would help his Dad get the car away from the curb, but he's in a hurry. Burris jumps out of the car after Charlie's gone for help. He leaves his father with the car because he's looking for the girl, the woman, the victim." Brawley nodded towards his partner, Detective Mickey.

Mickey picked up the banter. "So now, Charlie, he's in the library, passes near the picnic table but not near enough to see or hear anything. But, you two guys know what's going on, because you're there." Mickey pointed at Ralph Jay and Joe Birch.

"Who says? Ouch." Jay squeezed the little creep's neck.

"The witness says."

"What witness?" Jay asked.

"We'll get to that in just a moment," Mickey continued, "Charlie in the meantime, has the Woodbury librarian call the police to help out the motorist, Mr. Greyer, here." The detective pointed to the

Assistant Principal. "We've got a recording of the call, that's clear." Mickey gave Charlie an apologetic look. "We just got it yesterday."

"So Charlie goes back through the park, this time he goes by the picnic table. "What happens, Charlie?"

"I thought I saw or heard something."

"So Charlie sees something and goes to investigate, make a quick look, but turns out not so quick. He finds the Wallick woman, on the ground, panties off, skirt around her neck."

"She was raped?" Mr. Greyer paled.

"We didn't hurt her, we didn't rape her, she was okay when we saw her at first," Birch blurted.

Ralph Jay was dumbfounded. Everyone knew then that he had held back. He sat on the edge of his chair fuming at Birch who by now was a can of spilled oil, he couldn't stop leaking.

"We saw her, yeah, but she was talking to some guy."

Mickey slowed Birch down. "Okay, take it easy, we want the details. You saw a guy, a man, a boy, what? Where were you watching this from?"

Birch answered. "We was behind the trees because we was waiting for someone."

Jay blanched.

Birch continued, "It was someone that looks like the guy in the paper, the escapee that you haven't caught yet. Anyway, he was there."

"So what did he do?" Mickey asked.

"He was shaking her, arguing with her, hugging her, arguing with her again."

"What where they arguing about?"

Joe Birch continued, "We couldn't really hear them so maybe they was just talking, maybe not arguing. The guy kept hugging her, but she pushed him away. 'You left me, you bastard.' She screamed at him. Then we heard someone say. Hurry up, get over here, I need some help."

Brawley jumped in, "So you heard someone holler, and then what?"

"Well that's pretty much it. The guy said a few more words. I think he said, 'I'll find you later, I got to go help,' so he splits."

"So that's when you raped the girl?" Brawley asked.

"No, I didn't, I mean, we didn't do nothing."

"Did you get cute with her, kid? I mean you know, a little lady, in the park, it's late, you think maybe you're on to something?" Mickey asked Birch.

"No, it was nothing like that. Was it, Ralphie?"

Jay sat still.

"What about it, Ralph?"

"You tell them, you little wiseass. I should have thrown you out of the third floor window a long time ago."

Birch was stunned. "Look, so maybe I asked her what's going on — that's all."

"You scared her, running up to her like that. She fell and hit her head on the table." Jay squirmed in his chair, "And just then, Ruthie Grey comes up. She was supposed to meet her friend Becky in the library." Ralph Jay continued, "She says, 'What're you guys doing?' She was hysterical, went crazy, but just for a few moments, and then she leans over the girl, but the girl isn't moving. She puts her hand on her neck to feel for a pulse. Ruthie says, 'She's not breathing.' Now Ruthie gets crazy again, like another person, and then she changes back like that." Jay snapped his fingers. "Anyway, we hear somebody coming. But, Ruthie, she fools around with the girl's clothes. Like pulls her skirt up and messes with her panties -- it was weird."

Joe Birch couldn't resist embellishing the story. "'Get going you two.' Ruthie says to me and Ralph. So I pull Ralphie back among the trees and I see Bonarelli, but Ruthie has already split, man, like a ghost."

The detectives looked at each other. "We'll talk downtown, but before we go, you two," Mickey pointed at Jay and Birch, "where's the girl."

"What girl?" Jay asked.

"What girl? The one you're hiding, you know, Ruthie Grey."

"Ruthie?" Jay said, "We're not hiding Ruthie. We haven't seen her in over a week."

"Haw, they haven't seen her." Mickey winked at his partner.

Charlie stood still but stared at Detective Mickey thinking Damn, Mickey's doing that donkey laugh. Jay and Birch are in for it now.

"Okay fellas," Brawley opened the door, "You two, Jay and Birch, can take a little ride with us. Charlie and Bobo here can go back to class. Mr. Greyer, we'll be back to talk to you. You know the deal, find your son." He turned back to the door. "Let's go boys." The two detectives took both Jay and Birch out.

Bobo couldn't resist, "Hey you two, I hope you had a nice big breakfast."

Charlie and Bobo turned to leave.

"Charlie, I would like to talk to you for a few minutes. Bobo, you can go back to class now."

"No sir, Mr. Greyer, I'm keeping tabs on my cousin while your son is on the loose."

Mr. Greyer was embarrassed. He shut the door. "Sit down boys, I wish to apologize for all of this mess."

45

Find Those Two

Mr. Greyer told Charlie and Bobo how he tried to get his son, Willie, to turn himself into the authorities.

"He's always been a hot head, and never thinks things out. "My first wife, Willie's mother, had a big influence on the boy. Our divorce didn't help except to move him over the edge. My ex-wife had custody of Willie and I was never allowed to visit. He ran completely out of control.

"He remembered me when he got in trouble with the law. The police called me from California the night Willie and Dorothy Wallick were picked up. It's truly unfortunate about the girl, and then this murder or accident . . . I want to believe that it is really an accident.

"And, after the mischief in California, it was me who went there and straightened things out. California wasn't going to allow his and the girl's extradition. The State of Colorado had an earlier claim, they robbed a drugstore here, and we were able to get them back eventually.

"I don't know where Willie is now; he called me that night you stopped to help me in the park. He wanted to see Dorothy. He said he loved her and he had to see her, and then he promised me that he would turn himself in. I knew where she was, at that house behind the park. I couldn't dissuade him."

Charlie was full of questions, "So where is your son now? He keeps getting into my face and he's threatened my family. He's the one that hit my Grandfather Bonarelli. I mean he hurt him, and the family is really upset about it.

"And, he or the cousin, Ruthie, is leaving threatening messages. She put my Uncle Bernard and me in some serious trouble in the mountains. She shot at me. Where'd she get to?"

Mr. Greyer put up his hands, "I warned my brother that she was a little too keen on guns. But, let's start with that night. Willie saw Dorothy, heard me call after him and then he saw you. He was under the blanket in the backseat of my car. The next day he heard about Dorothy. He surmised since you came out of the park at about the time of her, uh demise, that you must have caused her death.

"We know that isn't the case now, but he's none the wiser. Ruthie knows, but she manipulates people. She probably hasn't told Willie the real story. I haven't seen him for days. He hasn't contacted me. The police think that Ruthie is hiding Willie, and that she's probably hiding with him. I think they are around this end of the city somewhere, but not in the school after I found him threatening you in the boy's room that day."

Charlie steamed, "I'm tired of being the goat, Mr. Greyer. My family has been threatened, I'm being dogged by both Willie and Ruthie, and you're the prime cause of it."

Mr. Greyer buried his head in his hands. He shook his head. "I'm sorry, I'm so sorry, Charlie. I've never been close to the boy. I wanted to help him, but I had no thought of the consequences. Poor judgment, that's all I can say."

"Bad judgment" Charlie raised his voice a little more than he would normally to an adult. He was taught to respect elders, but lately he questioned authority, and Mr. Greyer's 'judgment' pushed it too far. He thought that last tirade was a little too bold. I'll get him riled, show lack of respect that will help me with the rest of the semester.

"I've been a real jerk about this, Charlie."

Bobo nodded in agreement at which point Charlie gave him a look to cool it. He wanted to get out of Mr. Greyer's office.

"So, what are the chances the police will find Willie?" Charlie asked. "The police have probably discussed that with you. He's a chameleon, and Ruthie must be as good as he is."

Mr. Greyer thought for a moment. "The police will eventually find him and Ruthie. Ruthie's parents are frantic though I've assured them that she must be with Willie."

"That's reassuring." Charlie got up to leave, "I think I understand, Mr. Greyer, but I don't like it. I want to graduate in one piece. Let's go, Bobo, time for lunch."

They left the office to the grumble of Bobo's stomach.

"Man, can you believe that guy Mr. Greyer? A nogoodnick as Zel would point out. And, he's assistant principal?" Bobo turned towards Mr. Greyer's office, stuck his right thumb under his front teeth and popped a disdainful sign.

"Bobo, don't forget we're meeting Jewell and her girlfriend. Do us a favor, head Becky off before she gets into the lunchroom and spots us. Better yet, ask Zellie if he'll take Becky aside and discuss his physics exam or Einstein's theory, or anything to pull her off the trail."

"Didn't you tell Jewell this morning that you don't like to sneak around? What is this, you sneaky shit?"

"No, not sneaking, this is a political move. Congress can't meet today or there will be a filibuster in the lunch room."

"You mean a bust in the chops. Okay, I'll find Zellie, it'll take a few minutes. I'm still keeping my eye on you."

"It's cool. We're in a public place."

* * *

"Charlie, Bobo, This is Friday O'Day."

The two girls had found them in the lunchroom. Expecting the worst, Charlie looked for Becky. Zellie must have found her on the way into the lunchroom. Charlie couldn't help but to look around for her to appear throwing daggers.

"Friday O'Day?" Bobo couldn't stop his laugh.

"My parents have a sense of humor. I'm glad my last name isn't Knight." Friday smiled brightly at the two boys even if they proved bores.

Bobo recovered. "I'm sorry, Friday, I think that's a neat name. It's the O'Day that throws me, but I'll get over it. So you want to go to the dance with me?"

"Did I mention, Bobo's shy," Charlie pointed at his cousin.

The girls giggled.

"I don't even know you yet, Bobo."

"By the night of the dance, we'll be the best of pals. Oh, except, I have to watch out for Charlie. He's being followed by an escapee from the state mental hospital."

The five-foot-four, one-hundred-pound sparkling blonde girl gave a doubtful look towards Bobo, "Oh, that's original."

Jewell said, "It's a fact, Friday. I couldn't talk about it before, but it's known now that Charlie has been the target of Mr. Greyer's son, Willie Burris. The police, my father and his partner, are trying to find him. He's armed and dangerous."

"You mean he's got a gun?"

"Uh, no, I didn't mean that exactly. He's got a baseball bat. Charlie told me that Burris got into the Bonarelli's garage, hit Charlie's grandfather and took a bat with him. Charlie said it's the same bat that Willie Burris hit him with."

"Oh my God, how exciting, I mean, how awful -- I think."

Jewell smiled at Charlie as he rolled his eyes.

They ate lunch together and talked until the bell rang. Bobo grabbed Friday's elbow and walked ahead of Jewell and Charlie, talking Friday's ear off.

"Some bodyguard," Charlie said loud enough for Bobo to hear.

He turned his head towards Charlie. "Uh, not to worry, Charlie — eyes in back of my head," as he walked into a steel support post. Bobo went to the floor.

"Bobo! Everybody knows that post is there. Where's your head. You'd think intuition would've kicked in. Here, I'll help you."

"Oh let me," the blonde hoisted Bobo's dead weight off of the floor without so much as a deep breath. "Hey, Bobo, you've got some muscle in there."

Kids walked by giggling at Friday supporting Bobo's bulk.

"She's a gymnast; strong as iron," Jewell said.

*   *   *

Later that afternoon, they met again. "I'll take you home, Jewell. I'm working at Groban's tonight. Bobo's going to help me. How about you, Friday? Can we drop you off? You're safe, police escort."

"Police escort, you're kidding. Oh, right, sure, that would be great. I don't live too far from Jewell."

On the drive home, they made plans to pick the girls up at their homes, dance night. A plainclothes detective followed them from school to the girl's homes and to Groban's.

Bobo could hardly contain himself until they delivered the girls to their homes. "*Madonna*, Friday is a looker. She digs me."

"It must be the Band-Aid on your head, Bobo. The school nurse patched you up pretty good . . . makes an impression on the babes. Real men have zippers in their skulls."

"Nah, I think it's my love bump." Bobo tapped his crooked nose, broken in a boxing match the year before. "Just rub this in the right place and the girls scream my name."

*   *   *

On the night of the dance, Willie Burris was still on the loose, and Ruthie hadn't returned home. Becky told Charlie that Ruthie's parents hounded the police. They were convinced that Ruthie was in trouble, and if she was with Willie, she was being held against her will.

"Against her will?" Charlie asked Becky. "This chick is Ma Barker. She shoots, she swears, and I'll bet she chaws terbackee, too."

Becky tried to stifle her laugh, "Charlie, Ruthie's a little mixed up, but she's really sweet."

"Oh come on, Becky. I'm tired of talking about it. She's got to be found, and when she is, she'll be with Willie Burris."

"Okay, change of subject . . . I understand one of the junior girls has asked you to the Junior Sock Hop, huh, and you're going?"

"We'll I couldn't very well refuse. Her Dad is one of the lead detectives on the Willie Burris case. He's looking out for me now." He thought, Oh, Charlie, you speak with a twisted tongue, *un narratore*. "Yeah, it might be a good idea if I showed up at the dance, you know, kinda of act normal in case Burris thinks he's going to scare me, uh like that."

"Uh, like that, huh? Charlie, you've got a forked tongue, buddy. What father in his right mind would allow his daughter to go out with you if he knew you were a target? C'mon, get real. Oh, I get it, you're the bait again."

He didn't want to put it that way, "Yeah, it's something like that."

"C'mon, Charlie, that's stupid. The cops don't do that, not with their own family, do they?"

"No, no, of course not."

"See, I said you're lying, you bastard. You just told me a minute ago that you were working a setup. If I was a guy I'd kick you right where you live. Here all the time . . . ."

Charlie saw his cousin approaching; saved by Bobo, Charlie thought.

"Charlie, let's split, man, I'm taking, Friday . . . oh hi, Becky. Did Charlie tell you that I'm his official bodyguard now?"

"You're his bodyguard. Get real, Bobo. Do you carry a bucket with you in case of fire?"

"Oh, Becky, that's cruel. Behhhhhckeeeethatscruewell. I'm never going to live that story down, but a friend . . . oh I'm shattered."

"You better get your cousin out of my sight, you want to see shattered."

Becky steamed off. Charlie had never seen Becky so hot. He liked it.

"Wow, Charlie, is that smoke coming out of her ears? Never mind, she's a pal. She'll get over it. At least she's not like Ruthie, is she? That attitude . . . wow, Becky."

Charlie speculated, "Ruthie? What's going on with Ruthie? I'll bet she's hiding right around here. The night we drove around back of the candy company, I noticed a few of those older houses looked unlived in."

Bobo answered. "Yeah, I'll bet you're right. She could have run into any of those houses or a garage. Some of those houses have woodsheds, too. Let's go take a look."

"Nope, I'm tired of chasing *la raggaza*. Let the police do their job. We're all going to the dance and start getting things back to normal."

"Okay, she's history already."

46

The Chorus Sang

Bobo drove his car on the night of the dance. "Let's pick up Friday, and then we'll head over to Jewell's pad. I haven't noticed our police shadow tonight, have you?" Bobo beat on his steering wheel, as he sang to Buddy Knox and The Rhythm Orchids, *Party Doll,* coming through the car radio.

"Man, that's it, Friday, she's going to be my party doll."

"You're a sap, Bobo, and your little Jewish chick is going to rip your wheels off. I saw her in action at Groban's. She's got a killer instinct. Isn't she a professional roller racer; the kind that likes to duke it out on the racetrack?"

"No man, she's not a pro-skater, yet. She's working out though."

"Yeah, I know the type. Tough, she'll be trimming her mustache by the time she's twenty. I'd watch out for her. Turn here."

"I'm telling you, Charlie, me and Giselle, we're history. Up like Sputnik and down like a rock."

Charlie interrupted Bobo. "Okay, that's the house. I'll wait in the car."

Bobo left the motor running. A car came by with a four strangers in silk-looking jackets and pork-pie hats. Charlie thought it was probably a car club going to check out somebody's rod. He had daydreamed about the car he wanted since 1953. A red Buick convertible, chopped, was the coolest. He saw the car turn around and head back to where they parked. As it neared, Bobo and Friday came out of the door and he forgot about the car.

"Okay. We're off to pick up, 'The Jewell,'" Bobo said.

"Better leave it at, Jewell or JM, Bobo. She's sensitive about that name," Charlie warned.

"Oh, okay."

* * *

They drove the two minutes to the Mickey's house. Charlie felt the pressure. He was going to meet the Mickeys, formally. He rang the doorbell and Detective Robert Mickey opened the door.

"Hi, Charlie." He shook Charlie's hand. "Uh, I need to talk to you a minute."

Mrs. Mickey and Jewell walked up behind Mickey. Jewell waved and gave Charlie a big, "Hi."

Robert Mickey said, "This is my wife, Veronica." Charlie shook the mother's hand. He saw where Jewell got her interesting good looks. The mother was stunning with long jet-black hair, green eyes and a *Play Boy* figure at about five-foot, nine-inches. Both parents were dressed to go out. Unable to speak, Charlie stared at Veronica Mickey.

"Uh, Charlie, let me talk to you a moment."

"But, Daddy, we're going to be late if you need to talk. Can't it wait?

"It'll be quick."

Mickey took Charlie through a nicely furnished house and into a new kitchen.

Charlie looked around. *This policeman is doing okay.*

They talked; Mickey did the talking while Charlie nodded like his head was hinged.

"Okay, let's get the girls." As they went into the living room Mickey announced, "Mother and I are chaperoning the dance. We'll meet you there."

"What?" It was almost a howl. "Daddy, you didn't tell me. Mom?" Jewell protested.

"Last minute, honey," Veronica Mickey told her daughter. "I just learned about it an hour ago and had to rush to get ready."

Jewell blurted, "Oh so that's why you two are all dressed up. I thought you were going to a movie."

"It's okay, Jewell, I think it's a good idea until the police round up those two crazies," Charlie said.

"You mean Burris and that nutty girl, what's her name . . . ."

"Yeah, Ruthie Grey."

"We'll take our car and meet you at the school."

"But, Daddy, Mom, that's cramping our style."

"Not to worry, honey, we'll be chitchatting with the other adults. Now run along. You won't even know we are there." Veronica winked at her daughter.

Veronica flashed a smile at Charlie. He couldn't open his mouth, as he waved a limp goodbye. They got to Bobo's car where he was singing, and jiving Friday. She giggled and jived back.

Jewell looked at Charlie with a big grin. "Hey," she whispered, what did my Dad want to talk about?"

"Uh, oh you know, about Burris and so on . . . getting me up to speed."

Mickey told Charlie the police were going to be at the sock hop. "We think that Burris is in the area but don't know for sure." That was the real reason the Mickey's were going to be at the dance. Chaperones made good cover.

Charlie saw it again, the same car with the silk jackets that drove by Friday's house earlier. "Bobo check that car out." He pointed as it passed them. "Have you ever seen that car before?"

"Nope, never," Bobo turned to say something to Friday.

Charlie thought it could be a coincidence, but why had that same car been around twice in the last few minutes?

* * *

Noisy, the Junior Sock Hop at the school gym blasted music from a record player, and an occasional squelch of the P.A. as an acne-faced kid, acting as DJ, made announcements and called the tunes.

Jewell took Charlie's hand and squeezed. "Look, Friday, most of our class is here."

Charlie and Bobo were examined like germs on a glass slide; two senior wiseacres escorting junior girls. Charlie checked the frosted looks of some of the juniors staring at Jewell.

A boy came up to her and whispered in her ear.

"Are you writing a book?" Jewell retorted.

"Hey, babe, just checking," The kid threw up both hands and backed off.

"What's with him?" Charlie asked.

"Nothing, he's bad news. Hey, listen, *Whispering Bells.*" Jewell grabbed Charlie's hand and pulled him out onto the dance floor.

It still hurt to move fast to the Del-Vikings doo-wop.

"You digging this?" Bobo called from the dance floor.

A dull pain in Charlie's ribs reminded him that he wasn't quite healed.

"Wow, what a rhythm, really the most," Jewell danced well; she was getting into it.

Charlie broke a sweat under his suit. "I've got to get rid of this coat, Jewell, let's find a table."

They found an empty table and placed their things. She looked around the gym.

"I don't see my parents."

"Probably talking to somebody out in the hall," Charlie said, "I'll take a look." He walked just outside the gym entrance. The boy who had talked trash in Jewell's ear stood next to a hulk dressed in a blue silk jacket. "Joker's Wild" was written in chenille script over a colorful joker embroidered on the back of the jacket.

The smaller boy pointed towards the gym. The hulky, dusky-skinned, half-man-half-gorilla turned and glared at Charlie. Three more people walked up behind him, dressed in the same silk hotrod jackets. Charlie barely saw their faces for the funky pork-pie hats pulled over their eyes.

Those are the same guys that kept driving by when we were picking up the girls, he thought. That's not a hotrod club, a gang probably -- Jokers Wild?

Charlie melted back into the gym and the crowd. At the table he put his hand on Jewell's shoulder. "I don't see your parents, but I think something's up. You sit here for a few minutes. I need to talk to Bobo, back in a few?"

"What's up, Charlie? Maybe you better wait for my Dad."

"I'll be right back."

He found Bobo on the dance floor putting the moves on his date.

"Bobo, we need to talk. Somebody's been following us, and they're here."

A reluctant Bobo let go of Friday.

"We're sitting over there," Charlie pointed to the table where Jewell stared back at them with a worried look.

"Let's talk in the *bacasa*." Charlie led the way. "Look for four guys in blue silk jackets. 'Joker's Wild' is written on the back of the jackets. There's one guy, looks like King Kong."

"Hey, I know that name, some kind of gang," Bobo said. "I've only heard of them. Some big guy is the leader. He's called, 'Mook'."

"That must be his African gorilla name. You ever see this guy?"

"No, but I heard he's big."

"Fucking six-feet, and that's his waist size. Looks like a big hairball. He's out in the hall with his gang. I think they may be looking for me."

They went into the boys room.

Charlie put his arm around his cousin's neck, "Time for a plan."

Bobo went to the urinals, "May as well write the plan."

A boy standing next to Bobo laughed.

The door to the boys room burst open.

Three guys in Joker's Wild blue silk came into the toilets. A fourth, the Mook, came in behind, blocking the door.

"Bonarelli, now you're fucking mine."

Charlie looked around at Bobo, still at the urinals, who had turned when he heard the door. He peed on the leg of the boy next to him. The kid, disgusted, made a quick retreat into one of the stalls.

Willie Burris striding like an over-confident snake handler pulled a bat from under his silk jacket.

"So now it's my time to do a little damage to you like you did to Dorothy." Burris advanced.

By this time Mook, the human plug, was through the door, but someone from behind him shoved and he turned, to his credit, quickly and confrontational.

Burris and the two others turned their heads to see what was going on with the big guy. This gave Charlie a split second to think and defend what was coming.

He never liked that the doors on the boys' room stalls swung both ways. He'd taken a few beatings in the knees from wise guys who ran through the boys' room slamming the doors inward to smack an unsuspecting victim sitting on a toilet.

Quickly, Charlie grabbed the top of a stall door. Burris turned back towards Charlie quickly advancing with the bat poised over his head in a woodchopper's stance. Charlie slammed the outward swinging door with as much force as he could muster.

The stalls vibrated as Burris's nose and face contacted the door's edge.

Bobo shot past Charlie and into the person behind where Burris lay doubled on the floor, who was screaming, "My nose. He broke my goddamn nose." He passed out after that.

Charlie grabbed the bat, his stolen bat, from the floor.

Bobo had a guy by the jacket and slammed him against a wall and held on to him.

"Wayzzzzoutman –- I'm cool, man. No need to hit me."

"Yeah, you're cool. Bobo turned the guy around and pulled the silk jacket half way down the guy's arms. He pulled one sleeve loose and made a quick hogtie at the guy's elbows and kicked him in the back of one knee. Bobo's quarry went to the floor with a whimper. "And stay right there."

Somebody gave the Mook a bad time. "Kick my knee again you gimp fucker and I'll kill you for sure."

The Mook pulled out a switch blade knife and lunged towards whoever was in the doorway.

Bobo jumped the Mook from the back and grabbed the knife. The other guy, who was somehow overlooked, pummeled Bobo between his shoulder blades.

"Bobo, watch out," Charlie shouted, "I'll take care of him."

By this time the guy on Bobo's back had crawled up Bobo and was hitting him on the head with his fists. It looked like Bobo trying to fend off a beehive stuck to his skull.

Charlie jammed the fat end of the bat into the Mook's back. He let out a grunt. "Yeah, King Kong, I've got you now."

The Mook turned to Charlie who shoved the bat into Mook's ribs. The bat glanced off and the Neanderthal grabbed the end of the bat.

There was enough opening now for the person caught at the door to shove by the Mook.

"You got him, Bonarelli?"

"Huh, yeah? I got him." The Mook and Charlie played tug-o-war with the bat as Ralph Jay pushed by.

Jay ran up to where Bobo fought off the little-shit-storm pounding his head. Jay grabbed the guy on Bobo's head and plucked him like a grape.

The struggling person in Jay's arms kicked and screamed invectives enough to strip paint.

"Wow, this guy's got a tongue, Huh, Bonarelli?" Jay laughed as he turned the kicking and screaming devil into the nearest stall and hung him on a clothes hook by the back of his silk jacket.

The stalls shook and resounded with the person's kicks and screams. The guy's hat fell off and a long stream of dark hair fell out. A pink scarf had dislodged from the inside of the jacket as the person tried to extricate from the hook.

"Huh?" Charlie looked away long enough to see the wriggling body flail while flying a pink pennant.

"Ralph-you-stinking-piece-of-shit-bag-damn-you-to-hell-and-I-hope-somebody-drives-a-car-up-your-ass."

The chorus sang, "RUTHIE?" Charlie, Bobo and Ralph Jay called out.

Two policemen had come in the door and immobilized Mook.

A crowd gathered outside of the boys room; Charlie heard Detectives Mickey and Brawley, "Hey, back up, let us in there."

"Charlie, Bobo, what's going on in here?"

Detective Mickey saw the prone Willie Burris. "Willie Burris — it's him — and he saw Ruthie extricated from the clothes hook by the two uniformed police. "Ruthie Grey, too?"

47

Crazy as I Am

Jewell cried on Charlie's shoulder. "Oh, Charlie, I was so worried. I found Dad and he got more cops. God, I'm so glad that they got there before that big guy stuck a knife in you."

The police had cleared out the boys room and transported the Joker's Wild gang to the main city jail. Detectives Mickey and Brawley had to go downtown, too. Veronica Mickey sat at the table with the Charlie, Bobo, Jewell and Friday.

"Hey, let's not be glum now you guys." She tried to cheer everybody up. Robert should be done with that mess in a couple of hours. You guys go dance, and have fun. I told Robert that he had to take us all out for Pizza at Carl's after the dance. Friday, I'll call your parents and ask them if it's okay –- okay?"

* * *

The date turned into a debriefing session at the pizzeria.

Detective Mickey told them, "Those two cousins, Burris and Grey had been staying in an abandoned car-barn below the 16th Street viaduct. The uniforms checked it out. The place was a good hide-out. They had a camp stove, running cold water and lots of kerosene lanterns. The Joker's Wild gang was Burris's connection to the world. He was their leader before he went to the state mental hospital; he's a phony, and about as crazy as I am."

Veronica Mickey gave her husband a sideways look and a laugh. Jewell let out a "Haw."

The restaurant patrons looked over at the table of yappy, laughing, happy people.

A big weight lifted. Charlie felt like he had a future without daily body damage. He asked, "So why was Burris so bent on beating me to death, and what's with Ruthie? How'd Ralph Jay get involved?" Charlie asked questions before Mickey had all of the answers formulated.

"Long day," Mickey rubbed his eyes, "Let me lay this out so that I'm not blowing the case. I'll tell you what I can. Willie Burris connected Charlie right away with Dorothy Wallick's death. Ruthie perpetrated Charlie's involvement because she had a crush on Ralph Jay. She thought she was protecting Jay, even though it was Joe Birch who caused Dorothy to hit her head.

"So, Ruthie fed lies and deceit to her cousin Burris by saying she saw Charlie hit and assault Dorothy. Naturally, Willie Burris was out for revenge.

"But, Dorothy was already dead when Ruthie took it upon herself to make it look like the woman was assaulted. She pulled up the dead woman's skirt, took off her panties like she'd been raped and tore her blouse.

"If anybody belongs in Pueblo, Ruthie Grey does. She's a psychopath. And, her mouth, I can't believe the mouth on that little high school girl — kids today."

Charlie felt better when Robert Mickey didn't look in his direction.

Bobo colored and choked on a piece of pizza.

"Okay, so why was Ralph Jay there without his shadow, Joe Birch?" Charlie asked.

Mickey answered, "We've got Birch in juvenile hall. Ruthie had called Ralph Jay and said she was going, 'to get Charlie,' and that he shouldn't worry that the police would think he had done the crime. Ralph called the Bonarelli house and found out that Charlie was going to the dance.

He drove over to the dance to warn you. Just as he got there he saw the Joker's Wild gang follow you into the boys room. You know the rest.

"Ralph Jay told us that he was being stalked by, Ruthie and that's why she was in the park that night. He said she wouldn't leave him alone, and that he spent a good part of his days avoiding Ruthie Grey. He was relieved when she didn't come back to school. But, she started calling him. Ralph Jay was smart enough to report to us that the girl was calling him. So we knew that she was still around and probably okay. Anyway, it worked out, and I'm really sorry, Charlie, that you took the brunt of it."

* * *

Career Day came and went, and Charlie had already made a decision. The U.S. Navy promised him training, education, adventure and the opportunity to, "See the World."

The announcement that he was going to Great Lakes Naval Training Station, in Waukegan, Illinois at the end of the fall of 1959 was accepted by his family as an obligation he had to meet.

"I think you'll prefer the Navy over the other choices," Vince told Charlie. "I hate to see you leave, but it's your duty and I'm proud of you. We'll be okay. Your Nonna and Papa Bonarelli, and your aunts want to help. Your Grandmother Striker came through with round trip tickets to England for Jody and Sam. They'll be gone the entire summer. I'm glad that you'll be here for a while yet."

We'll go up to the ranch, near Marble, for a couple of weeks where your mother and I used to vacation. We'll do some fishing and horseback riding, it'll be a kick."

True to his word, Vince left his business in the hands of his capable assistant, Miss Mistletoe. They fished, rode horses, and most important, they talked.

Vince treated his son as an adult now, even though Charlie wasn't sure of himself yet. He had time to think about the last few months and his attitude about everything from his poor use of the English language and his relationships with family and friends.

Jewell and Charlie became closer. It wasn't the same thing he once had with Karin. He didn't smother her like a blanket even when the car steamed up as they felt each other all over. They were lovesick and thunderstruck, right on the verge of consummating their relationship in the backseat of Charlie's car.

Both Charlie and Jewell were petrified with the fear if he as much as pointed his penis in the wrong direction that Jewell would end up pregnant.

Charlie was doubly frightful of a possibility of living with the Mickey's on his pay as a part-time drugstore clerk.

His relationship with Robert Mickey improved. Mickey treated Charlie more like a son. Charlie thought during his active duty that he'd be out of Mickey's hair for a while, and his daughter was safe.

Charlie was smitten with Veronica Mickey. He was sunk, hooked through the lip like a big trout by the Mickey family. He was respectful. He didn't need that big detective pounding him black over his daughter and his slip of the tongue.

Charlie's body healed. He and Ralph Jay came to an understanding, and they both grew up a little more during the summer. Charlie's drumming got better and he picked up some nice work before he shipped out to boot camp.

"Why Waukegan and not San Diego?" Bobo asked. I hear it's colder than a well-diggers butt in the winter. You're going to be there when the weather changes, too."

"Just lucky, Bobo, I didn't have a choice." Charlie thought about how he would have liked to have gone to California. As it turned out he would see San Diego, in detail, later.

It was the end of October, and the whole family saw Charlie off at Union Station. Jewell clung to him until he pulled himself aboard a Burlington Zephyr, "I'll see you in a few weeks."

He watched his family and Jewell as the train pulled away from the station. They passed factories, backyards, and vacant lots before they got to the rural northeast into the Great Plains.

Behind Charlie, a woman's voice with a beautiful English accent asked the children about what games and books they would like to play. He turned around to see an attractive woman, and two elementary-age children digging through a big bag of books and lunches.

"Now Donny, do let Peggy have a look as well."

The woman lifted her head and smiled at Charlie.

He shifted back around facing his window as he felt his eyes well up. *You're a big boy now, Bonarelli — cool it.*

il fine

Author's Note

Whoever said, "youth is wasted on the young," had me in mind. I was a student at Denver's North High School, Class of 1959. Thanks to the tenacity and the belief of the excellent counselors, teachers, staff, and school friends who believed in me, I made it through by the skin of my teeth.

The characters are fictional, the locations are mostly factual.

The Barrel Drive-In was a well-known restaurant near the school. Although most of the kids hung out at another legend, a few miles north of the school, The Barrel fits the geography and the events. There is a plaque at the old location that says that the Cheeseburger was invented here.

Groban's, the name is fiction about a factual place. The former drug store location is still on the "West Side."

Highland Park and Woodbury Library still exist. There was a home for the blind behind the park. Carl's Pizza is operating in North Denver.

In October 1957, there was a breakout at the Colorado State Hospital of five felon-patients. Several years later, a girl was found murdered in park less than a mile north of Highland Park.

Any similarities to actual people are coincidental. No one person is intentionally targeted, and like all fiction, a writer writes a pastiche of fact and fiction.

I apologize to the native speakers of Italian, and Yiddish. My grandparents, I believe, spoke the dialect of Molise. The rest of the family, friends and Italians or Jews that I've had the good fortune to know spoke English-Italian or English-Yiddish, "Yinglish". We often mixed tenses, dropped articles or just made language up to suit the occasion. Also I have a great appreciation for and use of the late Leo Rosten's *The Joys of Yiddish* and *The New Joys of Yiddish*.

Thank you for your indulgence of a daydream long in the making.

Alan C. Iannacito

30813038R00223

Made in the USA
Middletown, DE
07 April 2016